KISSING KIN

ELSWYTH THANE

PEOPLES BOOK CLUB
Chicago

To
Harold A. Foster

CONTENTS

ACKNOWLEDGMENTS

The human memory is a tricky and unreliable thing, and the research for the background of this book, which lies within the experience of a great many people today, has therefore been as carefully done as for remote historical times. The English illustrated periodicals are the last word in accuracy and vivid coverage on the 1914-1918 war, and on current opinion during the growth of Nazism. I am grateful to Air Marshal Sir William Welsh, Air-Commodore Peregrine Fellowes and Mr. Francis Vivian Drake, who flew with the RAF during the first World War, for helpful comment and additional information on the pages concerned with early combat flying, which was so different from the work done by the Flying Fortresses and Spitfires in the recent past.

The summers in England which were an unalterable part of my life from 1928 to 1939 supply me with a certain personal viewpoint, but the opinions expressed by Johnny Malone and Bracken Murray in the book are drawn from the published record of foreign correspondents and statesmen in Europe during those years. No balanced estimate of the twenty-five years between the wars can be complete without a thoughtful study of Leopold Schwartzschild's *World In Trance*—a book which should be compulsory reading for every adult in the Western World.

Miss Barbara Hayes of the British Information Service very kindly made it possible for me to learn more about St. Dunstan's than is readily available in this country. Dr. Joseph Fobes gave patient and comprehensible answers to my queries about surgical details. And as always, Mrs. F. G. King and the staff of the New York Society Library have been endlessly helpful to me.

E.T.

CHART OF FAMILIES AND RELATIONSHIPS

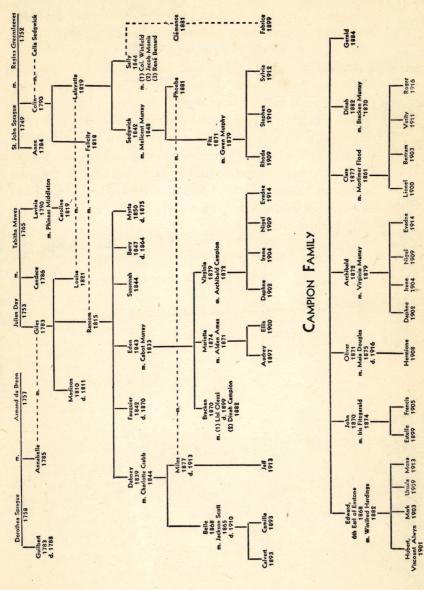

CAMPION FAMILY

THE SHOW GOES ON

1. *SPRING IN WILLIAMSBURG. 1917.*

THE TWINS DESCENDED FROM THE TRAIN IN silence, looking exactly alike in their young tautness and gravity, though there was nothing feminine about the set of Calvert's slender shoulders, and Camilla's fine-drawn face and colt-like frame were anything but tomboy. They had no luggage.

Still silent, they set out along the familiar arching green street which led to what, since Great-grandfather Ransom's death a few years before, had become known in the family as Aunt Sue's house, on the other side of town. By unspoken consent they avoided England Street, where the Sprague cousins lived. It was no day for family junkets and frivolity. They had run away from Richmond, to come here—sneaked out, in fact, by a series of fibs and childish maneuvers designed to deceive their trustful mother. They felt like rats, and they held their heads high.

The subtle psychological bond which exists between twins

from birth and reduces the necessity of speech between them
to a minimum amounting to thought transference, supported
them as they went. Almost without discussion, certainly without argument, their decision had been taken the night before
in Camilla's room, after their mother had gone to bed. Aunt
Sue was the one to ask. Aunt Sue always knew what you
should do, and what you must not do. Quietly and without
any fuss or foolish questions, Aunt Sue would help them to
sort themselves out and settle this thing which rode them.
To Aunt Sue they had fled, empty-handed and luncheonless,
as all the family were accustomed to do every so often, to say,
"And so I thought—" and "Of course *you* can see—" and
"*Don't* you agree—?"

She always told them, without any nonsense. And she
always saw, even if she didn't always agree. And in the end
you were comforted and sustained, even if you had been
wrong.

So they came to the gate in the white picket fence, with its
chain and cannon-ball weight, and creaked through it, and
marched up the path between low box hedges, their chins
well up. Old black Uncle Micah, Aunt Sue's butler, opened
the door to them with exclamations of astonishment and joy,
and escorted them to the dining-room where Aunt Sue was
just finishing luncheon.

"*Well!*" she said, and rose, and kissed them both soundly,
Camilla first because she was the girl, but Calvert loudest because he was the boy. And then she said, "Have you had anything to eat?" and when they shook their heads a look passed
between her and Uncle Micah and he bustled away kitchen-
wards.

Hagar, who was Uncle Micah's youngest, at once appeared
to lay two places for them with gleaming silver and old flow-
ered china, and Uncle Micah bustled back with food as hot
and lavish as if they had been prompt and bidden guests.

They ate hungrily, and Aunt Sue had another cup of coffee to keep them company. Meanwhile they assured her that everyone in Richmond was well, and agreed that the weather was very warm for March. They said how sweet Williamsburg always looked in the spring, and how forward the gardens were everywhere. They heard all the latest news from the Princeton cousins, who had done nothing notable, and from the London cousins, who were being bombed from the air by both Zeppelins and aeroplanes now, and from Cousin Phoebe, who was a nurse in France, and Cousin Bracken, who was a war correspondent.

And then Aunt Sue said, "Have you had enough to eat?" and they nodded above empty plates. She pushed back her chair and said, "Then come into the drawing-room and tell me about it."

They followed her, wordlessly linked in their twinship, linked too by their rather clammy, nervous hands which met and clung as they passed through the door behind her. She sat down on the sofa and they stood beside her, right hand in left hand, wondering how to begin, looking exactly alike. . . .

She cut the ground from under them briskly.

"I suppose you've got some idea you want to go and fight this war," she said, and they both spoke at once, overflowing with gratitude.

"Cousin Phoebe is already there, and—"

"Cousin Bracken's Sunday article in the *Star* said—"

"I thought so," said Sue. "And your mother thinks you're too young, is that it?"

"We're twenty-three," they pointed out resentfully, with one voice. And Calvert added, "We're the eldest. Eliot comes next, and he's only seventeen." (Eliot was one of the Princeton bunch.)

"And besides, Eliot would never get into the Army on account of his eyes," said Camilla, with a prideful glance at that perfect specimen, her brother, who didn't have to wear spectacles.

"I see," said Sue serenely. "Well, what do you have in mind to do about it?"

"I could be a nurse like Cousin Phoebe," said Camilla.

"I just want to kill Germans," said Calvert unemphatically. "I don't want to write about this war, like Cousin Bracken. I'm younger than he is, anyway. I just want to take the quickest and easiest way to get a gun and shoot me some Germans."

"There isn't any short cut to that, I'm afraid," said Sue, who could remember Manassas and San Juan Hill. "And nursing wounded men isn't very picturesque, you know, Camilla, except perhaps the uniform."

"Oh, I realize that," said Camilla quickly. "I know Cousin Phoebe's letters almost by heart, the ones she wrote last year from that hospital near Nieuport. But the sight of blood doesn't make me sick, and I always take care of Calvert when he's ill, and I don't need much sleep to get along, and I'm much stronger than I look, and lots younger than Cousin Phoebe."

"Mmmm," said Sue thoughtfully, her gaze resting on a big jar of blue iris which stood against the light.

"So we thought—" Calvert began anxiously, and simultaneously Camilla said, "So if you'd only—" and they looked at each other and then at her and waited. But she was silent so long, not seeming to be aware of their presence any more, that they went and sat down one on either side of her and each took a hand. "Honey, what are you thinking?" Camilla asked softly.

"I was thinking how familiar it all sounds," Sue said, not looking at either of them. "And how it keeps on happening to us, time after time. I was thinking about when Eden went to Richmond and scandalized everybody there by being kind to the wounded Yankees in Libby Prison. That was before your mother was born—even before your Grandmother Charlotte married my brother Dabney. And I was thinking of when they all went off to Cuba—your Cousin Fitz and Gwen had been married only a week, but she never tried to hold him back. And I was remembering how when this war started we all hoped it wouldn't come here—though Bracken always said we'd be in it before the end came. I remember thinking, back in 1914, They're all too young for this one—they were all born too late—except Calvert." Her hand tightened on his. "You see, I've known all along that Calvert would want to go."

"Ever since the *Lusitania*," said Calvert. "But mother—"

"I know," said Sue gently. "But it's hard for her, Calvert, with your father dead. You and Camilla are all she's got. You must be patient."

"We have been patient," Calvert pointed out. "It's nearly two years since the *Lusitania,* and how far have we got? Wilson has broken off diplomatic relations! Not declared war on Germany, mind you, nothing so impulsive as that! Just handed the German Ambassador his passports with a tactful slap on the wrist! 'Armed neutrality,' what good is that? I for one am not going to sit around any longer, I'm going up to Canada and enlist! I'm of age, and no one can stop me. It's done every day, the whole Canadian Army is stiff with Americans!"

"I don't blame you for feeling that way," Sue said fairly. "I've heard other people talk the same way, right here in Williamsburg. But as for Camilla—"

"Oh, please, Aunt Sue, I can't stay here and do nothing if Calvert is in it, I'd go crazy! And besides—what about Aunt Eden in the old days? And look at Cousin Phoebe now—and Cousin Virginia too, in London!"

"Their men are in it, Camilla. Virginia married an Englishman, and Phoebe—well, Phoebe is in love with one. It's different for them, and besides, they're older."

"Well, so shall I have a man in it!" cried Camilla fiercely. "My own brother, you can't ask for better than that! We're *twins!* We always do things *together.* I can't stay home and let Calvert take all the risks and discomforts, I've got to do my share! Else when he got back he'd know a lot of things I didn't, and I'd be *ashamed!* And if he got killed—and I'd sat safe at home—I'd *despise* myself forever!"

"I see," said Sue unargumentatively, and they waited, watching her. "And what about your music?" she asked then, for Camilla's singing voice had great promise and had been carefully trained, though family opinion was dead against her using it professionally.

"It will have to wait, like a lot of other things, till the war is over," said Camilla. "Nobody in Europe can stop to study singing now, why should I?"

"I see," Sue said again, and Camilla added in a sort of mutter, "If I had my way I'd cut my hair and go as a boy, the way Grandmother Tibby did before Yorktown!"

"Yes, but have you laid any other plans?" Sue inquired reasonably, and Camilla grinned, and Calvert laughed and said, "We thought Dinah would be the most help, to Camilla, at least, if we could get to her."

"If you could talk Mother round for us, that is," said Camilla. "Calvert doesn't care if he gets a commission or not, so long as he gets *in,* and soon. And I don't care what I do so long as I do *something,* right away. So we thought if we went up to New York and asked Dinah about getting a passage to England—"

"No doubt they could make use of you as a VAD at her sister's hospital down in Gloucestershire," said Sue.

"Or the house in London where Virginia is," said Camilla,

for the idea of a country mansion turned into a hospital seemed tame if one could be in London where the bombs came down.

"Well, we could ask," said Sue.

"And what about Mother?"

"I'll talk to her. You telegraph her and stay here tonight, and we'll write to Dinah so she'll be prepared. And tomorrow I'll go back to Richmond with you and have a talk with your mother."

They kissed her, one on either side.

"You're wonderful," they said, and her smile was a little rueful.

———

They spent the evening concocting the letter to Dinah in New York.

English Dinah was the sister of Edward, Earl of Enstone, and had married their Cousin Bracken Murray and come to live in New York where he owned and edited a newspaper. Bracken's sister Virginia had married another of Dinah's brothers, one who wasn't an earl, only a lawyer in the Inner Temple—a K.C. with a wig and a black gown and a single eyeglass. The cousins at home in Williamsburg and Richmond had never seen Virginia's Archie, but they all loved Bracken's Dinah, who always came to the family Christmases and birthdays and belonged to them from the first. Dinah was born a ladyship, but gave herself no airs, and was little and reddish-haired and wonderfully dressed and so in love with Bracken it made your throat ache to see them together.

They had been in England on their yearly visit to Cousin Virginia, Camilla recalled as she sat at Sue's desk writing down the letter to Dinah more or less at everybody's dictation, after dinner that evening—Dinah and Bracken had been in England when the war began, and because she had been delicate ever since losing her only baby Dinah had broken down completely under the strain of nursing wounded men during that first terrible winter in London when the Earl's house in St. James's Square had been turned into a hospital for officers and all the family wives had gone to work there as VAD's. So Bracken brought her back to New York and she was recuperating there when Cousin Phoebe suddenly decided to go to Europe in the spring of 1915—which was convenient because Phoebe had been able to leave little Jeff in Dinah's empty nursery. . . .

Camilla looked up suddenly from the letter, interrupting a well-rounded sentence of Calvert's about his necessity to go and shoot Germans. "Aunt Sue, what was that you said about Cousin Phoebe being in love with an Englishman?"

"Oh, dear," said Sue. "Well, you may as well know, if you're going over there."

"I thought she went abroad because a friend of hers who was married to a German prince hadn't been heard from after the war began," said Calvert.

"She did. But Rosalind is safe in England now—they got her out of Germany through Switzerland."

"I thought it was funny Cousin Phoebe didn't come back," said Camilla. "Who is it she's in love with? And why doesn't she marry him?"

"He's an officer in the British Army. And he had a wife."

"Aha!" said Calvert, not pleased.

"Now—you may as well both get this thing about Phoebe straight once and for all," said Sue earnestly. "Ordinarily it might not have come up. But you'll have to know all about it now, though your mother might think I was wrong to tell you. Phoebe fell in love with Oliver Campion in London years ago—the summer Edward VII was crowned. They didn't mean to—they were both engaged to somebody else before they met each other."

"*Well!*" said Camilla, sitting up. "It sounds like something in one of Cousin Phoebe's books. Tell us more."

"It wasn't funny, Camilla," Sue said quietly, and Camilla laid down her pen and came to sit beside her on the sofa. "Oliver was just as much in love with Phoebe, but they both tried desperately hard to do what they thought was right," Sue went on. "They decided they must get along without each other, as though they had never met. Oliver married Maia, as he was supposed to do, and went out to India with the regiment. And Phoebe finally married your Uncle Miles and settled down here in Williamsburg."

"I remember the night they announced it," said Camilla. "At a Christmas party at Cousin Sedgwick's. I thought that night she was the most beautiful thing I had ever seen, and I never could understand why she married Uncle Miles. She could have had anybody in the world, I always thought. She was rich and famous for her books and still young, and— and so sophisticated—and poor Uncle Miles always seemed so *dull,* for her to marry!"

"Poor Miles *was* dull," Sue agreed frankly. "She thought she wanted something like that. She thought it might save her, like an anaesthetic, from wanting Oliver. Because you see she and Oliver went right on being in love, no matter what they did. They were meant for each other. Sometimes it happens that way," said Sue gently, "and then you never do get over it."

"So she wasn't happy with Uncle Miles," said Camilla. "I was right, then. I never thought she could be. It was a mercy that he died, wasn't it!"

Sue sighed.

"I don't know, dear—if he had lived to see their baby—if Phoebe had had both him and Jeff to build a life on—she might have managed it the way she wanted to. But with Miles dying like that, so suddenly, she didn't know where she was again, she didn't know what to do with Jeff when she got him, or—how to go on. She didn't *want* Jeff, I began to think, without Miles too."

"So she dumped the poor kid on Dinah and went off to nurse soldiers in France," said Calvert, who sometimes saw things with an uncompromising eye.

"She went to find Rosalind, because no one knew what had happened to her in Germany, and it was a good thing she did too," said Sue firmly. "After Rosalind was saved, Phoebe just sort of—stayed on in England and France. I can see how it is. She wants to feel as though she is *doing* something. Even you feel the same," she reminded Camilla. "And Dinah is glad to have Jeff. She can never have one of her own, you know."

"And what about this Oliver?" asked Calvert. "Will he be wounded and brought into the very hospital she works in, do you think, and will she nurse him back to life like the story-books, and what about the woman he married?"

"I wish you wouldn't be flippant," said Sue gravely. "I suppose it does sound rather like a cinema to you—and you aren't accustomed to thinking of your elders as able to have emotions or romance of their own, are you. Phoebe's only thirty-six, even now. And I hope you don't think she and Oliver are enjoying themselves, these days. He was badly wounded during the first summer in France, and is at the British War Office now, doing Staff work. Phoebe is still drudging her heart out in a hospital near Paris, and Bracken says she will write the best book of her life if she lives through it."

"And Oliver's wife?" Camilla persisted.

"She died in an accident during an air raid in London last winter."

"Died?" cried Calvert. "Why, then they can marry each other after all and live happily ever after, just like the fairy tales!"

"I suppose they will marry eventually," said Sue without smiling. "But there isn't much time for fairy tales in Europe now, Calvert."

"Well, it just shows you, doesn't it," said Camilla thoughtfully. "Here's one of the oldest and saddest stories in the world, going on right in the family under our very noses. Everybody married to the wrong ones, and breaking their hearts, and living along just as if nothing was happening at all. Maybe Uncle Miles is well out of it, at that! What becomes of Jeff?"

"Bracken wants to adopt him and bring him up to inherit the newspaper, as he did from his father," Sue explained.

"I think that would be very heartless of Cousin Phoebe!" cried Camilla.

"Why would it?" asked Sue reasonably. "It's all in the family. And they can do more for him than Phoebe alone ever could. Bracken needs an heir and Miles doesn't—any more."

"Seems a bit hard on Jeff, all the same," said Calvert.

"I don't see why," Sue argued patiently. "He's only four now, and he's got nothing to lose, and he adores Dinah—and Bracken will be a father to him."

"Still, I should think Jeff would feel pretty queer about his family when he's old enough to think," said Camilla. "His own mother deserting him like that."

"But she *hasn't*—" Sue began, and gave it up. "It isn't as though she had run away with Oliver, or anything like that," she pointed out.

"No, but still—" Their obstinate young faces showed that they were not convinced. Camilla rose and returned to the letter on Sue's desk. "It will feel very strange, meeting Cousin Phoebe again, now that I know all this," she said. "Shall I see Oliver, do you think?"

"As he is Dinah's brother, no doubt you will."

"How many brothers has Dinah *got?*" demanded Calvert.

"Edward, the Earl," said Sue, checking them off on her fingers. "John, the M.P.—nobody ever seems to see much of him, and he has a vague wife and daughter. Oliver—he's a Colonel now, they say. Archie, married to Virginia. And Gerald, the youngest, a captain in the artillery, I believe."

"What a mob," said Camilla. "All married and all got children, just to make it more complicated!"

"All but Gerald."

"I'll never be able to keep 'em straight," said Camilla, to whom the ramifications of the Day-Sprague-Murray clan in America were as simple as a,b,c. "It will be nice to see Virginia again, she was always my favorite when I was little."

"I must say I look forward to Cousin Phoebe now," said Calvert irrepressibly. "Honestly, I never *dreamed!* Going round as though butter wouldn't melt, and all the time—"

"Calvert," said Sue, and "Shut up, Calvert," said Camilla, and "Oh, all right," said Calvert, "but all the same, it's great fun having a dark horse in the family. The rest of us are so rotten respectable!"

"You're forgetting Cousin Sally," Camilla suggested, and—"You'll never get that letter done," said Sue.

———

Their mother cried a little, but took it better than they had expected, once her worst fears had materialized, and they both wanted to go. And the end of the same week found them having tea in Dinah's drawing-room in New York.

Dinah quite understood that they wanted to go and fight the war. All of her own family were in it, and she often felt very cut off and frustrated because she wasn't in it too. The big Georgian country house whose bleak nursery and school-room floor she had left at barely eighteen to marry Bracken Murray had been converted by her brother Edward, Earl of Enstone, into a hospital for wounded men. Edward was ADC

to somebody on the Staff and didn't come under fire very
often. Their sister Clare worked at the Hall as a VAD, and
Edward's wife Winifred was in charge there, and ran the
whole thing very efficiently, everybody said. But then, she
would, Dinah always thought enviously, for Winifred was
brisk and competent and rather on the plump side, and running things came naturally to her—she even ran Edward,
who stood six feet two and weighed a good fifteen stone.
Edward's two sons were at Eton, but Hubert the elder would
soon be old enough for the Army.

The Earl's town house in St. James's Square, an oppres-
sively rococo mansion, had been an officers' hospital since
1914, and they were having quite a lively time there now
with the air raids, according to Virginia. Dinah was very fond
of Virginia, and they had worked together at turning the
London house into a hospital, back in that first dreadful autumn of the war. Together they had taken their VAD training, and Dinah cheerfully slaved long, backbreaking hours
at dull tasks in the scullery and lower regions, realizing with
preoccupied surprise as she did so that in the normal course
of events as the daughter and sister of the owner of the house
she might never have set foot behind the green baize door
which led to the servants' quarters where she now spent her
days. Not, as Virginia pointed out, that the schoolroom floor
where for generations the unconsidered young of the family
had slept and fed and learned their lessons offered anything
as comfortable as the housekeeper's room.

Dinah found it very hard to bear that Virginia was still on
VAD duty in St. James's Square, being bombed, while she
herself had one day collapsed ignominiously in the middle
of the kitchen floor and been carried off to bed and then sent
back to America to recuperate. Virginia must be very tough,
although she didn't look it, to stand so much punishment,
and her letters were still gay and undismayed, no matter what

happened, and Zeppelins were coming down all over the place now. Archie in the Judge Advocate General's department was not so far in any great danger, and that was a relief —it was fantastic to Dinah to think of Archie as being considered a bit old for active service, and he was very fed up about it himself. He was younger than Bracken at that, and Bracken as a correspondent saw much too much of the firing line to suit anyone but himself, and once he had nearly been taken prisoner.

This was Bracken's second war. Nearly twenty years ago he had gone to Cuba and followed the Rough Riders up San Juan Hill and nearly died there of a wound and fever. Dinah at sixteen had sat that one out in England, waiting for news of him, and now here she was in New York, and if Bracken in France got wounded again—

At this point Dinah would always seek the company of Jeff, who was the main reason she wasn't by now moving heaven and earth to get back to England because she was almost well again. Jeff was a windfall, for Dinah. He had been born at Williamsburg the summer before the war began, six months after the death of his father. Lost and restless in her sudden widowhood, bewildered by her unaccustomed motherhood, Phoebe had brought Jeff and his colored mammy to New York in the spring of 1915 and asked Dinah and Bracken to keep him with them while she ran over to Germany. She seemed to think it would be as simple as it had been before the war began, to pay a visit to Germany. She found out otherwise. And as the weeks slipped by and Phoebe did not return, Dinah in New York began to play a pathetic and dangerous game—she pretended that Jeff was hers for keeps. He was only two years younger than the baby she had lost would have been, and all the other wives in the family, both in England and America, had babies. It didn't seem fair to Dinah that she alone should have failed. Virginia had had four, with apparently the greatest of ease. And now Phoebe didn't seem really to want Jeff—everybody suspected that she had only married poor Miles Day to keep the wind away, when it was Oliver that she loved.

Bracken returned to France in the summer of 1915, and except for a few weeks in New York last winter he had been there ever since, with brief breathers in England. Now that the submarines were so bad in the North Atlantic, Dinah was quite willing that he should not risk the voyage just to see her. They had discussed her bringing Jeff to England, and delayed for the same reason—that and a recent illness which had made his diet important, and food was now becoming a problem in England.

Jeff came down to tea in Dinah's drawing-room the day that Calvert and Camilla arrived in New York. He was a grave, long-headed child, just turning four. Bracken had not seen him for months, but Dinah was careful that being brought up by women did not make a mollycoddle of Jeff. His light brown hair was cut boy-fashion, his clothes were simple, with breeches and no frills. His handclasp was firm and he looked you in the eye.

He accepted a cup of cambric tea—hot water, milk, and sugar—and a toasted muffin, and dealt with it tidily by himself without interrupting or seeming to pay much attention to the conversation. Camilla's eyes kept going back to him, and at last she said, "Honestly, how *can* she?"

"What?" said Dinah, knowing very well.

"How *can* Phoebe just *give* him to somebody else—*anybody* else—to bring up?"

"Don't you think I'm doing a good job?" Dinah asked anxiously.

"Yes, of course. He's wonderful. If Phoebe saw him now I bet she'd be sorry."

"That's what I'm afraid of," said Dinah with a little sigh.

"Well, she can't take him back now, can she, once you've adopted him legally."

"If she ever wants him back, we could hardly stand in the way," said Dinah, and Camilla gave her a quick, understanding look.

"Let's hope she won't, of course, for your sake. But what about *him?* How do you explain it to him?"

"I don't try."

"But some time—"

"He doesn't miss her, you know. He loves me in her place."

"What does he call you?"

"Diney. I'm not fooling him. He knows I'm not his mother. But he'd just as soon have me, truly he would."

"I don't doubt that," said Camilla. "What's this about Phoebe and your brother Oliver?"

"She'll marry him, I hope. He's earned it."

"Has he got children?"

"A daughter. She's nine."

"I wonder what she'll think!" said Camilla, and Dinah sighed again.

"She's just like her mother," she admitted. "I couldn't like Maia. None of us did. I tried, but I just couldn't *like* her."

"Did Oliver?"

"We-ell—" said Dinah with a rueful smile. "Anyway, he likes Hermione, and she adores him."

"Isn't it strange and—romantic," said Camilla unwillingly. "Imagine all this going on right in the family. Phoebe and Oliver all these years, in spite of Jeff and—what's her name again?"

"Her-*mi*-o-ne," said Dinah distinctly, and made a face. "Maia chose it."

"Oh, dear," said Camilla. "And would Phoebe live in England if she marries Oliver?"

"I can't imagine what Oliver would do in America—he's

Army," said Dinah. "Her books often had an English background anyway. She can go on writing them there. If the war ever ends."

"Speaking of the war," said Calvert, bringing them back to it firmly, and disposing of women's gossip.

━━━━━━━

When Camilla sailed for England at the end of the month, Calvert had already crossed the border to enlist with the Canadians and was training under canvas in the Laurentians. The first letters she had from him were gaily studded with Army slang and a few technical terms thrown in to impress her. It was plain that he was happy there, and was adapting himself with ease to the tough existence of a new recruit, walking his ten miles without falling dead, eating his dull, plentiful food with an uncritical appetite, forming friendships in the oddly assorted society into which he had pitchforked himself.

Camilla was very proud of him. She had known all along that he wasn't a sissy and would not be dismayed by bad weather or bodily discomfort and privation—but she had wondered about the strangeness, for that was her own difficulty. She herself was as brave as a lion, she was sure, and wouldn't mind submarines or bombs a bit, but she did dread homesickness and separation from Calvert. He, of course, had once been away from Richmond to school. But she, even while she was still under Dinah's wing, had felt suddenly unfledged and forlorn after Calvert went to Canada.

There had been a scurry to collect her overseas kit in time, for Dinah's appeal in Bracken's name to the right people in Washington had procured a passport for Camilla with startling promptness. Her luggage loaded with warm things to wear and with goodies for the family in England, she caught the boat—a small English liner—in a breathless state, and found herself launched, alone and still incredulous, on her adventure.

The announcement of America's entry into the war came by wireless during an otherwise uneventful voyage, and went to everyone's head far quicker than the champagne which was drunk to celebrate it. But Camilla was secretly glad that she and Calvert had both got away before it happened. Everyone said, on soberer thought, that it would be months before America could be of any practical help, even now, and they would both have gone mad if they had had to wait and cross with belated American units after all.

Camilla dropped off to sleep in her bunk on the night of April 6th feeling smug and excited and impatient—and a little dizzy with champagne. She and Calvert had beat the gun. They were in it. All the slow-coaches back home would be kicking their heels for months yet, wasting time. The war might be over before America had contributed much besides moral support. . . .

London was showing the Stars-and-Stripes when she got there, and in Flanders the Canadians had just taken Vimy Ridge with terrible losses. She was proud to say, "My brother will be coming over with the Canadians," even though it caught in her throat. She would see him again before he went into the Line. They always trained a while in England, but replacements would be badly needed now.

Mr. Lloyd George was Prime Minister of England, and had introduced what was described as a sort of war-time Lent, which was an honorable competition in voluntary self-denial, and he was regarded with general good will and so far with only a little misgiving. He had most of the faults and virtues of a born warrior and a constitutional democrat. He was boundlessly energetic and optimistic. After the rounded Parliamentary periods and sleek diplomacy of Mr. Asquith, he reacted on the war-weary British public like an astringent tonic.

Aeroplanes were doing more bombing than Zeppelins now, over England, and several were heard in London the first night Camilla was there, though nothing was dropped on the city and all the damage proved to be in Essex. She was sitting with Virginia in the little upstairs parlor where visitors to the St. James's Square house were received by the family, when the first low hum became noticeable.

"*What's that?*" said Camilla, and felt her heartbeats quicken.

"Oh, you'll get used to that," said Virginia without moving. "It's the Jerries again. Usually nothing much happens."

"Can we see them?" Camilla demanded above the sound of the guns which had wakened to duty belatedly in the Park. "Somebody must see them because we're firing back at them, aren't we?"

"You can look if you like," said Virginia, who was very tired. "But it's an awful fag to open the windows on account of the blackout curtains and turning off the lights, and so on." She reached for a cigarette from a silver box on the table, lighted it, pulled a chair round to face her own and put her feet up in its seat. "I wish I could remember a time when my feet didn't hurt right up to the knee," she added plaintively.

Camilla sat still and looked at her while cigarette smoke curled out across the room and the ground defence in the Park carried on.

"How long have you been doing that?" she asked curiously.

"Smoking? I forget. Quite a while. Archie doesn't mind, and it seems to help, I don't know why."

"Could I have one?"

Virginia nodded and pushed the silver box a few inches along the table.

"You will sooner or later. I've no objection." She yawned, covered up too late, and slid down in the chair. "I'm sorry to be so dull, my dear, but I've had a really grisly day. Three of our kitchen people have gone sick—some sort of bad tummy—and I had to help out there. You'll be a godsend, I'll never forget how we worked poor Phoebe when she turned VAD, though it was nothing to what she got later on in Belgium."

Camilla noticed that the hand which struck her match— her own hand—was not quite steady, and her knees felt queer. She envied Virginia's cast-iron composure with all that noise going on outside and that strangely naked feeling overhead, and thought, Give me three years and I can do it too. Casting about for something to pin her mind to, the way you fight off the first qualms of seasickness, she said, "Is Cousin Sally still at your house in the country?"

"Mm-hm. Indefinitely."

"Virginia, will you please tell me about Cousin Sally, she's a *total* mystery at home. What exactly did she *do?*"

"Some other time, darling," pleaded Virginia. "I really haven't the strength tonight to begin on Cousin Sally, it's much too complicated. We'll have a cup of weak tea, shall we, and some biscuits, and by then the raid will have drawn off and we can go to bed." She passed a fretful hand across her aching eyes and forehead, swept off the white nursing coif she wore and dropped it on the table.

"Virginia, you've got your hair cut short!" cried Camilla. "I thought you had, but I didn't—how *sweet* you look, doesn't Archie mind?"

Virginia ran her fingers through the short dark curls at the back of her neck.

"It's less trouble this way. And Archie says it looks much nicer than long hair when I wake up in the morning," she said complacently.

The blue VAD dress and white cap and apron made Camilla look very young and earnest. She found the work sheer, sickening drudgery, and had often to grit her teeth against the surge of nausea which was partly stretched nerves. Bedpans and blood-stained linen and greasy dishwater and dreadful smells—and then the hum of German aircraft overhead and the necessity not to show the slightest concern lest one be thought a coward. It was hardly fair, because the others had had plenty of time to get used to it. But everyone was kindness itself and pretended tactfully that she was used to it too.

The arrival of Pershing in France in May coincided with—and assisted—a wave of optimism born of the British campaign around Arras. The first American troops were soon in France—it was only a token force straight from the Mexican Border, lean, springy, eager men who inspired the remark that it might have taken a long time to get America into the war but it would take a lot longer to get her out of it. Bracken came back from France for a few days' rest and said things looked a little better—there had been some trouble in the French Army, but now that Pétain was boss he would have things straightened out in no time. Bracken was more worried about Russia, now many weeks gone in revolution. Russia's leaders still insisted that a separate peace was unthinkable, but Bracken said he didn't like the look of Russia. But then, Virginia reminded him, he never had.

The third anniversary of the shooting at Sarajevo passed, and Calvert arrived on Salisbury Plain with a new lot of Canadians. Camilla wanted to rush off to see him, and began looking up trains to Amesbury, but was persuaded to wait till he could get leave and come to London, which, late in August, he finally contrived to do. He was made much of in St. James's Square, and Virginia gave a theater party to see

Daddy-Long-Legs at the Duke of York's, and they all wept just enough to enjoy themselves, and had supper afterwards at Scott's, and tried to forget that now the Russian front had quite collapsed and America would never be in time to compensate for the loss of the Ally on the East. Soon the fresh German divisions which had been pinned down by the possibility that Russia might go on fighting after all would be streaming westward to be used against the weary, battle-worn men in the Allied trenches. And that would mean an endless demand for Allied replacements. And that meant Calvert and his new toy, the machine-gun.

The Canadians in Flanders were already famous for their snipers and their runners. Now they had taken the machine-gun to their devoted bosoms and did such deeds with it that conscientious correspondents like Bracken Murray hesitated to report them for fear of being charged with exaggeration. Camilla had to listen while Calvert talked of his gun like a man in love—had to look at diagrams and keep track of figures—almost expected to be swept off to Salisbury Plain to meet the beloved in person. The machine-gun was "she" to all its besotted crew. Like any exacting mistress, she was full of crotchets, and unless tenderly treated would jam at a critical moment, or just plain quit on you and there you were. But you knew all her whimsical ways and her complicated innards and her dirty little soul, and if you were on your way to France with a Canadian machine-gun battalion in the summer of 1917 your gun came just next after your God, and your girl, if you had one, was a poor third. Sisters—well, twin sisters always knew how you felt.

He confessed to them the last night that this was his Embarkation leave and he was off to France within a few days. Camilla, hard pressed by her own exhausting duties when he had gone, had less time to worry about him than she had anticipated, and the brigade he was sent to was then in a rest area behind Lens. His letters were great fun, and she read them aloud to Virginia. He had enough French to make friends with the civilian population, and the French Canadians in his battalion often turned things into quite a circus, particularly with the children they encountered. Gradually from his anecdotes and the second-hand tales of past heroism which had become legend in the ranks, one name began to stand out—his lance corporal, whose name was Raymond, though they were rather at a loss in London as to whether or not that was his surname. Raymond was an American too, who had joined up in Canada soon after the *Lusitania,* and had reached France in time to win his V.C. in the reeking mine craters roundabout St. Eloi, where he was the sole survivor of his machine-gun crew. During that endless fight he had repaired his gun again and again under blistering fire, and kept it shooting inside a mounting ring of German dead. He was completely cut off, but held his key position against three separate German rushes until the counter attack could come up behind him and consolidate. And then, soaked and muddy and spattered with blood which was not his own, moving in a sort of deliberate, stolid fury with no room for words, he had loaded up with hand grenades and gone out alone and cleaned up a still active German machine-gun nest which was raking the newly established line from a vantage point on the left. He brought back with him a whimpering wounded German by the seat of the pants and dumped him disgustedly for somebody else to look after. The rest of them, he said, weren't worth bothering about by the time he got there.

Raymond was kind of sheepish about his V.C., and it wasn't from him that Calvert had got the story of that day at St. Eloi. Since then he had handled his gun coolly and with deadly effect at Sanctuary Wood and Vimy. Three of his men had died at Vimy, which was the reason for Calvert's assignment to the crew. But Raymond never got a scratch. By all the odds it couldn't go on, and he was due for it soon. But Raymond wasn't worrying. He took what came.

Before very long it became obvious by Calvert's letters that they had gone up into the Line, though there didn't seem to be much doing just where they were, except for raids, mostly volunteer affairs to collect information, usually at night. Raymond, who moved as soundlessly as an Indian, often volunteered for raids. It gave him a chance to pick up things. He was passionately interested in the German fighting equipment, and when he went on raids always acquired respirators and small arms and whatever loose gear happened to be available, which later he took apart at his leisure to see how it worked and then put it back together again as good as new. He possessed a very good Luger, complete with its rifle-stock attachment, and a pair of officer's binoculars. And once when there weren't any Germans left in any condition to give information as prisoners, he brought back a disabled German machine-gun—not for the first time, apparently— and had been tinkering it happily in his spare time ever since. He said it would soon be in shape to do a little shooting for them in the opposite direction if they could find some feed for it next time they went visiting. . . .

Rain was their main trouble, Calvert wrote. Rain and mud up to the waist. You ate mud with your meals, and it got into your gun, which was worse. If Camilla thought *he* was crazy about the gun, she should see Raymond, who talked to it. "Here, what's the matter with *you?*" he would remark affectionately when the gun balked at a critical time and other people began to shout and swear. "You got the stomach ache?" he would say. "Somepun you et, no doubt." And he would start taking it apart with unhurried, gentle fingers, murmuring encouragement to it meanwhile, and he would find the trouble and mend it, and when the gun was together again he would give it an approving slap on the back and say, "Feel better now?" And the gun would go back to work, looking docile and smug about the whole thing because its feelings had been pampered, without names being called. You mustn't call your gun names and hurt its feelings when it had the stomach ache. . . .

The fighting around Arras and on the Aisne had been bitter but inconclusive, and in midsummer the tide of battle turned back into Flanders, so that all the old familiar places were heard of again—Messines, Wytschaete, and hallowed Ypres—the fateful Salient. The weather went mad, and the armies existed in a continual downpour and an ocean of mud. Still the Allies inched forward towards Passchendaele, beyond which their real objectives lay, and in ten weeks of grueling struggle and endurance they accomplished what had been allotted to the first fortnight. Passchendaele was still ahead of them.

———————

Early in October Phoebe came back from the hospital in France to marry Oliver at last. It would have been sooner, but he had been sent on a long inspection tour with his general, and then the Matron at Phoebe's hospital had collapsed and she couldn't leave while they were shorthanded because when she came away this time she was not going back. There would be plenty of work for her to do in London, where Oliver had taken a furnished flat near Westminster for them to live in till they could find a small house. The child Hermione was at Farthingale to be out of the way of the raids, which affected her nerves to the point of hysteria. Virginia remarked grimly that Hermione's mother had not been able to stand up to the raids either. A soldier's child, Camilla thought in some surprise, even if she is a girl—well, yes, and only nine—but her father must feel a bit let down. And then

Camilla would stiffen her own back and remember she came
of fighting stock herself, with no nerves to speak of. . . .

Phoebe arrived in London on a cold clear night with a raid
on. Oliver had dined with them in St. James's Square, in the
little upstairs sitting-room, and went off to meet the boat-
train looking like a schoolboy, Virginia said compassionately
when he had gone, all lit up inside, and God knows they deserved it, the both of them, and it was high time.

"Are all Dinah's brothers as good-looking as that?" asked
Camilla, on whom Oliver's brilliant dark eyes and ready
smile under the clipped mustache had made a definite impression. "And are they all so—*gay?*"

"Wait till you see my Archie," said Virginia smugly, and
then laughed at herself. "Well, he's not a bit like Oliver, so
far as that goes, I just happen to like him best. As a matter of
fact, they're all quite different. Edward is large and pompous,
and so is John, rather. Gerald—he's the youngest—is a little
more like Oliver, I suppose, but he wants kicking most of the
time if you ask me. Instead of being just naturally lighthearted, Gerald is downright irresponsible. A real trouble-
maker. Gerald would never love the same woman for fifteen
years, through thick and thin, the way Oliver has, either!"

Phoebe too was looking rather lit up inside when she arrived at the house with Oliver later that evening, after a
windy crossing from Boulogne. They had stopped somewhere along the way for supper, in order to keep the first
hour of reunion to themselves, and their happiness was a
piteous thing to see, it was so shameless and real and so—
young, Camilla thought, trying not to stare. As though
neither of them had ever been in love before. And that was so
in a way, because for Phoebe it was her first love back again,
her only love, and for him it was an almost hopeless dream
come true.

The All-clear bugles were sounding in the street outside

as they entered the blacked-out parlor, with its drawn curtains and the single lamp on the table and the coal fire—
Camilla hoped that was an omen for them. Phoebe kissed
her, smelling of Paris just as she had always done, and Camilla thought how like a girl she looked still, for all the blue
shadows round her eyes, and how serene. She took off her hat
and her hair was bound round her head in a wide smooth
band, still a warm brown except for a soft greying streak on
the left side. She was just enough made up, and when she
removed her gloves her hands showed carefully tended,
though the nails were short and unpolished.

Every move that Oliver made as he took her coat and
shifted a chair for her an inch nearer the fire, every glance
of his smiling eyes was like a caress. Whenever Phoebe looked
at him or spoke to him or said his name she shone with a
quiet joy. Camilla had never seen, or at least had never noticed before, how love could set a nimbus around two people
that was positively visible to the naked eye. They didn't hold
hands or use endearments, they were beyond that. It was
superfluous in the completeness of their comprehension of
each other. He sat down near her, watching her face, she
kept glancing towards him as she talked to Virginia, as
though to make sure he was still there, and she always found
his attentive, amused gaze waiting. Camilla, silent and observant on a hassock at the corner of the hearth, felt a stab
of envy like pain. For the first time in her life she saw love
as something desirable, something one could not oneself
bear to be without forever—and she felt bleak and forlorn
and left out in the cold because there was nothing like it in
her own experience, nor any prospect of it that she could see.

She rose obediently when Virginia said it was bedtime, and
they left Phoebe and Oliver there together by the fire—and
Camilla's feet ached and she was chilled and miserable and—
yes, *lonely*—unbearably, childishly, tearfully lonely, and not

for Calvert—climbing the stairs to her little room on the top
floor which had once been slept in by an under-housemaid.
She got into bed and lay there wide-eyed in the dark, thinking of the warm, firelit room below and Phoebe in Oliver's
arms—till hot tears of weariness and nebulous longing rolled
down her cheeks into the pillow. Lost in this strange new
misery, she never suspected that Virginia in a similar bare
little cell across the passage was sobbing into her own pillow
because there was no hope of seeing Archie before Christmas
and maybe not even then.

Phoebe and Oliver were married at a Registrar's office a
few days later, and neither Bracken nor Archie could get
to London for the wedding, and nobody came up from
the country because Cousin Sally had caught a slight cold.
Phoebe had no trousseau and there was to be no honeymoon
journey; they simply went home together to the little Westminster flat after the ceremony. Camilla had seen elaborate
church weddings in Richmond, had been a bridesmaid once,
and the whole business had seemed to her rather remote and
tiresome and not altogether in good taste, and she had even
been heard to remark that if her time ever came she would
elope. But as they watched Phoebe and Oliver drive away
together in a broken-down taxicab, each incandescent with
wordless contentment, she said to Virginia with a catch in her
breath, "Why didn't somebody tell me it was like that to get
married?"

"It isn't always," said Virginia, and put her hand through
Camilla's elbow and gave it an understanding squeeze. "I was
lucky too. And pray God that you will be. But I remember
the day Rosalind Norton-Leigh got married—" Camilla distinctly felt her shiver, and looked round in surprise.

"To the German prince?"

Virginia nodded, and her small, heart-shaped face looked
set and drawn.

"That was barbarous," she said.

"Barbarous—how?"

"She was afraid of Conrad. And he was a brute."

"Then why on earth—"

"She had to. It was a long time ago. Things were different then. There didn't seem to be any way out of it. Girls used to be so helpless—"

Camilla's chin lifted.

"I *couldn't* marry a man I didn't love," she said fastidiously, out of her new knowledge. "I just *wouldn't*. Nobody can *make* you marry somebody."

Virginia gave her a long, speculative look. She was a self-contained child, Virginia was thinking ruefully. One had learned very little about her in the weeks since she had come to live in St. James's Square. She worked hard and willingly, she was steady under the raids if a little tense, but that would doubtless pass. Looking back, it seemed to Virginia that the only man Camilla had ever mentioned was her brother. Twins were queer, of course. It might be that her devotion to Calvert had so far cheated her out of the usual boy and girl attachments. She had an almost aggressive virginity of outline, with her undeveloped figure and her pure, sharp profile. But her mouth was wide and tender and there was a reddish cast to her thick chestnut hair—the capacity to feel was there, Virginia thought, dormant still, perhaps, but surely not for long now. Her fingers tightened on the small sharp bones of Camilla's elbow.

"Are you by any chance in love with somebody yourself?" she asked lightly.

"Me?" Camilla's eyes, rather dazed with her own preoccupation, but utterly honest, met hers. "Heavens, no! Who would I be in love with?"

"Whom," Virginia corrected gently. "I just wondered. Shall we walk home, there's plenty of time."

Camilla fell into step with her.

"Did you ever feel like that?" she asked after a moment. "The way Phoebe looked just now, I mean."

"I never had to go through what they have endured," Virginia admitted. "Archie and I were free to do as we pleased from the beginning, and there wasn't even a war. But when he comes home on leave nowadays I expect I look pretty hazy myself, even at my advanced age."

"It lasts, then," Camilla said thoughtfully.

"Sometimes it does."

"I wonder," said Camilla, and her feet dragged a little, "if anything like that will ever happen to me."

"Darling—why shouldn't it?"

"I'm not pretty like you—nor clever like Phoebe. Calvert is the only man I've ever really known very well, or ever *cared* to know, I reckon. Father was always busy, and I don't seem to remember him very well, and I never thought much of Uncle Miles. Of course, Bracken is wonderful, but—you couldn't *marry* Bracken."

"Dinah did."

"Oh, well, Dinah's different, he would never have looked twice at anybody like me," Camilla said vaguely, stating a simple, self-evident fact.

"Doesn't do to be too humble, you know," Virginia advised sympathetically.

"It makes one **humble**," said Camilla. "To see a man like Oliver—and no doubt your Archie too—to see them *belong* to somebody that way, believing in that one person out of all the world, and the *responsibility* of being that person and living up to it—I should be afraid to **try**, I think."

"There's no reason for that," said Virginia briskly. "You could make some man happy with one hand tied behind you. I can't imagine what the Richmond boys have been thinking of."

"Oh, in Richmond there was always Calvert."

"But Calvert's only a brother, goose. He'll get married himself some day, and then where will you be?"

"Yes—I suppose he will."

"Lonesome?" asked Virginia kindly, and Camilla nodded with a tightness in her throat.

Growing pains, Virginia thought with compassion. Poor lamb, I've forgotten how it feels to be as young as Camilla. I never *was* as young as Camilla, I started having beaux when I was sixteen. She'll fall in love with some soldier before long, I suppose, and then God help us all, it will take her very badly when it comes. Well, she won't be the only one. Not Gerald, though, blast him. Gerald wouldn't do. Besides, he belongs to Fabrice, if she bothers to hang on to him. Camilla wouldn't stand a chance against Fabrice, any more than Jenny did. I must look round for somebody suitable for Camilla. There's young Lord Binley, but he's lost an arm. Or if only they hadn't killed Bertie Pakenham— She wants someone kind, like Archie. I want every girl to have someone like Archie, don't I! There's Adrian Carteret. He's still whole, and now that the Needham girl has got herself engaged to that colonel, Adrian must be rather at a loose end. I must try to get him down to Farthingale for Christmas. . . .

2. CHRISTMAS AT FARTHINGALE. 1917.

BUT CHRISTMAS WAS STILL A MONTH AWAY
when the indestructible Virginia slipped on the stairs leading to the scullery and was picked up with a broken ankle.
For the next few days she lay with her leg in a cast, fuming,
in the little cell at the top of the house which had served for
three years as her bedroom, and Camilla carried trays and
chamber-pots and tried to fill in round the edges of the large
hole left in the hospital routine by Virginia's absence from
below stairs. Then Phoebe moved in and took charge there,
persuading Virginia that she would be less trouble if she
went home to Farthingale until she could get round on two
feet again. Phoebe added that in view of the fact that Farthingale was under-staffed already it might be a good idea if
Camilla accompanied Virginia and stayed there to wait on
her while Virginia was more or less helpless, putting in any
spare time she might have in helping Winifred at the Hall.
   Camilla's disappointment at this tame interruption of

her war-time career in London was mitigated by her eager-
ness to see Virginia's Gloucestershire home, around which
so many family legends grew. The house called Farthingale
had been built by a remote ancestor and through a chain of
romantic circumstances which included Virginia's marriage
to Archie was now once more inhabited by descendants of
the original line. It lay in a fold of the Cotswold Hills not
far from the Hall, where the wounded soldiers were in possession—so that Farthingale had become the rallying place
for leaves, illnesses, and whatever leisure the war had left to
anyone on either side of the family.

It was to Farthingale that Bracken repaired now and then
on his brief visits to England from the Front, to catch up on
his sleep and his writing of articles which could be sent to
the New York paper by boat without having to pass the cable
censor. To Farthingale the children of Edward and Winifred
and of Clare and Mortimer Flood went for their holidays, as
well as Virginia's and Archie's four. And at Farthingale one
would find the fabulous Cousin Sally, who had been born a
Sprague in Williamsburg and was Phoebe's aunt, and who
had taken refuge in England in 1914 after living in France
for more than thirty years in what was believed by the puzzled younger generation at home to be sin. For all her zeal
to be of immediate use in the war, and to accustom her tense
young nerves to the sound of enemy aircraft over London,
Camilla could not help looking forward to Farthingale and
Cousin Sally.

They got Virginia a pair of crutches, on which she at once
nearly fell over backwards, giving herself a terrible fright,
and with motherly concern and already a touch of professional steadiness Camilla escorted her to Paddington Station,
helped her into the train, and settled her as comfortably as
possible with rugs and cushions. By a miracle the two other
occupants of their compartment got out at Oxford, so they

had it to themselves when by another miracle nobody else got in, and as the train moved out of the station Virginia said, "Now, about Cousin Sally," and Camilla was instantly all attention.

"You mustn't look like that," Virginia complained. "You'll make all of them awfully self-conscious and uncomfortable."

"All of whom?"

"Well—everybody. Cousin Sally, Sosthène, and even Fabrice, I suppose," Virginia explained rather vaguely.

"Is she—m-married again?"

"You would ask that!" Virginia murmured.

"*Well*, I do think this family gets more like a circus every day!" Camilla burst out. "Calvert has no idea what he's missing! Skeletons in every closet, and ghosts in the attic!"

"Nothing of the kind!" said Virginia rather sharply. "And please say cupboard in England or you'll be misunderstood."

"Won't you go right back to the beginning about Cousin Sally?" Camilla entreated.

"Nobody can remember that far back, unless it's Cousin Sally herself," said Virginia. "She's *got* to be seventy, but you'd never know it to look at her—almost makes you believe in those tales about glands and things the Viennese surgeons can do to keep one young. She's had three husbands, all of them much older than she was—at the time she married them, I mean—and all extremely wealthy, and they all died one after the other and left her all their worldly goods. Somewhere along the way, I'm not quite sure when, she had a child—a daughter named Clémence, who in time grew up, got married, and had a daughter of her own named Fabrice."

"Who is now at Farthingale too?"

"Yes, Clémence died and Sally has brought up her granddaughter, who is your cousin, don't forget!"

"How old is Fabrice?"

"Eighteen."

"Nice?"

"She is what I believe in Sally's day was called a minx," said Virginia, and lit a cigarette. "She makes eyes at all the men and most of them love it."

"She can't have Calvert," said Camilla jealously at once. "You mentioned somebody else."

"Sosthène."

"Well, who is he?"

"A lamb," said Virginia warmly. "He's got a dicky heart and can't fight—never even did his military service as a boy because of delicate health."

"Well, how does he come into it?" Camilla prodded, as Virginia seemed to have come to a full stop.

"It's hard to say," said Virginia slowly. "We none of us can quite make up our minds about that, and we've stopped trying."

"Where did you find him?"

"He came with them out of Belgium when they escaped."

"Attached to Fabrice?"

"No. Attached to Sally."

"*At her age?* How old is he?"

"About forty, I should think."

"You—don't mean they're—" Camilla for once was speechless.

"No. Who knows?" Virginia was leaning back, dreaming through the smoke of her cigarette. "He's devoted to her, in the most heartrending way. They seem to read each other's thoughts, they seem to converse without speaking, their hands seem to touch across the room. I suppose it's the French in him," said Virginia dreamily. "And what they've been through together."

"You don't suppose—he could be her son?" Camilla suggested. "Secretly, you know."

"No." Virginia shook her head. "That's one thing I'm sure

he isn't. Bracken says mother says Sally doesn't deserve it.
When they were girls Sally was known to be utterly heartless
and vain and a flirt. Either she has changed since then—or
she's got Sosthène fooled."

"And you *like* him?"

"We all love him," said Virginia simply. "You'll see."

"Fabrice too?"

"Not Fabrice, no. She doesn't get anywhere with him. He
is immune." Virginia put out her cigarette. "She's turning
the Hall upside down, though, with her taking ways," she
added, and her tone hardened. "*I* say she oughtn't to be
allowed to work there, but they're so short of help they have
to take anybody who offers. She shirks all the dirty little jobs
a VAD is supposed to do and flirts with the men and puts
them against one another for fun and generally stirs up
trouble, and we'll be lucky if we come out of it short of some
beastly scandal. I specially resent it because she's messed up
Jenny Keane's life without any conscience at all."

"Messed it up how?"

"Jenny was engaged to Archie's youngest brother Gerald.
They had grown up together—Jenny is the Duke of Apethorpe's daughter and lives at Overcreech House up Moreton
way—and while Gerald's not much of a match, being a
younger son, and Jenny is the Duke's only child, it's been
understood for years that Jenny and Gerald sort of belonged
to each other. Then Gerald took one look at our Fabrice and
went right out of his mind and asked Jenny to release him—
broke it off, mind you, without consulting anybody—and I
don't think Fabrice wants him now that she's got him—not
for keeps, anyway, and no more than she wants half a dozen
others. *She* means to make a good match, you can count on
that! Jenny's been perfectly splendid, and tried to pretend
she doesn't mind and didn't really want to marry Gerald, but
we all know better and the poor kid is killing herself over

at the Hall, doing all the kind of beastly work Fabrice ought
to and won't. Archie keeps wanting to thrash Gerald, but it's
Fabrice who ought to be scalped, she only took him away
from Jenny to prove she could do it—and everybody is a bit
crazy anyway, in war time, I don't suppose you can blame
anybody, really, no matter what happens. Gerald is in France
and the thing is temporarily more or less at a standstill just
now. Fabrice doesn't bother much about letter-writing, I
fancy!"

"He might get over it out there and come back to Jenny,"
Camilla suggested.

"He might. If only we could get rid of Fabrice while he is
away! Get her married off to some one else, or something.
You'll like Jenny, she's our sort. Dinah's sort. And the Duke
is a dear."

"Shall I see him?"

"Who, the Duke? Bound to, he's always around. Overcreech is lonesome for him, with Jenny at the Hall, and he's
got most of it shut up and lives in one wing all by himself
with a couple of ancient servants. Her mother is dead."

Virginia leaned her head back and closed her eyes, tired
with talking and the nagging pain in her ankle. Camilla sat
looking out the window, her sharp young profile flooded
with the pale clear light of the Cotswold country, green and
gold in the late afternoon sunshine. It didn't by any means
always rain in England, she had discovered, and even though
the unheated compartment was frigid with autumn chill, the
land was just as green as they said it was. Little grey farms
flashed past her eyes, and low stone walls and lovely rolling
fields and sudden wooded hillsides—the sky curved above
them, deep blue with hardly a cloud. And somewhere men
were dying. . . .

Her quick, keen-cutting mind jeered at the commonplace
reflection, which she told herself was bound to occur to any-

one with an ounce of imagination, beholding the remote peace of Gloucestershire. Growing up with Calvert kept one from sentimentalism, like another boy. And all these involutions of other people's love affairs were Greek to her, so that she approached them skeptically, warily, with curiosity rather than sympathy, and no wish to become involved in them herself. She had known young men in Richmond, of course, who admired her coltish beauty and were a little staggered by her forthright manner and uncompromising way of looking at things. Southern girls were not like that, as a rule. Southern girls made some effort to please. The young men decided charitably that Camilla's odd ways came of being twin to a boy, and were a little afraid of her.

And Camilla, wrapped up in Calvert and wanting no other company if his were available, had never felt the lack of the romantic interludes other girls of her age had experienced, and she had never yet seen any man to compare with her brother. Now Virginia's words left an uneasiness. Suppose Calvert met some one irresistible, like Fabrice. Suppose Calvert fell in love, enough in love to go out of his mind like Gerald, and forget his old loyalties and convictions. She, a sister, certainly had never meant to interfere with Calvert's marrying when the time came. But he must marry some one good enough for him, that was all. And who would be the judge of that—Calvert or his sister? With people like this Fabrice about, and France must be full of them, how would a mere sister count?

"The next stop is us," said Virginia, gathering herself together, and Camilla roused to lend a hand.

It was tea time when the motor wheezed its way up the drive in front of Farthingale—it was in need of repairs, and war-time petrol was not what it was used to—and the day was grey and chilly, but Camilla cried, "Oh, how beautiful!" like the right-minded person she was. Virginia recalled with a pang her own first sight of the old stone house with its rows of narrow mullioned windows and its sharp gables, and the smooth lawn sloping to the brim of a clear stream too wide for jumping, the further bank overhung with chestnut trees. No war then, thought Virginia nostalgically, and everyone was young and gay and there was no necessity for patience and fortitude and all those bleaker virtues life had thrust upon one recently. Lovely days, when first she herself had come to Farthingale; lovely days since then too, living here with Archie and the babies. When would such days come again, she wondered, or had one had all the best of it now for a long time to come, and would the babies, growing up, ever know the pure, unclouded happiness in which her own first youth had passed—not so long ago. . . .

"Who's that?" Camilla was asking, at sight of a strolling figure in a tweed knickerbocker suit and cap, which had paused near the front steps to await their arrival.

It was Sosthène, walking Cousin Sally's Peke and being patient while it did its duty at the edge of the herbaceous border. Bracken had presented the golden brown Mimi to Cousin Sally to replace another Mimi who had been left behind in France and might never be seen again and was endlessly lamented.

Sosthène stood still at the edge of the gravel sweep as the motor drew up, and when Virginia waved he lifted his left hand in a slow, gracious gesture of reply, and then, unhurried, at his ease, his white, even teeth showing in his smile, he advanced to open the car door for them.

"Anyone looking less like an invalid I never saw," he greeted Virginia with affection. "Was it a tedious journey?"

"We're chilled to the bone, that's all," said Virginia. "This is Cousin Camilla from Richmond."

"How do you do?" said Camilla gravely, wondering what she was to call him, as she stepped down into the drive beside him and offered a slim paw in a dark glove.

Sosthène bent and kissed it, glove and all, which was the first time any such thing had ever happened to her, and she was still looking astonished when he straightened and met her eyes. His were dark brown, with rather sleepy curving lids, and they were smiling too. Mimi, suddenly aware of strangers, dashed up to them and began to bark shrilly, dancing round their feet.

"Another charming cousin from America," said Sosthène above the racket. "Sallee is so pleased that you have come and has made me understand exactly how you are related to her. *Tais-toi, Mimi—que tu est folle—silence!* And now, Virginia, does one carry you into the house or do you want a stretcher?"

"I have crutches, but I'm terrified of them," said Virginia, handing them out.

He took them and passed them straight on to Camilla, and stepped up to the door of the car.

"Just put your arms round my neck," he said. "Don't be afraid. I won't drop you."

Virginia trusted herself at once to his competent hold and was lifted out with the greatest of ease, the heavy white cast dangling, while Camilla sprang to open the house door. Sosthène passed her, carrying Virginia, and she followed them, reflecting that he did not behave, or look, like an invalid himself. But as he set down his light burden on a bench in the entrance hall, Virginia said in some surprise, "You probably shouldn't have done that—I keep forgetting—are you all right?"

"Perfectly," said Sosthène, and an elderly maid appeared to take their wraps, and their bags went by in the hands of the chauffeur and up the stairs. "Tea will be waiting," Sosthène went on in his gentle voice, his accent more a matter of intonation than of vowels and consonants, and then he turned severely on the noisy little dog which still cavorted hysterically about them, shrieking its disapproval of the arrivals. *Mimi, en voilà assez!* Shut up!"

"That's done it," remarked Virginia as the barking ceased. "I keep telling you this dog doesn't understand French."

"It must learn," said Sosthène calmly. "Elvire doesn't speak English. Some one must come half way."

Elvire was Cousin Sally's maid.

Virginia announced that she would like a cup of tea before she went up to her room or tried to cope with the children, and a voice from the drawing-room doorway behind them said, "My dear unfortunate one—how have you supported the journey? And where is Dabney's granddaughter?"

"Oh, Cousin Sally!" cried Camilla, and went towards her impulsively with both hands outstretched. "I'm Camilla. Everybody sent you their love."

Sally took her hands in a firm clasp and looked at her with violet-blue eyes, unfaded beneath their thin shadowed lids with long, blackened lashes—Camilla thought she had never seen such beauty, a little worn but not ravaged by time, the red-gold hair piled into an intricate pompadour and high psyche knot like a crown, the fine skin, only a little loose, exquisitely made up, the throat still white and firm. Her velvet tea-gown was skilfully cut and draped over a trim figure with a high bust. It was all true. All the legends about Cousin Sally were true. She was eternal. Camilla's ardent young spirit prostrated itself promptly before this ultimate embodiment of romance and mystery, and she adored Cousin Sally at sight.

"You must tell me about everybody at home," Sally was

saying, and she had really more of a French accent than Sosthène, though she spoke her mother tongue. "So many that I knew best are gone."

Sosthène came towards them with Virginia in his arms again, headed for the drawing-room fireside where tea was waiting, and at sight of them Sally gave a small humorous cry.

"Heavens! What gallantry!" she remarked, more in admiration than malice. "I assure you in all these years, Virginie, he has never done as much for me!"

Virginia waved at her impudently over Sosthène's shoulder and was deposited with the utmost care in a large chair at the side of the hearth. Camilla came forward diffidently, stripping off her gloves.

"Her foot has to be kept up on another chair or something," she said, and Sosthène drew up the needlepoint bench from the hearthrug and raised the cast tenderly to place it there. "And there ought to be something warm to put over it," said Camilla.

"Dear me, it is going to be as much trouble as a baby!" said Sally. "Here, take this." And she handed Camilla a soft knitted shawl from the end of the sofa.

As Camilla and Sosthène stooped together over Virginia's cast on the hearth-bench, tucking in the shawl, their fingers brushed briefly. Hers were still cold from the drive, his were warm and firm. She glanced up in embarrassment, and his face, bent above the task, was serene and oblivious. How kind he was—how much trouble he took—no doubt he had got used to waiting on people, with Cousin Sally. Camilla, who had never been waited on in her life and had never cared to be, was suddenly envious of the women who were entitled to Sosthène's solicitude, and who took it entirely for granted with a smile and a light word of thanks.

Sally was pouring out their tea, seated on the end of the

sofa next the table. Virginia received her cup first, by divine right, and Sally asked Camilla what she wanted in hers.

"N-nothing, thanks," said Camilla, hasty and confused, for sugar was short in England now. "Just tea."

"Ah, then you are a real tea-drinker like me," said Sosthène, taking her cup from Sally's hand. "Sit here, close to the fire—your hands are cold—"

She followed him to the opposite end of the long sofa, and when she had sat down he gave her the cup and handed round a covered silver dish of hot muffins, scantily buttered, and then returned to the middle of the sofa with his own tea, placing himself between Sally and Camilla but sitting well back so that they could go on talking across him.

"And your grandparents? Just think, Charlotte and I were born in the same year. Both dead, are they not?" Sally was saying almost cheerfully. "Charlotte and Dabney—how well I remember—he was still on crutches at their wedding—it was in Richmond, during the war—men I danced with that night were dead the next day in the trenches below the city, where Dabney had already lost his leg—"

"And at the church," Camilla reminded her eagerly, for it was a story she had always loved to hear, "Grandmother Charlotte caught hold of the swing door, do you remember, so it wouldn't knock him over, and everyone pretended not to notice—"

"Yes, yes, how it all comes back," said Sally, with affection rather than sadness, but her violet eyes were weary. "What days those were—how young one was—how tragic one felt about it all—it was the worst war the world had ever seen— *every* war is the worst war, I find—yet Dabney and Charlotte lived long, happy lives in spite of it—that can be true, for those who survive—we must be sure that it will be true again. Sosthène, Camilla would like one of those cakes—"

He moved quickly, obediently, to hand the plate of cakes.

Camilla took one daintily, feeling like a child at a grown-up party. Her eyes went up to his face with the doubtful, apologetic look which was so often hers when Calvert was not there to lend her countenance. Sosthène's gaze, lowered to the plate he held and her young, slim, ringless hand accepting the cake, seemed unaware.

"Me too," said Virginia, reaching out to him and waggling greedy fingers, and he carried the cakes to her, saying, "A broken ankle does give one an appetite," and exchanged a laughing glance with her, and the line in his cheek beside his long, well-modelled lips was a sort of exaggerated lengthwise dimple.

"It does, it does!" Virginia asserted without shame. "There is so little else to do but eat, meals become terribly important. You get so *bored,* because you can't do anything!"

"A little dose of doing nothing will be good for you," said Sosthène, and turned back towards the sofa, but paused to exclaim, "Ah! All is discovered!"

Following his gaze, Camilla saw that the drawing-room doorway was full of children, and heard Virginia saying cheerfully but with a distinct note of resignation, "Come in, darlings, I was only snatching a cup of tea before I sent for you. Come in and finish off the cakes, you might as well!"

She held out her arms and the well-mannered young avalanche descended upon her—five of them, apparently, the eldest a slim, leggy, dark-haired girl who obviously belonged to Virginia. Eventually they were sorted out and presented to their Cousin Camilla from Richmond—Daphne, fifteen, the image of her mother with the same delectable heart-shaped face and closed, mysterious smile; Irene, thirteen, with reddish hair like her aunt Dinah's; Nigel, who at eight looked exactly like Archie minus the eyeglass; Evadne, a three-year-old with Virginia's brown eyes and Archie's fair hair, who was going to be the beauty of the family; and a shy, sallow child, the cuckoo in the nest, Oliver's daughter Hermione.

They all curtsied politely except Nigel who bowed gravely from the waist, and Camilla, overstrung and full of new sensations, wanted to cry. She was not accustomed to children, as she and Calvert had been the only ones at home, and she had no idea how to make friends with them, so she only smiled back and said Hullo, and as soon as the introductions were over Nigel asked if she had been torpedoed crossing the ocean. He seemed disappointed that her answer was negative, and informed her rather accusingly that Cousin Phoebe had been torpedoed and nearly died.

"I was lucky," said Camilla lamely.

"Do you write books?" pursued Nigel, whose standard for cousins was obviously high, and Camilla shook her head.

"She's the one who sings," Daphne came to her rescue. "Cousin Phoebe said so."

"Oh, sing something now!" cried Irene. "Sing something from America!"

"No," said Virginia, settling them all. "We're both of us completely frazzled out and we're not going to amuse anybody till after we've had dinner and a night's sleep. Buzz off, now, the whole lot of you, and after I'm in bed you can all come and kiss me Good-night if you like. We shall be here for weeks, so your time will come."

"Will you be here for Christmas?" Nigel demanded.

"It looks that way. But I shall have the cast off by then, I hope!"

"May we *see* the cast?" Nigel's eyes gleamed with ghoulish interest.

"Later," said Virginia, waving them out.

But Hermione had come to anchor near her chair.

"Will my father be here for Christmas?" she asked very

quietly, and Virginia patted the small sallow hand which was laid on her sleeve.

"I think very likely," she said.

"And—Phoebe too?"

"Yes, of course, if *he* comes. Now, get your cake and run along with the rest of them, there's a dear."

The other children were filing past the tea-table, each receiving a single cake from the plate Sally held out to them. Hermione joined them reluctantly, her face brooding and downcast. At the door they all turned and waved, and Virginia waved back, and when they had disappeared she leaned back with a sigh.

"I love them all passionately," she said. "But right now there are too many of them. And somehow since Hermione came five seems so many more than four! I do hope she isn't going to be tiresome about her father's marrying again, it would be just like her, though we've handled it the best we know how. Her mother was insanely jealous, do you suppose we're going through all *that* again?"

"Surely not at Hermione's age," Camilla said.

"It is a very short-sighted self-indulgence—jealousy—at any age," said Sally. "Tell me again the name of the man your mother married, Camilla—Ames, was it not?"

"No, no, that's the Princeton bunch!" cried Camilla, horrified. "We're the Scotts!"

"Ah, yes, so you are," Sally nodded gravely. "Richmond—of course—Scott. And you have a brother."

"Calvert. We're twins. That's why I miss him so."

"I had a brother," said Sally dreamily.

"Honey, you've still got him!" Camilla reminded her. "Cousin Sedgwick is very much alive in Williamsburg!"

"I know." For the first time Sally sighed, looking back. "I never thought not to see Sedgwick again." And just as the silence fell—"Sosthène, the child would like more tea. Bring me her cup, at once."

"No, really—I—it doesn't matter—"

This time his eyes met Camilla's as he stood above her—a look so deep and intimate and confidential that it was as though he spoke: *Let her pour the tea for you. Let her recover herself that way. You and I understand this.* And once more Camilla's cold fingers encountered his warm ones, as she surrendered the cup.

The jewelled white hand which held the teapot while the amber liquid flowed was not quite steady now.

"Nothing in your tea at all," marvelled Sally, and made a little face. "That is the way the Chinese drink it."

"And Sosthène," said Camilla, greatly daring, driven by her need to use his name for the sake of retaining the sense of old acquaintance which that long, silent exchange of looks had wrought. And then, losing her nerve completely and relapsing into her habitual childish embarrassment—"I don't th-think I have ever heard your other name."

"You will not need it," he smiled, returning her cup, and resumed his place on the sofa and took out a gold cigarette case which he offered to Sally and then lit both their cigarettes from one match and moved the ash tray nearer her hand on the corner of the table.

It did not occur to him to offer the young American a cigarette. And Camilla, who rather liked to smoke because it made her feel sophisticated and mature, hoped that Virginia would not call attention to the fact, and discovered that her patient was sitting with her head resting against the back of the chair and her eyes closed.

"Darling, are you all right?" cried Camilla, setting down her cup with a clink and darting to Virginia's side, remorsefully aware that she had forgotten for a few minutes, actually *forgotten* that she was in charge and was neglecting her duty. "Would you like some more tea? Or had you better have another one of those little pills?"

Virginia opened her eyes and said she thought she would like to go to bed if nobody minded. "And Sosthène is *not* to carry me up stairs," she added firmly. "With you in front and him behind I can manage perfectly well on my crutches."

The ascent was accomplished, not without a few minor alarms and some amusing comment from Sosthène, who walked behind with his hands holding Virginia's waist. Sally's maid Elvire, who understood massage, was waiting to put Virginia to bed, and Camilla followed Sosthène from the room and paused just outside her own door, to which he had escorted her.

"Does—do you think Cousin Sally is ever homesick?" she asked hesitantly. "For Williamsburg, I mean."

"I think sometimes she is," he said gently. "Especially now, with her comfortable life in France broken off. I am all she has left of the old days there—all there is of sameness and security. At her age she is bound to feel that."

"Yes, of course." Camilla lingered, fingering her doorknob. "Had I better not talk about America when it can be avoided? Or would she like to know that she's not forgotten there, and that we've all grown up wondering about her—" And then she remembered that the uncertainty they had all felt was vaguely scandalous. "N-not that we knew much about her, of course," she added, and wondered if she had not made it worse, for was not Sosthène himself a part of the mystery?

"Of all the people I have ever known, Sallee is best able to support life as it comes," he said gravely. "She does not repine. I would not have you raise any barrier between you of tact or evasiveness. Answer all her questions, tell her little stories of your life, give her all the news from there—you need not be afraid. Never let her feel that you withhold. More than anything else in the world she needs love and care and thoughtfulness and homage—as indeed we all do—but Sallee has lost so much more of it than most of us ever have— she has had so much more to lose—I try constantly to make it up to her, now that what she calls the starving time has come—it is a Virginia phrase, is it not?"

"It was the old word for famine in the colonies, I think."

"Yes—I had guessed. She is very brave—no one knows that so well as I do. But you can understand, I am sure, that for a woman of such beauty and such wealth—I do not mean only in the coin of the realm—to know that the sands are running out—"

"Is she ill?" cried Camilla, her eyes full of quick hot tears.

"No, no. And the last thing I want is for you to pity her. But you are young and strong and—full of life. And you are of her own blood. You can help me, if you will, to keep her feeling warm and cherished and beloved, as she must be to live at all."

"How? How can I?"

His shoulders rose a trifle at the ease of it—at the simplicity of his request.

"Talk to her—tell her things—ask her advice on your own affairs, even if you must invent the affairs—pay her little compliments—tell her she is beautiful!"

"She *is* beautiful!"

"Ah, yes, she is. You see, I do not ask the impossible."

"You mean you want me to take the place of Fabrice?" asked Camilla directly, and he gave her a long, smiling look with admiration in it.

"That is called catching on, I think," he said. "Virginia has doubtless told you that Fabrice is—a disappointment. We see very little of her here any more, we are too quiet for her taste. Sallee has hoped so much of you—I know that very well. And now that you have come, I can see that her hopes are all safe with you. You will be a breath of fresh air. But I keep you standing here, and you must rest before dinner."

"Wait!" She laid an impulsive hand on his sleeve and lifted it away again at once and felt her cheeks grow hot under his attentive, courteous gaze. "No, I—it doesn't matter—I'll ask you some other time—"

"We shall have plenty of time, and you must be tired now. The dressing-bell goes at seven and I should lie down until then if I were you."

He turned away, with a smile like a caress, towards the stairs and the drawing-room where Cousin Sally was. Camilla shut the door and stood a moment leaning against the inside of it, wondering why her heart was pounding as though she had run uphill. She had touched his sleeve to hold him there beside her—why? What was she going to say to him? What did he think of her, backing down like that? She felt a fool, a blundering, schoolgirlish idiot, all thumbs, abrupt, tactless, *gauche* would be his word for it. Left-handed. Was that what he thought of her now? *You will be a breath of fresh air. . . .*

Pressing cold, nervous fingers against her temples, she moved slowly to the bed and sat down on the edge of it limply, staring ahead of her at the cheery little coal fire which did its best to warm the spacious room—a room with old Chinese wall-paper and old Queen Anne furniture and a long view down the wintry garden towards the curve of the stream.

Camilla was not conscious of the room, which she would have explored with interest an hour before. Now she sat still on the edge of the bed, suddenly overwhelmed with weariness and a strange, paralyzing depression whose cause was not clear to her. She felt wrung out and hung up to dry. Well, why? It was not such a dreary prospect ahead of her, to be nice to Cousin Sally because Fabrice, who was her own granddaughter, was a washout. And there would be plenty of time, he said, to talk to Sosthène.

About what? They had absolutely nothing in common except looking after Cousin Sally—Sosthène didn't know or care anything about the family in America, there was nothing in her own reminiscences which could possibly interest him, except the bit of war-time London she had seen and the one bad raid she had gone through, but there was nothing in that to impress anyone but herself, it had happened to hundreds of other people. He and Cousin Sally had seen much worse, getting out of Belgium. She had nothing to offer him, there was nothing whatever about her own meagre, crude, childish, stammering self to interest him in the least. And she had to wait two endless hours before she could see him again. . . .

She had no idea how long she had sat there on the edge of the bed before there was a knock on the door and Sally herself looked in.

"Not resting?" she asked in surprise. "Sosthène said that he advised you to lie down before dinner. I only came to see if you had everything you wanted."

Camilla rose and went to put her arms around the slender, fragrant figure which had paused in the middle of the room.

"How *nice* you smell!" she said. "Is it you or your clothes? And wait till they hear at home that I have seen you at last and that you are just as beautiful as they always said you were!"

Sally's answering embrace was a little tense, but relaxed at once and she was smiling.

"You know, of course, that by all the rules I should by now be dying in a gutter," she remarked. "It's really very disobliging of me, but I've never been anywhere *near* a gutter! Be sure to tell them that at home, won't you!"

"They know it!" Camilla grinned, and Sally patted her cheek with a ringed hand.

"But that is not to say that you are to follow my example," she said.

"Cousin Sally, tell me honestly—would you do it all the same again?"

Sally's wide violet gaze went slowly away from Camilla's face to rest on the door, somewhere beyond which was Sosthène and this life, whatever it was, that they lived together. Her small head with its red-gold crown of gleaming hair was very high and proud.

"For the same ending—yes," she said without hesitation. "Don't think I have never had my bad times—don't think I have never shed bitter tears—but Sosthène said to me once, a long time ago it was, at our beginning, You shall never weep again, he said, and it has been so—even with the war, it has been so. I have lost my home, my old friends, perhaps my fortune—but with what I have left, there is nothing lost worth weeping for."

Camilla, standing beside her in a long silence, thought, I must lie down after all, before I drop—I wonder if it's influenza coming on—you feel very queer when that starts—

She made a blind, groping movement towards the bed, and Sally's arm was around her waist.

"My dear, you are half dead with fatigue and I stand talking here! Lie down, now, and let me put the eiderdown over you—like that—kick off your shoes, no one can possibly rest with shoes on—there—now close your eyes and drift a bit, you're bound to hear the dressing-bell, I tell Virginie it would wake the dead—"

The eiderdown was expertly tucked in, especially at the hollow of the back where it was so comforting, all but one light was turned out, and the door closed softly behind her.

Camilla lay very still, as though hiding from something that was bound to pounce if she gave the slightest sign of life. Her fingers were damp and icy, her heartbeats were deafening, she was cold and frightened and alone. Desperately she numbed her mind, tried not to think, determined not to realize the relentless thing which waited in ambush at the back of her consciousness. . . .

But not for long. There was no putting it off for long. It was gaining on her now—there was no refuge—no defence. It came. . . .

Oh, *no,* I must not think of Sosthène. . . .

———

Exhausted as she was, she had found it impossible to doze when the dressing-bell sounded brassily through the house. What a thing, she thought mistily, sitting up at once, and then lingering a moment, her head in her hands. What must I wear? The blue is best, but I was saving it for the Christmas party. That's a month away. I'll wear the blue tonight. No, you won't any such thing, you'll wear your old black, it's only family and there's no reason to put on any airs.

She swung her feet off the bed and stood up, feeling shaken and odd. There was another knock on the door and the elderly housemaid came in with a polished brass can of hot water and fussed round the wash-handstand, placing towels and soap.

"Will you want any help with your dress, miss?"

"No, thanks, I can manage, I expect you have all you can do these days."

"Thank you, miss."

She smiled, and went noiselessly away.

Camilla took the black chiffon dress out of the wardrobe— it had short sleeves and a full petalled skirt, with a pink velvet rose caught on the left hip—she had worn it to informal dances and family parties in Richmond for the past two years. Firmly she closed the wardrobe door and laid the dress on the bed. It was quite good enough for anybody.

She got out of her travelling clothes, pinned back her hair and washed her face and touched it up very carefully—Virginia permitted her a film of rouge on her cheeks and lips and a light dusting of powder, with the remark that she might as well begin, everyone came to it because of being so tired all the time and it was better than looking ghastly and heroic.

While she was brushing out her hair Camilla wondered what Calvert would say if she had it cut short like Virginia's —and decided to ask him next time she wrote. She caught hold of it just below her ears on each side and bunched it out experimentally. Its softness was becoming to her high cheekbones and sharp jaw line. She leaned closer to the glass, studying her face as she had never paused to do before. Wide open grey eyes looked back at her under high, curving brows—a long, straight mouth with childish, sensitive lips—the throat was too small, like the neck of a colt—the forehead was high beneath the heavy natural waves of chestnut hair. No great beauty—not by Sally's nineteenth century standards—but clean-looking—*bred*-looking—like a promising colt. Camilla, realizing none of this, made a face at herself in the glass and began to twist up her hair into the usual heavy knot at the back of her neck. It dragged away from her face—made her chin stick out, made her forehead higher. She tore out the pins and began again, attempting Phoebe's style with the wide smooth band of hair wrapped closely round her head. To her surprise it stayed up. She pulled it looser round her small ears, doubtfully. Would they think she was copying Phoebe? Did it matter if they did? No one but Virginia would know it was the first time she had worn it this way. And it did make her look less—less stick-in-the-mud-ish. Phoebe fastened hers with a square tortoise-shell pin either side. Camilla wondered if Phoebe would mind if she got big pins too. Oh, only when she was off duty like this, of course.

The rest of the time the bun was more suitable. Unless she had it cut. . . .

She put on the black dress and the black silk stockings which went with it, and the black satin slippers with under-cut heels, and looked at herself again anxiously—the new hair style made her taller—gave her fine-boned face and slender neck something she had never seen in herself before. The word her youthful humility of spirit forbade her was *elegance*. It brought out her inborn look of race. But the quite unconscious excitement which shimmered all round her was due to the presence in the house of a stranger she was resolved not to try to know better.

While she still hesitated before the mirror the brassy gong went again, and when she reached the drawing-room Sally and Sosthène were already there, Sosthène in a velvet dinner jacket with a black tie, Sally resplendently décolletée and covered with jewels. Virginia had decided to have a tray in bed, and Camilla wondered with a darting panic if she had to dine alone with these two, and instantly despaired of making sufficient adult conversation to last out the meal. Sally must have seen something of her consternation, for she held out a welcoming hand crusted with diamonds and said at once, "Come along, child, and have a glass of wine with us. Or has Virginie taught you to drink those horrible cocktails up in London?"

"No, I—don't as a rule take anything before dinner," said Camilla, and gave her left hand into Sally's warm clasp grate-fully. "Unless there's a raid on, and I need Dutch courage!"

"Such cold hands," said Sally, holding Camilla's telltale fingers between her palms. "How nice you look, my dear, Sosthène, we won't wait for the others, they must have bro-ken down somewhere. Pour the wine now."

Sosthène had risen from the sofa when Camilla came in,

and he went to the tray where a cut-glass decanter and frail stemmed glasses stood, and began to pour the sherry, while Sally continued to appraise Camilla's appearance with interest.

"Yes—very nice indeed," she nodded. "But a little *too* chaste, perhaps. Here, you must have these." She unclasped the necklace at her throat and held it out—a double strand of graduated pearls. "Stoop down, child, I'll put it on for you."

"Oh, *may* I wear it, really? I've always loved pearls better than anything!" Camilla knelt beside Sally's knees and felt the cool, satiny things slide round her throat and heard the click of the clasp in Sally's fingers.

"Wait, now—let me look." Sally's hand on her shoulder held her there, level with the smiling violet eyes. "Yes, that's right—now I must think—Sosthène, ring for Elvire."

He touched a bell at the corner of the mantelpiece and then came towards them, a stemmed glass in either hand.

"It's only sherry," he said as Camilla glanced up at him uncertainly. "You need it after the journey."

She took the glass and settled back on her heels, half against Cousin Sally's knees and half against the sofa, and began to sip.

"Is some one else coming to dinner?" she asked, feeling a little more hopeful.

"My dear, the most tremendous surprise!" said Sally. "Archie is on his way to Gloucester from Oxford, and has got the night here! He rang up from the Hall half an hour ago and said not to say a word to Virginie, he would just *arrive!* He's travelling by motor on some mysterious errand, and is going to bring Jenny Keane with him from the Hall. It will be more cheerful for you to have her to get acquainted with tonight, and nice for her to come away for a bit, she works much too hard."

"Perhaps she'd let me see over the hospital," said Camilla. "Some time when it's convenient, I mean."

"She would be glad to, I know. She thinks of nothing else nowadays, poor lamb."

"I'm longing to see Archie, and I'd have put on my prettiest frock for him if I'd known!" Camilla remarked, just as Elvire came in—a gaunt, middle-aged Frenchwoman who had been Sally's maid since the beginning of time.

Sally gave some quick, explicit orders in French, which Camilla only half caught, and Elvire, having said *Oui, madame,* three times without enthusiasm, went away again. They drank their wine and speculated about what was delaying Archie until she returned with a handful of jewels which she laid in Sally's lap and retired.

"Ah," said Sally with satisfaction, handing Sosthène her empty glass, and picked up a pair of tortoise-shell hair ornaments set with pearls, and a three-strand pearl bracelet with a diamond clasp. "Now we shall see. Hold up, child—the left side, I think—" With a light, expert touch she set the hair ornament at the edge of the smooth band which went round Camilla's head, and glanced at Sosthène, who nodded, looking on from behind the sofa with his glass in his hand. "Just one," said Sally, and put the other in Camilla's paralyzed hand. "You may have them both, in case you lose one, but you are to wear only one at a time, do you hear? Now this." She slipped the bracelet on Camilla's slim wrist and snapped its clasp. "These are for you to keep. They suit you."

"To *keep!*" cried Camilla incredulously. "Oh, no, just to wear!—just for tonight because—because of Archie—I couldn't possibly—"

"To keep," said Sally firmly, closing Camilla's fingers on the second hair ornament which she had thrust back impulsively at its owner. "Tomorrow we will go through my jewel-case and you shall choose whatever you like."

"But I *c-can't* own things like this, I can't have real pearls, they must be worth a fortune and I'm only—I'm just a poor relation from Richmond!" she finished hastily, trying to make Cousin Sally laugh with her, trying to make her see that such gifts were not for graceless young heathens from the hinterlands like herself. "We never *see* such things in Richmond, let alone wear them!" she hurried on. "Mother wouldn't *allow* me, she'd have them locked up—"

"Your mother is not here," said Sally. "Fortunately, it seems. I have many good jewels, my dear, they have always been a weakness of mine. Those which are suitable to your age and style you shall have now, while you are young enough to enjoy them, instead of—later. We shall have to do something about a dress, too. Not that what you are wearing is not very good. But something perhaps a little more—festive."

"But I *have* a better one, a blue one," Camilla assured her eagerly. "I was afraid it was too gay for tonight, I—should I fly up now and change before they come?"

"By no means," said Sally kindly. "You are right for tonight just as you are. Sosthène, I want for her an ivory brocade—"

There were voices in the hall. Archie and Jenny had arrived.

———

Archie was as different as a brother could be from Oliver, though his smartly cut captain's uniform became his slender body and easy carriage as though he too had been bred to it instead of to the legal gown and wig he had forsaken at the beginning of the war. Camilla liked him at once and was fascinated by the single eyeglass, which she had never seen done before.

The girl he brought with him was small and fair, with a relaxed composure of manner which Camilla admired and envied. Jenny was completely at home in Virginia's house, but then she would have been at home anywhere, she had a self-possession which came of generations of dignity and pride of place. She was simplicity·itself. But at the same time she was Lady Jenny Keane, the Duke of Apethorpe's only child. It showed in the way she held her brushed blonde head with its short gold hair curved under at the edges like a bell, and her small quiet hands, and her slow, rather deep voice with its pure vowels and perfect articulation. Jenny Keane was everything that Camilla desired to be—poised, groomed, self-contained, a little aloof—grown up. And yet Camilla doubted very much if Jenny was as old as she was herself.

They accepted a glass of sherry each and Jenny sat down by the fire. Just as Camilla was beginning to wonder if Archie was ever going upstairs to see Virginia she found his eyes upon her, and smiled up at him—reminding him as she did so of something pathetic that wagged its tail. He put his glass on the mantelpiece and went and sat down beside her.

"I was talking to Phoebe on the telephone a little while ago," he said.

"In London?" Camilla wanted to ask if anything had gone wrong in St. James's Square since she and Virginia had left it early that afternoon, but it seemed a silly sort of question, so she only looked at him and waited for him to go on.

"She asked me to bring you a message," said Archie, and took her hands in both his. "Hold tight, my dear—your brother has been wounded."

For a moment Camilla held tight gratefully, feeling herself go paper white, leaving a tense silence while she mastered a wave of giddiness. She had braced herself for this, of course, but not yet. Not so soon.

"Is it bad?" she heard herself asking at last.

"Pretty bad, I'm afraid."

"Are you breaking something to me? Is he—dead?"

"No. Wounded. He will be sent back to England, I expect, before long. I'm trying to get in touch with Bracken over there, he'll go and look him up and send us details."

"Was there any word from Calvert?"

"No. Telegram from the War Office. Came an hour after you left. Now, don't worry yet, my dear, we'll know more about it soon."

"Yes, I—I'm all right." Camilla's head came up resolutely. "Thank you for—did you come out of your way to tell me yourself?"

Archie grinned at her ruefully.

"Well, the truth is, I was moving heaven and earth to get a few hours with Virginia," he said.

"Of course, you—you must go up to her now." Camilla let go of his sustaining hands. "How soon can we hear from Bracken?"

"Hard to say. It will be a few days, anyway. Now, drink this up and try to eat your dinner." He took a fresh glass of sherry from Sosthène's waiting hand and closed her fingers on its stem. "Drink it," he insisted kindly, and she obeyed, and Sosthène took back the empty glass. "Jenny will stay here with you tonight if you want her," Archie was saying. "We thought you might need company, and she's been through a lot of this—she can tell you that most of the time there's no need to worry."

"I know," said Camilla steadily. "Lots of them get well."

"*Droves* of them, darling," said Jenny from her chair across the hearthrug, and Camilla was grateful that she didn't fuss and sympathize. "We'll pull every wire in the place and get him sent down to the Hall and you can come and help look after him."

Camilla stared at her with reviving hope.

"*Could* you do that?"

"Well, I have heard of such things," said Jenny. "We can

try, anyway. You know what a wizard Bracken is. Just like
him to take it up with the Prime Minister!"

Archie stood up, and Sally told him that it had been arranged for him to have dinner upstairs in Virginia's room,
and he said How marvellous, and was gone. Virginia's shriek
of joyful surprise as he appeared in the doorway of her room
was audible all the way down the stairs as the rest of them
went in to dinner.

Jenny was a big help during the meal, and the three of
them kept a rambling conversation going on around Camilla,
creating an atmosphere of usualness and calm which was very
bracing, while she assimilated the shock of Archie's news and
even found things to say herself. And meanwhile a corner of
her brain was thinking, I don't really feel anything yet—it's
like hitting your head very hard—it will begin to hurt later
—I'm really doing pretty well, so far—I'm not crying, am I—
I'm able to eat—why don't I *feel* more?—is it the wine they
made me drink. . . .

After dinner, having coffee in the drawing-room, she
found herself talking in a normal sort of way to Jenny about
the work in St. James's Square as compared to Jenny's job at
the Hall—and Jenny was saying she wanted to take regular
training so as to go out to France as a nursing Sister but
everyone was dead against it, she couldn't see why, as in
some ways the work was actually easier than the sordid
drudgery the VAD's got, and it was certainly more interesting. Sally at once said No, Jenny was much too young to
nurse great hulking men with dreadful wounds, that was
for married women—or spinsters who had lost hope. Jenny
laughed, and said, "How old-fashioned of you, darling!" and
Sally said that anyway the Duke was quite right not to permit
it.

"Besides, I *am* a spinster," said Jenny then, and her lips
closed defiantly on the word, not smiling any more, and she

looked back at Sally with her blue eyes very bright and dark as though the pupils had expanded, and her chin very high.

"Nonsense, you are *jeune fille*," said Sally flatly. "And the world is still full of men who have eyes to see and hearts to give."

"But I don't want a man," said Jenny wilfully, and the words came out very clean-cut and bitten off one by one. "I just want to be a nurse."

"All men are not alike," said Sally. "You may as well say you do not want a new hat. Sooner or later there is one which becomes you and you cannot resist."

"And so you wear it for the rest of your life?" flashed Jenny, and shook her head. "That's a rotten simile, darling—isn't it, Sosthène?" There were queer, angry sparks in her eyes, and Camilla, watching her from across the hearthrug, recalled Virginia's reference to Gerald Campion, who had jilted Jenny for Fabrice and was now in France.

"Well, yes, perhaps it was," Sally admitted easily before Sosthène could speak. "But it was to say that there are always more fish in the sea."

"All rather scaly, I'm afraid," said Jenny, still in that clipped-off way, not bitter, not flippant, but—disinterested.

"Oh, come, *come!*" Sosthène objected with affection, and "You have hurt his feelings!" cried Sally with mock concern.

"I'm sorry, just show me another Sosthène and I shall revise my opinions!" Jenny reached to pat him lightly on the sleeve. "But there is only one of these, and it is not for me!"

"Perhaps I can show you Calvert soon," said Camilla generously, for she liked Jenny for trying to jest about her hurt, and she knew already what it was to covet Sosthène, and he was not for her either.

"I hope you can, darling. And don't think I'm sour about men because I'm not. Some of them are lambs." Her lips were softer now, and her eyes smiled again. "I just want to be a nurse," she repeated, acknowledging her obstinacy with a little foolish gesture of both hands.

"Wait five years," said Sally. "And meanwhile, take Camilla over to the Hall and show her everything."

"I'd be glad to," said Jenny at once. "She could come back with Archie and me in the morning and I'll find a way to get her home during the day. Can you ride a bicycle?" she asked Camilla, who nodded. "Then you can borrow mine to ride home. It's only a couple of miles by the lane."

Camilla accepted gratefully, aware that they were devising something to occupy her mind until Bracken could be heard from, but willing to be stage-managed to that end. She had no desire to worry and wonder and wait alone. And during the visit to the Hall there would be less time to think of Sosthène as well. Already she was counting on Jenny to save her—Jenny, who had somehow saved herself from one of the worst humiliations a woman can bear, and could still smile and make jokes and hold her head high. Camilla hoped also to see Fabrice at the Hall. She was shamelessly curious now about the girl who could take a man away from Jenny. Any man. Gerald, as Gerald, didn't really matter. Gerald was only the pawn. The players were the now unimaginable French girl, Fabrice, and the little aristocrat across the hearth who had lost. Or had she lost? Nothing worth having, surely. But she thought she had, that was the thing. Whatever Gerald was worth, himself, Jenny had taken the beating. And Jenny deserved the best. Even Calvert would not be too good for Jenny. . . . I'm match-making already, thought Camilla. Well, it *would* be nice. For everybody. I'd like Jenny for a sister. . . . I never thought to say that about anybody. . . .

Camilla was able to accept the offer of Jenny's companionship over night with the same simplicity with which it was

offered. They had dined late, and by the time Sally had drunk
her coffee and sipped her *grand marnier* in front of the
drawing-room fire the clocks were striking ten, which was the
time she usually retired to her room. Sosthène always accompanied her up the stairs, her hand in his elbow, and was not
himself seen again until breakfast. Virginia, after tactfully
providing them with adjoining rooms, had tried not to in-
dulge in impertinent speculation regarding so early a disap-
pearance of two people who seemed unlikely to require
approximately eleven hours sleep each night. Once, prowling
the passage in the small hours caring for a sick child, she had
seen light under Cousin Sally's door and had distinctly heard
the murmur of Sosthène's voice—reading aloud.

To Camilla, Sosthène's contented early departure from the
drawing-room was the last devastation of a bludgeoning day,
and she was left alone with Jenny in front of the fire under a
weight of depression too crushing for tears, her gnawing
anxiety about Calvert complicated by a guilty preoccupation
with the absorbing stranger whose mere presence had seemed
to hold her together and ward off a childish collapse into pre-
mature grief and panic. While Sosthène was there she had
to behave well. Now that he was gone, disappointment descended on top of apprehension, until it seemed she could
not breathe, and the long night was still to be got through.
But how wicked, thought Camilla, how heartless and de-
praved, to allow the sharp edge of her fear for Calvert's life to
be gummed up with thoughts about anyone else, about a
person Calvert had never even seen, a person who was nothing to her, nor ever could be. . . .

"You don't feel like going up to bed yet, do you," Jenny
was saying, and Camilla shook her head gratefully though she
had had a long day herself and would have known, if she had
stopped to think, that Jenny must have been up before six
that morning. "Shall we turn on the gramophone? Or would

you rather play cards? I know just how you feel, but you'll get your second wind pretty soon, I can promise. The thing is just to keep going till that happens, and then you can bear it."

"Jenny—" Camilla reached for her blindly, and Jenny's warm hands closed over hers.

"Yes, darling—Jenny's here to sit it out with you, however long it takes. Want to cry on my shoulder?"

But Camilla straightened, her jaw set. It was Calvert coming on top of this strange new confusion about Sosthène that made one so desperate, but one couldn't talk about that to Jenny. It was needing Calvert more than ever because of Sosthène that made his wounding so much worse. It was the necessity to put Sosthène out of one's mind that left those echoing empty spaces for fear to take root in and made one such a snivelling coward about Calvert. . . .

Camilla stood up abruptly and walked away from the sofa where Jenny sat.

"I'll be all right," she said tightly. "It's—a bit sudden— and I was tired to begin with—I'm sorry to be such a baby, I'll get used to it pretty soon—"

"We may get good news from Bracken sooner than you think," said Jenny, and went to the gramophone in the corner and dropped the needle on the record that lay there, without looking to see what it was, and the sparkle of a Chopin waltz danced out into the quiet room. Camilla listened, statue-still, staring at the fire, her face between her hands. And when the record ended, "More," she said without moving, and heard Jenny turn the record. By the time the B Flat Mazurka dripped away into silence Camilla was able to look round at Jenny and smile.

"That was my first grown-up piece," she said. "There was a while when I was sick to death of it. Now I've come full circle and dearly love it again. It brings back all the old-time family parties at Williamsburg, when we each had to perform and show what we had learned since the last time. I remember how proud I was the first time I played that and got through it without tripping, and they all clapped and Cousin Sedgwick said 'Bravo!' and Mother mopped her eyes, I can't think why, and Calvert winked at me because he'd said all along I could do it—"

The brave, bright words faltered, and Jenny said quickly, "You don't know how I envy you growing up in a big family like that, and how wonderful it seems to somebody like me that there can be a whole party, enough for dancing and music and applause, without ever going outside the family! Of course with us there is Uncle Ralph, that's Father's brother, and his wife, and their son Godfrey, he's at Harrow now, but they live up in Leicestershire and we hardly ever see them—most of the time there's only Father and me, and while we're awfully good pals it's not very many, is it! I mean, when I play to Father it sort of echoes, and he'd never dream of saying Bravo!"

"Do you play Chopin?" Camilla asked with interest.

"Oh, yes. The first one I learned was the one he did for the little dog, remember?"

"The D Flat Waltz. Is there a record of that there?"

"Don't think so. But I'll never forget how it goes." Jenny snapped on a light over the grand piano and her fingers scampered into the gay little tune, imparting an impudent stress and exaggeration all their own, which drew Camilla to the bench beside her and they finished together in a dead run, with Camilla's right hand an octave higher than Jenny's, and broke into schoolgirl laughter.

"And remember this one?" Jenny said then, slipping into a Nocturne, and Camilla said, "Yes, do go on," and sat with her cheek against Jenny's shoulder, listening till the end, when Jenny slid along the bench and said, "Now you play something new from America," and Camilla played an Irving Berlin tune from *The Century Girl,* which she had seen with Dinah in New York before sailing. When that was finished Jenny said, "Have you seen the new show at Daly's?" and played one of Miss José Collins' songs from that and they sang it together, and Jenny said, "We're pretty good, let's give the boys at the Hall a concert some time."

Camilla said she'd like very much to sing for them if they cared about that sort of thing.

"They'd love it," Jenny assured her. "They're the best audience in the world, and they're sick of all my tricks, they've seen them so often, you must come and perform for them. We're planning a lot of doings around Christmas time, and we'll need your help."

Camilla said she'd be glad to be of some use.

"Good," said Jenny. "Some of us are going to dress up and play the fool, they always love that, but they know good music when they hear it. You must brush up on all your Southern American songs because that would be a novelty for them— *My Old Kentucky Home,* and all that. You don't happen to play a banjo, do you?"

"Calvert does," said Camilla wistfully.

"Well, who knows, we might have him here by then! Tell me, shan't we skip down to the kitchen and make some cocoa and have it here in front of the fire before we go to bed?"

"Yes, let's," said Camilla, and set her teeth against a resurgent tightness in her throat and a stinging in her eyelids, and followed Jenny through the dark, quiet house to the tidy kitchen, deserted for the night, where she set out cups and biscuits on a tray while Jenny dealt efficiently with the range and a sauce-pan and milk and cocoa.

"It's a funny thing," said Jenny, stirring briskly at the stove, "but cocoa always does more to restore one's morale than any amount of brandy ever could. I suppose it's the business of *making* it, and coping with a fire and raising a cheerful noise with the china and so forth. There was a time when I simply lived on cocoa, because the motions I went through to make it seemed to keep me from having to scream. I got quite bilious from it finally, but I never gave up and screamed."

"Did it last long—your bad time?" Camilla asked, her head bent above the tray.

"Long enough," Jenny answered frankly from the stove. "But finally I grew some sort of a scar tissue, apparently, because I'm all right now, I really am. I daresay Virginia's told you about the man I was engaged to falling in love with somebody else," she continued steadily. "You don't have to be tactful about it, goodness knows it was no secret at the time! There was no point in my trying to hang on to him, of course, if that was the way he felt. But all the same, it wasn't the sort of thing you expect to have happen to you, was it!" the slow, beautifully formed words went on. "It's your pride that gets broken, I think, as much as your heart. You begin to wonder what's wrong with you. If your man is killed, that's clean and definite and can happen to anybody—you can still hold your head up. But if he just decides in cold blood that he prefers somebody else after all, you feel sort of—black and blue for a while, and you want to crawl away and hide. Not that I would rather Gerald had got killed, I don't mean it to sound that way—" She took the sauce-pan off the stove and poured the cocoa carefully into the tall china pot on the tray and carried the sauce-pan to the sink. "You know, this is very funny, I've never been able to talk about it before to anyone, not even Virginia—I suppose it's because you're in trouble too—and if my own experience can keep you from going to pieces—"

"H-how did you know I—" Camilla began and caught her breath.

Jenny turned at the sink, with the tap running, and gave her a long, surprised look.

"I meant your brother's wound," she said, and turned off the tap and came to Camilla at the table. "Is there something else?"

"No—nothing—I—"

Jenny laid a hand on Camilla's arm.

"Darling, have I put my foot in it somehow? I never meant to say anything—"

"Jenny, do you think Sosthène is—was ever in love with Cousin Sally?"

There was a long silence in the kitchen. Jenny took her hand off Camilla's arm and began to fiddle with the things on the tray beside them. Finally she said, "It's hard to tell, isn't it. Of course one can see he's devoted to her—"

"But I meant—"

"I know." Jenny dried the sauce-pan with care and hung it up, switched off the light over the sink and returned to the table where Camilla stood. She picked up the tray and paused with it in her hands between them, and Camilla's eyes met hers honestly across it. "Darling," said Jenny like a mother, "if I were you I wouldn't—think about Sosthène. Just don't *start* thinking about him, darling—there's trouble enough to bear without that. Turn out the light, will you?" And she walked out of the kitchen, carrying the tray.

A few minutes later, sipping cocoa in front of the fire, Camilla said, "You've felt it too, then—that thing about Sosthène."

"Yes, of course, everybody does, you know. In a woman it's called charm, I don't know what the word is for the masculine equivalent. But the difference with me is that I'm not in danger of falling in love with it, and you might. That's why I thought I'd better warn you. Don't."

"Oh, no!" said Camilla quickly, and felt her cheeks get hot. "He's—I couldn't!"

"If you take my advice, which of course you won't," said Jenny levelly, "you'll be careful not to fall in love with anyone while the war is on. If you want to be any good for anything, I mean. Since I got over Gerald and nobody matters to me any more I've been much more useful, both to myself and the hospital. You can put your whole mind on your job, which at the moment is working ourselves into a coma every day to do as much as we can for any mother's son who happens to be in our care. And there's less wear and tear on your own nervous system too, because you get a sort of impersonal viewpoint like an old nursing Sister, on even the worst cases, and you don't use yourself up with praying the same thing won't happen to someone you love. That's one reason I want to nurse in France—I haven't got a brother or a lover at the Front, and there isn't a soul in the world to divide my attention from the nameless cases as they come in. I'm emptied of all personal feeling about this war, I could become simply an efficient machine with a woman's touch, and that's what a good nurse ought to be. I'll tell you something nobody else knows—they let me work in the operating room now, at the Hall. One of the surgeons always asks for me because I can do anything he wants without getting sick—just like a real Sister with years of experience."

"That's wonderful. I couldn't trust myself," Camilla confessed. "I still dread going round with the dressing-tray. I never thought I would, but the very first time I did it I ran into a series of amputations and—well, I didn't disgrace myself, but it shook me, I don't mind telling you!"

"That's because you've never had an amputation yourself," said Jenny lightly. "Not literally, of course—but since that business with Gerald there's part of me that just isn't there any more. I don't feel anything, except now and then a sort of ghost-pain, where it was."

"But you will fall in love again, some time."

"I hope not!"

"But after the war——"

"After the war I should like to go on nursing if they'll let me. The wounded aren't going to just get well overnight, you know, when peace comes. There will be years of work—my whole lifetime, perhaps—caring for the men who fought in this war."

"But—that's like being a nun——!"

"Oh, far from it, I shan't renounce the world, or take any veils or vows or anything like that. But I'd much rather live the way I am now, it's much more comfortable than ever again to see anyone have the power to make me feel the way I felt about Gerald. It was too naked and ashamed," said Jenny, pouring out another cup of cocoa. "It's too completely terrifying to discover that you have no defences against some other human being, and that he can do exactly as he likes with your life and all you can do is stand there and wring your hands."

"But if he's kind——"

"Oh, Gerald was *kind*," Jenny assured her unemotionally. "He's no monster, he didn't *want* to half-kill me, he just made a mistake, and he was no end sorry about it, but that didn't keep me from nearly bleeding to death inside, for months. And even suppose he hadn't made a mistake, suppose the man I loved had been killed instead—I could be proud, yes, instead of humiliated down to the ground, but that part of my life would be just as cut off as it is now."

"But people fall in love more than once——"

"Not me," said Jenny firmly. "Once is enough, thank you very much. I'm not going to walk the plank again, not for anybody!"

"Virginia is happy," Camilla maintained obstinately.

"Virginia is pre-war. And I wouldn't like to be in Virginia's shoes if anything happened to Archie now. Darling, don't think I'm laying down any laws on anything!" Jenny added anxiously. "It's only myself I'm talking about. People are going to go right on falling in love and letting themselves in for untold agony and doubtless untold happiness, no matter what I think or say. But all that's not for me. I've thrown in my hand. I'm cured. Everybody else in the world can do exactly as they please, but from now on I'm just going to sit here and watch, I'd rather not play."

Camilla felt that what Jenny was saying was somehow all wrong, but she was not yet of an age herself to make any patronizing remarks about wait-and-see or time-will-tell. She considered Jenny's attitude an awful waste, because Jenny was so pretty and understanding, and some man would be done out of a delightful wife if she held to her determination not to love anyone. But it was Jenny's life, after all, and she had a right to run it any way she chose. Her unhysterical viewpoint on her own future, which was in no way martyred resignation or bitterness, but merely a deliberate choice of what she was sure she wanted from now on, left Camilla feeling childish and muddled and insecure. Camilla had no idea so far what she wanted, or expected, from her life. Without Calvert at her side she was rudderless and lost. She had never faced the necessity, at Richmond, of making decisions without him, or encountering any situation where he could not tell her what to do. It was time, she decided humbly in Jenny's stimulating presence, that she grew up and began to think for herself.

They finished the cocoa and biscuits and went upstairs to bed, swinging linked hands like old friends, and found Jenny's overnight things laid out in Camilla's room. Jenny asked if she would rather be alone, to which Camilla gave an emphatic negative, and they undressed together with easy chatter about what was going on in London these days, and how Virginia's accident had happened, and the amusing or exasperating things which could happen to a VAD. And soon after the light was out Camilla slept, and to her own surprise never woke until the morning sunlight was streaming into the room.

———

Because Camilla had never visited the Hall as Phoebe had before the war began, when the young Earl had just married a coal heiress and the great house was gay with parties for the hunting, and Winifred's famous balls, its altered aspect was no shock to her when she arrived there the next morning with Archie and Jenny. Nowadays its wintry park and gardens were full of wheel-chairs and blue-clad men on crutches and canes, and the red-caped forms of their attendant nurses, all making the most of a mild sunny day.

Camilla had by now acquired a professional interest in the equipment and management of hospitals other than the one in St. James's Square, and was eager to see what Winifred had made of this one. They said Good-bye to Archie, who departed on his mysterious assignment—said by him to be very dull—in Gloucester, and Jenny led Camilla through the mansion as a distinguished visitor, introducing her to Winifred and some of the Sisters, stopping to chat with patients who eyed the attractive young American with respectful admiration. They paid a special visit to the wounded Canadians, none of whom happened to have been in Calvert's outfit, but who were interested to hear that she had a brother who belonged to a machine gun.

Most of the ground floor rooms and those on the floor above had been turned into wards, and the morning room, which was next to the garden room with its commodious sinks and drains once used for the care and arrangement of cut flowers and household plants, had been converted into the operating room. The equipment here was so ample and so exceedingly up to date that it was a surgeon's joy, and the great Sir Quentin ffolliott himself had come down from London more than once to perform his remarkable operations. The baroque dining-room near by, with its elaborate plasterwork and coved ceiling and long windows facing east, was now the surgical ward, and shapeless muslin bags covered the nude statues which postured in the deep shell niches around the walls. The white drawing-room, its Gainsboroughs and Hoppners and crystal chandeliers all swathed in muslin, was the medical ward, and the blue drawing-room, which was smaller, housed the eye and head cases. The Gobelins had all been removed from the tapestry-room on the garden front, and Winifred used it as an office for conducting the business of the hospital and the interviews, often tragic, with relatives and friends of the patients. The gun-room, more or less intact in its comfortable leather furniture and oak panelled walls, had with the addition of more chairs and a piano and a gramophone become the recreation room. The billiard room, minus its table and appurtenances, but retaining its deep cushioned window-seats, contained the beds of the more active convalescent patients who could get about somewhat on their own and who took their meals at a big table in what had been the servants' hall. The spacious ballroom, which was always hard to heat, had the wheel-chair people. The family bedrooms had been stripped of their personal belongings and turned into small wards for special cases and for occasional officers sent down from the London house to convalesce in private.

The energetic Countess of Enstone and the Earl's sister Clare were pigging it cheerfully in former parlourmaid's bedrooms on an upper floor, appearing punctually in their starched nursing dresses to pull their weight and a bit more with the rest of the staff. One tremendous concession the Hall made to its hard-working VAD's, most of whom before the war had not known what it was to dress themselves without a lady's maid—each of them had her own cubby-hole of a bedroom, however bleak and ill-heated, to herself. Jenny and others of her age and kind, tormented by personal grief or anxiety, sometimes found this cherished privacy about all that stood between them and the breaking-point during the difficult settling-in period each one of them had to go through —learning to do without mere bodily comfort, to say nothing of recreation or companionship—learning to focus on each day as it came, without expending useless energy on remembering yesterday's tragedy or dreading tomorrow's possible bad news—learning not to see behind their closed eyelids in the dark the hideous, quivering wounds they had handled, nor hear again the sounds wrenched from brave men by agony. It required a whole new nervous system, these girls had learned, to become a successful VAD. And no matter how strong-minded you had proved yourself about not turning away from the kill in the hunting-field, nor how useful you had been the time your mother had bronchitis, nor how brave you had been about your own broken collar-bone, the things you saw in the surgical ward left you hanging on to the edge of the sluice in the garden-room, sick and shaking and ashamed.

After all the introductions and the chat, and even a brief glimpse of the great Sir Quentin himself, who was down for the day and with whom Jenny was obviously a favorite, one name was still missing. Camilla knew that Fabrice worked here as a VAD, but hesitated to ask for her lest Jenny should think it was plain low-down curiosity—which in a way it was. Just then Winifred said blandly, without moving her lips, "Ah, here is our little angel of mercy, she's a sort of cousin of yours, isn't she?" and gave Camilla a sidelong, malicious glance.

A girl was coming towards them down the surgical ward, to which they had returned after the tour of inspection. She was small and very slight and rather pink and white in the face, Camilla thought, with too much curly dark hair showing round the edge of her white coif. She was pushing a trolley full of cups of broth which she was dispensing with a great deal of graceful bending over beds and patting of pillows and laughing backward looks which brought answering grins and some informal retorts from the men as she passed.

"Always scattering cheer, wherever she goes," said Winifred, *sotto voce,* at Camilla's ear. "I'm sure I don't know what we'd *do* without her, she does perk us up so, the self-sacrificing darling!"

"Well, they do seem to like it," Camilla remarked, watching.

"They do, God bless them, I'm telling you they *do!*" Winifred agreed promptly. "Don't think for one minute I'm complaining. Just a little ray of sunshine, that's what it is!"

"Wini-fred," drawled Jenny with a rueful smile, and Winifred turned on her heel.

"Go and introduce them, I'm busy," she said, and walked away.

As they approached the trolley in the center aisle, Fabrice left it and came forward, both her hands held out—frail, curving hands with tapering wrists lost in the bulky starched cuffs.

"You must be my new cousin from America," she said before either of them could speak, and the words were lightly touched with a French accent. "How nice it is to meet one more of my charrrming family. My dar-ling, it is *trrrragique* about your poor brother, but we must always hope for the best until we know to the contrary!" And she kissed Camilla prettily on both cheeks with the sort of tenderness due to a chief mourner.

Camilla, who had to stoop to receive the caress, found herself withdrawing from it as soon as common courtesy permitted, heard herself saying rather brusquely, "We hope Bracken can arrange to get him to England soon."

"Ah, yes, that makes them well when nothing else can." Soft brown eyes rayed with black lashes looked up at her sympathetically, small warm fingers pressed clinging comfort on hers. "The sight of a familiar face, like a sister's—it brings them back from the door of death sometimes! Send him to us here, and we will pamper him and get him well for you."

Camilla, who felt perfectly capable of pampering Calvert in London herself if she had the chance, thanked her politely and said the broth would be getting cold.

"And then *I* shall hear!" cried Fabrice archly, and sent a dazzling, inclusive smile down the row of beds on their left. "Sick men are such tyrants! They would as soon run your feet off as not!" She caught up a cup of broth in fingers that made the thick white china seem almost too heavy to hold, and carried it to the man in the nearest bed, who watched its approach greedily. "This is the one we call Grison, don't ask me why!"

Camilla, who saw that the man had grey hair, smiled perfunctorily, and Jenny standing beside her said in an expressionless tone, "Well, I think that's about everything. I must go and change now. Will you stay to lunch, or do you think you ought to be getting back?"

Camilla said she thought Virginia might be needing her, and Jenny accompanied her to where the bicycles lived in an empty stable, and saw her off down the lane to Farthingale. Pedalling thoughtfully along the frosty ruts, Camilla argued with herself that everything Fabrice had said was entirely in order and if it had been said by anyone else would have given

no offence whatever—and heard herself resolving inwardly
that if Calvert could heal as well in St. James's Square she
would keep him there for more reasons than one, commission
or no commission. Not that he would be likely to be taken in
by Fabrice. He would dislike her at first sight, and that too
would be bad for him.

━━━━━━━━

Bracken's letter arrived within the week, written from a
big base hospital near Boulogne.

It will be difficult to write this without pulling out all the
stops (he began.) It's a common enough story these days,
goodness knows, but when it happens in one's own family
somehow one wants to choke up.

I traced them here without much difficulty—both Calvert
and his buddy Raymond. I expect you've heard about Raymond before now. I found them lying in adjacent beds,
pretty well done up but still able to grin and very glad to
see me.

To come to the point, Calvert's right leg is badly shattered
and he is in a complicated sort of cradle-thing hung from
the ceiling and can't be moved for some time—weeks, in
fact. There is a great deal of pain, which he bears cheerfully as long as they will allow him to keep the leg, which
he has a decent hope of doing if no further complications
set in. I know this is dreadful news, but it could be much
worse, and I put it baldly because we are all realists these
days, and there is no sense in beating about bushes.

We should never have got him back at all if it had not
been for Raymond, who already has the V.C. or this would
have got it for him. They were on night patrol feeling out
one of the farms on the way to Passchendaele Ridge, and
ran into a sharp fight in which their officer was killed,
and before they could consolidate were suddenly counter-
attacked and forced back from the position they were trying

to hold. It was dark and raining hard, there were no tapes, of course, and except for Raymond's almost Indian sense of direction they were totally lost in no time. Three of them and a badly wounded man who had to be almost carried were left trying to find the captured pill-box in their rear which served as a dressing-station and battalion headquarters, when a shell-burst killed the third man outright and completely disabled Calvert with this wound in the leg. There weren't any medics or stretcher bearers in an affair of this kind, no communication trenches, no shelter or bearings, not even wire, just there, to serve as a guide. Raymond had two wounded men on his hands, neither one of whom could walk alone, and it would soon be dawn. He made the other man as comfortable as he could in a shell-hole half full of water, said "I'll come back for you," and took Calvert on his back. He found the pill-box by some miracle, and then, though it was beginning to be daylight, he went back for the other man. The usual morning *strafe* had begun, plus the usual snipers, and he had to crawl, half dragging, half pushing the half-conscious man through the mud. As they approached the pill-box some one there saw that Raymond had been hit in the shoulder so that one arm was useless, and went out to help him. That night they were all three carted off with other wounded to the rear, and thence to hospital at Boulogne. Raymond has a compound fracture of the shoulder from shrapnel, and moreover almost bled to death before he got proper dressings. He is worried now because there is no feeling in the fingers of his wounded arm—he is a man who works with his hands, and the loss of even partial dexterity in one of them would be a terrible thing for him. I want Virginia to find out where this particular wound can best be cared for—they say here that a series of operations will be necessary and are doubtful even then. We must leave nothing undone for this boy. Even apart from his devotion to Calvert, he is worth saving, and must have the utmost we can find for him in care. . . .

Virginia said at once that Sir Quentin ffolliott was the man
for Raymond's arm, and machinery was set in motion for
Raymond's immediate transfer to England, though that
meant separating him from Calvert, who could not be moved.
A little reassured by Bracken's letter, Camilla resigned herself to a Christmas without her brother, and found that she
was able to breathe again. As usual, she craved the piano for
comfort, an indulgence she had had very little time for since
her arrival in England.

Finding the drawing-room deserted on a rainy afternoon,
she began to play over to herself some of Calvert's favorites
in his quieter moods—Strauss, and Brahms, and Schubert—
German music, though the Germans had done their best to
kill him. That was one of the things it was useless to puzzle
over. They had written music that he loved, that he and she
had learned together in the cool, shaded drawing-room in
Richmond. She began to sing softly, intermittently, mindful
of the silent house where people were having a mid-afternoon
rest—pretending that Calvert was there to hear, lying on the
sofa as he might be some day before long—remember this?—
and this. . . .

The *Cradle Song* faded into silence in the middle of a bar
—she turned, her hands still on the keys—Sosthène stood in
the doorway, listening. Camilla felt the helpless blush surge
upward across her throat to her hair.

"I—didn't know anyone was there," she said breathlessly,
and her lips were not steady, while her fingers turned cold
and damp on the keys.

He came on into the room slowly, and Mimi pattered im-
portantly beside him, having been for her outing along the
herbaceous border.

"You have a beautiful voice," he said, not casually as one
pays a compliment, but almost reluctantly as though render-
ing judgment. "It has been trained."

"Well—only in Richmond. I was—just singing some of the things Calvert likes." The words were hurried and uncertain in her own ears, and she had to choke back an impulse to deny again that she had sung for anyone's benefit, for she had truly believed that he was upstairs with Sally, and her newly self-conscious pride would have forbidden her to set any such obvious schoolgirlish trap for his notice as to be found singing to herself on a rainy afternoon. She struck a few notes at random, and rose awkwardly from the bench.

"Ah, no—please go on—unless you would rather that Mimi and I should go away?"

"Not at all, I—I had just finished." It sounded ungracious. She dropped back on the bench again, her hands in her lap. The very rims of her ears felt hot, as though with a fever. "What would you like to hear?"

"While we were outside in the drive we thought we heard Solveig's Song," he said, seating himself with deliberate ease on the near end of the sofa. "But only scraps of it reached us. Could we have that again, please? Mimi—*écoute donc! Ici.*" The little dog subsided at his feet. They were waiting.

A sudden third-person serenity descended on Camilla. Her fingers found all the right notes, her voice rose clear and steady from a throat she would have sworn was paralyzed. She sang as at a début, possessed by the born performer's magical reflexes surmounting panic and the weakness of the flesh. The song ended and she sat quietly, her head bent, not daring to meet his eyes though she knew he watched her.

"That was—exceptional," he said quietly after a moment. "I had no idea you had such a voice. Do you intend to use it professionally?"

"I don't know, I—wanted to once, but the family is against it. And now with the war and all, I—don't think much about it any more."

She heard him rise, felt him approach, looked up to find

him leaning on the corner of the piano at her left, his thin
hands loosely clasped, his head bent sidewise to see her
averted face.

"It breaks your heart a little—not to be allowed to sing,"
he said.

"Well, I thought so once. But now it doesn't seem to matter
so much. Why did you say that?"

"When one has a great gift one suffers not to use it. Your
voice is a thing to be shared. It would be very stupid of anyone, even yourself, to deny that."

Self-consciousness dropped from her like a cloak. She
raised her head and looked him in the eyes, her own self
looked out at him, without foolish barricades and pretenses.
Worship sat in her gaze, for anyone to see, the blind, unreas-
oning, humble devotion which the first sight of him had
kindled in her uninitiated heart. It was Sosthène who was
startled now, for she had been to him so far only an angular,
unawakened girl with haunting eyes. He saw her suddenly as
a woman, willing and aware of him. And there was no place
in his life for such a woman. His life was ordered and complete, without impulses or urges or uncertainties. His life,
beyond its present unvarying routine, was over. He had been
content to have it so. Apart from Sally, he had no life. This
girl, just by lifting her face to him, had knocked out a window in a solid stone wall. The sun shone through, but
there was also a draft. What she said was commonplace
enough, though, and he groped hastily for the commonplace
answer.

"Then you think," Camilla was saying, "that I should go
on studying when the war is over?"

"I have no right to advise you," he managed to reply in the
same casual tone. "It is always a mistake, I think, to encourage anyone to become a professional artist. The odds are too

heavy against recognition, the work is too hard. And you don't look very strong."

"Oh, but I am," she assured him. "I'm strong as a horse, really. Calvert's just the same. Thin, but indestructible." She smiled. It was a confidential smile, the first he had ever had from her without some sort of apology in it. Her music had released her, at last, from her dread of self-revelation. Let him know. He had to know some time. She couldn't live, and never let him know. She felt lightheaded with relief, and freedom. Her cap was over the windmill. She was through pretending with him. She had delivered herself into his hands. There was no need for him to answer, nothing for him to say. He had seen. She was quite sure that he had seen, though he had made no response. They need never speak of it, she had no desire to drag it out in the open. For her it was enough that now she had nothing to hide from him. She had no idea that she was laying upon him a burden he would not know how to bear.

"Perhaps you would do best to forget all of this," he was saying compassionately, and then as the quick shadow fell across her face, "All except when I say that to me it is a lovely voice—young—fresh—very warm and real. May I hear it once more, or are you tired?"

Her fingers moved again on the keyboard. She looked down, smiling to herself, choosing his song, basking in a strange, illusive happiness. She sang *Depuis le jour.*

"And why was I not told that we had a singer in the family?" demanded Sally into the silence which followed, and they turned to find her standing where Sosthène had stood, in the doorway. Camilla frankly started, but Sosthène's movement was casual and slow as he took his elbows from the piano and went to meet her.

"Perhaps because there has been so little to sing about, these days," he said.

"You have been well taught, my child," said Sally, advancing on the piano. "In Richmond, I suppose. We must find someone to go on with it here."

"Oh, I mustn't—not in war time," Camilla objected. "I go back to London to the hospital right after Christmas, you know—and my time will be full then without singing lessons." She sat still on the piano bench, looking up at Sally. Her back was very straight. She did not intend to allow Sally to pay for her training, in any case. The least she could do now was not to be beholden to Sally in any way. She was not jealous of her. That would be absurd. She was not a rival of Sally's, for Sosthène. That too was absurd. She reserved to herself the right to love him, so long as it did Sally no harm. But it seemed to her bad taste in the circumstances to accept favors from Sally. Young and strong and ignorant, she stood apart from them both now, convinced that her life was her own to live as she saw fit, taking advantage of nobody, islanded in fierce honor and self-respect. Sally would never have anything to reproach her with, as long as she lived. As long. . . . *No, you must not think like that, I forbid it.*

"Ah, yes, the war," said Sally, as though she had forgotten it. "The war will not go on forever. Then we will go to Paris. I know just the man." She glanced at Sosthène and nodded. "Marinelli. If he is still alive."

"You take a great responsibility, my soul," said Sosthène. "You condemn her to a hard life."

"That depends," said Sally, "on what she wants to make of it."

"I'm not afraid of work," Camilla said at once. "But Calvert may need me. We'll see what Calvert says." The old, comforting formula. Calvert would decide.

Meanwhile, she devoted all her spare time to helping with the elaborate Christmas preparations at the Hall. Jenny, whose work was with the eye and head cases in Ward B—the blue drawing-room—was sewing the red gauze stockings which would be hung on each man's bed on Christmas Eve, to contain cigarettes, fountain-pens, note-paper, chocolate, pipes, and similar small treasures a sick man finds comfort in. Camilla would go and sit with her, working on the colored paper garlands which were to festoon Ward F—the ballroom —which had a small platform at one end for the entertainers and would have the Christmas tree at the opposite end. The delighted wheel-chair people could all be pushed into one corner and a lot of cots moved in for those who were able, and the convalescents could have a group of gilt chairs. For the ones who had to stay in bed where they were, there was to be a procession, with carols, just before tea on Christmas Day.

Camilla found it very touching that the weary, overworked nurses and staff of the hospital should give up their precious leisure to these additional chores designed to amuse and comfort the homesick, suffering men in their care. Sometimes her eyes would fill with tears when she glanced up at Jenny's pale gold head bent above her needle, the soft belled hair falling forward along her jaw, her small, work-worn hands so deft and busy while she absent-mindedly hummed a snatch of *King Wenceslas* or *Adeste Fidelis*. Jenny was so vulnerable still, in her young armor of hard-won composure—so infinitely pathetic and so unbelievably brave, and would so have resented anything like pity. It was always Fabrice who bent charmingly above the men in the wards and their fumbling, earnest attempts at painting or cutting colored mottoes and greetings, and the simple small tasks which could be delegated to them in assembling the decorations. It was Fabrice who rallied the discouraged and clumsy ones, and laughed at the bad jokes, and fanned the jealous rivalry in festive design between the wards. Ward G—surgical—was going to have an elaborate trellis effect of green ribbon and holly clusters. The recreation room was to be graced with some highly colored humor in painted mottoes and devices more or less suitable to the Christmas Season, and had laid violent claim to a box of paper mimosa and wisteria which came to light when Clare and Winifred went up to rummage in the attics for the trunks where costumes for charades and private theatricals were kept.

Among the convalescents was a man with both legs off who had the knack of writing catchy little tunes with topical jingles, and a minstrel act was inevitable, and the piano in the gun room went all day. It was Fabrice who rehearsed with them tirelessly to the neglect of her other duties, and it was Jenny who sat in apparent contentment, humming scraps of carol music, among the patient forms of her blinded or bandaged head cases, sewing the endless red stockings.

Camilla found herself regretting that it was not Calvert's injury which required the attention of Sir Quentin, so that he would have been sent to England instead of Raymond, who of course deserved the best and was expected to arrive in London a few days before Christmas, at the same time Bracken returned from France. If Raymond was well enough he was to be brought down to Farthingale for the Christmas festivities, and then sent on to the Hall for the operation, assuming that Sir Quentin would take the case.

No one knew yet whether Archie could get leave or not. Almost everyone—even Fabrice?—cherished a secret guilty feeling, perhaps not quite a hope, that perhaps Gerald wouldn't. Bracken was due for a rest, and Phoebe and Oliver would come down from London for the day. There was to be a family party at Farthingale with all the children on Christmas night after the hospital celebrations were over and the men tucked up for the night. They would roll up the rugs and turn on the gramophone and dance, said Virginia, who had begun to get about with a cane now. And after all, having Raymond there would be the next best thing to having Calvert, and they must all be very nice to him and make him feel from now on that it was his home too, because they owed Calvert's life to him. . . .

A letter from Calvert, dictated to his nurse at Boulogne, arrived for Camilla in the middle of December.

Bracken says Virginia has invited Raymond to Farthingale for Christmas (he wrote) and he left here in the hospital ship this morning. I wish I could have come with him, but I'm sure he won't feel strange there for long. He isn't accustomed to a big family like ours and may find it a bit overwhelming at first, so be a tactful darling and look after him, won't you. His mother died when he was born, and his father brought him up, with a maiden aunt to do the housekeeping. They weren't very well off, I'm afraid, and his father died just before Raymond enlisted. That was one reason he went, he said they both felt very strongly about the Germans and when his father didn't need him any more it seemed the obvious thing to do—to go and kill some Germans for him. So you see Raymond is rather alone in the world, but he doesn't feel it the way we would, I suppose, as he's never known anything else. I think he's a little scared at the idea of coming there without me, and he has asked a great many questions about you, and I've promised him you will be a sister to him too!

I probably ought to warn you that he hasn't read a lot, the things we have, I mean, so don't start quoting at him the silly way we do at home, because he can't follow, I found that out very soon. I don't know what sort of schooling he has had, but it doesn't matter—he knows more than I ever will, and when things look worse and worse, and the air is stiff with bullets and the ammunition is running out—Raymond just goes stolid and steady and *tough*, instead of swearing or dithering, and somehow it comes out all right. I've seen him deliberately take down the gun and repair it and put it together again as though he had all the time in the world, while the rest of us were holding off the Germans with rifle fire, and I personally was shaking like a leaf. Nothing flusters him—unless meeting all the family will; and you must help him through that. Don't let Virginia heckle him, will you. He gets on all right with Bracken.

You have got to get his arm fixed up somehow amongst you, because he wants to fly, now that I'm out of things for good and the old gun crew are all gone. Bracken says that as soon as a Medical Board will pass the arm Raymond can put in for transfer to the RAF, which would mean weeks of training in England, and I like the sound of that as we might see something of him on leave now and then. Please don't be put off if he only blinks at you—he never speaks unless he has something to say, and all the impulses have been trained out of him long ago. He is the most completely controlled person I ever knew, probably because he has been in this war since 1915 and has seen about all there is to see and nothing can ever surprise him again.

There isn't much use in my writing all this, because you will have the sense to see what he is without my spelling it out for you. I can only add that I would rather be like him than anybody I ever knew. And nothing you can do is too good for him.

Sister says I have to stop now, for fear of getting tired. It's beastly not being able to see you at Christmas time, but I shall be well enough to travel soon and perhaps they will give me a bed in the St. James's Square house and we can see each other every day. . . .

Camilla read the letter more than once, and pondered it a good deal. Raymond's reception by the family, and his reaction to it, were so much on Calvert's mind that he had said almost nothing about himself, but it was obvious that even if he kept his injured leg there would be no more fighting for him. One couldn't help being relieved about that. But Raymond meant to go on, in the Flying Corps. Raymond must have the use of his arm, if it took every surgeon in England.

She sat knitting her brows over the letter. What was it that Calvert was trying to say about Raymond? What was between the lines? That about his schooling—and not being able to quote. . . . "Perhaps he means that Raymond says 'ain't,' " Virginia suggested lightly when Camilla showed her the letter. "Why doesn't he tell us what part of the country he's from, at least?"

"It wouldn't matter to Calvert now," said Camilla.

"If he hadn't any grammar? Or if he came from Missouri?"

"Nothing would matter. He must be one of the family from now on."

"Absolutely, I quite agree. What's this about my heckling him?"

"Well, you do sort of—*quiz* people sometimes," Camilla reminded her uncomfortably.

"I do not! At least not on purpose. Now, don't you worry, you and Calvert, I'll make as much fuss of this Raymond boy as though he was Archie, no less! What shall we have for his presents? The fountain-pen? Does he smoke a pipe, do you think?"

"Wasn't there a wrist watch sort of left over?"

"A very nice one. Do you want it for him?"

"Yes, please. And the tortoise-shell cigarette case."

"We *are* going to make an impression!" said Virginia. "I was saving that for Bracken."

"Bracken has dozens of cigarette cases. If Raymond's been hard up all his life he's got to have nice presents. Calvert would want him to."

"Whatever you say," said Virginia agreeably. "There's a little gold lighter too, while you're at it, that doesn't belong to anybody in particular so far. I don't suppose there's time to get it initialled now. What's his other name?"

"I don't know," said Camilla rather blankly. "I don't think anyone has said."

Phoebe rang up from London a few days later to say that Raymond had arrived in pretty good shape and had been put straight to bed. Sir Quentin had seen him and would take the case. Bracken was there when Sir Quentin came and got round him as Bracken usually could and arranged to drive Raymond down to the Hall when he himself came to Farthingale. Raymond must go back to bed there and rest until Christmas Day, when if all was well he would be allowed to get up and attend the party at Farthingale. The first operation was to take place at the Hall on the day after Boxing Day. If successful, there might be only one after all.

"I see," said Virginia at the other end of the telephone. "Phoebe, what's he like? We're all dying to know."

There was just the fraction of a pause, while Phoebe seemed to choose a word.

"He's sweet," she said. "Worth any amount of trouble."

"I see," said Virginia, still pretty much in the dark.

Because he was surgical, Raymond was given a bed in Ward G at the Hall and was therefore not in Jenny's charge. And as Fabrice was no good with dressings—she had once fainted dead away across the patient when required to hold an amputation stump—she had been assigned to Ward E (medical) though the Sister there would not trust her with respirations and temperatures. This left him quite outside the family beat except for Clare, who was on night duty in Ward G and who reported to Virginia by telephone the morning after he arrived that he had given her one dazzling smile when she spoke to him and promptly gone off to sleep like a baby and been no trouble at all.

"One of the lucky ones without nerves," she said. "It's amazing."

"But, Clare, what's he *like?*" pleaded Virginia.

"How can I tell, he's been asleep," said Clare. "He's not good-looking, if that's what you mean—except for his eyes."

"What about his eyes?"

"Light blue—or grey—and the rest of him very dark—very weather-beaten. He looks right through you," said Clare almost resentfully.

"And then goes to sleep."

"Exactly."

Virginia sighed.

"Well, I suppose we shall just have to wait," she said.

Bracken had not been much use either when he arrived at Farthingale after depositing Raymond at the Hall the night before. He described the wound in some detail, and Sir Quentin's opinion of it. He approved the presents they had set aside for the guest. He didn't think Raymond had a wrist watch, and he was positive that he smoked a pipe. When questioned further, he seemed, for Bracken, somewhat at a loss.

"You'll soon see for yourself," he said. "You must form your own opinion of him, you're bound to anyway, no matter what I say. I like him. Nothing I wouldn't do for him. He's older than Calvert, you know, and—hard-bitten. He's been through more than two years of this war in France. You have to be tough, for that."

Tough. Weather-beaten. Slept like a baby. Looks right through you. Sweet, said Phoebe. Hard-bitten, said Bracken. Where were they?

Camilla first saw him on Christmas Day when she went over right after the midday meal to assist at the entertainment, where she was to sing American songs. He had been allowed to dress for the visit to Farthingale, and so wore khaki instead of hospital blue. His right arm was in a sling, but to Camilla's surprise it had been passed through the sleeve of his shirt and tunic. There had been a slight rumpus about that, as the Ward G Sister could have told her, and Raymond had won, for he refused to go to any party with a dangling sleeve and unbuttoned tunic.

Camilla found him in the gun-room, which was full of Christmas greenery and the noise of the gramophone in the relaxed period just after lunch and just before everybody assembled in the ballroom for the entertainment, which was causing a good deal of bustle around the edges. He rose at once to meet her as she appeared in the doorway—six feet and one half inch of him, and *big,* not slender though not too heavily built—with powerful shoulders and eyes the color of a knife-blade in a brown, weather-beaten face; an uncompromising kind of face, rugged and used-looking, with deeply cut lines from the blunt, straight nose to the rather heavy, obstinate lips which drew a little across the even curve of strong white teeth. An unruly plume of straight dark hair had been brushed and brushed, but would not lie flat. He was not good-looking, maybe, but he was impossible to miss in a crowd.

"You're Raymond," she said, and advanced smiling, with her hand held out.

"Yes, I'd know you anywhere for Calvert's twin sister," he answered. His voice was very low in the noisy room, and she realized too late that he had only his left hand to offer, so that their fingers met in an informal, apologetic way which made for friendliness. His were warm and firm, but let her go at once, and there was an old-fashioned deference in his greeting, without any obsequiousness, which seemed to confer on her the rank of royalty. His look was long and level, as though to see if she was all that Calvert had said she was, a searching of her character as direct and unself-conscious and uncompromising as a child's.

"I can't tell you how pleased we are to get hold of you," she said with all the sincerity she knew.

"I'm sorry it had to be me instead of Calvert," he replied simply. "I would have traded places with him if I could."

"I believe you would, at that," she said, looking up at him, and he gave a rueful little shake of the head.

"I sure did hate to leave him there like that," he said.

"We'll get him over here too, pretty soon, they think. He's looking forward to being in England while you're training for the Air Force."

"If they can get me fixed up," he said gravely. "I wouldn't desert the gun as long as one of the old crew was left, honest. But they're all gone now—I and your brother were the last. And he's through with this war, you know."

"Yes, I—gathered that."

"He's swell," said Raymond gently. "You don't have to worry about him. Whatever happens, he'll come through—you can count on that."

"That's the kind of thing he's been writing about you."

He gave again that rueful shake of the head.

"We' been through a lot together," he said.

There was something in his speech, a sort of elision rather than an accent, that Camilla could not place, but she was no good at guessing accents, she hadn't travelled enough. It might be New England, for all she knew, or somewhere in the West. Phoebe ought to know. For some reason one felt shy about asking him where he came from, as though it was none of one's business unless he chose to speak of it first himself. She laid her hand impulsively on his good arm.

"We can never thank you enough for what you did," she said.

"He'd have done the same for me," said Raymond with conviction.

"Oh, there you are, Camilla," Winifred's crisp voice cut in from the doorway behind them. "Come along, everybody, stop that row and take your places in Ward F for the show."

The gramophone stopped abruptly with a squawk and there was a general movement towards the door.

"I've ordered a car to take you and Raymond to Far-thingale after the carols," Winifred went on to Camilla. "The other girls are in the procession—you can see it best from the main hall when the program in the ballroom is over, and still get away in time for tea at Farthingale. Jenny can leave with you, to drive, but Clare and Fabrice will have to help with the men's tea here and I'll send them over later, just before dinner. They can dress first, and save a lot of bother. Raymond, you've got your arm in the sleeve."

"Yes, ma'am," said Raymond unargumentatively. His voice was very gentle, his eyes were wide and level.

"Remember what Sir Quentin said," Winifred cautioned him. "The wound can open, and then you're in for trouble. Don't go mucking about with the bandage yourself. I've arranged for you to sleep in one of the private bedrooms here tonight, so as not to disturb the ward when you come in late. All three girls will be driving back with you, and one of them will help you to bed. I'll speak to Clare about it. You're not to try to straighten your arm in any circumstances."

"No, ma'am," said Raymond stolidly, and Camilla was conscious of a sudden impulse to hug him, sternly repressed.

"Come along, then, they're going to begin," said Winifred, and they followed her to the ballroom.

———

Calvert was wrong when he said that Raymond was scared about going to Farthingale, though Raymond himself might have used the word loosely regarding his own sensations. Leary, came a little nearer to it, for Raymond was always cautious about unfamiliar ground. A hospital, yes, that could happen to anybody, they meant to be kind and you did as they said and remembered to be polite to them. You hadn't got to be friends with them too, you could keep them outside. But places where you were a guest, more might be expected. If they took you inside, because of Calvert, you couldn't very well insist on them staying outside. And they weren't the kind of people Raymond was accustomed to. There was an earl somewhere amongst them, and some of the women had some sort of fancy title, and the men were all officers. And it wasn't as though he was related, like Calvert. Would they be expecting somebody *like* Calvert, which he wasn't nor ever would be? What if he had to eat a meal with them, with only one good arm and a lot of forks? With Calvert there he wouldn't have minded so much. But Calvert's sister was, after all, only a girl.

So far he had done all right, and nobody had got acrost him, except maybe the one they called Winifred, who was a bit of a tartar. She had a right to be, she owned the place, you couldn't blame her if she knew it. She wasn't coming to the Christmas party, as her husband couldn't get leave, and somebody had to stay and run the hospital anyway. He suspected that her absence would probably be O.K. with everybody.

Bracken would be there, which was the next best thing to Calvert, but you couldn't be absolutely sure what Bracken was thinking behind that poker face of his. He was all right. But if you made a mistake, he'd see it. He'd cover up for you, but it would be there. Bracken was used to a lot of forks.

Sitting beside Camilla in the little gilt chairs in the ballroom, laughing at the minstrel jokes, bewildered by the charades, enchanted with any and all of the music, Raymond was aware in his middle of the sensation which always grew there just before the whistle blew in the dawn. Farthingale in time for tea, in a car with two strange girls. It wasn't exactly that Raymond was shy, and he had never heard of an inferiority complex. It was just that he liked to know his ground, and choose his company. For the sort of women he was encountering here he had a deep-rooted respect and admiration, but he had always kept to what he considered his place with them. Outside. For the other sort he had a manner of his own, which could be kind or rough as the occasion called for, and which kept them in their place. Outside. From the moment Camilla's slim hand rested on his sleeve, these familiar barriers had begun to go a bit hazy round the edges.

He had crossed some sort of threshold. If Camilla had told him he had gone through the Looking-glass he wouldn't have known what she meant, for he was not acquainted with a little girl called Alice. But already, with Camilla's elbow brushing his in the cramped space, and the faint scent of flowers which seemed to come from her clothes—bewitchment was beginning. His outer defences against the things she stood for—hitherto so unattainable as not even to have been desired—were crumbling.

Then Camilla rose and left him, taking her turn on the program. She sang three songs—*My Old Kentucky Home,* as requested by Jenny, *O Susannah!,* and *Swing Low, Sweet Chariot*—the men were completely enchanted and would not let her go, stamping, clapping, cheering, and beating on the floor with their crutches and canes. For a moment she stood uncertain and half laughing, shaking her head, unbearably touched by their enthusiasm. Then she started *The Long, Long Trail,* and got them to sing it with her, which released a lot of pent up emotion and made everybody feel better. Raymond appreciated her poise and warmth, and the clear, true tones of her voice. She was wonderful, he decided, and Calvert had a right to be proud of her. He smiled up at her with an increasing informality as she returned to her chair beside him.

Soon after that with a final burst of applause the show ended and the ballroom began to be cleared so that the carol procession could assemble and start from there. He accompanied Camilla into the main hall where convalescents and other people were lingering to see it pass on its way to the wards. Already the early winter twilight had blued the windows, and at a signal the few lights which had been turned on winked out and the ballroom doors opened. The chorus of untrained women's voices rose softly, gained confidence, swelled into ardor—

> *"God rest you merry, gentlemen,*
> *Let nothing you dismay,*
> *Remember Christ our Savior*
> *Was born on Christmas Day,*
> *To save us all from Satan's powers*
> *When we were gone astray;*
> *O tidings of comfort and joy. . . ."*

They walked single file in their starched white aprons and high-collared blue dresses, with the misty white coif haloing their heads. Each one carried over her shoulder a pole on the end of which was a lighted Japanese lantern. They moved forward slowly, like a wedding procession, singing as they came. Most of them were young, some of them were pretty, all of them were worn fine by anxiety or grief or sheer weariness. None of them were crying, but the eyes of the people who saw them spilled over, and the men who lay in the long rows of beds looking up at them as they passed up each aisle and down the next, so that no one but could have reached out and touched their crisp skirts—and many did—those men wept unashamedly.

Raymond stood beside Camilla, unable to move, unable to speak, gazing after them, and felt her hand creep inside the elbow of his good arm and rest there, friendly and firm and understanding. They waited till the procession had wound its gracious way through Ward G and again passed in front of them on its way to the staircase. He glanced down once and saw that her cheeks were shining in the soft colored light from the lanterns. Without thinking, he pressed his elbow a little against his side, cherishing her hand which lay there. Her eyes came up to him dazzled with tears. She tried to smile, and they both looked away.

The tune had changed as the lanterns bobbed daintily up the ornate staircase towards the rooms above, a Jacob's ladder of song.

> *". . . .*
> *Peace on earth and mercy mild,*
> *God and sinners reconciled!*
> *Joyful, all ye nations rise,*
> *Join the triumph of the skies;*
> *With th' angelic host proclaim,*
> *Christ is born in Bethlehem!*
> *Hark! the herald angels sing*
> *Glory to the newborn King. . . ."*

It was a long time before either of them found words, and the last lantern had passed the landing out of sight from below. Then Raymond said in his quiet voice, "Wasn't that pretty. I never saw anything like that in my life before."

"You couldn't see it outside England," said Camilla, and blew her nose.

"Who are they?" he asked. "Where did they come from?"

"They're just the girls who work here day after day."

"They weren't trained to sing like that?"

"Oh, dear, no, they're just singing the songs they've all

sung every Christmas since they were children. There isn't a professional singer among them. There was a duke's daughter, though, and the sister of an earl—one of them was my cousin, and one was Virginia's sister-in-law."

"The little one that came third—with the yellow lantern," he said gently. "I noticed her both times. Wasn't she cute?"

"That's Jenny," said Camilla with satisfaction. "She's coming to the party tonight."

"She is?" He slammed shut the breach. "Don't you tell her I said anything."

"Why not?"

"She might not like it. It was pretty fresh, I guess."

"You be nice to Jenny, if you get the chance," Camilla told him. "She's had a beastly time, and she works harder than anybody. I wouldn't dare be sorry for her, but she almost breaks my heart."

"Did somebody get killed?" he asked sympathetically.

"Better if he had, I think! Somebody jilted her for another girl!"

"Somebody what?"

"She was engaged. He asked to break it off because he had fallen in love with another girl. Maybe you don't realize what that kind of thing would do to Jenny."

"I expect she'd feel like she'd been kicked in the teeth."

"That's about it," said Camilla. "She's got over it now, of course. But this is the first party she's been to in months, and it's time she had some fun."

The men's tea was going in and there was a cheerful clatter of cups from the wards when Jenny joined Raymond and Camilla at the foot of the stairs a short time later, carrying a dressing-case with her evening clothes in it. She had changed out of her uniform into a blue wool frock. Her small white face was framed by the sable collar on her coat and her pale hair curved loosely against her jaw under a little fur hat.

When Camilla introduced them Jenny held out her hand and Raymond took it in his left, and said, "How do you do?" with the same grave courtesy which to Camilla had suggested the old-fashioned formality of a court bow.

Camilla got into the back seat with Raymond and Jenny drove, chatting over her shoulder. Raymond beheld the gay lighted façade of Farthingale without comment, and they entered on a little flurry of welcome and festivity, and Camilla said, "This is Raymond, Virginia. Don't let's make him shake hands all round, there are too many of us."

"By no means," Virginia agreed, giving him her own hand, so that Raymond again responded with his left and she kept their fingers linked in a friendly way as they went on into the bright drawing-room, which seemed to the stranger to be packed with people, a great many of them children.

His first quick, guarded glance took in the tall, glittering tree against the dark windows at the far end of the long room, the log fire, the shining silver and white linen of the tea-table near the hearthrug, the handsome, friendly faces all turned expectantly towards the late comers. Virginia led him forward, saying, "This is Calvert's Raymond, everybody, and I'll leave you all to introduce yourselves to him as he gets round to you, just don't smother him, that's all. This is my husband," she added, laying her other hand on the sleeve of a slender, fair-haired man with a single eyeglass who came forward to meet them, and Archie said, "Awfully glad to have you here, old chap," and Raymond said, "Thank you, sir," to the captain's uniform of his host, and was drawn on to the sofa beside the fire. "Cousin Sally will give you a cup of tea," said Virginia, and Raymond found himself gazing down at that astonishing woman, seated beside the tea-table. Her hair was an artificial red, elaborately dressed, her face was painted and powdered, and she shone and sparkled with jewels which he knew were real. She was the most beautiful thing he had ever seen except on the stage, and her violet eyes were smiling up at him as though it was the most natural thing in the world that he should stand there before her with only one good arm, to be given a cup of tea.

"Come and sit here beside me, my child, till you are a little recovered," she said, and touched the sofa beside her. "How do you like your tea? Just as it comes, and very strong?"

"Yes, ma'am—thank you—as strong as you like."

"See, we will make room here on the corner of the table and you need only raise the cup—" Her ringed fingers moved deftly on the silver and china, beautiful dark tea flowed from the spout into a fragile cup.

Raymond remained on his feet beside the table, not awkwardly, not in the least defensively, but not in any unseemly haste to claim the privilege of seating himself beside her. And then he felt a hand laid on his shoulder from behind and Bracken's voice said, "How about a slug of rum in the tea, old boy, just till you get used to us?"

Virginia, Archie, and Sally were facing him as he turned from them to Bracken, and the three of them witnessed the small miracle those few words wrought—the dark, rugged face of the stranger was transfigured by a smile so radiant, so trustful, so completely glorified by recognition and affection that they all felt afterwards as though their jaws must have dropped. It was just the smile that Raymond kept for his friends, but it had not been seen since Bracken had taken leave of him at the Hall several days before.

"Hul-*lo!*" said Raymond, without in the least raising his voice. "I'm glad to see you!"

"I'll bet you are!" said Bracken sympathetically. "Sit down here—" He pushed Raymond gently on to the sofa beside Sally, who placed a cup of tea on the corner nearest him, and lifted a silver-mounted glass jug from the tray and removed the stopper.

"It is a barbarous drink—rum in tea," she murmured. "But you shall have it, all the same. Now I have made it too full."

"No, it's all right—it's wonderful," said Raymond politely, and raised the brimming cup with an absolutely steady hand, glanced over it at Bracken, and then with a little inclination of his head at the rest of them, who watched him as he drank. "Well, it *is* rum!" he remarked in pleased surprise after the first swallow, and set down the cup again. "I never saw it come out of a thing like that before," he added, nodding at the silver-mounted jug.

"No doubt it tastes just as good out of a tin cup where you have been lately," said Sally, and offered him a plate of thin, crustless sandwiches. The split-second's hesitation which told them that he had never seen sandwiches like that before either was instantly covered by his ingrained composure as he accepted the nearest and bit into it.

Bracken turned a chair and sat down on it, his back to the fire.

"I'll have another cup, Cousin Sally, if I may—rum and all," he said easily, and reached past Raymond to the sandwich plate.

"So shall I—to keep you both company," she said at once, busy with the cups. "*Without* rum!"

Raymond, lowering his cup again, found a small boy standing before him, gazing up.

"You're the one who saved Cousin Calvert," said the child solemnly, and for the first time Raymond showed embarrassment.

"Well, I guess you'd have done the same as I did in my place," he said.

"This is Nigel," said Bracken. "He belongs to Archie and Virginia."

"Hullo," said Raymond, who was unaccustomed to children

and therefore talked to them as though they were adults, which is what they like best.

"Hullo," said Nigel. "Can I see your wound?"

"I don't know about that." Raymond appeared to give it due consideration. "They won't let me monkey with the bandages, you know."

"Did the bullet go right *through?*"

"No, I wish it had. It was shrapnel, and they had to dig it out." .

"Did it hurt?"

"Well, I wasn't there all the time. They gave me some chloroform."

"Nigel, do not stare at a guest," said Sally, and "That'll do for you," said Bracken, turning the child round by the seat of his breeches. "Buzz off, now, and let a man enjoy his tea."

Nigel departed with no animus whatever to report his findings, and a voice over Raymond's shoulder said, "Don't let me interrupt—don't move, old boy, don't move, I just want to introduce myself—"

Raymond looked round to find a portly grey-haired gentleman with a luxuriant mustache leaning on the back of the sofa beside him.

"I'm Apethorpe," said the gentleman with a fatherly smile. "Just want to say Cheerio, you know, and jolly glad to have you with us, and all that rot, you know—"

"Thank you, sir—"

"Jolly glad you could get here for Christmas, old boy, makes it a bit merrier, what?—I say, Sally, is there any more tea going?" He drifted on to the other side of the table. "Jenny says she'll have a cup, if it's no bother—"

Other people came and went as Raymond drank his scalding, rum-laced tea, told him their names, made him welcome, and were lost sight of again—a dark, pretty girl who looked like Virginia—a quiet French chap in civilian clothes—Calvert's cousin Phoebe whom he had seen at the London hospital and her husband who was a colonel, no less, and with red tabs too—and so on. Raymond gave them each his level, searching look and the grave formality of greeting which acknowledged without servility his newness to their circle and his gratitude for their hospitality. But Virginia, who had seen his spontaneous reaction to Bracken's presence, was bemused. He's beautiful, she heard herself thinking, to her own surprise. When he smiles like that, he's *b-beautiful* —and and so *young*. And she tried not to watch him from the fringes of things, waiting for the smile to come again, which it didn't, because Bracken was the only one there that he had proved. At last, irresistibly drawn to him, she returned to the fireside sofa. Raymond rose at once with his instinctive good manners, and Bracken stood up too.

"I don't really know if you're up to all this," she began uncertainly. "I was very firmly told that you were not to overdo it tonight, and I think it's time Bracken took you along to his room for a rest and a smoke before dinner."

"Please don't worry about me," said Raymond earnestly. "I feel fine, honest I do. You've got a—a very interesting family here."

"No doubt you could think of a shorter and simpler word," said Virginia lightly. "Just brush the young ones off if they're a nuisance, but you must realize that you're the first hero they've seen and they're very excited about you."

Raymond gave a sort of gasp of laughter, as though for once he really was surprised, and glanced at Bracken.

"I'm afraid somebody has given them the wrong idea," he said. "Like I told your son—anybody would have done the same as I did."

"I'm sure of it," Virginia agreed soothingly, and patted his sleeve. "You go along now with Bracken and have a breather.

We shall be sixteen at dinner, with presents afterwards and then music and dancing. You'll need your strength!"

———————

As they went up the stairs together and reached the sanctuary of Bracken's bedroom, Raymond said, "You'll have to sort me out some, I guess. Who was the kind old bird with the mustache?"

"That's the Duke," said Bracken, stripping back the pale green counterpane from the bed and unfolding the satin eiderdown. "You tuck up here a while—I'll take your boots off."

"Duke?" Raymond repeated. "I oughtn't to lay down here with my clothes on, ought I?" He folded up on the edge of the bed abruptly as Bracken knelt and lifted one foot from under him, resting it on his bent knee. "I could do that myself. A *real* duke?"

"None realer," said Bracken, busy with the laces. "Apethorpe, he is. Lives just the other side of the hill in a big house called Overcreech, and gets lonely with everyone away at the wars. Take it easy, now, I've got nothing else to do, and you must last the evening out. Don't be afraid of him, though. He's just like anybody else and wants to be friends."

"Gee," said Raymond. "I'm dining at the same table with a duke, am I?"

"What's more important, you're taking your hostess in to dinner."

"What does that mean?"

"Means you're the guest of honor, over and above the Duke. Let's have your other foot."

Raymond was looking alarmed.

"What do I have to do?" he asked. "Couldn't I sit by Camilla?"

"She's on your other side. You don't have to do anything

special, it's just Virginia's way of paying you a compliment."

"Well, gee," said Raymond again. "I don't know if I—"

"Lie down and put your feet up," said Bracken, piling up the pillows. "Shall I fill a pipe for you?"

"Please," said Raymond, fishing it out of his pocket. "Say, she said something about presents, and I didn't know—I never had a chance to—"

"It's the custom at these Christmas parties for the hostess to have a little parcel for each guest," Bracken assured him. "But the guests don't have to give her one—usually theirs have been sent on ahead. The family presents were all opened this morning. You aren't supposed to give anybody anything. Jenny and Clare and Fabrice weren't here this morning either, so you'll all probably have several apiece."

"All the same, if I'd known I'd of brought her something," said Raymond, and Bracken glanced up to find the dark, fenced-in look on his face again, drawing deep lines downwards from his blunt nose, the lips gone heavy and obstinate, the brilliant eyes hooded with their heavy lashes. " 'Twould have been only polite if I'd brought her something," he persisted, and Bracken thrust the filled pipe at him and struck a match.

"Now, don't be an ass, what chance have you had to go shopping? Anybody knows that. I don't think you realize what it means to this family to have you here," he went on. "I wonder if you've any idea what this evening would have been like if nobody had brought Calvert in safely. You've made us all the greatest gift a man possibly could—because we are not mourning a dead boy here tonight. Can't you see it like that?"

"Thanks," said Raymond after a moment. "I'll try to. Only —he should be here instead of me."

"He'll be here, finally. Meanwhile, let them make a fuss of you, they love it."

"They're all so kind," Raymond marvelled, his teeth set on the pipe stem. "The one at the tea-table—why, you'd have thought I was the King, or something. Who was she?"

"Cousin Sally. A character. She's lived in France as long as anybody can remember, till the war began. We're pretty proud of her, one way and another. Sosthène belongs to her, you know. And Fabrice is her granddaughter."

"I don't think I know which one Fabrice is."

"You will!" Bracken promised. "Watch out for her, too. She'll try to flirt with you."

"Yeah?" said Raymond with a guarded upward glance.

"Don't fall for it, that's all," said Bracken. "It's a habit she has."

"There's one they call Jenny," Raymond said, and the shielding lashes came down again.

"Ah, well, now you're talking!" said Bracken. "You're all right with Jenny, she's a little trump. We must all rally round Jenny tonight, as a matter of fact, because Fabrice will be here and it was Fabrice who stole Jenny's boy."

"It was?" Raymond puffed on the pipe a moment. "Is he here too?"

"Not yet. May turn up. Got a perfect right to be here, of course, he's Archie's youngest brother. If he does arrive, Jenny mustn't be left a minute without a partner. You can help us out on that because you won't be dancing. Help to keep an eye on her, I mean, if the rest of us happen to be out on the dance floor."

"I will," said Raymond.

"Fabrice will probably go to work on Adrian Carteret because he's new," Bracken said. "She always goes for a new man, and being a captain, he ranks you. Virginia will be livid, because she got Adrian expressly for Camilla."

"Oh?" said Raymond, lifting his eyes again.

"Virginia always match-makes," Bracken explained. "It

doesn't mean anything, and it very seldom works. But Camilla doesn't seem to have a beau, so Virginia, who abhors a vacuum, couldn't rest till she'd rounded up somebody like Adrian, who doesn't seem to have a girl at the moment. We're gossiping like a couple of old nannies, aren't we, but it's a bit tough on you to walk into so complicated a family with blinkers on! The least I can do is give you your bearings."

Raymond nodded gravely.

"About this dinner," he said after a moment. "Will there be a lot of forks?"

"Oh, that's easy," Bracken reassured him. "You just work in from the outside. Left to right on the forks, right to left on the knives. You'll come out even. There will be champagne. I don't suppose I have to tell you that's tricky stuff."

"It is?" Raymond's attentive gaze rested again on Bracken's face.

"Like some women," Bracken explained, "it seems mild and harmless. And then—*boom!*"

"I'll remember that," said Raymond gratefully, and just then a brass gong resounded through the house and he sat bolt upright from the pillows. "What's that?"

"Not a fire. Just the dressing-bell. Take it easy. People in uniform don't have to change." Bracken did not add that it was for Raymond's peace of mind that this decision had been made. "It gives the girls a chance to pretty up, that's all." He rose lazily. "I'll just have a wash and be out of your way in the bathroom."

When he returned Raymond was dozing comfortably against the pillows. But there was a tightness round the corners of his mouth as they descended the stairs a half hour later and Bracken said, "Stagefright?" "I wish I had both hands for this," Raymond replied stoically, and Bracken said, "Don't worry, the girls will see you through."

And they did. Seated at the end of the long table between
Camilla and Virginia, who had the Duke on her other hand,
Raymond found dinner less of an ordeal than he had expected. Jenny was half way down the side facing him, and he
watched her discreetly as the meal went on—saw her laugh
at the colonel with red tabs as though she had known him all
her life (which she had) saw her touch glasses gaily with the
French civilian in white tie and tails as the champagne went
round, saw how her eyes crinkled up when she was amused,
and how her firm little chin stuck out when she was serious
—you wouldn't trade her in for six of the other one, he con-
cluded, for Fabrice's obvious prettiness and soubrette ways
had not impressed him during the brief encounter he had
had with her in the drawing-room before dinner. Fabrice was
stuck on herself. He knew that kind, whichever side of the
tracks they came from. This Jenny was a mouse of a girl, kind
of helpless and damp behind the ears still—the kind of a
girl that got kicked in the teeth.

With an effort, he withdrew his attention from Jenny and
returned it to Calvert's sister. He liked Camilla. She was all
right. Looked you straight in the eye, and didn't put on any
la-di-da. None of the people here went in for la-di-da. They
had money and they lived like lords—some of them *were*
lords—but they were regular. You knew where you were with
them. Even the Duke. You wouldn't expect a duke to be so
friendly. There wasn't anything they wouldn't do to make
you feel at home. No snobs here. They said you were one of
the family and by golly you were. But you knew in your own
soul that you didn't really belong. Comes midnight, and your
coach turns back into a pumpkin, and you wake up in the
hospital with an operation hanging over you. Jenny worked
at the hospital, but not in the surgical ward. Well, what if
she did, or didn't. Just looking at her wouldn't get you anything but a headache. And Jenny, with real pearls around

her little neck and a dress all fluff and shimmer and hair like washed gold—such *clean*-looking hair—Jenny belonged here. You didn't start thinking about Jennys, at your age. —But what sort of bum could she have loved, to lose him to a—not that word, at this table—like Fabrice!

"I haven't really been neglecting you," Camilla was saying beside him. "Captain Carteret has been telling me what happens when you transfer to the Air Force. He was in the cavalry."

Raymond looked at the man in Air Force uniform who sat beyond her—the enviable man with a commission and pilot's wings on his breast. Raymond's face was dark and withdrawn, for the idea of flying was very dear to his heart and not a thing he cared to discuss with just anybody. He didn't need to be told that he had a long way to go, from being a lance corporal of a machine-gun crew. The blue eyes which met his were frank and smiling.

"Do anything I can to help, of course," said Adrian Carteret, with a glance at the bandaged arm. "I shall be at the training school at Reading for several weeks more. Camilla has promised to let me know how you go on with that arm. Sir Quentin is a wizard, he'll fix you up in no time."

"I hope so, sir."

"Drive a car?"

"Yes, sir."

"Ride a bike?"

"Yes, sir."

"Good shot?"

"Yes, sir."

"Well, there you are, that's the sort of thing they ask you, you're practically *in!*"

They all laughed, and Raymond's face softened. They were so kind. He had never seen such kind people.

"The trouble with me is, I hate machinery," Adrian confided cheerfully. "I mean, it terrifies me. I'm perfectly certain to be killed by my own bus some day, simply because it won't listen to reason."

"Don't you even like automobiles?" Raymond ventured incredulously.

"Not very much. That is, not when they go wrong, because I'm not one of those chaps who can fiddle about under the bonnet and start her up again. I suppose you got along all right with your gun?"

"Oh, yes," said Raymond, unaware that the most subtle of social tricks had been played on him in all kindness of heart, as the other man confessed himself a duffer at Raymond's game.

"He repairs it under fire," said Camilla, from Calvert's letters.

"I know that kind!" Adrian nodded. "Everyone else going to pieces all round, and this fellow sets to work with a spanner and a pair of tongs and pretty soon the beastly thing is as good as new! We want all that sort of thing we can get in the Air Force."

"I'll be there," said Raymond recklessly.

"Sure to be." Adrian raised his glass. "See you at Reading next!" he said.

Camilla snatched up hers.

"Reading!" she cried.

"Reading," Raymond echoed politely, and they all drank to it.

At the end of the meal when everybody rose, Raymond watched the women leave the room together and glancing at Bracken for enlightenment found the men of the party gathering in at Archie's end of the table, where decanters of wine were being placed and cigars handed round. The Duke turned up at his elbow and maneuvered him into a chair, and they had a long, intelligent discussion about deerstalking and guns, although Raymond had no idea how it got started. He had accompanied his father on a hunting trip to Canada every autumn since his tenth birthday, and had even once got a moose. The Duke was delighted with him, and issued a cordial invitation to come up to Scotland for the very first shoot after the war ended. Raymond thanked him solemnly, and the Duke poured out another glass of port each and they drank to the day.

"Feller knows all about deer-huntin'," said the Duke, catching Archie's eye. "Wasted on the Army, what? Must get him into the Air Corps where he'll be safe. Anybody knows they can't go up when it rains, and it always rains in France, so there you are, eh, Carteret?"

"You're entirely right, sir. Air Corps never does any work," Adrian agreed, and Raymond looked slowly from one to the other and joined in the general grin. It was his own form of humor—rude, understated, low-voiced, and mendacious. He felt suddenly more relaxed and at ease then he had at any time yet that evening.

———

Meanwhile most of the drawing-room had been cleared for dancing, with the rugs rolled up and the furniture grouped more closely round the fire, where Clare on the sofa beside Virginia was saying, "Well, what do you think of him, after all? He seems to fit in pretty well."

"Yes," Virginia said thoughtfully. "I somehow had an idea he would."

"I must confess I wondered," Clare said. "Boys like Calvert who go in as privates form some very strange friendships. It's all right out there, of course. But if Camilla should be taken with him—" She dropped her voice still lower. "—it could happen, you know—you feel you want to know a bit more about him."

"I don't suppose anyone would object very much if she should be taken with him," Virginia replied after a moment. "Such a thing must have occurred to Calvert, at least, when he sent him to us. You can see that Raymond wasn't brought up quite—quite—the same, but he has great dignity, and the old lines of demarcation, or whatever you want to call it, are going pretty fast these days. Besides, I think he could learn almost anything."

"He could learn grammar, anyway," said Clare, and Virginia shot her a baleful glance, for she thought it unkind of Clare not to ignore his few small solecisms as she herself had tried to do even in her own mind. "What part of America does he come from?" Clare continued with an entirely friendly interest.

"I don't know."

"Have you any idea about his people?"

"None. All we know is that he saved Calvert's life, he's presentable, he has nice manners, and nothing is too good for him here."

"Oh, I quite agree with you that he's presentable," said Clare, and Fabrice, who had ears like a fox, said clearly from across the hearth, "Are you talking about the new boy Calvert has sent us? *I* think he's charrrming. Not *quite* out of the top drawer, of course, but definitely charrrming. And what shoulders!" Her big eyes rose expressively to heaven.

Not a woman in the room but looked at her with open dislike, while a little silence fell and Virginia's hostess sense measured the reassuring distance between the drawing-room hearth and where Raymond sat behind the closed door of the dining-room. Then Sally spoke incisively.

"I have always said that you had the mind of a chamber-maid, Fabrice. What a pity it is that you are no longer young enough to be sent out of the room when you say the wrong thing!"

"What was wrong about what I have said?" asked Fabrice with her ingénue pout. "I admire him tremendously. He would be very difficult. But I think worth some trouble if you succeeded."

"That will do," said Sally coldly, and Fabrice laughed round at them in malicious schoolgirl triumph.

"Oooh, I know, I know, he is for Camilla!" she assured them. "I will not interfere, I promise!" Her bright, cruel glance flicked Jenny's still face in the firelight, reminding them all of her power. "I shall have my hands full anyway, by ten o'clock this evening, you can be sure! I have promised Adrian every other dance, and when Gerald comes he will want them *all* himself!"

"Have you heard from Gerald?" The question came sharply from Clare, for he was her brother and she had had no message from him.

"Certainly, a wire from London last night. It was to be a surprise. He stopped in Town long enough to clean himself and sleep and carry out some sort of wager with three friends who are with him. Tonight he comes here."

"You might have told me," said Virginia. "Will he want to stay here?"

"It was nothing to do with you," Fabrice shot back tactlessly. "He will want to stay at the Hall, of course, to be near me. I told you it was a surprise." She glanced at the clock and took out a little gold powder-box from her beaded bag and became absorbed in her complexion.

Sally shrugged expressive shoulders. No one looked at Jenny, who sat without moving, gazing into the fire, her untouched-up face a mask of composure. Camilla moved closer to her instinctively, and Clare said with an attempt at casualness, "Gerald *would* wangle Christmas leave at the last minute, I never saw anything like his luck! Here come the children."

The babies had been put to bed, but the schoolroom set were allowed to come downstairs for the presents and a few dances. It included Virginia's Daphne, just turning sixteen and already a beauty, and her sister Irene, and Clare's two boys, Lionel and Bertram, from Eton. Oliver's Hermione was only ten, but had seen so little of her father lately that she was allowed to stay up a while in the hope that she would begin to adjust to his marriage to Phoebe, which she showed every sign of resenting on her dead mother's behalf.

Phoebe wisely did not pursue her with attentions, and it was Irene who took the place beside Phoebe to ask for news of Jeff in New York, for all his English cousins were curious about Phoebe's baby son who was living with Dinah. There had been some talk about bringing Jeff and Dinah to England in the spring, or at any rate the minute the war ended—but Phoebe knew from Oliver that far from being almost over the war was about to enter a new and terrible phase; it was no secret at the War Office that a German spring offensive was shaping up very fast. Such a dismal subject was forbidden on a night like this, however, so she said nothing of it to Irene. For tonight the family was to feel secure, the children should be shielded from grown-up apprehensions, and life must appear to be as normal as possible. As for Dinah and Jeff, however much they were missed—and she knew Bracken's heart was sore from their absence—however much they might feel themselves exiled from the places where things were being done and from the people who belonged to them, they were safe and they had the right food and they were spared a lot of things it was only right that a few cherished ones should never know.

With Irene's hand curled confidingly in hers, Phoebe glanced ruefully at the group of youngsters lighting the candles on the tree. During the next few months Lionel would begin his military training and then go out to France.

Soon Daphne would start her VAD service at the Hall. They were all growing up into it, the ones who had been just children when the war began. Not her own Jeff, of course. Jeff was only four, though it seemed twice as long as that since she had seen him last. But by the time Jeff was Lionel's age—her mind stopped on the edge of the abyss, peering ahead—what would it be like in 1930? Where would they all be by then? Would even Oliver make a guess at that?

With relief she heard the men's voices returning across the hall from the dining-room, and rose impulsively as Oliver entered and went to meet him, with Irene's hand still in hers.

"Hullo," he said, and his kind, penetrating gaze rested on her troubled face. "What have you two been talking about, to look so solemn?"

"We aren't solemn at all, we were saying how nice it would be when Aunt Dinah and Jeff could come to England for a visit," Irene told him innocently, and Phoebe added, "By summertime, we were saying," and squeezed his arm. "Dinah loves the summer here."

"Oh, yes, by summertime, I should think," he agreed easily, for this was Christmas night and Irene was listening.

Camilla, supporting Jenny merely by being a loyal presence at her side, watched Sosthène go straight to Sally, needle to the magnet, and heard again in her own mind Fabrice's thoughtless words—*Raymond is for Camilla.* In her preoccupation with the overwhelming thing which had happened to her since she met Sosthène, Raymond had hardly appeared to Camilla as a man, as a romantic possibility not at all, though at one time the man to whom she owed Calvert's life would have seemed no lower than the angels. Her awareness of Sosthène had blotted out all other men from her consciousness. Besides—who *was* Raymond? Calvert's friend. But before that. Before he saved Calvert's life—who was he?

Standing beside Jenny, who was still seated by the fire, she watched him come towards her, with Bracken at his elbow, down the long room. Bracken would have to do something about Jenny—they must all do something about her—when Gerald came. Even Raymond must throw himself into the breach. There must be no smallest chink around Jenny for Fabrice's darts or Gerald's careless cruelty to penetrate.

"We're all to sit down and behave while Hermione carries round the presents," Bracken said confidentially when they arrived at the hearth. "She has been chosen for that office, I gather, not because she is the most popular person present, but because she is the youngest. Archie is going to read off the names."

"Phoebe doesn't like you to say things like that," Camilla rebuked him. "Hermione can't help being Maia's daughter."

"No, but she does rub it in, rather," said Bracken, who had shared the family aversion to Oliver's first wife.

Jenny looked up at him, her round chin jutting.

"Now, Bracken, do be careful, if a child like that once gets the idea that people have a down on her it can ruin her whole life."

"*I* didn't give her any such idea," said Bracken contrarily. "She must have worked it out herself."

"Sh!" they told him.

Archie and Hermione were standing by the lighted tree at the end of the room, and everyone settled unobtrusively into whatever seat was nearest and Raymond felt himself pulled down on to the fireside bench by Jenny's kind little hand on his good arm as she made room for him there beside her.

"Your Grace—my lords and ladies—boys and girls, what-nots and so forths—er—pray silence," Archie began in an exaggerated Inner Temple drawl, slim and monocled in tailored khaki, with Hermione in a white crêpe de chine dress and strapped slippers very self-conscious beside him. "On

my right hand you will perceive a somewhat—er—youthful
and—er—not to say beardless embodiment of Father Christmas. But I may assure you that the tokens about to be delivered to you by the hand of this—er—delightful deputy are
nevertheless guaranteed all wool and a yard wide and have
arrived via the usual reliable channels direct from the shop
at the North Pole." At this point he looked sharply at Hermione for confirmation and she managed to nod mutely,
twisting her fingers together in an agony of embarrassment.
"Therefore," Archie continued briskly, taking pity on this
incomprehensible child who, unlike his own, had no sense
of fun and could not toss the ball back to him, "therefore,
without further delay we will proceed to—er—proceed.
Everybody must open his parcel as soon as he receives it—
that is to say, no hiding it away till next Christmas, or any
nonsense like that." He stooped and lifted a square tissue-
wrapped package from the top of the heap beneath the tree
and peered profoundly at its label through his monocle.
"Well, now, that's very awkward, this first one seems to be for
me. Couldn't I just—" He made as if to tuck it well under-
neath at the back.

"Open it!" everybody yelled at him.

"But if I stop to open mine now it will hold up everybody
else—"

"Open it!" they yelled at him, and "Oh, very well, have it
your own way," he grumbled, and plucked at the silver ribbon which tied it.

Hermione, almost forgetting herself in a child's rapture
over presents, anybody's presents, leaned towards him, join-
ing in the suspense. Camilla, the only one besides Virginia
who knew what was in the box, and who had herself chosen
the exact spot most likely to be under Archie's hand at the
beginning, suppressed a giggle. Archie reached the box inside
the paper, removed the lid, and lifted out a barrister's wig,

scrupulously copied in every detail in bright carroty red
hair. A shout of joy went up, and Archie, not a muscle of his
disciplined face betraying his own hysterical amusement,
gazed round at them between benevolence and censure.

"I call that very thoughtful of somebody," he remarked.
"You have no idea how naked I feel without one of these
things." He adjusted it solemnly to his head, and flipped
out the little ribboned queue behind. "Well, now," he said,
and caught Hermione's eyes and winked at her so that she
squirmed and sobered and remembered that she was in the
limelight too. "Now if only you had a long white beard we
could do this right, couldn't we." He stooped and solemnly
chose another parcel from the heap. "Miss Camilla Scott,"
he read deliberately, "of Richmond, U.S.A." He handed it
to Hermione for delivery, adding in an audible aside, "That
will be the beautiful young lady in blue chiffon on the sofa
by the fire."

Hermione made the journey across the bare polished floor,
wearing a rather smug smile and walking affectedly because
everyone was watching her, and Virginia thought, "Why *is*
she like that? Mine never were. Oh, God, is she going to
curtsey to *each one* of us as our turn comes?"

"His Grace the Duke of Apethorpe," Archie read out as
Hermione returned to his side again, and she set forth on the
new mission to the accompaniment of rustling tissue paper
in Camilla's hands and a spontaneous cry of *"Oh,* Virginia!"
as a silver filigree vinaigrette scented with very modern
French perfume came to light. "Miss Irene Campion," Archie
announced next, and weighed it in his hand before Hermione took it. "Feels like chocolates to me. Does it rattle?"
They shook it, their heads together. "No—not a sound. Soap,
maybe." He sniffed it. "Well, I suppose she may as well
have it." Hermione was off again. "Now, this one," Archie
continued impressively, "this one I claim the privilege of

presenting myself. You won't need to guess whose name is on it." He left the tree and carried Sally's gift ceremoniously between his hands and laid it in hers with a little bow. Her upward smile into his face had all the practiced coquetry and charm of a vanished era, as well as the warm, magnetic thing which was just Sally, secure and radiant in the midst of the homage she was so accustomed to that it was like the air she breathed.

The gifts went on, some beautiful, some comic, some quite valuable, all appropriate and chosen with understanding and care. Raymond, seated beside Jenny on the hearthrug bench, watched while she unwrapped first an expensive-looking little powder-box and then a bottle of French perfume—and lowered his nose obediently when the stopper was offered him to sniff. Muguet—lilies-of-the-valley. It suited her. He watched her dab it behind her ears, and the delicate fragrance enveloped them together in a new intimacy. Then he looked down to find Hermione standing before him with a ribboned parcel extended. He took it slowly in his left hand with a glance at Virginia as though for permission, and a quiet Thank-you to the child's punctilious curtsey.

"Shall I undo it for you?" Jenny said, laying her own things aside, and he kept his eyes on her small deft hands while a jeweller's box opened to reveal a gold wrist watch with a link bracelet.

The sight of it caught him by the throat, made a stinging in his eyelids. It was the sort of gift they gave each other. And they had given it to him. The room by now was a pandemonium of tissue paper and joyful cries and hilarious laughter as the unwrapped gifts multiplied and no one waited any more to see some one else's knots untied. He looked up at Jenny, and she saw the tears in his eyes as she sat holding the watch for him.

"But I can't take it," he said, very low. "They shouldn't do that, it's much too good, I can't—" His eyes went back to the watch. The famous name of its maker on the dial looked up at him. His inborn passion for fine mechanism made him want the watch more than he had wanted anything for years. It was the watch he had promised himself some day, and now here it was, in Jenny's hands, while the cheap open-faced turnip-seed which his father had carried and which lost twelve minutes every day no matter what you did to it ticked in his pocket.

A light hand fell on his shoulder.

"That's from Calvert," said Virginia. "Let Jenny put it on for you." The hand patted him once, and she was gone again.

Jenny lifted the watch from its white satin bed and held it out, waiting. He raised his left hand to her and felt the cool metal bracelet click into place.

"They're only trying to thank you," said Jenny. "Put yourself in their place. They only want to give you the earth."

"You think it's all right for me to keep it?"

"Of course."

"Well," he said, still doubtfully. "Whatever you say."

Archie's pleasant voice droned on, more presents came to Jenny, and to Raymond came the tortoise-shell cigarette case and the lighter, without initials, and a large mechanical insect made of tin which when wound up with a key clattered futilely along the floor waggling its large green wings but unable to take off. Next to the watch it was his favorite gift, and he made Jenny wind it again and again, as pleased as a child that it actually performed, even in his hand.

He was beyond surprise now, beyond an uncomfortable sense of obligation, beyond anything but a kind of speechless bliss he had never encountered before. He was one of them, lost in the happy, careless shuffle, submerged in the family tide of laughter and bad jokes and good fellowship. He wasn't a guest. He wasn't a stranger. He was inside. Accepted, ignored, pampered, forgotten—one of them. Just like they said in the beginning. One of the family.

"It's wonderful," he said to Jenny, his eyes wandering over the bright, noisy room. "Aren't they wonderful? I never knew there was anything like tonight in the world."

"I know how you feel," Jenny said quickly. "I feel the same way about this house, because I never had a family. My mother died when I was born."

"That's queer," said Raymond. "So did mine."

They stared at each other. It seemed a very deep, inevitable bond between them.

"I should have been a boy, though," she added finally.

"I think I like you better as a girl," he remarked consideringly, as though the choice rested with him, and her eyes crinkled up in her laughter.

Somebody dropped the needle on the gramophone and the dancing began. Jenny was carried off into a waltz by Bracken, and was taken from him by Archie, who still wore with dignity and unconcern the red barrister's wig. Oliver danced with his daughter Hermione, and the Duke led out a rather flustered Irene, and Adrian danced with Daphne, who lost her heart to him as utterly as only a sixteen-year-old girl can, and when he guessed her age as seventeen her evening was completely made.

Word went round that the cold buffet was ready in the dining-room, mostly potted meat sandwiches—not rationed —and sweet biscuits, but there was a punch bowl as well, and a beaming maid had begun to circulate in the drawing-room with a tray full of sparkling champagne glasses.

A machine is a machine, and before long Raymond was running the gramophone. They had gone through all the dance records once and were beginning on them again when he found Jenny standing beside him with a glass of champagne in each hand.

"I'm sorry you can't dance," she said. "Let somebody else tend that thing for a while." And she offered him one of the glasses she carried.

"I just had some of this," he said, but he thanked her and took it, and they drank while their eyes held across the brims and the record came to an end. He had to set down his glass to start a new one, saying into the opening bars of *The Merry Widow,* "I could dance left-handed."

"How do you mean?" She set down her glass and faced him, willing to try.

"Like this." He slipped his right arm out of the sling, leaving it bent up towards his shoulder, and put his left around her waist. "You hold my right arm up," he said, and her hand closed quickly on his as he backed her neatly on to the dance floor.

"So you're ambidextrous," she said, surrendering easily to his guidance.

"What's that?"

"It means you can use either hand equally well."

"Oh, yes. I was a left-handed kid, and at school they made me learn to use my right instead. It's kind of convenient sometimes."

"Have you ever danced the wrong way round before?"

"No, that never came up before. Does it go all right with you?"

"It goes perfectly." He had a strong natural rhythm, and she leaned confidently on his encircling arm at the turns. "Are you sure you ought to?" she asked after a minute.

"You know something?" said Raymond, ignoring her question. "I can feel your fingers in mine. There was a long time I couldn't feel anything in that hand. What does that mean?"

"It must mean you're getting better."

"I sure hope it does."

"Hi, Jenny, don't let him do that!" said Bracken, brushing past them with Fabrice in his arms. And a moment later Clare swept by with the Duke and cried, "Don't let him use that arm!" as she went. Jenny faltered in her step and looked up at him, realizing that she knew very little about his wound.

"We'd better stop," she said, and felt his clasp tighten masterfully around her.

"Whose arm is it?" he wanted to know, and then, wiping out the dark obstinacy on his face, came the transfiguring smile so few people ever saw. Jenny caught it for the first time at a distance of only a few inches and it knocked the breath right out of her, leaving her limp and pliant in his hold, obedient to every shift and turn of his big body, without the will to resist him even for his own good. He was having such fun. Anything that could make him look like that couldn't hurt him. Anything that made him look so—so *young.* "I'll need this the day after tomorrow," he was saying. "They can't take this away from me, even with chloroform." His eyes went possessively over her hair, so near he could almost feel its softness against his cheek, over her upturned face in a deliberate glance like a caress, with a pause on her lips like a kiss. "You've got the cutest chin," he said. "I bet you can be stubborn as hell."

"Well, so can you," she said without embarrassment.

"Yep—that's two of us," he agreed at once. "Two stubborn people, I guess."

"Stubborn or not, when this record ends you're through dancing for tonight. And it's ending now."

She returned with him to the gramophone and helped him slip his arm back into the sling, and he wound the machine with his left hand while she turned over the record. He knew now how wrong he had been. While they were still dancing, there had been a prickling in the wound, a growing smart, a flash of pain, and now he felt a slow spreading warmth. As he set the needle he was wondering desperately how he could get away without Jenny's catching on, get out of the room, get off somewhere alone and not spoil the party. . . .

There was a shout from the doorway, and Gerald stood there—captain in the Royal Horse Artillery, tall, dark, laughing, very naughty and very brazen about it. Fabrice flung herself at him with a joyful scream, the rest gathered round to greet him, and Raymond realized with relief that Bracken had arrived to help look after Jenny.

"Let's all go have something to eat," said Bracken, and moved them towards the dining-room, collecting the Duke with a lifted eyebrow on the way.

As they passed the staircase in the hall Raymond fell a little behind, then stepped quickly aside and mounted to Bracken's bedroom. Closing the door carefully behind him, he made for the bathroom. The wound had opened and was bleeding hard.

━━━━━━━━

After a decent interval in the dining-room Bracken began to wonder about Raymond. Then he began to worry. And finally Jenny agreed with him that he had better go upstairs and find him.

Raymond was sitting on the edge of the bathtub dripping scarlet splotches on to the white porcelain. He had undone his tunic in an effort to get it off which had been too much for him alone. The right side of it and the shirt beneath it was dark with blood. He looked up defensively as Bracken appeared in the bathroom doorway.

"Please don't say anything about this downstairs. Could you get me back to the hospital without anyone knowing?"

"I wouldn't dare to try," Bracken replied promptly.

"You've got to have that seen to at once, but it's too much for me. Stay where you are and *don't move.*"

From the top of the stairs he could see Jenny hovering in the hall. He beckoned to her and she came running up.

"He's bleeding," said Bracken. "In my bathroom. Can we get a doctor to come over from the Hall?"

"Let's have a look," said Jenny competently. "Which room are you in?"

"The green one."

Jenny had a look—just one—and said, "Send Phoebe and Virginia up here, quick. Then ring up the Hall and ask Dr. Butler to come at once—say I asked you to—say it's an emergency—a bleeding wound which may go into shock before we can get it stopped. Ask him to bring whatever he needs, there's nothing here, and to bring me a nursing dress, I'll take night duty. And ask him to hurry."

Bracken vanished without comment, and Raymond raised his head slowly to look up at her. He was drawn with pain and his color was already bad.

"I'm sorry about this," he said rather thickly. "I'm sorry to take you away from the party—"

"Nonsense, we're used to this sort of thing, we'll fix you up. Stay right where you are while I get the bed ready. Can you stick it a few minutes more?"

He nodded, and she went into the other room and began to strip back the bed. Phoebe arrived breathless from running upstairs, followed by Virginia, limping, and they rushed off again to bring rubber mats and mackintosh sheets from the nursery cupboard, towels and hot water bottles. By the time Bracken returned from the telephone the bed was ready and he helped Jenny to get Raymond out of his clothes and into a pair of his own pyjamas. Dr. Butler was not in at the Hall, but was believed to be dining at the rectory. They were trying to find him.

Raymond collapsed gratefully against the pillows and lay with his eyes closed, looking rather done for. Jenny rolled a towel and wadded it under his armpit, pressing the arm against it, but the blood kept coming. His shoulder-cap bandage was soaked bright red, and Phoebe said, "It looks like the sub-clavian artery to me. Put your finger on it." Without hesitation Jenny made pressure on a spot above the collar-bone, and they watched anxiously. It was hard to tell at once if the flow was slowing up. For all Phoebe's experience in front-line hospitals, it was somehow Jenny who was in charge here, and Raymond was aware in a growing mistiness that she had fastened a towel over the front of her dance-frock which was already blotched and stained. It was Jenny's small hands which were red with his blood, it was Jenny who had pinned herself to his side to maintain the pressure on the first rib. He opened his eyes wider and looked up into her face, brightly lit by the lamp Phoebe was holding above them.

"Please don't bother," he said foggily. And then, when she turned her head to smile at him, "You'll spoil your dress—"

"Hold tight," said Jenny. "The doctor's coming."

They kept the linen wad pressed under his arm, they kept the bed warm with hot water bottles, Jenny kept her fingers hard against his collar-bone. Their faces were white and strained, and Raymond's had got quite grey, and a creeping cold was gaining on him, but the bleeding had finally stopped.

He wavered in and out of consciousness, and always when he opened his eyes Jenny was there, her soft hair falling forward along her jaw, her bloodstained hands firm and quiet on him, her chin sticking out. Stubborn, he thought, but could not get the word past his teeth. Too stubborn to let me die, I guess. . . .

But the mists closed in again, and he never knew when the doctor came, and never felt the morphine injection. The lamp was still burning when he roused again to find a clean new bandage in place and the covers smooth above him. He had no strength to stir, but there was a movement beside the bed, quick fingers were laid on his pulse, and he caught the smell of good cigar smoke. The doctor, he thought, gratefully. He got here, then. Where's Jenny? She was not within the range of his half-open eyes, so he tried to turn his head a little to look for her.

"That's right," said the doctor. "Coming round nicely now. Better get some nourishment into him soon."

With a great effort Raymond raised his eyelids a little further, but his head weighed too much to move.

"Well, you did give us a fright," said Jenny on the other side of him. "I suppose now you'd like breakfast?"

He tried to smile, he tried to see her—but his eyes closed again in spite of him—he heard something a long way off about chicken broth—and the next thing he knew he was swallowing it.

"There," said Jenny. "That's the stuff, isn't it. Have some more."

He swallowed again. It wasn't hot enough to burn his tongue, but hot enough to comfort. It took Jenny to serve broth at the right temperature. He could see her now—holding the bowl and spoon for him—wearing her blue VAD dress and white apron with her hair hidden under the coif.

"Hullo," he whispered.

"Hullo, darling," said Jenny.

He remembered that he had heard her call Bracken darling, and even the Frenchman. It was a way Jenny had. It didn't mean anything.

More broth went down. He dozed again, with that lovely stuff inside him, and the day passed in a haze, punctuated by a visit from Sir Quentin, who humphed at him and hurt him a good deal and said A fine thing, and now they would have to wait a few days.

When he had slept off Sir Quentin he found Virginia sitting beside the bed knitting, and supposed that Jenny had gone back to her regular duties at the Hall. That being the case, it didn't seem advisable or tactful to ask Virginia about her, so he ate docilely what was given him and drifted off again.

It might have been hours later when he opened his eyes on lamplight, and there was Jenny. This time his head turned towards her on the pillow.

"I thought you'd gone," he murmured.

"I'm on night duty," she said. She had been reading a book by the shaded light, and her coif and apron were spotlessly fresh. She laid down the book and took his temperature and pulse and wrote them down while he watched silently. Then she went to a little spirit stove which had been installed on a table against the wall and heated some broth and brought it to him. He stirred as though to raise himself and she said quickly, "Lie perfectly still, I'll feed it to you."

"How long has it been?" he asked, for he had pretty well lost track of things.

"This is the third night. You'll be all right now."

"Was I pretty bad?"

"You almost got away from us," said Jenny.

"It was you," he said, looking up at her between spoonfuls. "You were right in there pitchin', weren't you. Your hands were all over blood. Did it spoil your dress?"

"Yes, I'm afraid it did."

"I'm sorry," he said.

"The dress doesn't matter. We won."

"We won, eh." His eyes rested contentedly on her face. "That was quite a party, wasn't it. They can't ever take that away from me now. Champagne—and a real duke—he asked me to come shoot deer on his place in Scotland—and I danced with you—didn' I."

"You certainly did."

"You got an awful cute chin," he said. "It sure was stickin' out that night before the doctor came. You put up quite a fight for me—didn' you."

Jenny carried the empty bowl back to the table and left it there.

"You've talked about enough," she said.

"Jenny," he murmured, and she looked round inquiringly and returned to the bed.

"Want something?"

"I just wanted to say it. D'you mind?"

"Of course not." She straightened the sheet, and sat down again in the arm chair beside the bed, facing him. "Go to sleep now."

"Must I?"

She nodded, and picked up the book.

"What time is it?"

"Just on three."

He remembered the new watch. It was still there on his wrist and had been kept wound by somebody.

"Where's my bug?" he asked suddenly.

"What?" said Jenny.

"My mechanical bug. I wouldn't want to lose that."

"It's there on the dresser, perfectly safe—along with the other things."

"Could I have a cigarette?"

"Then will you go to sleep?"

He nodded, and she lit one for him.

"Does this make any difference to the operation?" he asked after the first puff.

"Puts it off a bit, that's all. You'll have to stay very quiet for a few more days."

"I won't—lose my arm now?"

"No." She saw the shadow of dread in his eyes and understood. "Have you been worrying about that? You mustn't."

"He didn't say anything about it when he was here?"

"Not a word."

There was a silence.

"I sure played hell with your Christmas holiday," he said then.

"There wasn't any holiday. I had only the one night off."

"Keeping you up all night," he muttered. "Spoiling your dress. What are they doing over at the hospital without you?"

"They'll get along."

"Bet they'd like to shoot me. Well, they can't take it away from us, can they—that dance we had."

"You paid quite a price for it. I should have known better myself. I should have stopped you."

"It was worth it," he said, his eyes on her face. "Worth just about anything it costs me. I'm sorry to put you to so much trouble, though."

"Maybe it was worth that too," said Jenny.

"I'm glad you said that," he whispered. "I can go to sleep on that, I guess."

She took the stub of his cigarette and crushed it out. He closed his eyes and was gone, as completely as a baby—or a soldier.

Jenny sat watching him, the book in her lap. In the lamplight his sleeping face was relaxed and defenceless, and his color was coming back to normal. It was a kind, generous mouth with deep corners and strong curves, and a slight draw across his teeth. His lashes lay black and heavy on his cheeks, which still had a boyish roundness under the dark three days' beard. His straight black hair was rumpled like a child's. I'll have Bracken shave him tomorrow, she thought. That always perks them up. He's got to have one of the private rooms at the Hall, after the operation. I shall make them let me go on looking after him. He's used to me, and Camilla and Virginia will be going back to Town from here.

Winifred had rather grudgingly sent over some of Jenny's things from the Hall, and Jenny and Virginia were taking turns with Raymond until he was well enough to be moved, early in the new year. Jenny discovered now that she apparently had no intention of returning to Ward B and her head cases until Sir Quentin had finished with Raymond, and she regarded herself with some surprise. It never mattered to her what sort of cases she had, as a rule. They were all soldiers, and they all needed her and were grateful and good and polite. This Raymond was no different from the rest, she told herself, sitting beside him while he slept. Other men watched her with the same pathetic endurance, the same childlike worship in their eyes, and usually they asked to call her Jenny. Other men had unruly dark hair and powerful shoulders. Other men knew and hid the dread of amputation. Other men had won the V.C.

But it was no good. No other man was Raymond.

Now, this won't do, she lectured herself, sitting very still with her head against the back of the chair, watching him. This isn't what we intended. It's not fair on all the others. You've always been dead against having favorites in the wards, you might as well be Fabrice if you start thinking like this. You are less useful to them all if you are preoccupied with one, I've always preached that.

You put up quite a fight for me, he said. But she had fought just as hard for other men's lives, men who were strangers to her. So was Raymond a stranger, if it came to that. She had seen him first on Christmas Day. A little champagne and they had danced together and it had nearly killed him. Not much of a record, was it. *Whatever it costs me, it was worth it,* he said, and he meant that, he was in no condition to turn off mere pretty speeches. And she had answered him impulsively in the same key. Worth the dress, yes, to save Raymond alive. But Phoebe could have done it just as well. I wonder. He knew it was me, working on him. Maybe that made a difference to him, when the turning point came. Maybe we both tried harder because we were doing it together. He had to want to live. Sometimes they are too tired, and don't care. He'll get well now. He wants to. I want him to. Are we going to fall in love?

That's the trouble with night duty, she thought without moving. You have so much time to think, and you imagine things. He's probably got a girl at home, several of them by the look of him, he could have pretty well anything he wants, I should think. And I'm cured of all that. I don't want to fall in love, not ever again, not with anybody, certainly not with a stranger, you'd never know what might pop out at you from the time before you knew him. He's not a boy, he hasn't come all this way without—without— Well, he's left a girl in America, anyway, of course, waiting for him and hoping. It wouldn't be fair, he must go back to her, where he belongs, and I belong here, with the wounded. It was just the champagne, the other night, and the party. We were all very gay and trying to forget that it was only for one night. . . .

Worth whatever it costs me. . . . Well, even then, even if he meant that, there's nothing in it for either of us, I'm just another girl to him, he's just another wounded soldier. *Two stubborn people.* . . . No, no, it won't do at all, you've just got over it once and stopped hurting, for heaven's sake don't let's begin again, you'll only be sorry. But with him— would it be worth whatever it cost me . . . with him . . . even if it didn't last. . . . No. Nothing is worth what it

cost me last time. No one else shall ever matter to me like
that again. I'm better off as I am. All right, so I'm afraid.
Not of him. Of that thing inside me that bled and moaned
and ached and agonized and wouldn't give in and decently
die—that thing they call your heart, but it might just as well
be your stomach, that's where you're sick, and you can't eat
for fear of its coming up, and it feels as though you've swallowed a stone—heart sounds better, when it's love, but your
stomach makes the fuss. So I'm a coward, for fear it will hurt
again. All right, I am, I'd rather die than go through again
what I went through about Gerald. I'm going to keep myself together now and be useful, and keep my mind on the
war till it's won. Raymond will be more useful too, in what
he has to do, if he isn't thinking about me. No good could
come of it for either of us, only misery. He hardly knows
what happened tonight, or what we said. Tomorrow I shall
keep out of sight till he's gone to sleep, and just nip the
whole thing in the bud. . . . Oh, darling, you look so *trustful,* lying there, but it's the only way. . . .

———

Camilla returned to Town with Phoebe and Oliver, but
Virginia and Bracken were remaining at Farthingale till
after New Year's Day. She sat looking out of the train window, rather silent and preoccupied, during the journey.
It would be quite a while before she returned to Farthingale,
she knew, for she was badly needed in St. James's Square
and when the spring offensive started things would be much
worse. And there would be Calvert to look after too, pretty
soon. It was bound to be weeks, even months, before she saw
Sosthène again.

They had been alone together only once since the afternoon at the piano. He did not dance at the Christmas party,
but whether it was because Sally did not or because he was

not allowed to by his doctors Camilla did not know. A man
with a bad heart can live forever if he is careful. There was
very little sign of carefulness on Sosthène's part, beyond
great moderation in eating and drinking and an unostenta-
tious avoidance of physical exertion. It was impossible not
to wonder how ill he was, especially if you spent your life
nowadays nursing, and impossible not to wonder if everything had been done to make him well. Sally must surely
have seen to that, there was always plenty of money.

Camilla was anxious about what Calvert would think of
this strange, swift bondage she owned to Sosthène, and wondered how she could ever explain it to him—excuse it to
him was the better word, perhaps, for she knew uneasily
that at least until he had seen Sosthène for himself Calvert
would not approve. And yet, if she didn't tell him at once,
it would be the first time there had been a secret between
them. No one else knew but Jenny—and Jenny wouldn't
give her away. They had not mentioned it again since that
first night in the kitchen, but there was no doubt in Camilla's
mind that Jenny had more than once caught her eyes on
Sosthène's face, or read correctly a restless mood of depression which everyone else conveniently blamed on her worry
about Calvert. Poor Raymond's collapse at the party had been
a handy thing, really, for it had removed Jenny from the
dance just at the awkward time of Gerald's arrival. It was
impossible not to like Gerald, even in his shameless infatuation for Fabrice—not just because he was so handsome and
so impenitent, but because he was so happy in it and might
be dead next week. You only wanted Fabrice to be kind to
him, and not tease him too much, and not brag of her con-
quests at the Hall. You couldn't be hard on a man who had
only three days' Christmas leave in England. Gerald was gone
now, on his way back to France, and Fabrice was back at the
Hall handing round the eternal broth and tea. And Jenny,

who had got over it anyway, was staying on at Farthingale to look after Raymond till time for his operation. Jenny was still there in the house where Sosthène was. . . .

To occupy her mind in the train going back to Town, Camilla began to compose the letter to Calvert about Raymond, so as to reassure him about the chances of saving the arm in only one operation if all went well, and Adrian Carteret's confidence that the Air Force would accept him as soon as the Medical Board gave the word. "He has the look of a good flyer," Adrian had said. "Wouldn't fluster easily, I should think."

She could safely tell Calvert that they had all liked Raymond, and Jenny had taken him under her wing and promised to see him through the operation and report to London daily. Camilla's mind was at peace about leaving him in Jenny's charge, you couldn't do better than that. I wonder, she thought, gazing out the train window, if it had not been for Sosthène—. Well, it's too late now, she thought. There will never be anyone for me now but Sosthène. I must get used to that, somehow. Jenny got used to much worse. Sosthène will never let me down. It's just a matter of trying to live without him. After all, I haven't got much to lose, because there hasn't been anything—except that day at the piano—he liked my voice—and this morning before the others came down to breakfast. . . .

She had come into the dining-room a bit early, having finished her packing, and found it empty, and was helping herself to something hot from the sideboard when Sosthène came in, also early, with Mimi at his heels. Sally always breakfasted from a tray in her room.

They said Good-morning and she sat down at her place and began to eat while he still pottered round the hot plates on the sideboard. She had no longer that first agony of nervousness in his presence, nor the first insatiable craving for it. She had steadied a little, resigned herself and relaxed a little, now that she must no longer conceal from him her headlong, schoolgirl worship, the knowledge of which apparently caused him no self-consciousness, no desire to avoid her, and no inclination whatever to take advantage of it. He seemed to accept with a fatalistic compassion the fact of her having fallen in love with him. It was impossible to tell by a glance or a flicker of expression on his serene, secretive face if he felt in himself the faintest response to her emotion. The time would come when this attitude of his would be to her the ultimate exasperation, but not yet. So far it was only a relief, giving her time to assimilate her own unfamiliar sensations in the friendly vacuum of his unfailing kindness and patience.

He sat down with his own plate on the opposite side of the table.

"So you are off to London this morning," he said. "We shall be very quiet again hereabouts after today."

"Don't you ever come up to Town yourself?" she ventured.

"Not often. It is very tiring for Sallee, and there is no point in her exposing herself to the raids."

He obviously had no idea of ever coming to London without Sally. Camilla wondered if they were ever separated, but to put such a question to him would only sound petulant and childish now. She sighed, and he glanced at her over his fork.

"It might be that your brother should come here to convalesce," he suggested gently.

"Yes—eventually, perhaps. And I might come with him for a few days."

"It is lovely here later in the year. You should see Gloucestershire in May," he said.

"I wonder what will be happening by then," she murmured. "Will the war be over, do you think?"

"I'm afraid not so soon."

"They think there will be another offensive, don't they —by the Germans."

"Any time now."

"Sosthène—we *are* going to win this war, aren't we?"

"But naturally," he said with conviction. "Only not just yet. Germany has not yet sufficiently spent herself. We must have patience."

Their eyes met across the table—the old world and the new—wisdom and youthful folly—discipline and ardor—and once again there passed between them that current of complete comprehension, in which he recognized the tribute she paid to him, and with a sense of inevitable desolation allowed it to lie there unclaimed.

"Yes," said Camilla, obedient to his discretion. "I will try to be patient."

She was trying now, as she sat in the railway carriage with Phoebe and Oliver. She was telling herself that her time would be very full when she got back to London, and with Calvert coming as well she would have a lot of extra things to do. She was trying not to think about Gloucestershire in May, or to promise herself that perhaps in four or five months she could go back with a good excuse—Calvert's convalescence—and see Sosthène again. She knew that any letters which passed between them must include Sally—there was nothing he did that did not include Sally—and the knowledge of Sally, unsuspicious and content, in secure possession of his company morning, noon, and night was the hardest part of all to bear.

———

At Farthingale, Raymond progressed slowly with only one brief relapse. Sir Quentin made another visit and expressed satisfaction. Winifred set aside the yellow bedroom at the Hall for Raymond's use after the operation, and as it was a slack time she undertook to leave the two other beds in the room empty for a few days, inquiring sardonically on the telephone if she should also have the red carpet laid down for his arrival. To which Jenny replied easily, "Shut up, darling, you know we promised Camilla nothing would be too good for him."

"And I suppose," said Winifred in a resigned sort of voice, "she wants you to look after him while he's here."

"Well, yes, she did, rather," Jenny admitted, though she hadn't meant to and instantly regretted it, and then drew a breath of relief because after all Winifred had suggested it herself.

She was finding Raymond not a very easy person to nip in the bud—not because he was at all obstreperous but rather because he was the opposite. There was nothing to rebuke him for. He never tried to catch her hand, for instance, he never asked favors or wanted to beg off the things that were required of him—he was always polite and docile and respectful. But his eyes, grey as a winter dawn, missed nothing she did and seemed to follow the least movement of her hands and the changes of expression on her face with affectionate care as though memorizing what they saw. And his smile, when it came, was as intimate and possessive as a caress.

He always woke at least once during the night while she sat beside the bed, and she gave him broth or tea and a cigarette, and they exchanged a few quiet sentences, and he slept again. He made very little trouble even for his day nurse, Virginia reported, and when he did not sleep seemed still withdrawn into some quiet world of his own, disinclined for conversation, mute about his experiences in France, until Virginia said to Bracken that she had never known a man more courteously untalkative than Raymond was. She asked him if he wanted to read or be read to, and he listened gravely while she read off a dozen titles from the bookshelves in the corner of the room. Most of the miscellaneous collection which had found its way there obviously meant nothing to him, but he recognized with pleasure an old Jules Verne which he said he had read with his father years ago, and asked to see it again.

Virginia brought the volume to the bed, mystified, and he at once became absorbed in it. She noticed that he read slowly and thoroughly, turning the pages without haste, handling the book with respect, closing it and putting it out of harm's way under the edge of his pillow when the tray with his dinner arrived. He was taught to take care of things, thought Virginia with a maternal tenderness. Books were not easy to come by in his father's house. It was another fascinating clue to his unknown background—that books were not casual possessions to be thrown about and left with odd markers in them. Virginia herself, well educated as she considered herself to be, had never opened a volume of Jules Verne in her life, and could not imagine anyone, except possibly Archie, who might have done so. Barrie, Bennett, Wells, Kipling—he passed them all up. But Verne was an old friend. I'd better try him with *Swiss Family Robinson*, thought Virginia.

Before December thirtieth the family party had dwindled, but neighbors were coming in for the evening and the rector was invited to dinner, and there would be champagne to see the New Year in. Raymond dozed off that night by nine o'clock, and roused again a little before midnight to find Jenny in the bedside chair reading his Jules Verne.

"Do you like it?" he murmured, the first indication she had had that he was awake.

"Yes, I do," she said stoutly, though it had bored her a little, and she rose to take his temperature and pulse.

He surveyed her with visible amusement, his lips pursed

over the thermometer which silenced him. When she removed it he said gently, "You're awful cute sometimes."

It was the sort of remark she knew it was wisest to try to
ignore, so she began to heat his broth on the spirit stove, her
back to the bed. When she returned with it he lay looking up at her in his unembarrassed absence of chatter, and
she heard herself saying, "What's cute about reading Jules
Verne?"

"It's no book for a girl," he explained, still amused.

"I suppose you think I can't understand anything but
The Prisoner of Zenda!"

"Who was he?" said Raymond.

It was the sort of *impasse* she had encountered with him
before, when to explain seemed ridiculous and to try to pass
it off was embarrassing. Sometimes it was almost as though
they had been educated in different languages, so that things
which were commonplace to her were complete blanks in his
mind, and the things which must have held a similar place in
his own experience were to her as remote as Mars. When
this happened she always pointed it out to herself as evidence
that it was quite impossible for them to fall in love with each
other, as they had nothing upon which to base even any sort
of permanent friendship. She had always heard that in order
to have any real success with a man you must have interests
in common and if possible mutual friends, and above all that
you must never step out of your class. So by all the rules she
and Gerald had been perfectly suited to each other, and look
what happened. The same thing was not true of Gerald and
Fabrice, and that was one of the reasons that their affair was
frowned on. And yet the gulf between them was nothing like
so wide as the one which separated herself and Raymond.

She would get this far in her fine reasoning, sometimes, and
then the whole thing would collapse into a desire to laugh a
reckless, giddy sort of laugh which meant *What of it?* Or it

would dissolve slowly in a warm wave of feeling which meant *I don't care*. But nothing of all this ever showed in her serene, smiling face with its tilted chin, and she would answer as she answered now, almost without inflection, saying the obvious thing.

"That's the kind of novel schoolgirls have to hide under the mattress."

"Did you?" he asked interestedly, and she nodded. "What is it about?" he insisted with curiosity.

She found herself trying to describe to him the intricate plot of Rudolph Rassendyl's impersonation of the Ruritanian king, and to her surprise Raymond followed it acutely. When she bogged down and gave it up he asked to read the book all through, and she promised to find him a copy for after the operation.

At this point Bracken arrived in the doorway carrying a tinkling bucket of ice with a half bottle of champagne in it and two glasses. He peeked in cautiously and then when he saw that Raymond was awake he entered, and set the bucket and glasses on a table.

"We're getting ready to drink the New Year in," he said. "Here's yours. Mind you join in when we start singing." He wrapped a napkin round the bottle, popped out the cork for them, waved his hand and hurried back down stairs. Raymond looked inquiring.

"Don't you do that in America?" Jenny asked. "Here we always open a bottle of champagne, and when twelve o'clock strikes we join hands to make a circle and sing *Auld Lang Syne,* and then everybody kisses everybody all round and drinks a champagne toast and the New Year is officially in."

"It sounds like a nice idea," Raymond said, and the clocks all over the house began to strike and downstairs somebody started *Auld Lang Syne* on the piano and broke off abruptly as the player was gathered into the singing circle.

Jenny's hand closed warmly on Raymond's as she stood beside the bed, and her clear voice rose to join the others which floated up the stairs. At the end of the verse she bent and kissed him.

She had meant it to be just a quick friendly gesture—she had no idea how by a slight turn of his head on the pillow, a tightening of his fingers on hers, it became a declaration, by both of them, of a full grown devotion neither of them could deny. The demand of his lips on hers reached far deeper than any kiss of Gerald's during all the months of their engagement, left her warm and shaking and brimming with heedless happiness. When she straightened at last, beyond his reach, and stood looking down at him, pink-cheeked and with bright, defiant eyes because she didn't care what happened to her now, she was enveloped in his smile.

"Happy New Year," said Raymond softly. "And as they say in your army, what price champagne!"

Lightheaded, lighthearted, beyond doubt or reflection, Jenny brought two full glasses to the bedside and gave him one.

"In France," said Raymond, lifting it to the light, "they tell me they kiss the brim instead of touching glasses." He did so, his eyes on hers, and she did likewise, and they laughed contentedly and drank. "That's wonderful stuff," said Raymond on a very cheerful note. "It does a lot for you, that stuff. Anybody'd think I'd already had mine, wouldn't they!" He sipped again, and laughed again, to himself, and his face was young and gay and—as Virginia had already noted—beautiful. "How I had the nerve!" he marvelled. "I never thought I had the nerve. You might've murdered me."

"No," said Jenny, and sat down in the chair and leaned her head against the back, holding her half empty glass. "No— I liked it."

"Did you, dear?" He lay very still, watching her. "Oh,

Jenny, did you—honest?" His eyes, when she only turned her head against the back of the chair and gave him a long, silent, shining look, were anxious. "It's hard for me to believe," he said simply. "I—know what I know now, but it's hard to believe."

"What do you know, darling?"

"You feel the same way about me—that I feel about you. Don't you. And it's not the champagne. Is it." And when she only sat smiling at him mistily, the half empty glass in her hand—"How could it happen, like that?" he wondered. "You don't know anything about me. I didn't even save your brother, because you haven't got one. So far as you're concerned, Jenny, I'm just something the cat brought in."

Her head moved slowly, lazily, in negation, against the back of the chair. She felt relaxed, at peace, safe in some unimaginable haven, but it was not the champagne.

"You're what I love," she said steadily, for Jenny never could do things by halves. "I didn't want to. I tried not to. I never meant to love anybody again."

"I know. Camilla told me. But it won't be like that with me." His dark, expressive face was full of compassion.

"I don't care," Jenny murmured, smiling. "So long as it's you—I just don't care. I'm lost—nothing matters—I'm past praying for, darling. I don't know how you did it, but—it's done."

His brows drew together in a half scowl, his lips tightened, and he looked at her straightly under his lashes.

"I'm kind of surprised myself, you know," he said with a gentle belligerence. "On my side, I mean. I' been around quite a while without anything like this happening to me."

"You weren't—you haven't got a girl back home?" She looked down, turning the glass in her fingers.

"No." It was a simple statement, truthful and sincere.

"There's nobody got any claim on me, if that's what you mean. Nowhere."

"I'm glad."

"Not that it would have made much difference if they had, I guess. This would have wiped it out. Any sort of claim. Knowing what I know now. Good thing I'm free, though, isn't it. Dear—" It seemed to be the strongest word in his vocabulary. "I don't feel quite right about this, not till I get my wings. Everybody's been swell to me here, don't think I don't know that. I don't want to seem to take advantage."

"B-but—"

"When I've got a commission, like that fellow at dinner—when I can fly, I'll feel different about it then. But honestly, I don't dare face your people before then, they'd have a right to kick me down stairs. Do you understand what I mean?"

"Yes," said Jenny with the new meekness happiness brought, understanding that she was not yet to consider herself engaged. "Only—sometimes people get killed learning to fly, and—"

"Not me. For me it will be pie. You'll see. Once I get this arm fixed up—" he stirred restlessly. "Once I get past that Medical Board, with this arm—"

"Which reminds me," said Jenny. "Time you went to sleep." She rose and set their glasses on the table, and returned to straighten the bedclothes. As she bent over him he lay quietly awaiting her kiss, and she gave it with no further demand, and smoothed back the straight dark hair. "Goodnight," she whispered, and he smiled at her and his eyes closed.

She sat down beside the bed, and picked up the volume of Jules Verne and held it open in her lap, dreaming. Gerald had been sponged from the slate.

Sir Quentin announced modestly after the operation that it had been entirely successful and that the arm would not suffer any permanent damage. Pressed for details, he estimated the convalescent period as six weeks—maybe more, maybe less—Medical Board within two months, anyway.

Jenny wrote to Adrian Carteret and when his reply came she counted up on her fingers. Application for transfer to the Air Force by March first—some delay, anything up to thirty days, spent at some Canadian Army depôt in England on light duty, with a summons to London for interviews at Adastron House—another Medical Board—orders to report to ground school, and about six weeks there—flying school by mid-May—two months more—a few days terminal leave— and back to France by early August. Not long. Not long enough for the war to end before he returned to it. But longer than a lot of people could look forward to, nowadays, for love . . .

He mended slowly, with a great deal of weakness and exhaustion to overcome. His own helplessness exasperated and terrified him, for he had never known illness before. Except for his innate courtesy and obedience, he was not a good patient, for it was inconceivable to him that he could not do things for himself, that he could not even sit up in bed except for short intervals at the beginning. He watched the weather wistfully through his window-panes, and a mild sunny day would set him fretting to be outside, and when he was promised a wheeled-chair outing in the garden as soon as he was strong enough he looked at first incredulous and then chagrined. "Can't I *walk?*" he asked childishly, and found when he tried it that he couldn't, not with any degree of certainty, because his legs were made of cotton wool and gave under him.

When he was out of danger and there was no more need for night duty he saw more of Jenny as day nurse. She could no longer devote herself exclusively to him and now had the care of two shattered Flying Corps men who had been put into the other beds in Raymond's room. One of them could not see, and the other, horribly burned, cared very little about anything any more. Jenny tended them tirelessly, and they stayed alive and that was about all.

Compared to them, Raymond was soon almost robust, and he was content to wait his turn, lying very still while his eyes followed her and he thought what it would be not to be able to see her, to have to wait in darkness for the sound of her step and the touch of her hand. So long as I can see her, he would think, looking his most stolid because he was ashamed of his own thoughts. Just to watch her ought to be enough for anybody like me. And then at last Jenny would get round to him, and they would smile contentedly at each other, for there was never any embarrassment between them at the things his weakness required her to do for him, only the simplest gratitude and patience on his part and cheerful efficiency on hers.

She brought him books and flowers and little tid-bits of her own, to enliven his long, tedious days, for although he never complained of it she felt in him more than in any other man she had ever served the sense of captivity, and the male humiliation at being bedridden and confined. Sometimes she could sit a little while by his bed and talk, their fingers clasped on the counterpane. It was an intimacy of glance and laughter and speech neither of them had ever known with anyone else.

Raymond brought with him into a hospital cot the essential dignity and unself-consciousness of a woods creature— Jenny possessed the same quality as the result of generations of breeding and gracious living. Both were innocent of the

pretences and inferiorities and little doubts of the so-called
middle class, the bourgeoisie, the in-betweens. Jenny from
the furthest citadel of society, Raymond from beyond the
pale, recognized in each other a kindred simplicity and in-
tegrity, spoke the same spiritual language, smiled the same
friendly, confident smile into each other's eyes. There were
no barriers between them to be broken down. They both
began at the same place—an utter inner honesty which entertained no misgivings and felt the need of no apologies or
self-defences. Both expected to be taken at their face value,
and took each other so. Neither gave any sort of masquerade
performance for anyone's benefit, or their own. Both were
accustomed to the liking and approval of their own world.
Both possessed the essence of self-respect, which means an
effortless composure.

Zenda went very well with him, the fights and the love
story as well, and roused his interest in the art of fencing,
which was new to him. Jenny said that Archie belonged to a
club in London and had once been some sort of amateur
champion and could tell him more about it than she could.
Lots of people learned sword-play still as a kind of hobby,
she explained. It was a good way to keep fit if you had to be
shut up in Town. Raymond could see that, and Archie went
way up in his estimation. He was frankly disappointed in the
renunciatory ending of the story and was inclined to argue
with it, not so much because the lovers were parted as that it
offended his practical side. "They didn't do the country any
good, keeping a man like that alive to rule it," he said, intent
and scowling. "The other guy would have done it better, and
everybody would have been happy. The real king wouldn't
last, he was no good anyway."

"Would you have had them kill the king when he was
helpless?" she asked, watching him.

"He wasn't worth all that trouble they took to save him,"

he maintained obstinately. "Not from any point of view. He was no good to the country, and he was no good to his wife."

"Would *you* have killed him, if you'd been in Rudolph's place?"

Their eyes held. His were heavy-lidded and without light, his lips were full and suddenly rather coarse-looking—a terrifying face, Jenny thought suddenly at the back of her mind—his anger would be a dreadful thing, there's a brute in him—and something in her own expression must have flinched, for he looked away from her, down at their clasped hands.

"It's only a story, isn't it," he said.

"Raymond—how does it feel to kill a man? I mean, right after you do it."

"You mean Germans?" he asked, his eyes on their hands.

"Well—yes, of course. I don't suppose you've ever killed anyone else, have you?"

He shook his head slightly—a small, bored movement. His fine fingers, bleached clean with weeks of hospital tending, moved gently on hers, caressing each separate knuckle absently. Deep lines ran down either side of his mouth, his heavy brows were drawn—a brutal face, thought Jenny, spellbound, without a trace of the smiling, almost diffident man she had come to look for in him.

"I had two buddies before Calvert Scott," he said at last. "And he's the luckiest of the three. You can't see your own friends get what I've seen—let alone the thousands you don't see—and not do what you can about it. And for me, that's kill Germans, wherever I find 'em. And I make sure they stay dead too." His eyes came up suddenly to her face. She had never seen, in his own worst hours, such naked pain as she saw there now. She sat looking back at him silently, into his eyes, and all the time his fingers were warm and kind and slow on hers. "If you don't make sure of them they'll like as not shoot the stretcher-men," he said.

"Seeing the wounds we get here, I—sometimes feel as though I'd like to kill a few Germans myself," she said faintly.

His smile broke, he even laughed quietly at her, his head pressed back into the pillow, his face was suddenly transfigured and young again, her hand was enfolded and crushed close in his.

"You with that chin sticking out!" he said affectionately. "Any German I ever saw would turn right round and run like hell! Wouldn' he!" His glance brushed her lips, and lingered there.

Jenny lay awake that night thinking about the other Raymond she had seen, lost in his grief and pity for his own dead comrades and the primitive need to avenge them. Startling as the glimpse had been, it touched something fundamental in her own nature which had had no opportunity to respond to the light, understated talk which was all that the men she had known hitherto permitted themselves regarding the war. A leashed but still savage force had surged through the quiet air of the hospital room when he spoke—something that had not yet been entirely bred out of the New World. Jenny heard it like a rush of wings, with a quickening of her blood. And she lay with her slim hands clasped over her breast and surrendered again to the tingling awareness that she had delivered herself over, without reservation, to this ruthless, tender, unpredictable stranger from nowhere.

Sir Quentin made his rounds again next morning, and at the end of the day when Jenny was on her way to the room with a tea-tray in her hands she met him coming out. Quick anxiety showed in her face, for the other two men in the

room were not his cases and a second visit could only have
been on Raymond's account. She paused with the heavy tray,
looking up at him, and asked if everything was all right.

"I just looked in to tell that Red Indian of yours that he
can go out in a chair tomorrow if this rain ever stops," he said.
"Face lit up like a Christmas tree. Thought he was going to
hug me. What's the matter with you?"

Jenny was blinking at him.

"What you called him. Has he been talking to you about
Germans?"

"No. Why? Does he scalp 'em?"

"You weren't serious, were you?" she persisted, too preoccupied to smile.

"About his being part Indian?" Sir Quentin looked at her
more closely in the dim corridor, her slight body bent back
under the weight of the tray, her anxious eyes scrutinizing
him. "No, I wasn't, really. But I could well believe it, couldn't
you?"

"I never thought about it," said Jenny.

"Just a dash of Indian," said Sir Quentin casually. "A lot
of them have, and don't even know it. Americans. Especially if they come from the West." He added a few directions
about the proposed outing, said a cheery Good-night, and
waved her on with the tray.

Jenny entered the room looking a little dazed, and found
Raymond taking an excessive interest in the weather,
though the sky outside his window was leaden and unprom-
ising. She gave the blind flyer his tea, and found that the
other man, as usual, preferred only to be let alone, and came
finally to Raymond, whose eyes were bright and expectant.
He noticed at once that she had something on her mind, and
became watchful and silent himself. Finally he said, very
low, "Is something wrong?"

Jenny said No, of course not, and saw that he was not satis-

fied. Something in his deep, unself-conscious reserve and her
own British training still made personal questions impossible
to her. And then quite unexpectedly he gave her an opening.

"Sir Quentin was very pleased with you," she was saying
to reassure him. "He's a dear old thing, isn't he."

"He's swell," said Raymond simply. "I never felt about
anybody the way I feel about him, except for my own father,
and he's dead. Sir Quentin makes me feel like a kid again."

"You ought to tell him so. He'd be very touched."

"I couldn't do that," Raymond said instantly, backing into
his shell.

"Darling—where did you grow up?" she asked with some
diffidence. "I can show you Overcreech some day soon, when
you're better—my life is all here, where you can see it. But
you never tell me anything about yourself."

"What is it you want to know about me? You only have to
ask." But his face became guarded and withdrawn.

"Well—I'd just like to know where you grew up," she repeated rather breathlessly.

"In a place called Indian Landing, on Lake Champlain,"
he said explicitly. "I bet you don't even know what state
that's in."

Jenny confessed that she didn't.

"It's in New York State. Did you ever hear of Fort Ticon-
deroga?"

Jenny thought she had, vaguely, and Raymond grinned at
her with affection.

"We took it away from the British once," he said. "I admit
they got it back, later on, and ruined it for us. It's ours now,
though, what there is left of it!"

"Oh, was that in the War of American Independence?"
asked Jenny intelligently, and he laughed.

"Is that what you call it over here? Never mind, dear,
we're on your team now, aren't we."

She realized that she had answered her query about himself in words of one syllable and then turned it aside, so that she knew very little more than she had in the beginning. And while she was reflecting on this, he asked abruptly, "What else did you want to know?"

"About your father," she experimented.

"He died just before I joined up in 1915. My aunt kept house for us—Aunt Emma—she lives there in the house still, and she brought me up. Anything you don't like about that job you'll have to take up with her, I guess."

"I think it was a very good job," Jenny said promptly, and he was visibly pleased.

As the silence fell between them he was trying once more to see Jenny at Indian Landing, sitting on the front porch in the summer evenings in one of the shabby rocking-chairs with faded cushions—or lying in the ugly, comfortable hammock that always hung there—Jenny with an apron tied round her waist helping Aunt Em can peaches—Jenny across the table from him at supper under the hanging lamp made of marbled green glass with gold bead fringe—Jenny in his old room among his boyhood treasures which he never showed to anybody. . . . No. No, it wouldn't ever do. She didn't realize. He could imagine from what he had seen of Farthingale what the house called Overcreech would be like (if it wasn't like the Hall itself) but there was no way for Jenny to imagine Indian Landing. . . .

And because he knew now that he would have to tell her, some time soon, that it wouldn't do, that she couldn't possibly live there, that they had only been kidding themselves, and because he hadn't the heart to do it yet and drive that trustful, shining happiness from her face, the look he turned on her was more than ever compassionate and fond, and Jenny dissolved under it into a blissful mist and caught at his hand beside the tray.

"It wasn't that I *cared* where you came from," she said unsteadily, clinging to him. "I mean, I only cared because it is part of you, and I've missed so much of you—if it was just a *manger,* I wouldn't mind so long as it gave me you!"

"You mustn't say things like that," he murmured, surprised and shocked by what seemed to him like sacrilege in her vehemence. "I'm just a—just something the cat brought in."

"Don't you talk like that yourself!" she cried, turning angry in a breath as though some third person had belittled him. "I answered that once before, remember?"

"Don't you stick out your chin at me!" he said delightedly. "Want to scare me into a temperature, or somepun?"

Jenny stood up and removed the tray from his bedside, still bristling, while he lay and grinned, and hope stirred rebelliously within him. She was so real, so down to earth, with him. If he got the commission—if he was a good pilot and got his name in the ace class—if he kept all his arms and legs till the end of the war—if Jenny went on feeling this way about him till the end of the war—if a miracle happened . . .

He might, he supposed, have dared to ask Camilla to marry him, if they had happened to fall in love. Just because Jenny was English was no good reason to treat her differently. Maybe they wouldn't have to stay in Indian Landing forever—maybe they could start a better business somewhere else—somewhere bigger—would Jenny like Buffalo? Or would it have to be New York? He wasn't sure about tackling New York. It was a tough place to get along in. Or maybe he could get a job—like his father had always said he should—a big job building engines, designing engines, maybe—that paid—it would take more schooling than he had had, of course—night school—he'd done it before, he could do it again—he should have worked his way through some college, like his father had wanted him to, instead of tinkering all those engines—would Jenny wait—how long could he ask her to wait—she didn't realize the difference between them now, but she would if she saw Indian Landing—over here, there was no way she could realize how and where he had grown up. . . .

Raymond took a deep slow breath, and hope had its way. Get well first—get the commission—and then try to talk to Jenny again, try to tell her what it would mean to them both —try to face her folks at the house called Overcreech—she had mentioned a father more than once, and said she was the only child. Come to think of it, he didn't know so much about Jenny, except what you could see—except going by Farthingale and the presents they gave and the clothes they wore. Indian Landing was bound to be an awful come-down for Jenny. But she was real, Aunt Em would like her . . .

Get well. Get the commission. Get the war over. Then we'll see.

─────────────

Two days later it cleared and warmed up, and the gardens were full of slow figures in hospital blue, limping along the paths, riding in wheeled-chairs, sitting on cushions on the benches in little knots with a Sister's white coif in attendance.

Raymond made his way with Jenny beside him from his room and down the staircase to his chair and sank into it with relief, quite willing that she should do the rest. She took him out the south door on to the stone-flagged terrace, from where they looked down to the river bank on one side and the formal paths of the sunken garden on the other, with a long lawn between. Jenny unfolded a small stool and sat beside him in the sun, and they talked foolishly for a while in a relaxed state of intimacy which was hampered in the room where the two sick, unheeding men lay.

"There's Fabrice," he said out of a companionable silence. "Who's she got this time?"

"A new one," Jenny sighed, watching the progress of a strolling couple in the gravel path below—the man on crutches, the nurse beside him with her hand on his arm, her face upturned to his.

"Wasn' I lucky," said Raymond, slurring his speech as he was likely to do in moments of emotion. "Wasn' I lucky to get you for my nurse instead of her!" He smoked a moment, ruminating. "I'd of broken her neck for her inside a week," he added, "even if I'd been half dead."

Jenny laughed softly.

"I'm surprised at you," she said, trying to look it.

"No, but honest," said Raymond, "what does she think it gets her, to lay it on like that?"

"It gets her what she wants, usually," Jenny reminded him, and he glanced at her under his lashes.

"Well, that's all right with us," he remarked. "Isn't it?"

"It most decidedly is," said Jenny, and touched his hand briefly. "Darling—I want you to know. I'm not in love with you because I lost Gerald. I'm in love with you *in spite* of losing Gerald, which is much harder. And I'd be in love with you even if I hadn't lost Gerald, and wouldn't that have been a mess!"

"You would?"

She turned her face to him in the sunlight.

"You know I would."

It was the sort of cue, though unconsciously given, that the men of her acquaintance would have risen to with appropriate gallantry and an apt reply. Raymond, being deeply moved, allowed it to pass in silence, his eyes on the figures below them, all near enough for recognition but far enough to be out of earshot. And when he spoke it was with the exasperating irrelevance she had learned that he used to cover his own emotion when it had got too much for him.

"Which one is the duke's daughter?" he asked.

"Wh-what?" said Jenny stupidly.

"Camilla said one of the nurses here was a duke's daughter. I've always wondered which one she was."

"Why?" groped Jenny.

"Well—I was interested. She'd come next below a princess, wouldn't she?"

"I—suppose so. A long way below."

"Do you know her?"

"Pretty well," said Jenny helplessly.

"Will you point her out to me some time?"

"You might be disappointed."

"How do you mean?"

"It's—only me," said Jenny apologetically.

There was no sound at all from him, but the impact of his realization drained the color from his face and froze on to it an expression of sullen resentment. At last his eyes turned from her slowly, out across the gardens, as though she was no longer there.

"I—thought you knew that," said Jenny, and her voice sounded small and hurried in his silence. "It didn't occur to me that you didn't. That is—Father was at the Christmas party—I thought you knew he was my father."

Raymond got out a cigarette and lighted it lefthanded with the lighter which was a present from Virginia. He used it with the carelessness of habit now, but with a still unfailing satisfaction. He said nothing. He felt sick with shock and the necessity to revise a number of ideas very swiftly without letting it show in the outside.

"Raymond, what's the matter? I didn't mean it to sound as though I was trying to—to play a joke on you, or anything, I honestly didn't know you hadn't got it straight. It's not important, anyway, why do you—why on earth are you so angry?"

He made a move as though to rise, and she laid a quick hand on his shoulder, holding him in the chair.

"Please don't get up, if you walk into the house they'll notice and ask questions. Why are you like this? Raymond, *look* at me, I don't understand—"

He looked at her remotely, from a great distance.

"I'd like to go back to the room," he said.

"But we can't talk there—"

"I don't want to talk."

"But—*why* does it matter to you so much?" she cried, bewildered. "It's no crime in this country to be a duke's daughter, it's done every day!" She flung out both hands in a little funny, futile gesture, trying to laugh into his rocky face. "Can't you ever forgive me?"

"For not telling me who you are? No."

"But why *should* I *tell* you, I'd have felt an awful fool suddenly to say, out of the blue, By the way, I'm Apethorpe's daughter. There'd be no point in that, why do you *mind* so much?"

"You let me fall in love with you."

"*Let* you! Well, I like that! I fell in love myself! What's that got to do with it?"

"The girl I fall in love with, I want to be able to ask her to marry me. She might say No, because I had a dud arm, or because she didn't want to live in a place like Indian Landing. But at least I could ask her."

"Well, go ahead and *ask* her, and see what happens!"

He turned from her again silently, letting out a gusty sigh of smoke, looking out across the gardens, waiting to be allowed to return to the sanctuary of his bed.

"Is it because you think my father's got a lot of money and you haven't?" Jenny asked anxiously. "Because a title doesn't mean money any more, you know. Actually, we're poor as church mice, and after the war we shall probably have to let

Overcreech the year round and live in a pokey flat in London. Nobody's going to mind if you're poor. I'm poor too."

"You don't understand," he said wearily, not looking at her.

"No, I don't!" cried Jenny. "Please try to explain!"

He turned to her then, squared round to face her, not touching her, half a world between them.

"Listen," he said quietly. "Listen, now, and let's not talk about it again. Indian Landing is a one-horse town that nobody ever heard of. My father kept the livery stable and feed store, and I had a machine shop at the back. A little while before he died we put in a gasoline pump and I began to do automobile repairs. We were going to open up a garage annex. We'd bought the land, and we'd ordered the lumber to build when he died. I gave up the idea and went into the army. When I go back I expect to build that garage, the way we planned it, and operate it the best I can without him. The house we lived in is mine now, a little way down the street, and Aunt Emma is still there to cook my meals and look after me. We haven't got even one maid, we never could afford to hire any help for her. The house has ten rooms and a bathroom, and we wired it for electricity ourselves a few years ago. It's pretty old and by the time I get back it will be all out of repair. I'll have to work on it myself, my father taught me how to do things, I don't have to call in the plumber and the carpenter and so on. You see—if I'm ever going to get anywhere beyond that garage I've got to go back to school when I get out of the army. I want to design and build engines, but I don't know enough, I have to learn more mathematics and a lot of things you never heard of. It would be years before I could give you a better house, or a good car, or the kind of clothes you're used to. You'd be the wife of a common garage mechanic in greasy overalls, if you married me, how long would you last at that?"

"Forever," said Jenny, looking down at her hands in her lap. "If you wanted me."

"You haven't got any idea what you're talking about," he said roughly. "It was crazy enough anyway, when I thought you were just anybody, like Camilla or—or Virginia. I let myself be that crazy, against my own judgment—I tried to think that when I got my commission and did some flying it might be all right. But I knew better all along. And I know better now, and so do you."

Bright tears were dropping down on her clasped hands in the sunlight. She kept her head down, unable to speak.

"Don't cry," he said more gently after a moment. "I'm sorry I spoke so harsh, but I don't like to feel like a fool."

She drew a long, shaky breath, but made no other move.

"There's no reason for you to feel like that," she said. "*I* knew who I am, all along. It doesn't make any difference to *me.*"

"It does to me."

"You see, I don't—care where I live," said Jenny through quivering lips, "if you're there too. I don't care what I wear. I'll learn to cook and be a help to your Aunt Emma, and I could learn to make my own clothes. You wouldn't have to be ashamed of me, I could learn." And when astonishment left him silent she hurried on, looking down at her glistening fingers. "This is me, Jenny Keane, without my ducal pride— asking you to give me a chance to go on loving you. When this war is over, if it ever is, dukes aren't going to matter, there won't be any big houses like Overcreech left to us, death duties will take them all—nobody's going to care whose daughter I am, and we needn't tell them in America, nobody would have to know."

"But, dear—" And at the old loving note in his voice again she raised her face, shining with tears, piteous with hope, and his heart turned and cramped inside him and he threw away the stub of his cigarette because the hand that held it was shaking. "—can't you understand, it's because of *you* that I can't do it, you couldn't live like that, I couldn't ask you to."

"What's wrong with living like that?"

"You aren't used to it, you couldn't—"

"I wasn't used to amputations and bed-pans and people dying in my hands, when this war began. But I am now. I'm used to being a nurse. After that you can't scare me with Indian Landing! And I don't care if it's the outskirts of hell, I'd be with you!"

"Oh, poor Jenny," said Raymond, making no move to touch her, and she gave him her tear-wet fingers clasped tensely round his.

"Don't hold it against me," she pleaded, trying to smile. "I know you think I'd be useless and homesick and an expense, but I wouldn't. If we were hard up, I'd get a job while you went to school—everybody's going to have to get a job when the war is over, nobody's going to have any money. I wouldn't be a nuisance, truly I wouldn't!"

He sat a long moment looking down at her hands on his. Then he said slowly, "Do you remember one night at Farthingale while I was sick there, Virginia came in with a letter she'd just got, and told about that fellow who had married some girl out of a tea-shop? And you both said how it wouldn't do, because she didn't even know how to speak right, and how upset his family was because he'd thrown away his prospects?"

"Yes, but he—"

"How's that any different from your marrying me, except that it's the other way round?" he asked reasonably. "Be honest, now, what would Virginia say if you told her you wanted to? What would your father say?"

"Father asked you to come to Scotland for a visit," she reminded him rebelliously.

"As a guest, yes. Maybe just to make me feel good, and because it was Christmas."

"Honestly, Raymond, I believe you're a worse snob than Fabrice!" Jenny accused him, with an uncertain laugh, and he said, "You haven't answered my question."

"I don't know what Father would say," she confessed. "But I'm not afraid to stand right up and tell him tomorrow. He couldn't but see the difference between you and Gerald, anyway!"

"And how about the difference between me and somebody like that Adrian Carteret?"

"I'm not in love with Adrian Carteret!" she retorted.

"Well," he said kindly, and withdrew his hands from hers, "let's not worry about it any more now, shall we?"

"But you'll promise not to—"

"I can't promise anything," he interrupted firmly.

"Promise to go on loving me," said Jenny, and caught his eyes, and he looked back at her, still a little remote and cool.

"I've got no choice there, I guess," he said.

Knowing that he was unconvinced and dangerous still, she rose and dried her cheeks with her fingers and wheeled him back into the house. When he reached the room and stretched himself gratefully on the bed again he realized with a kind of horror that he was shaking all over, and cursed the weakness of his own limbs. It was lunch time, and Jenny went away to fetch the trays, and he lay very still with his eyes closed, fighting dizziness, and saw behind his closed lids the little town of Indian Landing, baking under a summer sun.

3. *SUMMER IN GLOUCESTERSHIRE. 1918.*

AS THE HOSPITAL IN ST. JAMES'S SQUARE WAS for officers, Calvert was sent to another one way up in Camberwell, and Camilla had to be given extra time on her days off in order that the long bus trip each way would not eat up the few hours they might spend together. His leg could be saved, but there would be a long and painful convalescence.

Camilla, sitting on a hard ward chair beside his cot with her fingers laced in his, saw with agony the change in his beloved face, the hardening round the mouth, the vertical lines between the eyes, the sharp, somehow pitiful jaw line. This was what war had done to him—war and pain and patience and steadfast courage. Calvert had grown up, since she saw him last. Something of him had escaped her forever. There was something new to be learned in him.

It wasn't until her fourth visit, when he was noticeably improved, that she realized that as usual he was thinking the same thing she was.

"You're different," he said slowly, looking up at her from the pillow. "You've—got all grown up while I was away. There's a lot to catch up on between us, isn't there."

Her fingers tightened on his and she nodded.

"It's hard to know where to begin."

"You're breaking your heart over something," said Calvert, with his dreadful insight. "It couldn't be the music, still?"

"Heavens, no, I've given that up. For the duration, anyway."

"Don't you ever sing any more?"

"There's not much time for it, Calvert." Her lips closed on the memory of the rainy afternoon at Farthingale, and Sosthène leaning on the piano.

"That's what I mean," said Calvert at once. "That look on your face. Where did it come from?"

"I don't know," she said, her head bent, for it was hard to tell about Sosthène at best, and this seemed no time for it, in the open ward, and Calvert ought not to be worried yet. . . .

"You do know. So do I, I think. You've fallen in love with somebody while my back was turned."

"I don't see why you—"

"You're softer. You've got tears to shed." The low voice from the pillow paused while her tell-tale eyes filled. "Perhaps I shouldn't have mentioned it."

"You've got to know some time, I reckon."

"I guessed right, then. It was only a guess."

She nodded mutely.

"Somebody you nursed?"

She shook her head.

"Somebody in France?"

"Oh, Calvert, it's going to be so desperately hard to explain. Let's wait till you're a bit better."

"I'm better enough," he said briefly. "I'd rather know

than wonder any more. Have you got into some kind of mess?"

"No. At least—maybe you'd call it that."

"Don't let's have mysteries," he said gently. "I'm not such a crock I can't hear about anything that's happened to you. Who is this bird that makes you cry at the drop of a hat?"

"You remember I wrote you about Sosthène."

"Cousin Sally's beau. Yes." He waited. Then it dawned. "Not—*Sosthène!*"

"Please don't jump to the wrong conclusions, I only—"

"But, Camilla, for the love of God—"

"Don't swear at me, Calvert, it—it isn't anything. It can't ever *be* anything. I don't mean it to be. But—it's happened, that's all. I can't go back of that. I can't—*not* be in love with him. I don't think I want to."

The boy in the cot might have said any one of a dozen futile, indignant, or commiserating things, and been wide of the mark. As usual he chose the only right thing and said it in the right way, almost without expression, reserving judgment so obviously that instead of going on the defensive or becoming apologetic she could answer without self-consciousness.

"What's he like?" said Calvert. "You've given me only the haziest idea in your letters—or perhaps I just didn't pay enough attention to that part."

"I don't know how to tell you," she admitted quietly. "When you see him I think you'll understand. He's gentle —and civilized—and disciplined—and kind. He knows how I feel. But he pretends that he doesn't. We both pretend that like mad."

"You haven't talked it over with him?"

"There's nothing to say."

"Then how does he know?"

"I let him see. I couldn't help it."

Calvert lay turning it over in his mind.

"How could it happen?" he asked at last. "You knew from the first that he—"

"That he belongs to Cousin Sally," she nodded. "Don't think I *meant* it to happen! It was like coming down with influenza. You can feel it creeping up on you, you know exactly what it is, and no power on earth can stop it. I'm finished, Calvert. Done for. There's nobody else."

"What about him?"

"He belongs to Cousin Sally," she repeated doggedly, like a lesson she had learned. "I've no right. I've no place. And I have to let her like me, and give me things, and do kindnesses for me. It's not her fault, and she must never suspect. She turned out her jewel case and made me presents, with Sosthène looking on. I had to smile and take them and thank her. I have to try not to hate them, because they stand for the wrong thing. I have to be *fond* of Cousin Sally—I *am* fond of her—and because Fabrice is a disappointment to her she has turned to me. It's damnable. She's so happy with him—so possessive—so serene. You couldn't ever do anything to hurt her. You just have to bite on it." Her breath caught in her throat, and she hurried on. "You know, it's a queer feeling, I—never thought it would be me. I always thought you'd be the one to fall in love."

"Give me time," said Calvert rather wearily, suppressing the hope that he would manage a little better than she had.

"It's a nice thing to hand you before you're on your feet again," she said ruefully. "Anyway, that's all there is to it. And there's nothing anybody can do about it. I'm not asking for advice—or sympathy—or anything like that. I'm just telling you the facts. Don't worry about it—I mean try not to. I shall get used to it, I suppose."

"I wish I could see him," said Calvert with a restless movement which brought prompt pain.

"You will, fairly soon. When you can travel you're to recuperate at Farthingale. I might get a few days there with you. Like old times together." She tried to smile. "Don't take it so hard, Calvert. I'll live through it. Jenny lived through much worse. If the war ever ends I'll go back to my music. You can live on music, they say."

"Do they?" He smiled up at her palely. "You've still got me," he reminded her.

"Thank God."

"Thanks to Raymond, too. What's the latest from him?"

"His letters aren't much, are they! He's still at Reading, I gather, learning flight theory and map-reading, and fretting to get up into the air and fly. He's due for week-end leave in London soon and it looks as though Jenny might be coming up about the same time to see the dentist. Virginia says we'll have a real party if only we can match up dates—the first party since Christmas, theater, supper, champagne, dancing, everything! And I'll bring them both here to see you," she added in quick compunction because Calvert could not come along.

"Is Jenny coming up on account of Raymond?"

"Oh, no, it just happens that way. But as she nursed him through the operation they got to be very good friends, and we can make it a sort of reunion and celebrate Raymond's recovery, Virginia thought." She reached out and laid her hand along his thin cheek in a pitiful gesture. "You will be well enough for the *next* party," she promised.

───────

Camilla's careless assurance that Jenny's visit to the dentist had no connection with Raymond's leave beyond coincidence was evidence that his obstinate discretion still ruled their lives. His few letters from the depôt and the School of Military Aeronautics at Reading were sparse and formal and utterly exasperating to Jenny. His withdrawal from their first swift intimacy had persisted throughout the remaining days of his convalescence at the Hall, and except for one desperate, hasty kiss before his departure, which caught them both off guard, she had little comfort with which to face the long days and nights when he had gone.

Another man came into his bed in the yellow room, and she returned to her head cases in Ward B, and sank again into the dreary hospital routine. The brief, bright episode seemed finished, snapped off by his stubborn pride and ingrained sense of the fitness of things. He remained convinced that it was not his place to make love to the daughter of a duke, and he seemed willing to break her heart to prove it. Bewildered and hurt by his firmness, which amounted to hardness, Jenny pointed out to herself over and over again what always happened if you fell in love, and refused to permit herself the luxury of tears.

Her pride came into it too—not only ducal, but feminine pride. She had offered him something, everything, in fact, and he had not accepted. There had never been any condescension in her feeling for him. But her upbringing was at last getting in the way a bit. Jenny Keane had never been a suppliant, and was not by nature meek, and generations of her ancestors had been accustomed to give lavishly and graciously favors which were received with due appreciation. Gerald, her equal in rank and background, had wilfully affronted her feelings as a woman. And now Raymond's behavior according to his own lights amounted to almost the same thing. Jenny's punished but naturally imperious spirit strove against this second humiliation with growing resentment, not at Raymond, she would remind herself desperately, but at circumstances which could somehow contrive to inflict on her this second ordeal of denial.

And then, when he had been several weeks at Reading, came a letter mentioning the prospect of a week-end in London soon. *I might go to see Virginia in St. James's Square,* he wrote in his firm, slanting hand. *And if you had happened to come up to Town just at that time to go to the dentist, let's say, or to do some shopping—we could say Hullo without anyone thinking twice about it, couldn't we?*

It wasn't much, but it set Jenny's heart beating again, and a trip to the dentist was with some difficulty arranged to coincide with Raymond's week-end. Their visits to Calvert's bedside were made separately, Jenny with Camilla, Raymond on his own, and they did not meet there.

Virginia's party was overshadowed by the news from France, where the long-dreaded German offensive had opened with the bombardment of Paris on Easter Sunday, followed by violent fighting on the Somme. Bapaume had gone back into German hands—Peronne—Montdidier—Armentiéres—Wytschaete, where Oliver had got his wound the first summer of the war—Messines—the terrible toll went on. The Germans were using gas. Rheims was again being pounded. The lines around flattened Ypres were drawing back. The rubble-filled streets of French villages which had long been secure behind the Allied lines were deserted, and refugees twice homeless were on the road again. The British Air Force was taking heavy losses, and every man still in training in England was under double strain in his anxiety to take his place in the thinning ranks of the fighting pilots.

The London theaters were full, though, for men on leave from inferno and women stretched to breaking point with uncertainty needed surcease from their own thoughts. The wounded were pouring in at Charing Cross again, and hospitals were overflowing, and the faces of nursing Sisters and VAD's were drawn and heavy-eyed. A bit grimly, Virginia made her arrangements for a night off for herself and Camilla, knowing that the two girls would profit by a change, however brief. They all put on their prettiest clothes and dined early at the Savoy and went to see *Going Up,* in which Miss Evelyn Laye sang like a lark and wore a pink charmeuse frock which was much admired.

Afterwards they went where there was music and dancing and a gaiety that was a little forced, and they drank champagne as promised by their hostess, and Jenny danced with Raymond. This time his right arm was firm and close about her waist, and they were both a little quiet and thoughtful.

"Takes you back, doesn't it," he said, looking down.

"We've come a long way since then," she answered.

"We've got a lot further to go. I'm trying for Upavon."

"That's fighter training," she said quickly, aware that he had aimed highest of all, for the stiffest course there was.

"That's what I want," he said cheerfully. "One of those new single-seater Camel planes—there's where you can really have some fun."

"When you're gazetted and posted to Upavon—*then* will you be satisfied?"

His arm tightened ever so little.

"We'll see," he said gently.

He called on Calvert at the hospital in Camberwell next day and found him full of Jenny's visit with Camilla. Calvert wanted to know all about that Christmas house party he had missed, and complained that Raymond never told him anything in letters. Had Raymond heard the story about Jenny and Gerald and Fabrice? Had he seen Gerald? Had he seen Fabrice? Look at Jenny—what kind of siren *was* this Fabrice?

Raymond gave a succinct Anglo-Saxon opinion of Fabrice and then apologized because she was Calvert's cousin.

"Oh, well," said Calvert philosophically. "Jenny's better off without him, I expect. She deserves better than that."

"She certainly does," Raymond agreed, and lighted cigarettes for both of them.

"She was your nurse for a while, wasn't she. What luck for you! Nothing like that around here!" said Calvert disgustedly. "Why can't *I* go to the Hall?"

"You could. Just tell 'em you want to," said Raymond.

"Not while Camilla's stuck here in London, I'd never see anything of her." He grinned frankly into the brooding face above him. "That Jenny girl is just about what I've been looking for," he confided.

"She is?" said Raymond, and breathed out smoke.

"She's pretty cute," said Calvert reminiscently. "Of course I've got to be sure of my leg first," he added as an afterthought.

"It'll be all right."

"They think so. And they fixed you up, didn't they."

"Yep. I'm all fixed up."

"Like your new job?"

"It's wonderful."

"Poor old gun."

"She won't forget us," said Raymond.

"About this Jenny," said Calvert, reverting shamelessly to what was uppermost in his mind. "I'm not fooling. I can't wait to see her again."

"Her father is a duke."

"So I hear," said Calvert unconcernedly. "Did you meet him?"

"Yep."

"How was he?"

"Nice."

"Lady Jenny," mused Calvert affectionately. "Sounds kind of cute, doesn't it." And as Raymond, who had learned that on the outside of an envelope she was Lady Jennifer, said nothing, Calvert rambled on. "Dinah was a ladyship too, but that didn't stop Bracken. Of course this leg could stop me."

"Your leg'll be all right," said Raymond.

"You keep on saying that and it may come true. How would you like to have Jenny in the family?"

"That would be swell," said Raymond.

"Well, there's no harm in trying, is there, once I get on my feet again. Of course Jenny might have other ideas," Calvert conceded with another confiding grin. "Something tells me *I* never will. She struck me all of a heap, somehow. I wonder what Camilla will say."

"It will be all right with her, won't it?"

"They're great friends, I think she'd be pleased. Better pleased than I am about her, anyway. Did you see much of Sosthène at Farthingale?"

"The Frenchman? No, not much." Raymond looked an unasked question, and Calvert nodded grimly.

"We haven't any secrets from you. Did you notice anything between him and Camilla?"

"No. That would be kind of a funny set-up, wouldn't it?"

"I'm pretty worried about it. She's taking it too hard. Nothing I can do, of course, till I can see for myself. He's not a bounder, is he?"

"I wouldn't think so," said Raymond cautiously.

"Not like Gerald?"

Raymond's black brows and heavy lips expressed his wordless estimate of Gerald.

"Maybe Gerald's going to get what he deserves, with Fabrice," suggested Calvert hopefully.

"You're right about that."

"And Jenny—what does Jenny deserve?"

"The best," said Raymond, feeling for another cigarette.

"Which is better than me," said Calvert lightly. "Oh, well —I reckon Jenny's going to have a chance to turn me down, anyway."

"You might get a shock," said Raymond. "She might take you up on it."

"Did you notice anybody in my way?"

"Nope," said Raymond, and his lighter flared, and his fine hands cupped the cigarette between his lips. "So far as I know, nobody is going to stand in your way."

———

Camilla went down with influenza in May, and was shipped off to Farthingale, very shaky, to recover, along with Calvert, equally shaky and on crutches and in constant pain. They arrived on a day of drizzling rain, and Sosthène came to the station in the car to fetch them, driven by the aged gardener-chauffeur. Camilla was absorbed in assisting Calvert to negotiate the step from the train to the platform and did not see them until Sosthène's voice said at her elbow, "Let me help, if I can."

Calvert, who was facing the platform, felt her fingers tighten convulsively on his arm as Sosthène reached out to steady him on the other side, and he stood between them as Camilla said faintly, "It's Sosthène."

"How do you do?" said Calvert, with sangfroid for two. "Awfully good of you to come and meet us."

"The car is just there," Sosthène told him gently. "Take it slowly—Bickett will see to the luggage—was it cold in the train?"

"Bitter," said Camilla, playing up. "We had rugs, of course. But I'm looking forward to a cup of tea."

"It will be waiting," he promised.

Calvert managed with difficulty to clamber into the back seat, Camilla got in beside him, and Sosthène covered them both with a fur-lined rug and himself took the seat beside the chauffeur. Sliding back the glass, he sat with his arm on the back of the driving seat, chatting with them through the opening, giving the news of the country family and the Hall, asking easy, interested questions about London.

Camilla, her cold fingers clasped in Calvert's comforting hand under the rug, replied with an effort at a similar casualness, and Calvert joined in helpfully, though he looked drawn with weariness and pain. Sosthène's serene, secretive face showed nothing but the most normal and polite pleasure at their arrival, and a total unawareness of constraint. Camilla appreciated once more his utter self-possession and at the same time felt an unreasonable disappointment. Apparently it meant nothing to him in the way of a personal emotional upheaval that she had come back to Gloucestershire. In the face of his smiling Continental composure, her own wild heart beat seemed childish and absurd, and she wondered if Calvert would ever believe now that she had not imagined that Sosthène knew and had accepted her feeling for him.

The car drew up on the gravel sweep in front of the house and old Bickett got down rather stiffly and opened the door to the back seat. Sosthène came round the other side and together they helped Calvert down with his crutches and he began a slow progress towards the shallow stone steps, supported by Bickett. It was only then that Sosthène turned back to the car, just in time to extend a steadying hand as Camilla stepped down on to the gravel. It was only then that their eyes met in a long look, and she was conscious of the lingering clasp of his fingers cradling her hand, enfolding her wrist above the short unbuttoned glove she wore.

"You are so thin," he said pityingly, and his gaze moved intimately over her face and throat and shoulders. "You have been very ill."

"Yes, it was beastly," she admitted, smiling up at him. "And I go on being so wobbly even now that it's over."

With a glance at the two slow figures climbing the steps ahead of them, they moved towards the house, her left hand still held by his right as he drew her arm through his.

"You want cossetting," he said in his low, unemphatic voice. "We shall see to that here."

"Oh, Sosthène, what a heavenly word!" she cried. "Where did you learn it?"

"Cossetting?" He was a little surprised. "Have I said it wrong?"

"No—we don't say it at all at home—that is, I must have heard it, because I know what it means, but—"

"It must be one of Sallee's words," he said easily. "I seem to have known it always."

"How is she?" Camilla asked, while another question twinged through her: Has he known Cousin Sally *always?*

"Just the same. Ah, there—you see?" He nodded towards the open doorway, where Sally stood with welcoming arms outstretched to Calvert, who was gently enfolded as he reached the threshold. "Now she will have a new slave," said Sosthène complacently. "One has only to ache ever so little somewhere and Sallee becomes a ministering angel."

"Poor Calvert aches quite a bit," said Camilla briefly, suppressing a quick reminder that she was the nurse.

By the time Calvert had had his tea in front of the drawing-room fire and been helped to bed, Camilla was telling herself firmly that it was a good thing she hadn't got a jealous disposition. For Calvert was frankly enslaved and bedazzled and loving the experience. The two older girls came down to the drawing-room for tea, and hung devotedly above their wounded cousin from America, even to the neglect of his invalid sister, but it was Sally he talked to and listened to and looked at. Once more Camilla watched the Sally legend coming true, exactly as it had happened to herself. It never failed, she thought ruefully in her chair at the corner of the hearth. Calvert would be on Sally's side if—if there were ever any necessity to take sides, which of course there wouldn't be. . . .

She looked up to find Sosthène standing at her elbow with a dish of hot scones, saying, "You must eat another. They have been very generous with the butter today."

Because it was not in her to refuse anything he suggested, she took a scone and bit into it obediently, though she found it difficult to swallow with his kind, searching eyes on her face.

"Last time it was Virginia with a game leg," she said rather at random. "Remember? You made such a lovely fuss of her, I was quite envious."

"This time it is you I am concerned about," he answered with a rueful smile.

"Do I look so awful?"

"You look very breakable," he replied. "And quite transparent."

"I hope not that," she murmured, and his eyes lit and answered the implication in her steady look, as she added simply, "I never try to hide anything from Calvert anyhow."

"No, I can see that you have not," he agreed, and she wondered if something in Calvert's level scrutiny had already warned him that her twin was abreast of things.

He turned away, smiling imperturbably, to replace the scones on the tea-table in front of Sally, and there was no further exchange between them before the complicated business of getting Calvert up the stairs began.

Calvert was to have his dinner on a tray in bed, and Camilla went in to help him with it before going down for her own. She had changed into the same old black dress she had worn on her first night here last winter, and her hair was bound round her head because Calvert was not keen, he said, on short-haired girls.

"You look sweet," he said, eyeing her from the pillow.

"Sort of shining—and very sweet. I didn't think I was going to be sorry for him, but I am."

"You *do* like him?" she entreated.

"I'm afraid I shall. I didn't want to. I was hoping to be able to feel that you had made a mistake and it would soon blow over."

"And now you don't feel that?"

"Not that you've been an utter fool, if that's what you mean."

"You see what he is. You see why I—"

"Easy, now. I've only had a dozen words with him so far. Does Jenny know about this?"

"Yes, she spotted it. She says it's best not to care about anybody till the war is over. She says the way to be most useful is to have no particular feelings for anybody—that makes the best nurse. Of course it isn't as though Sosthène were in the war."

"Jenny's not in love with anybody, then—since that business with Gerald," he remarked thoughtfully.

"No. After Gerald she doesn't want to be. She says she's not going to walk the plank again for anybody."

Calvert grinned.

"That's one way to put it," he said.

"You like Jenny, don't you, honey."

"I sure do."

"I wanted you to. Calvert—somebody like you could save Jenny."

"I've got this leg."

"But if it gets well—it *will* get well—don't let her waste her life, Calvert. Just because she's been kicked in the teeth."

"Think she'd look twice at me?"

"You'll have to work at it, Calvert—she's made up her mind not to fall in love again."

"Mm-hm," said Calvert thoughtfully. "How do I start?"

"Be very kind—and patient. Don't rush her."

"What chance do I get, anyway?"

"She'll come over to see me—tomorrow probably. She comes on her bicycle from the Hall, during her time off. It's not very much, of course, but sometimes she gets away for dinner, or an hour in the afternoon. And since I've been ill, it will seem natural for her to come here instead of my going there. I can say you have to be amused."

Calvert grinned again.

"Poor Jenny," he said. "Cards stacked against her from the start. I'm glad you're on my side."

Camilla looked down.

"One of us may as well be happy," she said.

So Jenny, unsuspecting and kind-hearted, spent most of her free time at Farthingale amusing the invalids there. She was not unwilling. It was fun to play and sing with Camilla for Calvert lying on the sofa under a rug. They had all read the same books and liked the same authors and had the same shaped joke. She loved Camilla dearly, and she thought Calvert both pathetic and charming, and she had another reason: Where Calvert was, there would be news of Raymond; where Calvert was, Raymond would come for his leaves.

But before long it began to dawn uneasily on Jenny that behind Calvert's natural Virginian gallantry of manner and his own particular brand of affectionate foolery there lay a deeper feeling for herself. At first she hoped she was wrong and tried to pretend even to herself that she hadn't noticed. But as Calvert's leg progressed and he felt a little surer of ultimate recovery his spirits rose and he stopped trying to conceal his love for her.

Then there was a day when Calvert got a letter from Raymond announcing five days' leave on his transfer to Upavon, and accepting the often repeated invitation to spend it at Farthingale. Calvert felt he ought to be able to report progress in all directions when Raymond came. He seized a time when Sally had claimed Camilla's attention upstairs and he was left alone with Jenny in the drawing-room, with no very clear idea how to proceed.

"It will be good to see Raymond again," he began at random, playing with the fringe on the edge of the woollen rug which covered his legs. "They don't come any finer than he is."

"No, I'm sure they don't," she agreed, half hoping, half dreading that he would go on talking about his idol.

"I expect you got to know him pretty well, while he was at the Hall."

"Pretty well, yes. I had two other men to take care of at the same time, but they weren't much trouble, poor dears."

"Was Raymond trouble?" he grinned.

"He tried not to fret. But it was agony to him to lie helpless in bed so long. He was like something tied up by the leg."

"You got him well, though."

"Oh, yes. And you'll get well too, you'll see."

"If I do," said Calvert recklessly, playing with the fringe, "I'm going to ask you to marry me."

"Oh, no!" cried Jenny quickly, for she had not seen it coming. "I mean—I—" She stopped miserably. None of the things she could once have said were any good any more. I don't want to play, I'd rather sit and watch—I'm cured—I've thrown in my hand—all that is not for me—once is enough—it was all lies now, because of Raymond. There was nothing to answer Calvert with except an unvarnished refusal. And that, for a man just crawling up the slope of life again, was cruel and unfair.

"Camilla told me something about how you feel," Calvert

was saying, not looking at her. "I can understand how that is, of course, but I'm hoping I can change it for you. I'm hoping I can teach you to trust me enough to let me try to make it up to you for what you've been through. I want to take you home with me, Jenny, and make you forget the war and all that went with it. You've done your bit, anyway, at the hospital. As soon as I'm sure I won't be a nuisance to you with this leg, I want to start taking care of you. We'll go to Williamsburg, where Aunt Sue is, and you can have a good rest and eat Southern cooking and everybody will adore you. It's a pretty town, with white houses behind white picket fences, and the voices of the darkies are happy in the streets. They make the best servants in the world, loyal and funny and affectionate. You'd like Williamsburg better than Richmond, I think, we spend a lot of time there, though Mother won't give up the house in Richmond. We haven't got much money on our side of the family, but we don't seem to need much, somehow. You'll be all right with us." His eyes came up, honest and a little shy about the awkward subject of money. "You won't starve, anyway," he said earnestly, "and if I find I can write books like my cousin Phoebe, we might do pretty well. Anyway, I want to try. Will you come, Jenny?"

"Oh, Calvert, you make it sound very nice, but—" Tears stood in her eyes. The obstinate memory of another voice beat against Calvert's drawling words: My father kept the livery stable and feed store—my father taught me how to do things, I don't have to send for the plumber and the carpenter—you'd be the wife of a common garage mechanic in greasy overalls. . . .

"But what, Jenny? We could always come back to England for a visit when you get homesick. Dinah always comes back. Bracken's got more money in a minute than I have in a year, of course, but I can still afford steamship tickets for two now and then. I'm not asking you to emigrate."

"I know, darling, I know, it isn't that, but—"

"What is it, then? Are you afraid? You're safe to love me, honey, I'm yours for keeps, you know. Jenny, you're crying! Do you still love him?"

"Gerald? No, of course not!"

"I'll make it all up to you," he pleaded. "Just give me a chance. I'll take care of you, Jenny, I'll give the rest of my life to it. There's nothing else I want to do, but make you happy, and never see you cry again. I love you so, Jenny—"

And that other voice in her wilful memory, offering nothing, promising nothing: When I go back I expect to build that garage and operate it—it would be years before I could give you a better house—you couldn't live like that. . . . And her own voice, desperate and broken: I could get a job—I could learn to make my own clothes—I wouldn't be a nuisance. . . . And Calvert's Virginia drawl:—white houses behind white picket fences—the best servants in the world—I'll take care of you—I'll make you happy—I love you so. . . .

Had Raymond ever spoken of love, or happiness, or care, like that? But it was Raymond she wanted still. And inside of a week she would see him again. She wasn't engaged to him. He had asked for no pledge from her, nor given any assurance of his own. She had no right to take refuge behind him from any new proposal of marriage, for he had made none himself. She was bound to him only by her own stubborn devotion, not by any act of his, and he would doubtless point out his renouncement of her if confronted with a rival claim. He stood back, aloof, enigmatic, mysterious, a stranger in all his ways, making no concessions and no appeals and no demands. Her heart was in his strong, fine hands, but hers were empty, he had given nothing in return. She felt newly bereft and humiliated and bewildered, to realize that she had no plausible reason now for refusing Calvert. I am in love with somebody else, she could say. And then— Are you going to marry him? Calvert would have the right to ask. I don't know, was all she could answer. Why don't you know? He won't ask me—he won't have me. Then why bother about him—I'm here—I'll take care of you—I love you so—why bother about him, Jenny, who is he? And if she told him it was Raymond who stood between them, what would Calvert say? What did men do who loved each other and wanted the same woman? What would Raymond do if he saw that Calvert— The mere idea brought a sort of panic. He was sure to see. Or Calvert in all innocence would tell him. What would Raymond do then?

"I suppose it's much too soon," Calvert was saying on the sofa. "Camilla warned me not to rush you."

"D-does Camilla know how you feel—about me?"

"Oh, yes—Raymond does too. He said so far as he knew there was no one to stand in my way with you. Is there?"

Jenny rose and walked to the window and stood there looking out blindly. Her hands and knees were shaking. Calvert had been and done it.

"Please say something, Jenny," suggested a patient voice from the sofa.

"It's because I don't know what to say. It does seem a bit soon, doesn't it, we haven't known each other very long."

"I'll wait, then. I'll ask you again. But I think as a rule people know right away, don't you? I did. Of course there's my leg. Everything depends on it."

"It's got nothing to do with your leg," she said firmly, returning to the sofa. "You took me by surprise. The British are awfully slow, hadn't you noticed that?"

He sat up, and caught one of her hands in both his, and kissed it.

"I'll be good," he promised. "I'll try not to worry you. But it's such fun to be in love, Jenny."

"Is it?" she said, looking down at him ruefully.

"Try," he said. "Promise me to try."

That too stuck in her throat, for she dreaded to encourage him even a little. He was very attractive, with his hair rumpled from the pillows, his fine-drawn boyish face upturned to her, his grey eyes confident and dancing. He would be easy to love. Life with him would be gay and comfortable and perhaps lavish. There was nothing easy about Raymond, dark and inarticulate and unimpulsive. Nothing but to let him go. Jenny's chin lifted.

"For me, it's got to come without trying," she said gently.

———

The day before Raymond arrived at Farthingale Camilla got her feet wet on a walk in the garden with Sosthène and Mimi and began to sneeze again and some anxiety was felt. She was not allowed to go to the station in the car which would meet Raymond's train, and a telephone call to the Hall met with a firm reply from Winifred. Jenny's afternoon off was tomorrow. Today she could not be spared. Raymond would have to find his welcome on the mat at Farthingale and not at the train. At Camilla's croaking insistence Jenny was brought to the telephone.

"Honey, you've got to help us out over here," Camilla told her hoarsely. "I'm laid up again with a temperature and Calvert is tied to the sofa and it's going to be very dull for Raymond if you don't rally round."

"I've only got tomorrow afternoon," said Jenny, and her heart began to beat.

"Well, let's think of something," Camilla entreated. "I suppose you couldn't get a car and run him over to Gloucester or Cheltenham or somewhere, just for a treat?"

"No petrol for a jaunt like that, I'm afraid. If he can ride a bicycle I could take him to Overcreech and give him tea there, but that's not very exciting, is it."

"That would do nicely," Camilla assured her. "Just to break the monotony here, you know. You could show him over the house, and your father liked him at Christmas time, didn't he?"

"Father is in London, unfortunately. But he left the housekeeper and a couple of maids at Overcreech. I'll ring up and warn them that we're coming, shall I?"

"Unless it rains," said Camilla. "I do think it would be too bad for Raymond to be stuck here the whole of his leave with two complete crocks like us."

"I'll do what I can," said Jenny. "Lend him a bicycle and send him over here about two-o'clock tomorrow and we'll go on to Overcreech. He can see the pictures and the garden and they'll give us some sort of tea—"

"And then you could both come back here for dinner. I'll come down stairs tomorrow night if it kills me."

"I'd have to get back to the Hall before dark on a bike."

"Stay the night here. I can always lend you things."

"Well—I'll ask."

"Ask for Sunday too, while you're about it."

"I can try."

Jenny hung up the telephone, marvelling at the resourcefulness of Providence. It was hard on Camilla to have got a relapse, but it gave her, Jenny, an afternoon with Raymond —perhaps a chance to block any nonsense on his part about Calvert. And to have Overcreech all to themselves might make all the difference—a chance to talk to each other without eyes and ears all round them, a chance to behave for a little while like people in love in normal times. Tea in the panelled parlor, with the sun streaming in through the windows, and the door shut on the war. Jenny's heart was beating fast.

He was well now. He could put both arms around her. . . .

Raymond, confronted with the well-meant plans for his entertainment, protested that he would be perfectly happy at Farthingale with them all day, and was reminded that nobody ever missed an opportunity to see Overcreech House, famous for its picture gallery and its gardens. He subsided meekly, feeling that somebody somewhere was not giving him an even break on this thing. An afternoon alone with Jenny, even with a couple of bicycles between them, was full of risks he had no desire to encounter.

She was waiting when he arrived at the Hall the following day. She gave him her hand and her smile, and led the way to the stables where her bicycle lived, and they set out along a deep lane towards Overcreech. When they stopped to rest, sitting on the grass beside the road, he told about the training he had had, and they discussed what was ahead of him— gazetted Flying Officer now, he wore a single gold stripe, and if he passed in his technical subjects would be eligible for the CFS at Upavon and advanced fighter training. By the time July was out he would have won the right to fly a single-seater Camel over the lines in France. The German ace von Richthofen had been recently killed, his red plane crashing behind the British lines after a general dogfight. "The b-so-and-so claimed eighty of our planes, so we bury him with full military honors," said Raymond in disgust.

Jenny watched and waited with a growing hopelessness for any sign from him of their former intimacy. He was cool, impersonal, respectful, and withdrawn, as though she was the Queen—or a duke's daughter. Gradually the light went out of her face, and she became passive and polite like a disappointed child. It was gone. The thing they had had together was swept away by this passion of his for flying, his single-minded absorption in the job ahead of him. He had left love behind. He had no need of it now that he was well.

She had ceased to matter to him. It might as well be Gerald
all over again. And because she cared so much more this
time, it was going to be much worse. Later, when she had time
to face it, it would be. In the meantime, a cup of tea would
help.

Jenny rose from the grass, very much on her dignity, a
thing he had never seen before. She had not interrupted
him, but she had quietly closed a door on the subject of
German aces and their boastful records, as compared to the
less publicised anonymous exploits of the RAF fighter pilots.

"If we don't get on our way," she said, sounding to him
a little more clipped and British than he was accustomed to,
"the hot scones they promised me will be spoilt." And she
was off before him down the lane.

Raymond followed, looking dark and closed in. He knew
very well what he had done, he had seen it happening while
he talked, and had deliberately pressed home the point of
his blade, as he had braced himself to do. He had hurt her,
enduring a double anguish while he did so. But when it was
over, and he had gone to France, Calvert would still be here,
and Calvert was the sort of person for Jenny to marry. She
would be safe with Calvert, and this crazy interlude with
himself would finally be forgotten. Not by him. No one would
ever fill Jenny's place with him. But he would probably
not have long to get used to living without her anyway, and
he would be pretty busy. It was unlikely that he would ever
have to see her married to somebody else. To come right
down to it, he would just as soon be let off that. And if the
worst happened to him, the less she had to remember of the
love between them the better for her.

Following Jenny's bicycle through the tall wrought iron
gates of Overcreech House, he looked up to find the ornate
façade before him. That it was in the best Jacobean style
would have conveyed nothing to him. He only knew that it

was more impressive than Farthingale and more homelike than the Georgian vastness of the Hall.

It was a gem of a house, as Jenny well knew, and her pride of it was not entirely dimmed by the fact that it was no longer going to be as much fun to show it to Raymond as she had always thought it would be. Tea was laid in the panelled parlor, where tall vases of pale blue delphinium stood. The housekeeper had provided lavishly, but Jenny found it difficult to appreciate the delicacies the good woman had contrived. Raymond ate a bit of everything politely, and drank two cups of tea, and discussed the news from France, which was not good. After a month's lull another violent German thrust had been launched on the Marne front. Soissons was gone—and Neuilly—and it was hotting up round Montdidier again. He took some time to explain his own preference for the small fighter plane as against the bombing jobs—in a Camel, he said, you could go right down to the level of the housetops and machine-gun German troops jammed between the walls to great effect, while it took tons of bombs to damage a city to any extent, besides killing a lot of non-combatants, which was a waste of effort. It was troops you wanted to kill. They were the people who shot at you, weren't they? Well, then.

So that was the way the door was shut on the war, Jenny thought angrily as the afternoon slid by and away from her forever, with no word of love from him, no advantage whatever taken of their first opportunity to be quite alone together without being overheard. And remembering how she had promised herself the feel of both his arms around her, to warm and uphold and sustain her in the time to come, her cheeks reddened and her mouth tightened, and she listened numbly, making few remarks of her own, and he fought off a growing compassion. Her day was ruined, he knew. Better that than her life.

After tea she escorted him punctiliously through the picture gallery, famous for its Van Dycks and Gainsboroughs and a glowing, breathing Opie of the fifth Duke as a boy. Raymond took it all in gravely, and no one would have suspected that it had never before occurred to him that paint and canvas could survive in beauty and grow in value for two hundred years. He thought the Romney Duchess looked exactly like Jenny, and she admitted that her father had always thought so too.

Finally, in ever increasing constraint, they set out again down the avenue and through the gates in late sunshine on the bicycles. When they had come almost in silence to a secluded grassy spot in the lane, already in deepening twilight, Raymond reached out and caught her handle-bars and brought both machines to a halt. She looked round at him doubtfully, still astride, one foot on the ground.

"Come and sit down," he said, feeling for a cigarette, and he sat down first under some trees, motioning her to the place beside him. Jenny followed him obediently, her back very straight. His lighter clicked, he returned it to his pocket, and took both her hands in his. His face was soft and smiling now, but Jenny's eyes were on their hands, and she did not see.

"You feel pretty bad, don't you," he said gently, watching her. She did not answer. "Don't, Jenny. Don't feel bad about me, please. If I had any doubts before, and I hadn't, I'm sure now. You and I—we just don't belong together. It's tough now, I know. But you see what I mean—don't you. When I look at that house of yours—and then think of Indian Landing—"

"I don't think houses have much to do with it any more," she said, looking down.

"They have a lot to do with it. I've been hard on you today

—hard on myself too—I had to be. You'll forgive me, some time. It's the only way I could do it."

"Do what?" she asked quickly and caught his eyes, and saw his face gentle and young as she loved it. "Oh, Raymond—I thought you'd stopped loving me!"

He made no answer, maddeningly, where denial was urgently needed, but sat playing with her fingers in his, his face turned from her again.

"But you haven't," she persisted. "I saw it again just now. You *haven't.*"

"I'm no good to you," he said slowly. "I've told you that, can't you see? There's a guy back there at the house where we're going that's right for you. Forget about me, why don't you. I'd only make you sorry you ever heard of me."

"It's Calvert I'm sorry about," she said.

"Why? He's going to get well. He's your kind. I'll be going back to France in a few weeks, with a job on my hands. You don't want anything to do with that, you've seen how it is for these women with men in the Flying Corps. You know what can happen as well as I do!"

"So I should fall in love more comfortably with a man who is going to stay in England, and not have anything to worry about!" she challenged, and again he was silent. "That's *childish* of you," said Jenny with some heat. "As though I was shopping round for the easiest way to be in love! As though I could change overnight for my own convenience! What do you think I'm made of?"

To her angry amazement he looked up at her and laughed, he caught her chin between his thumb and finger and turned up her face to his and kissed her lightly on the lips and let her go.

"Got your dander up," he remarked with satisfaction. "I can always get a rise out of you, can't I. You can make it sound that way, I guess, if you try," he went on seriously, "but it's not what I mean. I'm only trying to think of you and your future."

"Without you I haven't any future," she told him simply. "Without you, I would go back to where I was before you came—"

"Just where was that?"

"—where I had nothing to look forward to but what I'm doing now, turning myself into a kind sort of machine to make wounded men as comfortable and happy as possible —other people's men—trying not to think beyond that, day after day, trying not to have any emotions of my own, or any hopes, or any memories. Just being alive from day to day, without any particular reason, because there was nothing else to do—"

"Was it as bad as that?" he said incredulously, watching her. "You're too young to feel like that. What makes you think I can change it? What makes you think you'd be any better off with me?"

Jenny looked up at him.

"Because I love you," she said.

It was one of the cues he did not take up, wrapped in his own dark thoughts. He shook his head slowly.

"Now you do," he said. "But things are all out of joint now. There's a war on. If you'd met me in the ordinary way, none of it would have happened. If you hadn't saved my life that night—"

"Phoebe was there too, to save your life. I didn't do anything."

"It wasn't Phoebe I saw beside me every time I came up."

"I terribly wanted you to live. Even then, I—couldn't let you go."

"Why?" He waited, his eyes on her face, patient and kind

and puzzled. "Why me? What is there about a guy like me for you to—" He stumbled and evaded. "—to care about?"

"I don't know. But whatever it is, it's nothing to do with you, or me, separately. It's bigger than that. I don't see how you can draw so sharp a line between us, anyway, we aren't so different as you seem to think. We speak the same language, we come of the same stock. Do you know anything about your ancestors?"

"Not very much. There's no picture gallery at Indian Landing."

"That's not what I meant," she said patiently. "In Virginia they have a phrase I love, I heard it first from Phoebe—if people have got the same blood to some degree of cousinship they're kissing kin. If your great-great-grandfather was a younger son, he may have gone out to America to make his fortune. Lots of them did. Your great-great-grandfather and mine may have been cousins—neighbors, anyway. Most of America has got to be in some degree related to most of England, because in the beginning they were, and their descendants must be still kissing kin. Perhaps you've only come back home after a couple of hundred years—Cousin Raymond." She lifted her face for a kiss.

"I don't stand a chance with you," he said, muffled, and his arms went round her, and he tipped her back against the grass and buried his lips in her throat. Jenny lay still, spent and flooded with happiness. His lips moved upward across her cheek to the edge of her hair, and he drew her closer against him with a swift, cradling movement. "I give up," he whispered, against her hair. "I don't know what's best any more. I only know I love you."

He had said it. She stirred a little to slide an arm around his neck, for Jenny never could do things by halves, so that soon it was Raymond who drew away, rather abruptly, and sat up, feeling for his cigarettes. As he lit one, his fine-fingered hands with their neglected nails were not quite steady. The sun had gone down and the lane was dark and deserted.

Jenny lay on her back, gazing up into the boughs above their heads. Relief and a sense of release were sharp as a pain, within her. Everything was all right now. He had said it. He loved her. Still.

"We'd better get moving," he said, sitting beside her with his cigarette.

"Not just yet," she sighed.

"What are you thinking?" He leaned on one hand, so that his face hung above her, shutting out the treetops and the sky.

"Just—Raymond," she said, and he kissed her again and again drew away voluntarily from her response.

"You're lucky it's me," he said. "Don't kiss anybody else like that, will you, in a dark lane."

Jenny laughed confidently, lying where she was.

"I'm not likely to," she said. "Shall we tell them now, at Farthingale?"

"No," said Raymond, his face turned from her in the twilight.

There was a silence.

"I'd rather," she ventured then.

"There's nothing to tell," he said, and Jenny sat up.

"But you said—"

"I know, I said I give up, didn't I. And I do. If you still feel like this when the war is over, and if I'm—still worth anything to you—we'll get married."

"When the war is over!"

"That's what I said."

"B-but, *Raymond*—"

"I bet you'd marry me next week, wouldn' you."

"Yes—of course I would," she answered breathlessly.

"Not me, you won't," said Raymond. "It would be awful easy for me to take you up on that, the way you are. But I'm not going to. Remember those two guys they put into my room at the Hall? The one with the burns, and the one with his face shot away? D'ya think I'm going to take a chance on handing you something like that myself?"

"It's a chance everybody has to take these days."

"You don't have to. Because I'm going to see to it you don't. Understand?" He turned to her and found both her hands and gathered them hard into his till it hurt. "Don't think I don't want you, before I go. But this is going to be just between you and me—till we see how things come out. Then, if anything happens to me, you're still free, and there's still Calvert, or somebody else. And if I come through all right, and you want to go on with it—we'll see."

She leaned against him, her forehead pressed against his sleeve, her hands in his.

"It's not—*enough*," she said. "I'm proud of it—I want everybody to know."

"It's the only way I can do it at all," he said. "Even that way—don't seem quite right to me. But it's the best I can do now. You got right under my guard, didn't you. I had this thing all figured out a different way. Doesn't do much good to make up my mind with you around, does it." He raised one of her hands and held it hard against his face, not kissing it. "You know how to make it pretty tough," he said.

"And there's another thing," she said against his sleeve. "I don't think it's fair to Calvert."

"It's just as fair to him one way as another," he maintained. "Besides—he's going to live through this war. He can afford to take it easy for a while."

"Raymond—don't get any sort of idea that if you're killed I'll marry Calvert and be happy," she told him shakily. "I couldn't—possibly."

"He's a lot easier than I am," he warned, and her head came up with a jerk.

"I told you I wasn't looking for something easy!" she cried in exasperation, and he caught her up, laughing, his cheek against hers, rocking her in his arms.

"Don't get so mad," he said delightedly. "Gosh, you've got a temper!" He held her a moment, tense and silent. "We're going to do this my way," he said then. "That don't seem right to you, does it. I ought to be the one to give in. Lots of people would always let you have your way about everything. I'm not like that, and that's your bad luck. When I come up against something I don't quite know how to deal with, I always get the bit in my teeth. That's what I mean about being hard to handle. See?" She was silent, crumpled in his arms, her face hidden. "Want to quit now?" he asked gently. "There's still plenty of time." Jenny shook her head. It was the only move she made. "Remember what I said, then. If anything happens to me, you aren't committed to anything, and nobody ever needs to know we were in love with each other. This is just a dream we both had, but you aren't to go on thinking about it, if it ends. You're not to grieve, Jenny, I don't want to be the cause of any sorrow for you, dead or alive. That's why I was so leary about this whole thing, dear, I couldn't see anything in it for you but trouble, one way or another. Don't think I mind a little trouble for myself—I've had trouble, I'm used to it. But I don't want you to cry, Jenny, I—" He broke off, and bent his head. Jenny was quivering with sobs, soundless, but her slight body was racked with them in the circle of his arms. He put his fingers to her cheek and they came away wet. After a moment's horror, he sat holding her quietly, his face against her hair—and it went through his mind that if he lived a week or a century, he would never know complete forgetfulness of this moment in the lane with Jenny crying against

his heart. He had never known anyone to cry like that before
—without a sound, but shaking and trembling, and tears
coming like rain. In all his compassion, it never occurred to
him to alter his own decisions or soften his inflexible determination not to see her bound to him in any way until he
was sure of his own survival, whole. Their life together, if
ever they had one, would be complicated enough, at best.
And at the back of his consciousness crouched the relentless
knowledge of the odds against him, piled up now for over
three years. It was fantastic to suppose that they would see
each other again, after he went out to France the next time.
And in that case, the less he took from her now, the freer
she would be when it was over. And it seemed to him that
life itself ran out through his fingers like water into dry sand,
while he held Jenny and waited for her to stop crying.

They were late to dinner, and explained that Jenny's bike
had broken down and Raymond had repaired it by the light
of the lamp on his own. He gave a highly technical description of the trouble, and no one questioned its veracity.

That evening he heard Jenny play and sing for the first
time, in the informal concert she and Camilla did so well at
Calvert's insatiable request, and Raymond knew a further
enchantment, for he had a deep, untutored love of music.
He sat listening with a pipe between his teeth, his head a
little sunk, guarded, almost mute, while every now and then
the memory of those moments in the lane played through
him like lightning shimmering down a cloudy sky. She would
have been his, he had only to take her. He dwelt recklessly
on the idea, while Jenny sang. Fire and trust and joy, submis-
sion and rapture, were in that eager little creature for his
claiming. For no one else the same. She had never felt like
that for Gerald, he knew. She had learned it because of him.

Dizzied, but obstinate, he clung to his determination to leave her free. Even if she never felt quite the same again—was it just being romantic, he wondered, to think that neither of them ever would? —something would come to her, some one was sure to make it up to her, in some degree. Better if she came to that without a ghost in the way. So he sat, withdrawn and silent, smoking, aching with love of her, convinced of his own doom.

And Jenny, unable to catch his eyes for any fleeting glance of mutual understanding, baffled by his lack of response to her own effervescence, confused by Calvert's open idolatry of herself so shamelessly displayed against the seeming indifference of the man she had kissed in the lane, felt her evening crumbling beneath her just as the afternoon had begun by doing, and she was angry and afraid. Where were his tenderness and his laughter, where was the look she had brought back to his face which made him young and defenceless and her own? And she began to grope distractedly about in what had been said and done since their return for any cause of offence on her part—should she have told them anyhow, to prove her pride in him?—or had she been too careless still and given it away somehow so that he was displeased?—or did he think she led Calvert on, or was she being too off-hand with him, whom neither of them wanted to hurt? It was difficult to know how to behave, with both of them in the room. What had gone wrong again? What had she done? Or not done? She had never before known this bewilderment of unspecified guilt, this numbing uncertainty of herself and distrust of a beloved person—except with Gerald. And if Raymond, loving her, as she had been so sure he did, could do exactly the same violence to her pride and her confidence as Gerald had done, what was the good of anything?

Once more the bright dream wilted in her hands and music

died in her and Camilla was left playing alone, for her throat would not let her sing. It *isn't* fun to be in love, Jenny argued passionately with Calvert's light words of a few days before. Not with Raymond it wasn't. And it was a perilous thing at best, to care too much what any one person thought or did. Raymond made it harder, you never knew what went on behind his brooding silences. Tonight his face was heavy and sombre, his eyes were curtained by their thick lashes, his generous lips were closed on the pipe stem. A new misgiving darted through Jenny's troubled consciousness. She had been playing well, singing anything they asked for—pleased to entertain, happy in her modest drawing-room accomplishments. To Raymond, was that further evidence of the Duke's daughter, educated, self-confident, perhaps to Raymond conceited with herself?

Jenny left the piano and wandered, suddenly listless, towards the sofa where Calvert lay, unconsciously turning for support to his steadfast admiration. Overwrought and let down, she wanted to cry, and despised herself accordingly. It's no *use,* she thought, we're too far apart to start with, I won't go on, I won't be made miserable again—by *anyone.* I won't care, I won't try, I won't hope, any more. It doesn't do. It's too difficult for us, just as he says. . . .

With Calvert's eyes upon them both, Raymond had not moved nor glanced up as she passed close to his chair. Camilla's fingers wandered on the keys, playing nostalgic bits of this and that, and drifting on. Calvert offered Jenny a cigarette, and though she seldom smoked she took it, and he struck a match. Raymond stirred, and gathering himself together knocked out his pipe. He had no words, even if he had felt free to speak, for the tumult inside him, and he dared not look at her with Calvert there.

Jenny had wangled permission to stay the night, and soon

after that they helped Calvert up the stairs and Raymond went into his room to help him to bed.

When she came down stairs in the morning the door to the front steps was open, and Raymond stood outside in the early sunlight with a pipe. He turned and saw her hesitating in the hall and said Good-morning with his odd formality—and then, as he came towards her she saw that his face was alight with his love, and she stared up at him, her lips parted on words that never came.

"What's the matter?" he asked in honest surprise.

"Why were you so strange last night?" she blurted, still confused and resentful.

"Strange?" He was at a loss. "What did I do?"

"You sulked all evening. I thought I must have done something you didn't like."

For a moment he looked at her without speaking, and she felt him exercising a deliberate patience and restraint. Then he glanced up the stairs behind her and out the open door, and moved her towards it, his fingers briefly touching her elbow. When they reached the steps outside, and his quick glance found a deserted drive and empty windows, he said very quietly, "You know I have to be careful, everyone was there. If I'd shown what I was feeling last night I'd have given the whole thing away."

"You mean you—*liked* it?"

"Liked what?"

"The music—and the clowning I did. It wasn't just showing off, I only—we always try to put on a show for Calvert, he enjoys it and his days are so long and dull the best we can do."

"It was wonderful. I loved it."

"You—?" She gave a breathless little laugh. "Oh, darling, I thought you didn't! You were black as a thundercloud, you wouldn't look at me, you didn't say anything—"

"I didn't dare. Don't you see, I—just didn't dare." His eyes were steady. "I won't ever forget a minute of last evening. I didn't know you could sing like that, I—"

Sosthène came round the corner of the house with Mimi, still out of earshot. Raymond's face changed at once, and he took a casual step back from her.

"I've got till Tuesday here," he said very low. "Will I see you again?"

"Oh, *yes*—I'll get some time off on Sunday somehow."

"Remember, now—I've got to be careful. But that doesn't mean I don't love you. Look out, he's coming."

Jenny recovered to answer Sosthène's smiling greeting. Camilla ran down stairs calling out that Calvert was ramping and would Raymond please go up to him.

After breakfast they said a casual Good-bye, with everyone looking on, and Jenny departed on her bicycle for the Hall, sustained by the thought of Sunday.

But the few hours they had in each other's company then passed like minutes, much as the evening had gone, and they faced the parting suddenly with no more time together. Jenny was longing for one more look from him, a dozen words, the briefest kiss, when she heard him saying to Camilla, "I'll get the bike and ride part of the way with her, it's getting dark."

There was that dangerous moment when Camilla might have said she would go along on another bike, but Calvert was looking rather exhausted by too much exertion and she had no thought of leaving him. Awed by their good fortune, they left the house by the garden door and went round to the stables where the bicycles were. When they had ridden almost in silence to the same place in the lane, they stopped without words and faced each other gravely in the fading light.

"Don't look like that," he said compassionately. "I'll have another leave, before I go to France."

"I *will* see you again?"

"Yes, dear—you will." He glanced up and down the empty lane and took her in his arms. "It's been wonderful—I'll always remember those songs you sang." He kissed her, hard, but briefly. "Don't cry, Jenny. The war's going to end some time."

She clung to him silently, her face buried against him, tearless but trembling.

"Don't, Jenny—what can I say—don't."

"You could say you love me!" she cried in almost hysterical exasperation, hating his deep reserve, longing perversely for evidence that he suffered too, and she beat his solid shoulder with one small clenched fist.

The result lifted her right off her feet, up into his arms, and the kiss he took while all the breath was squeezed out of her was so long and possessive that she broke it herself. But Raymond went on kissing her, again and again, till they were both spent and shaking, and then he said, "Now see what you've done," and stepped back from her, his hand going automatically to the pocket where his cigarettes were.

Jenny dropped down on the grass at his feet, sitting in a little huddle with her face hidden, and heard the rasp of his lighter, and caught the first whiff of smoke on the still air. He did not sit down beside her, but took a few steps up and down the edge of the road, and his voice came coolly from a little distance.

"We mustn't stay here any longer, they'll be wondering about us. And you mustn't go back to the Hall crying. Get up, Jenny."

Slowly she got to her feet, her head down, groped for her hat on the grass, and came towards him where he stood beside the bicycles. He took the soft tweed hat from her hands and set it gently on her bright hair, bent to brush some leaves from her skirt, and then held the bicycle for her. She looked up piteously into his face and found in his eyes a flicker of almost paternal amusement.

"I told you it wasn't safe to kiss a man in a dark lane," he said gently. "Smile, Jenny."

She tried to.

"Good-bye," she whispered, and he shook his head.

"So long," he said in correction.

Her bicycle was waiting. She mounted, watching his face as it was now, for her, and then rode away without looking back.

4. AUTUMN ON THE SOMME. 1918.

IN JULY THE FIGHTING FLARED AGAIN IN France, with a new German drive on Paris, which was held at the Marne with terrible losses on both sides. And then Foch made the first small move in his long-planned, long-awaited counter-attack which was designed to grow and grow, until almost imperceptibly at first the tide had turned, and the Germans began an orderly but still costly retreat. They were not beaten, they were still fighting hard. The Canadians were in it, and the tanks, and air fighting was intense and continuous. But the Allies progressed. Soissons was recovered, and Montdidier—Albert—Thiepval—the old familiar, agonizing names again, but now they were coming home.

In the midst of it, Archie got influenza on a trip to the north of England, and died before Virginia could reach his bedside. The family was stunned. Not Archie. Archie never made anything of being in the war, Archie had one

of the dull, safe jobs. Archie with his light touch, his under-
statement, his straight-faced foolery—his diffident, flaming,
shame-faced adoration of Virginia, which always so far out-
matched his traditional British off-handedness. Archie's
children waited in a white-faced, tear-stained group for the
arrival of their white-faced, tearless mother. And Virginia,
viewing with concern their piteous self-control, held out her
arms to them and said, "It's all over, darlings, and now we
can have a good cry together—" And they did, and felt better
for it.

Raymond was sent to France on twenty-four hours notice,
without time to return to Farthingale for good-byes. He had
completed his training at Upavon with distinction and was a
full-fledged Flying Officer with a gold stripe on his sleeve
and wings on his breast, and with fighter pilot qualifications.
He would be thrown straight into the air with the best of the
Royal Air Force against the best the Germans could produce.

Calvert swore with disappointment because they would
not see him before he went, Camilla said it wasn't fair, and
Jenny turned white and became very busy during the ensu-
ing days at the Hall, so they saw very little of her.

A man who has been handed a new single-seater war plane
with a scarlet nose and told to fly it to a certain spot on the
map of France and keep in formation while he does so, has a
number of things to think about more immediate than the
girl he loves or his own problematical future. There were
five of them, and their Flight Commander, sitting in their
machines on that sunny August morning in the south of
England, with a mechanic facing each propeller. Raymond,
first on the left, laid his hand on the control stick which was
all his, and grinned over the side at the little group of pilots
and ground people who had gathered to see them off, and
whose turn was not yet or who had unfinished business with
the Gothas which came to England. Despite the slight crinkle

of nerves in the pit of his stomach, he was awash with pure joy. He had his wings, he had his machine, he knew his job, he was on his way.

The shout of the man who was waiting to spin the Flight Commander's prop reached his ears on the warm wind— "Contaxer!" "Contact!" The Flight Commander's engine roared, the prop spun, the chocks came away, he was up. Raymond fingered his stick. One more plane, before him. Away. *"Contact!"* It was his own voice, answering. His own engine sang, the wind was in the wires, the stick came back, he was in the air, circling for height and position.

Easy, confident flyer though he was, it was a busy time. She was very sensitive on the controls, and to keep his place in the group took all his attention—not to overhaul or be overhauled, not to deviate from the course sidewise or up-wards—a cloudbank awaited them over the Channel—down to three thousand feet where there was clear air again—a few ships on the water—and then both coasts were in view, Eng-land's knotty with coves and capes, France's sweeping in a long curve to the corner at Grisnez—Calais, there below, and a right-hand swing following their leader—the straight, white tree-bordered roads of France—the spider-web of canals— down at the depôt of St. Gregoire for oil and petrol, and the man ahead bent an axle and tore a tire in landing.

Raymond put her down lightly, with a conscious neatness, entirely in order. Later in the afternoon, with the damaged plane mended, they flew southward, along the British lines, into country which became a scorched wilderness of war— dented roads, mottled fields, burnt, scraggy woods. Ghostly Ypres was still recognizable. And then, with the brownish strip of trenches winding through the desolation it was familiar ground to Raymond—St. Eloi, and Messines, and Armentiéres. He leaned over the edge of the cockpit, peer-ing down. He had come a long way since that time in the craters at St. Eloi. Arras, and the long, straight road from Albert to Bapaume—scrap heaps that once were villages—the sparkling ribbon of the Somme—an aerodrome below—the Flight Commander headed for it, the group streaming behind him—an exhibition landing—and champagne in their honor at supper in the mess. He had come a long way from Jenny too.

They were posted to a fighting squadron whose job was to patrol inside the German lines and knock down anything they encountered there—no bombs to carry, no reconnaissance to make, no lumbering camera planes to escort—no red tape. Just go out and look for trouble. You were sure to find it. Raymond began at once to feel at home.

The air war was on in earnest now. In 1914 the British pilots had gone up in anything that could get off the ground, with nothing to shoot but their own side arms. It was two years before they began to catch up, and after last spring's Bloody April their losses were only now again evening up, with fast new planes and a new crop of pilots. They had discovered in the interim that German infantry didn't like being fired on from above, to the extent of utter panic, and low-flying tactics against ground personnel had become a craze with this squadron.

That first evening in the mess Raymond heard how only yesterday a whole trenchful of Boches had surrendered to Fenton, there—a fair, tousled boy who chortled round his pipe at the memory—by waving handkerchiefs and anything white to stop him flying up and down two hundred yards above the trench and spraying them with maching-gun bullets. The lines lay close together there, and by waggling his wings and motioning with his arms he had managed to convey to his own side that they should move in and take possession. It was still funny in the mess. And then there was the story about the new baby pilot—glances at the recent arrivals

—who flew berserk and dived through the Bapaume barrage of anti-aircraft fire and let off a hundred rounds into the town square at eight hundred feet and raced away pursued by rocket-shells—no, Bapaume had not surrendered—yet. Troop trains were fair game too—the engineers shut off the steam and tried to become invisible, but Middleton, there, had chased one for miles and finally derailed it before he ran out of ammunition.

Ground strafing was a welcome change from the comparative boredom of patrols and dogfights at ten thousand feet. Anyway, there were no rules to this game, nor any precedents, because no two air fights were ever alike. You could only go by hard experience and practice, learning as you went. Raymond knew now that he had come to the right place.

There were a few first precepts, of course, which every cub pilot was taught. Blind sporting courage wasn't enough, you had to know wind and sun and deflection, you had to know what your own plane was capable of and to guess your enemy's intention in time. Willingness was no good without knowledge, and on top of that experience. Always dive out of the sun; time and direction both go from you in cloud; the plane that fell behind in a group attack was cold meat to the Fokkers; in a general dogfight the man you get seldom sees you, and you seldom see the man who gets you; get on his tail and watch your own; never jump out when you catch fire—stay with it and put her down if you can. The rest of it you must learn the hard way, by trial and error.

Pilots on maiden flights nearly always tried to do too much and became a nuisance to their mates and sometimes casualties in consequence of overeagerness. Mindful of his manners in his first flight over enemy lines, flying next to last in a group of five, Raymond nevertheless managed to land a burst in a scarlet Fokker which was already in difficulties, during a brisk scrap with eleven enemy planes. It went down in flames behind its own lines, and he knew then for the first time the sickness in his own stomach, the shuddering horror of fire which comes to every pilot sooner or later, and often grows to an obsession and a nightmare. *Shot down in flames.* Now he had seen it. He was still shaken, still adjusting himself to realities, when he felt his own plane hit and saw ominous holes in the left wing. Instinctively he yanked the stick and the plane stood on its tail while he emptied his drum into the Fokker as it roared past and over him. It was hit, but it turned and came at him again.

He dived sharply under the German's fire, kicked over the rudder, pulled up hard, the stick in his tummy, the sky a dazzling blur, completed the loop and straightened out. The German was still there, and now the Flight Commander, anxious about his fledgling, was coming to join in. Raymond banked, gave him room, and circled back. His left wing was damaged, wires hung loose, a strut had been carried away, his engine was shirking. The Flight Commander dived on the red Fokker, spitting bullets, and the German seemed to stumble in mid-air, and then fell like a dead leaf past Raymond's plane, so near that he could see the blood on the pilot's face. He let it go, the Flight Commander's kill, and found that the other enemy planes were drawing away. Had enough, he thought with a sober sort of elation, and thereafter had all he could do to get back to the aerodrome right side up, shepherded by the rest of the group, all a little the worse for wear, but none missing.

Their aerodrome was next to a decrepit little village with a still beautiful church, and the squadron's tents were pitched in a leafy orchard with field kitchens and mess hall adjacent. As Raymond left the hangar that first day, a muddy infantry battalion was arriving from the trenches for a few days' rest and recuperation. The weary, grey-faced men distributed themselves without much commotion among the cottages and barns and went to sleep. Raymond regarded them with compassion and drank a cup of hot tea in his comfortable quarters with almost a feeling of guilt. He had been one of them once. He knew how it felt to come out of the Line too tired to do anything but drop in your tracks.

During the following week, the infantry, clean and shaved and polished, visited the aerodrome and watched the planes come in and crowded round to count the bullet holes. Mess courtesies were exchanged by the officers, and stories were told, and the gramophone ground through its repertoire. And then, in a pelting cold rain, to the tune of *The Long, Long Trail,* they marched out again on their way back to the Line, jaunty enough now, but leaving a silence round the aerodrome, where no one would have changed places with them.

Raymond, with the rather enviable reputation of having been scared into a magnificent loop in the first minutes of his first fight, had settled down to the business of ground-strafing with that special group of pilots who were at their best under five hundred feet, machine-gunning whatever they spotted, troop columns, transport, trains, officers' cars —those whose particular joy it was to swoop along the trench or road, panicking the Boche.

He caught a large general once, riding alone in his dignity in the open tonneau of a staff car—and flying at an angle which threatened to nose-dive the plane into the ground, Raymond drove the car into the ditch and the general and his chauffeur up the bank into the woods—"For his size, he sure made time up hill," said Raymond later in the mess. He found a troop inspection by some Boche brass hats once, going full swing, and turned it into an ant-hill by diving on the field and frolicking back and forth two hundred feet above it till his ammunition gave out and five waspish Fokker triplanes bustled out to chase him off. He got away with some holes in his tail and a derisive waggle of his wings. Raymond always waggled at the end of a fight—salute to the fallen or swagger of triumph?—he flew alone, and no one knew. He never returned to the aerodrome with unused ammunition, but always disposed of it in a final zigzag over the enemy trenches and then hedge-hopped home. Finally, when he had been with the squadron about a month, there was the affair of the lavender Fokker.

The color of the plane irked him—it had lavender wings and a pale green fuselage, which seemed a bit girlish for a war, and it always went for Raymond, or perhaps he was first to single it out. Anyway, the feud was on, and they spent a great deal of air time chasing each other's tails on a dozen different days with no decisive result. By common consent in the squadron the lavender plane was regarded as Raymond's particular pigeon, and they left it to him whenever it appeared.

There was a day when young Fenton got in the way and went down in a sickening spiral with smoke coming out of his engine. Raymond saw him drop, apparently out of control, and was taken with one of his stolid rages. He flew head-on at the lavender one with his gun blazing—they said later in the mess that he would have rammed the thing if its pilot had not lost his nerve and dived—but Raymond made a tight turn almost on his wing-tip and found himself at last above and behind. There he stayed, spitting fire, while the German zigzagged and twisted and dived from seven to two thousand feet.

The duel took place directly above where Fenton's shattered plane had landed in an open field far behind the German trenches. Again the Fokker dived, so steeply that it seemed unlikely he could ever come out of it in time, and Raymond roared after him. A few hundred feet above the ground the lavender plane miraculously flattened, and came down right side up. Raymond circled low, and saw that Fenton was clear of his burning plane and apparently unhurt, running towards the German.

It was a desolate piece of land, bare of habitation, with no roads running through it, and not another living soul was visible. Raymond descended and made a tidy landing between the other two planes, and Fenton swerved towards him, waving. Together they ran at the German plane, where nothing stirred. The pilot was dead in the seat, and the plane had landed itself on a lucky fluke or by some reflex of the dead man's hand. "Well," said Fenton philosophically, "he's no use to us now. Got room for a passenger? I'll hang on to the cowl, my bus is done."

"Take mine," said Raymond, and began to haul the dead man out of the cockpit.

"Are you going to fly that thing in?" asked Fenton, assisting with the pilot's booted legs.

"Let's give her a spin," said Raymond, climbing in. The Fokker engine answered. "What a lot of gadgets," said Raymond, and began to play with them, and the engine died. "Oops, wrong one," he said. "Spin it again." Fenton spun it again, and this time it caught and held. "Now, let's see," said Raymond, and was busy for several moments on the dashboard. "Mm-hm," he said at last. "Why, a child could take off in this thing. What's that for? Oh, I see." He mumbled at it a moment more, and then put his head over the side. "Can you fly a Camel, by any chance?" he inquired politely.

Fenton, with suppressed mirth, said he could.

"Then you escort me home," said Raymond.

"You'll catch hell over the lines, but I want to see the Old Man's face," said Fenton, and climbed into the Camel.

The two planes rose easily and headed westward. The dog-fight had petered out and the group had gone home, sad about Fenton, uncertain where Raymond had got to. The two flew high with cloud beneath them. When they came out of it they had got off the course and were behind trenches which were held by the French.

The girlish Fokker, chaperoned by the red-nosed Camel, which waggled anxious wings in incomprehensible signals, brought the poilus out of the dugouts and there was some popping off with guns. Raymond circled and came down, and Fenton followed. The French ran up with revolvers, all agog. Raymond's head appeared over the side and he removed his goggles and asked in pure French-Canadian for the loan of enough petrol to get home to his aerodrome. They recognized the accent and the uniform, and began to laugh. An officer arrived, and saw the joke. Hospitality overflowed. The visitors were borne off to battalion headquarters, a small chateau nearby, and champagne appeared, while the story spread.

They were long overdue at their aerodrome when they finally arrived there, just in time to rescue their names from the list of missing. The Flight Commander came out in his pyjamas to see and hear for himself, and there was more champagne in the mess.

━━━━━━━

Just as each pilot had his secret dread—blindness, maiming, being wounded and taken prisoner, and in Raymond's case, fire—there was hardly a man in the squadron who had not some talisman he held in superstitious favor, without which he would not fly. For one it was his old cavalryman's riding crop, another carried his baby's worn-out shoe, some wore lockets and religious medals. For Raymond it was always Jenny's most recent letter, buttoned inside his tunic. Each one was carefully destroyed when its successor arrived, so that no trace of her remained behind in his possessions.

Jenny wrote exactly as she pleased, without self-consciousness or caution. Her letters were spontaneous, artless, full of news of the people he knew, full of her love and confidence in their future. He read and re-read them with a mixture of rapture and embarrassment and incredulity. Any one of them spread their secret on every page—a girl's steadfast devotion to a soldier was nothing new to the censor. But Raymond's letters to her, addressed to Lady Jennifer Keane, and passing under the eyes of his C.O., gave nothing away beyond the most casual friendship and respectful admiration on his part, and were a perpetual exasperation to Jenny, who longed for one unguarded sentence from him to cherish in her loneliness and fortitude. It was all a part of loving Raymond. You did it at your own risk and you came all the way to him. Her headlong, imperious spirit chafed under the further discipline of their one-sided correspondence. Sometimes in a wilful mood of retaliation she tried to write in the same vein, but always tore it up and began again—it wasn't his fault—he was thinking of the C.O., who was bound to recognize her name—he wasn't in the habit of writing love letters—he'd never learned to let himself go on paper—oh, well, he was Raymond, that was all.

She kept his letters in the bottom of a bureau drawer, and re-read their arid pages hungrily and folded them again with gentle, lingering fingers, for the paper had once been warm under his hand and she had nothing else of him to touch and hold. As usual he hid behind his preoccupation with flying— his letters to her harped on his idea of inventing a plane with no blind spot, a gun that could fire *down,* an escape device such as a reliable parachute so that an uninjured pilot need not be carried helplessly to his death by a disabled plane, and something about a wireless telephone which she made no attempt to understand. She knew that he spent most of his spare time in the workshop at the aerodrome, along with several other crackpot pilot inventors, working on ingenious gadgets of one kind or another which were to revolutionize flying after the war. It would be just like him to hit on something really sound, Calvert always said, for he also got letters full of flying and the workshop. No one would be at all surprised if Raymond invented a new gun mount or some such useful gag, which would be worth a fortune if he only saw to his patents. Raymond was a wizard with machinery, Calvert would remind them with pride, you should have seen him doctor the gun when it went back on them. . . .

At this time the blind spot had become Raymond's particular preoccupation, and he gave a lot of time and thought to rigging up a mirror attached to the cowl which would show him his own tail and eliminate surprise attack from that quarter. His was the first machine in the squadron to wear one in combat, but after some skepticism and irreverent comment other men began to see its advantages and wanted mirrors on their own planes. To his obstinate conviction that there must be some easier way to find your way home, particularly after dark, than by compass and shaded landing lights, there seemed to be no answer so far—except possibly a better compass. . . .

Meanwhile his score rose to seventeen and his rank to acting captain, and the ground people claimed that they could recognize his flying style anywhere. Even the little French dog which had attached itself to his heels and understood the *patois* he talked to it knew when Raymond was coming in and would run confidently up to the right plane, ignoring all the others, and be waiting in an ecstasy of welcome when he climbed out. He always nursed and valeted the plane himself when it returned to the hangar, and his mechanics were inclined to stand back respectfully. He and the plane were one. It was not she to him, it was not even we. I've got a bad skip somewhere, he would say, crawling stiffly out of the cockpit. Or, I've been holed in my tank, for God's sake. Or, I've got a damned great piece of lead in my breech block and can't shoot any more today.

Lens was again in Allied hands, for the first time since 1914, the Americans distinguished themselves at St. Mihiel, Germany had lost practically all the ground she had taken in the dreadful spring offensive, and the Hindenburg Line was rumored punctured. Gradually it became apparent that the front was not going to stabilize again in the usual way. The Germans were on the run.

The airmen realized it first, gunning the roads choked with eastbound German transport, reporting supply dumps ablaze in the rear of the German lines, noting a thinning of the air squadrons which came up to meet them. A cautious, unspoken something which was not yet optimism was felt around the aerodromes, a sort of rising tension—once more—twice more—how many more times would they go out to combat? What were the odds remaining to them, what were their chances now, of living through it after all? Once more, twice more—deep, deep into Germany and out again, still whole, still flying, still chalking up their growing score. . . .

When St. Quentin was taken, a ghost city emptied of its 50,000 souls carried away into captivity by the retreating German army, even the civilians at home in England began to realize that something had broken, and that it was not another false dawn—the Germans were rattled now, desperate, disorganization was setting in, peace proposals were being made—they wouldn't talk peace while they were winning. But there was little visible rejoicing in London and Paris. People went about their daily lives a little grimly, unwilling to go off half-cocked. Austria wanted terms, Bulgaria collapsed—Dixmude was gathered in, then Passchendaele. . . .

Until at last even Raymond began to look ahead, or rather had to try not to think ahead, and had to suppress within himself a rising hope where the knowledge of Jenny lived. It almost began to look as though he might be some good to Jenny after all.

It was just another day's work when he went up on a foggy afternoon in the middle of October for a look round behind Cambrai. He was paired with Fenton, and they ran into a flock of seven German planes and took them on. Fenton went down early in the fight, this time for keeps, and Raymond ticked off two Germans to keep him company. Four more drew off and limped away, but the fifth hung on. For what seemed like hours, but was only minutes of air time, the duel went on, in and out of cloud, diving, climbing, zigzagging, saving ammunition for the kill—Raymond's controls were giving trouble and the plane moved sluggishly, so that he got a spray of lead over his shoulder which struck the dashboard and broken glass from the instruments spattered up into his face.

One fragment struck and cracked the left glass of his goggles, and a warm trickle ran down into his collar, and there was a prickling pain from temple to jaw. Missed my eye, he thought. That's luck. He was losing height rapidly, and the German was still there, apparently as fresh as ever, crowding him. Another burst of lead struck his engine and flame flickered up where the tracer bullets landed, and his stomach fluttered with his own particular private dread —fire. Blood was running into his goggles now, so that it was hard to see, and his lips were salty with it. The engine coughed and quit, and there was a screaming of wind in the wires as he fell, and the machine-gun behind him chattered on.

Getting dizzy, he thought impatiently—falling too fast— tail going round—makes your head swim—I shall be sick in a minute—bleeding like a pig, everything's red—no, it's the fire, gaining—I heard of a man who got out on the wing and flew lopsided and kept the flames the other side—not for me, I can't see well enough—wisht I was a German now, they have parachutes—sometimes—if I get out of this by God I'll invent a parachute that will work—I'll never fly without one again, after this war is over, it's suicide—mustn't jump without one, though—got to take what comes, but there must be an easier way to die than this—wires shot away, damn him, I can't get my nose up—poor Jenny, we almost made it, didn't we—I wonder what's below, won't know till I hit it— ground coming up very fast, but I can't see much—can't see beyond my own prop—did he get my eyes?— well, here it is, *shot down in flames*—so now I know—let's not blackout yet, I might still manage a pancake—

He landed hard, with a crashing jolt, and heard the roar of flames in the silence that followed, and flung himself over the side of the cockpit with another sickening jar and began to crawl.

A long time later he roused slowly, unwillingly, and put up a hand to the sticky mess where his goggles were—jagged pain made him gasp as he pulled them away, feeling as though his face came with them. Was it dark, or was he blind? He waited, motionless, holding his breath—a few feet away in front of him the ground was streaked with moonlight. Some sight remained to him, then. He raised his head by main force—saw the broken, ragged boughs of a small copse, and the smouldering ruin of his burnt-out plane.

They'll come for me, he thought, and dragged himself to his knees. They always come—for souvenirs. Must get away from here. His head throbbed and reeled, but the idea of hiding persisted in him, holding him to consciousness. Crawl off into the woods a bit, away from the plane—no one could tell that he hadn't been burned up in it—get away—hide— no time to rest now—keep moving. . . .

He paused, listening. Footsteps, light and uncertain, were

coming towards him through the dim moonlight. No German walked like that. He waited, gasping with effort, laboring against the pain and dizziness. A small dark-clad figure showed in the faint glow near the plane, cast a shadow among the shadows under the trees.

"Mam'zelle," said Raymond quietly, and with a little sound quickly stifled she ran towards him.

He was flooded with anxious, whispered French and answered in the accented Canadian speech he had learned from his first gun crew. She understood, her hands were warm and strong, she mentioned her father's barn, not far away, the hayloft, bandages, a light, some food—sanctuary. There were no Germans near by, she said they were beyond—to the west. No main roads ran near. They might not come for the plane, they were seldom seen any more in the neighborhood, though it was said they were nearer now than they had been. Some town had been retaken by the Allies—yes, some town the Germans had held a long time—they would fall back—but not yet—there would be time for him to rest a little—to eat—to dress the wound—yes, yes, time to hide, he was to leave it to her—her father was willing, she had told him she was coming out to the plane with the cart—he was old, but very brave—he would be glad—he would help them decide what to do.

Hazily Raymond allowed her to help him to his feet, swayed, bore heavily on her thin shoulder with a mumbled apology—it was of the height and fragility of a child—and devoted himself to the grim task of putting one foot in front of the other over rough ground in the dark. After what seemed like hours of this, they came to a lane and a crude cart. He fell into it, and it moved forward jerkily at a snail's pace, raising all the echoes. Years later, hands pulled him out again, held him up, urged him forward until he sank into sweet dry hay and fainted again.

Pain forced him awake, and he was lying on his back in the hay with a lantern being held close to his head, and the girl was bathing the wound. The warm water in the basin beside him was the color of blood. He lay still, breathing rather noisily, and heard her say, "I am sorry—sorry you woke up —I have got to sew it. I will do the best I can."

He looked up at her in the lantern light—he could still see with his right eye—and her young face was perfectly white, even the lips, with dark, dilated eyes.

"Don't worry, it can't hurt worse than it does," he said grimly, and saw the gleam of the needle and the length of thread between her hands, and blackness closed in again.

The sharp bite of wine on his tongue came next—he coughed and swallowed with difficulty. An arm was behind his head and the cup stayed at his lips. "Once more," the girl's voice said gently. "Try to take a little more." He swallowed again, and again, and she eased him back against the hay. The wound was covered with a bandage now, which came over the whole left side of his head, and there was a strong smell of wine everywhere, for she had used it to sterilize, having nothing else.

"Is my eye gone?" he asked as soon as he could find the breath to speak.

"No. But the wound runs very close, and there will be a long scar. I did the best I could. It took seven stitches. You have lost a lot of blood. You must stay quiet a while."

"I can't stay here. It will mean trouble for you if they come this way."

"Trouble!" Her voice was scornful. "We are used to that!"

"What's that noise?" he said, listening. "Guns!"

"Yes. Nearer now. We think they are on this road. My father has gone to find out what he can in the village."

He tried to sit up, and she pressed him back gently into the hay.

"Not yet. It is still a long way off. My father will warn you in time. As soon as you are able to travel we will take the cart—I will go along as protection—"

"Where?"

"There is a way—others have escaped—if we are not already cut off."

"How many others?"

"Two that I know of. Of course we cannot always be sure that they are successful. But we try."

When she had gone away with the lantern he lay very still in the dark, tense with the effort to think clearly. Once he had known very well exactly what he meant to do if anything like this happened to him. Now his carefully laid plans were all a jumble of pain and darkness and confusion and urgency, and he could not sort them out behind the jumping agony in his head. The idea of Jenny's letter returned to him first—it was buttoned as usual inside his tunic. He fumbled a hand in to it—rather a short one this time, written on thin bluish paper. Impossible to touch a match to it in the midst of all this hay. He set to work patiently in the dark, with short intervals for rest. When he had finished, the letter lay in minute shredded bits, a mere mouse's nest of fragments in the hay.

Then after another long pause a second duty occurred to him. With unbelievable effort, he roused again and removed his identity disc and pushed it down, down into the hay. What else?

While he was wondering the day broke, and the girl returned with soup in a little pail and a hunk of bread. The guns seemed less noticeable in the dawn, and there was no news. Her father had not returned. She sat beside him patiently in the hay, while the hot, still hours slid by with the mutter of gunfire—gave him water to drink, and presently a bit more food—boiled fowl, a mouthful of cabbage. It was growing dark again in the barn when he heard her stir and said uneasily, "Are you going?"

"Not for long. I hear my father, I think—at last."

Noise grew and grew outside his consciousness—confusion, voices, commands—a rumbling of motor cars and tramping of many feet—too late now—the retreat was upon him. He heard the girl's voice, high, shrill, hysterical—heard something like a slap, and she was still. Men poured into the barn, rustling through the hay, shouting, swearing, barking orders —men who spoke German.

Hands were laid on him roughly, he was pulled to his feet, stood sick and swaying while a light was flashed in his face. Fenton would have minded this more, perhaps, as his particular nightmare was being taken prisoner—had Fenton died, or was it happening to him too, somewhere? German orders were incomprehensible, but German manhandling was easy enough to understand. Too many of them had hold of him at once, he tried to keep his footing, stumbled, and they let him fall heavily, striking the bandaged side of his head on a German boot, so that oblivion came again.

5. CHRISTMAS AT FARTHINGALE. 1918.

SHOT DOWN IN FLAMES. THE NEWS CAME TO
Calvert at Farthingale in a letter from Raymond's CO only
a few days before the Armistice. Two specks in the sky above
him which Raymond never saw turned into two Camels
which arrived in time to engage and down the single Fokker
which had done for him and to mark the inaccessible spot
where he fell, and his burning plane. Dreadful news, which
quenched the family excitement and joy over the end of
the war and laid a heavy hand on the preparations for a
Christmas that in spite of the loss of Archie would hold for
some of them reunion and fulfillment. Virginia was being
what everyone called Magnificent, and there was hope that
in Oliver's and Calvert's case no permanent damage had
been done. Even with Archie's death, they knew that for so
large a family they had got off very lightly.

Dinah arrived in England with Jeff almost simultaneously
with the Armistice, and was staying at Farthingale where

Bracken came for a brief holiday after witnessing the doings at Paris which ended hostilities. Phoebe had not seen her infant son since she sailed on the *Lusitania* three years before. He was five now, a thoughtful, dignified child with his father's long head and Phoebe's level eyes. Dinah had played fair and not tried to usurp his mother's place. He was quite clear in his mind as to his relationship with Phoebe, and understood that she had gone to help nurse wounded soldiers as Dinah couldn't do, because Dinah was such a crock and had fainted in the middle of the floor and been sent home—just in time, as it happened, to keep him company. Phoebe's photograph had kept her image plain, and he recognized her at once and went to her without hesitation when she entered the living-room at Farthingale on a November afternoon.

It was Phoebe who was self-conscious and uncertain of her welcome, idiotically nervous of this meeting with a child who even at her breast had seemed a stranger after his father's sudden death. It was not that she didn't like children —but she had had very little experience with them at home or in her bachelor-girl days in New York before her marriage, and she was not instinctively a maternal woman. Children were people to her, not toys or puppies, but people from a slightly different world with which she was not on intimate terms. She got along well enough with Virginia's on her rare visits to Farthingale by treating them with respect or letting them alone, and they admired her and were polite and flattered when she made conversation with them. Unlike Dinah, whose heart had never grown up, Phoebe had no inborn knack with children. And she had always been a little afraid of Jeff as a baby for fear he might be sick, or start crying, or she might drop him, or do the wrong thing.

She had reckoned without the unaccountable lump which rose in her throat at sight of the sturdy, independent little figure which advanced across the carpet to meet her. Phoebe went down on her knees and held out her arms, wordlessly, and Jeff returned her kiss without shyness or reservations.

Then he saw Oliver.

None of them quite believed what happened then, but they all witnessed it, all of them gathered in the drawing-room that drab autumn afternoon at tea time—Sally was there, and Sosthène, Dinah and Bracken and Calvert, and Virginia who had come down from London with Phoebe and Oliver for the first week-end of Dinah's homecoming. No one had yet said, "This is Oliver." No one had time. Oliver had come into the room behind Phoebe and paused a little distance from where she knelt for Jeff's greeting. When Jeff's eyes first fell on him, over Phoebe's shoulder, the child left her without ceremony, his face alight with something like recognition.

"Hullo," he said informally, and Oliver said "Hullo," and held out both hands. Jeff put his hands in Oliver's and looked back over his shoulder at the rest of them, smiling and confident, and somehow very proud. "It's Oliver," he told them gently. "My mother's married to him." And he looked up again into the composed face above him, at the red tabs and bright ribbons on the breast of the khaki tunic. "Are you a general yet?"

"Not yet, old boy, give me time," said Oliver easily, not showing any of the surprise which had immobilized everyone else in the room, at Jeff's assumption of lifelong acquaintance. With his arm around the child's shoulders, they moved together towards the fire, and Oliver sat down in a big chair, Jeff leaning on the arm of it beside him.

"Will you teach me to shoot off a gun?" said Jeff, as though resuming a conversation between old friends.

"Absolutely."

"You aren't wearing one now."

"Don't need one at home like this."

"And ride a horse? Will you teach me to ride a horse?"

"Positively. If we can find one that will stand up."

Jeff laughed, and swung on the arm of the chair.

"You're just like I thought," he said. "Have you got a dog?"

"Not just at the moment. We'll attend to that now that the war is over. What kind of a dog shall we get?"

Beyond the two by the fire, who had become oblivious to them, the family pulled itself together, searched each other's eyes, and tried to rationalize its feelings.

Oliver had given them the cue—Oliver the soldier, fatalistic, more or less unread, but accustomed to the margins of human behavior at times of crisis, as well as to the humdrum routine of the Regulations. Oliver was willing to accept without any fuss that he was somehow already known to the child Phoebe had borne to another man, rebelliously loving himself every step of the way. Oliver warned them by his own casual behavior not to make a song and dance about it and create hurdles in Jeff's mind.

Phoebe, her moment of brief glory rudely shaken, rose from her knees where Jeff had left her and went to sit rather shakily on the sofa beside Sally. There was nothing rational, ever, about anything to do with herself and Jeff. The whole thing was some sort of fantastic mistake, a wild Olympian joke, a perpetual boomerang, just because she had married one man in spite of loving another and had tried conscientiously to be a wife and mother and build a life of her own. When Miles was snatched away like that, she was adrift again, rudderless, confused, frustrated, still loving Oliver, still drawn to him, forsaking all others—until on another fall of the cards it was suddenly possible, and their life together had begun. It had seemed as though Jeff, the stranger, the accident, the left-over from that brief interlude with Miles, would have no place here. And now look.

"But he must have seen a photograph of Oliver," Sally was saying gropingly.

"I haven't got one," Dinah told them with some reluctance. "Oliver won't sit. Oh, a few snapshots, of course, but he's never taken any notice of those."

Tea came in just then, followed by an assortment of children from upstairs who had been banished till after Jeff's first meeting with his mother had been safely accomplished —Virginia's Irene, Nigel, and Evadne, and Oliver's Hermione, who went straight to his chair and flung her arms possessively about his neck and kissed him. Jeff looked on at the greeting with frank interest, and Oliver said, "You know, Hermione was my daughter before I married your mother."

"Then I must be related to her," said Jeff, ready to be pleased.

"You are, yes, in a sort of way, I suppose."

"Not *blood*-related," Hermione corrected at once. "You're my step-brother. That doesn't mean anything."

"Means you belong to the same family from now on," Oliver told them firmly. "It's rather a large family—room for everyone in it. And that somehow reminds me—" Shedding the children, he rose and went to Phoebe where she sat beside Sally, who was pouring out tea. "Kendrick is in London. Remember him?"

"Yes, of course." Phoebe looked up with a reminiscent smile. "On the *Lusitania*. Rather a dear. I'd like to see him again."

"Saw him myself this morning before I left town. He'll be round about for a while, he's had a bad go of influenza. He has promised to do everything possible about tracing Raymond through the Red Cross at Geneva, but he says that if

Raymond got gathered up in the retreat there's no telling where he is now or when we'll hear. Unless he is able to let us know himself, that is."

"You mean, if he wasn't killed in the crash," Calvert said steadily.

"Yes. Wounded or a prisoner, he may still turn up. A lot of missing people are turning up, you know."

There was a little silence, while the tea cups went round. *Shot down in flames,* the pitiless squadron record ran. *Missing, believed dead.* The words were almost audible in the firelit room behind the clink of china and silver. *Shot down in flames. . . .*

"He was one of the ones we needed to go on with," said Sally after a moment.

———

Camilla had steadfastly resisted the temptation to devote herself to Calvert at Farthingale by relinquishing her work at the St. James's Square hospital. Calvert was progressing as well as could be expected, pampered by Sally and Virginia's household, sustained by Sosthène's male presence and the week-end or tea-time visits of Camilla and Jenny. But just as Jenny had wisely prophesied long ago, the wounded were not miraculously healed over night by the Armistice, the hospital drudgery must go on, and the need for nursing would abate only slowly. Jenny was kept so busy, she said, that they saw very little of her, and for all their devotion to her the twins never suspected what the news about Raymond had meant to her. Her thinness and whiteness made Calvert's heart ache, and a new listlessness in her manner had set Camilla worrying that Winifred was demanding too much of Jenny's strength as a willing VAD, but Jenny scoffed at the idea of a holiday and assured them that she was as strong as a horse.

Camilla too had found a certain refuge in the hard work in London, convincing herself over and over again that to see Sosthène only now and then and from the necessary distance was no real help to her longing for him, and that she was better off away. Both girls from different reasons and unknown to each other felt a growing dread of the Christmas season as it came upon them with its burden of memories from the year before.

Archie would not be there to read off the presents, and as it was impossible to conceive of anyone else doing it in his place the ceremony was tacitly dispensed with. The tree, fully trimmed, would stand in its accustomed place at the end of the drawing-room, but the gifts would all be distributed informally during the day. The floor would be cleared for dancing as usual, and the gramophone would make a cheerful noise. Dinah and little Jeff were entitled to a semblance of the old-time family Christmas. Bracken would come back from Paris, Oliver and Phoebe would come down from London, bringing the convalescent Kendrick with them for a breath of country air after his influenza, and as many as could be spared from the Hall were of course expected. Jenny had tried unaccountably to beg off, but as the Duke had accepted with enthusiasm she was overruled and would have to come. And there would be enough children present to keep the day from bogging down.

Although two people were missing from last year's dinner table the total count, with Edward home and the Floods both there, would be higher this time. Camilla looked slowly from face to face as the soup came in, noticing that through some freak of absent-mindedness on Virginia's part or some deliberate intention, most of last year's guests had been put in the same chairs that they had occupied a year ago. Calvert was in Raymond's place tonight, between herself and Virginia. Sosthène had taken over Archie's duties as host. But

Adrian Carteret was on her left again, with young Daphne
beyond, wearing her seventeen-year-old-heart on her sleeve
for him, which he seemed to find both surprising and touching and he was handling it very well. Fabrice was between
Gerald and the newcomer, Kendrick, whom everybody at
once liked very much for himself as well as because he had
stood beside Phoebe while the deck of the *Lusitania* tilted
and sank beneath them. He had a quirky, laughing face with
pointed eyebrows, and carried himself like an officer-born
in the becoming Red Cross uniform he had worn all through
the war, driving ambulances he himself equipped and presented a little faster than they could be shot out from under
him. An only son, he had drawn freely on the resources of an
old Philadelphia family fortune, and had also spent himself
recklessly in the service of the wounded. When he went home
he would be regarded as a hero, and he more or less deserved
it, but it would never go to his head. Nothing went to Kendrick's head, not fear, nor liquor, nor women.

Within a few hours of his first meeting with Fabrice, the
family had begun to watch with a growing interest which
threatened soon to become breathless, as it dawned on them
one by one that he was actually laughing at her. Not un-
kindly, not rudely, but as though he found her inexpressibly
funny, like something on the stage which was not meant to be
quite real. She at once smelled his money, and she liked his
looks, and she began accordingly to flirt with him. Instead
of falling flat on his face as he was expected to do, Kendrick
not only flirted right back at her but went her one better
at it, as though it was a kind of game, as though he was
one move ahead of her, as though he had played the same
scene before. Bracken was the first to catch on, and he murmured delightedly to Phoebe, "He's got her pitch and queered
it. He's treating her like a high-priced tart, and she's falling for it." Phoebe grinned at him. "Oh, is that how you

treat them?" she said. Gerald was sulking, but nobody felt very sorry for him.

Jenny in her chair next to Oliver, wearing a pretty frock and her mother's pearls, was trying not to think at all, but it wasn't a success. A year ago this very minute she had been scarcely aware of Raymond sitting beside Virginia at the end of the table—the place where Calvert sat now, trying to catch her eyes across his glass. But the relentless evening stretched ahead of her with its inevitable milestones—the way Raymond had come towards her, with Bracken, when the men returned to the drawing-room—his delight over the watch and the mechanical insect—the winding of the gramophone between glasses of champagne—the strange, gay, exciting left-handed waltz—Bracken running up the stairs to see what had become of him—her own first sight of him on the edge of the bath-tub looking sick above the scarlet splashes on the porcelain—Phoebe's anxious face and her own aching arm as she sat beside him with her fingers on the artery—the long battle for his life after the doctor came, and the pale, triumphant dawn—suppose Raymond had died then, under her hand—better for him like that, perhaps—better than being shot down in flames. . . .

Oliver was saying something to her. The eyes she lifted to his face were swimming helplessly with tears.

"Everybody feels like that tonight, for one reason or another," he said gently. "Drink your wine."

She obeyed him silently, and knew that he noticed how her hand shook.

"It's worse for Virginia," she got out as soon as she could. "It's worse for her than for anybody here. Archie was—" She gulped and steadied again. "—was such a lamb."

"Well, we had him," said Oliver with a sigh. "They can't really take him away from us. And I expect he was very tired."

"Yes," said Jenny. "Everybody's tired enough to die, I think." But her mind fumbled and refused the comfort his words might have brought. They can't really take him away from us. No one you have loved, that is, can be entirely lost. But no one knew she had loved Raymond. Virginia had the support and sympathy of all her world in her grief. She could talk about Archie, she could always say, Do you remember how he used to . . . Do you remember when he said. . . . Do you remember the day we all . . . But there was no one for Jenny to talk to about Raymond except Calvert, and that wouldn't be safe. Raymond was lost to her because there was no one to share his memory with, or her own grief. She had to bear it alone, locked up inside her, till she choked to death. . . .

"My dear kid," said Oliver's quiet voice, "count ten, and take a deep breath. If you begin, it will set us all off, you know."

Jenny answered him automatically, out of months and years of difficult self-control, since long before Raymond.

"I'm all right," she said, and lifted her chin, and gave him a rather shaky smile. "And anyway," she added defiantly with a glance across the table, "it's not what you think."

"Oh, that," said Oliver easily, comprehending. "Nobody thinks about that any more. Take a week off. Phoebe and I had in mind something ridiculous like Cheltenham or Malvern—not for the waters, of course, just to rusticate. Come with us."

"Thank you," she said with real gratitude for his kindness and no intention of accepting it. "We'll see what Winifred says."

"I can tell you that beforehand!" Oliver replied darkly.

In the drawing-room after dinner with the gramophone going and what Virginia had begun with a pathetic matronly air to call the Younger Ones dancing to it, Phoebe looked round to find Kendrick slipping into the place beside her on the sofa.

"*Well!*" she said, and raised her eyebrows at him. "You do seem to be enjoying yourself!"

"I never had so much fun in my life," he said simply.

"Are you serious?" she asked with a lingering incredulity, and he grinned impudently back at her.

"One can't be serious about Fabrice. But I'm going to marry her, if that's what you mean."

"You're—!" Phoebe was speechless.

"Are you surprised?" asked Kendrick, pretending to be surprised that she was.

"But she—she's—"

"I know she is!" he chortled. "Nobody ever was more so! Like one of those unbelievable little creatures in a French farce that you want to buy as a souvenir and take home in your pocket! I've always thought that if you could tame one of those bits of nonsense and have it round the house—" He lit a cigarette and threw the match into the fireplace with an expert, carefree flick. "Of course I shall probably have to lay her across my knee now and then, but nobody minds that."

"How will Philadelphia react to her, do you think?"

"It won't get the chance to do any reacting for some time to come. I shall be going back to Geneva next week—there's still a lot to be done there. Geneva, I promise you, will be only too pleased!"

"So you really have got the courage to take it on," she murmured.

"Sure I have! She only wants a good spanking, and I'm the man to attend to that!" He laughed, but his eyes were tender. "She's the most divinely *obvious* thing I ever saw. But once she learns who's boss—I'll be a lucky guy!"

"Well, if you think so—" Phoebe said uncertainly.

"Should I do it right and ask Aunt Sally first?" he inquired.

"Yes, I think you should," she agreed, to see what would happen, and he rose at once and crossed the room to where Sally sat, and made her a little bow.

"Madame—I do myself the honor to demand your granddaughter's hand in marriage."

Sally was not taken by surprise. She rested upon him her deep violet gaze and nodded slowly.

"It will serve her right," she said, and Kendrick laughed and kissed her hand with easy grace and went off to where Fabrice was bickering prettily with Gerald in a corner, and asked her to dance.

She accepted with alacrity and a sidelong glance at Gerald, and Kendrick murmured against her hair as they danced away, "Congratulate me. I am going to be married."

He could not see her face, and it was a moment before she said coolly, "To whom?"

"To *you'm!*" he crowed, and swung her in a wide pirouette and swept her back again closer than before. "I have just spoken to Granny, and received her blessing. *You* have nothing whatever to say about it."

She chuckled, and her cheek touched his.

"How crrrrazy you are!" she said admiringly.

"That's what *they* think!"

"Who?"

"Your family. 'Why on earth do you want to marry *her?*' is written all over them. But *we* know why, don't we."

"Do we?"

"Because it will be fun." The words were warm against her ear. "Because you're up against somebody your size, this time, that you can't lead round by the nose, and life is going to be very exciting and full of surprises—for both of us."

"Will you give me a diamond ring?" she whispered.

"Down to the knuckle!"

"And a pearl necklace?"

"Down to—"

"Please!" squealed Fabrice, and melted against him, weak with delight and surrender, and Virginia, who had always considered herself unshockable, looked at Phoebe, who made a resigned sort of face.

Sally, brooding beautifully on the sofa, murmured to Sosthène, "I could not have chosen better for her myself. She will learn a thing or two now!"

And Sosthène said, smiling, "Will he beat her?"

"Ah, no, there will be no need. She will worship him. It is in her to worship, on her knees. She needs the high hand. And she will be a good wife to him after a while, you will see." The shadowed violet eyes travelled on among the dancers. "Daphne too—and that Carteret boy—so soon. She is very young—but as I remember, Virginia was young too, and never once looked back."

"There is supposed to be another woman for him—widow of a brother officer, I believe," remarked Sosthène, who knew everything by a sort of osmosis, but rarely made revelations.

"Are they promised?"

"Not yet, perhaps."

"Then no harm is done," said Sally. "After tonight it will be Daphne, for him. It is very flattering to a man when he has not seeked it—sought, do I mean? —and when she is so young. He is taken, you see? He is a little sorry—one is always sorry for the very young. He is kindness itself—he feels a little unworthy—he wants her never to be unhappy because of him. It is a good beginning, always. No man of any worth can be anything but humble when the woman, especially so young, is made so happy and so shining just to see him."

"Then you do not subscribe, *mon âme,* to the old rule that says man should always be allowed to pursue while woman flees?"

"Ah, bah!" said Sally, and flicked his sleeve with her fingers. "*You,* that was born knowing, you ask me that! If she does not cling—if she does not demand—if she is just, oh, so happy to see him—it is irresistible. *You,* that have always known that!"

"Since my cradle." He smiled into her eyes.

And Camilla, dancing by in Bracken's arms, saw the smile and felt it like a cramp in her heart, and thought with something like exasperation, Why do I care so much? Why do I care *at all?* It's not being jealous, it's nothing so simple as that. To be jealous you must have some hope of possessing something and dread to lose it. I have never possessed anything of Sosthène. But to see them like that together is always like having something snatched out of my hands again—something that was never there. Each time I have *less,* like taking something away from nothing. Mathematically, you can't do it. I've no right to Sosthène, and he has no need of me. Or—has he? Confronted again by the blank high wall of mystery which surrounded Sosthène and Sally, her thoughts fell back from it again, confused and embarrassed. You didn't think about that, whatever else you did. You didn't allow yourself to speculate, or even to contemplate. You hid your eyes and covered your ears. What was between them was nobody's business but their own.

But if this—this obsession for Sosthène, if you agreed to call it that, was just some sort of hallucination, like a school-girl crush, which came of unnatural war tensions and fatigue, in times when everybody was a little off center anyway, oughtn't it to begin to die down pretty soon? Oughtn't she to be able by now to see it for what it was, and dismiss it, live through it, get free of it, and be herself again in a more rational, familiar world where Calvert was all she really cared about, and after him the music she was born with? It was humiliating to go on being enslaved by emotions she had hardly known existed, to a man who had never made the slightest return—well, yes, he was kind, he praised her music, his eyes lingered, his lips smiled—but surely one could not be in love with a man one almost never saw alone, and who could not speak one word to acknowledge one's devotion?

Camilla knew very little about love, for her reading had not been in that direction, and she had received few feminine confidences. In her ignorance she had tried at first to label her feeling for Sosthène infatuation, and waited for it to die for lack of nourishment. More than a year, now—and the enchantment still held her fast. What would Bracken think if he knew? Bracken had an answer to most things. But if she told Bracken this he would surely doubt her sanity. Even Calvert seemed puzzled and uncertain what to say, and they seldom referred to it in their most private talks. It lay there between them, the first shadow across their common path— her love for Sosthène.

Calvert's case was simple enough. Calvert wanted Jenny, and Jenny was free but kept on saying No. They couldn't quite see why. She was tired, of course, and probably couldn't think quite straight. Nobody was thinking quite straight any more, it was the war, and then the end of the war, and a sort of keyed-up let-down. Calvert was trying everything they could think of—he offered to stay on in England, where she could go on with her work among the wounded—he offered to take her right out of England, to Williamsburg or the South of France, and make her forget the war—anything, anywhere, in the world. But Jenny went on saying No. Calvert had bad times when he thought it was because of his leg, which would never be right again. But they both knew better than that. Lots of Jenny's friends were marrying men much worse off than Calvert. Jenny said No because she didn't love him. To Camilla that was incomprehensible. Sometimes she was angry with Jenny, and sometimes she was sorry for her. And sometimes she couldn't help wondering if Gerald was still at the bottom of it. . . .

The music stopped abruptly, and Camilla looked about

her, dazed by her own wandering thoughts. Kendrick and Fabrice were standing in front of Sally, looking radiant and self-satisfied. Sosthène was handing round glasses of champagne. Fabrice and Kendrick seemed to have got engaged. Camilla's eyes met Calvert's across the room and saw that his face had gone quite white. She knew then that he too must have wondered if Gerald was not still at the bottom of Jenny's No.

━━━━━━━

Farthingale was so full of reunited married house guests who had to be together, and assorted single ones who could not be expected to share a room, that Camilla and Jenny had overflowed contentedly enough on to the top floor, where each had what was once a housemaid's bedroom. With Virginia's diminished war-time staff there was plenty of that kind of accommodation, and in Virginia's house such quarters were far more comfortable than in most grander establishments, like the Hall. Next door to the two girls was the smiling, competent Melchett, whose name was Lucy, and who had slept in that same small room since before Virginia came to the house as a bride, and who tonight had put hot water bottles in each of their narrow white beds and laid out their nighties on the turned-back covers and was now tactfully invisible behind her own door.

The girls climbed the last flight of stairs wearily, in silence, and kissed each other good-night with affection in the passage, neither of them inclined for a bedtime chat. Camilla felt unaccountably exhausted and her light was soon out.

Jenny had forgotten to bring up anything to read, and the former inhabitant of her room had not gone in for literature. A yellowing copy of *The Queen*, forgotten in one of the dresser drawers, presented little of interest, except a dismal reminder of the faraway days when people hunted and had new clothes and dined out in formal dress. Jenny dropped it on the floor beside the bed and lay and stared at the ceiling, which is never a wise thing to do at any time. From the other side of the partition against which her bed was set, came the gentle rhythm of Melchett's virginal snores. On Camilla's side all was at once reposeful silence.

Well, Christmas was over at last, and Virginia had got through it splendidly, and the children had had a good time, and it looked as though they were rid of Fabrice, and Gerald was left holding the bag, which was probably just what he needed, and he would doubtless not take it too hard, and Adrian Carteret was rather gone on Daphne, as anyone could see, and nobody would object to that when the time came, it was very suitable. Lucky Daphne. Lucky Fabrice. Don't grudge it them, somebody has a right to be happy now. Not for Camilla, though, and not for Jenny. Not for Calvert either, if he persisted in being in love with the empty husk which was Jenny Keane. It was a pity one couldn't somehow see one's way to oblige anybody so nice and so deserving as Calvert. No—oh, no, it wasn't to be thought of, first because one would feel such a hypocrite, second because it would keep Raymond always like a knife in one's side, twisting, when the only thing to do was to try and let him go now, try not to remember and grieve and ache, try to close a door on that part of oneself and be of some use without him. And thirdly—it was something she tried never to think of but never succeeded—thirdly, Raymond might still be heard from, even now.

And at the obstinate, painful stirring of that old, forlorn hope, Jenny put out the light and turned on her side and hid her face in the pillow and lay still, waiting for it to subside again. One mustn't begin thinking about that. . . .

Men did still turn up, though, the insistent whisper in her brain went on. Men who had lost their memories, or their identity discs, or had been taken deep into Germany with the retreat and had not been reported to the Red Cross in the confusion. Men still came back, every day. . . . How many men? What were the odds, now? But they *did* come back, and German hospital and prison records did get lost and burned in the retreat. . . . Thousands of women, telling themselves the same thing tonight, and for how many of them would it come true?

Shot down in flames. But they didn't *have* to die, when that happened, they sometimes—yes, they were sometimes like the man with the burns who had been in the yellow room after Raymond's operation—they lingered for weeks in agony and then died in spite of all you could do, and they were better off dead—and in Germany now nobody was going to bother to do much about men like that. . . .

Jenny pulled the pillow over her head and lay tense and motionless, at grips with the old, inevitable horror—Raymond in a German hospital, burned as she had seen men burned, untended, longing for death, and nobody doing the little that could be done for him—Raymond, dying of burns alone in Germany, with no one to care for him. . . .

She knew that this was morbid and cowardly and hysterical —all the things she most despised in other people. But in her present overwrought condition, once it got started like this she could only live through it, like living through a pain, till it let go. Raymond—even his name was solid and comforting—Raymond, help me again—help me to bear it and not make a sound, I mustn't give us away now. . . .

Teeth set, hands clenched tight, she fought again with quick, shallow breaths the need to fly all to pieces just once, and sob and moan and make a noise, an undignified, humiliating, luxurious, grovelling noise. He got well for me once—

he could do it again—he knows I want him back, no matter what's happened to him—there's nobody else, if there isn't Raymond—it's this not *knowing*—it's the burns I've seen, it's the other men dying in spite of me, it's the *helplessness*, it's not *knowing*, it's *imagining* things—Raymond—*Raymond*. . . .

In the next room Camilla woke with a start and sat up in bed, listening. The sound went on, like some one crying —and yet not like any crying Camilla had ever heard before. It must be Melchett, crying—had Melchett lost some one in the war? Or was it—Jenny! Camilla landed on her feet on the floor and reached for the light and her robe.

In the passage she met Melchett coming uncertainly out of her own door in curlpapers and a flannel nightgown. They stared at each other a moment, frozen, in the dim light which came from the open doors behind them, with Jenny's room between them, where the sound was.

Melchett opened dry lips.

"It's—Lady Jenny," she whispered.

"Yes—do you think I ought to go in?"

"Somebody ought—miss. She'll be ill like that. Hadn't I better slip down to the kitchen and make a pot of tea?"

"Oh, please do," said Camilla, thankful for the homely, sane presence of the kindly little woman. "Yes, bring up a tray—leave it on the floor outside the door, and then try to get your sleep, I'll see what I can do."

She tapped on the door, got no reply from within, where the sound never stopped, turned the knob quietly and entered the dark room.

Jenny lay face down in the bed with the pillow over her head, gasping, sobbing, strangling, moaning, making uncouth, subhuman, animal noises of grief that Camilla had never imagined before. She closed the door and knelt beside the bed without turning on the light, removed the smother-

ing pillow and laid a gentle arm across Jenny's shoulders.
There was no pause in the terrible crying, and there were
words in it, or seemed to be. Shrinking a little, but forcing
herself to hear, Camilla leaned closer. The slim body under
her arm shook and shuddered, the hand flung out against
her was damp and clammy. She caught it in her own warm
one, bending over the bed. Gradually the word dawned on
her, one word repeated again and again, in an ecstasy of hopelessness—*Raymond—Raymond—Raymond*. . . .

Camilla crouched there on her knees, taking it in. So that
was it. Raymond. And no one had guessed, least of all Calvert. Raymond and Jenny. Since when? How? During the
nursing, of course. And afterwards on the day they went to
Overcreech—they hadn't had much time. But why not *tell*
anyone? Because of Calvert? That was foolish of them. *Raymond*. She felt quite numb.

For the first time then Jenny seemed to become aware of
a presence in the room. She lay suddenly very still, panting,
shivering, like a trapped thing, trying to hold her breath.

"It's all right, honey," said Camilla softly. "It's only me.
You should have told me long ago, and not tried to bear it
alone."

"He didn't want me to—tell—" Her voice came swollen
and unrecognizable.

"Didn't—? Why not?"

"He wanted—his commission—first—"

"Well, he got it."

"He thought—he seemed to think—he wasn't—good
enough—"

"Oh, nonsense, we all loved him!"

"You can't change him—"

"Were you engaged?"

"If he came back—we were going to—be married—he
promised—if he came back whole—don't ever let him know—

I did this—I'd be ashamed—it's only because of *not knowing* —if he was hurt they won't take any care of him there—you know what burns are—I—I get to imagining things—"

"Of course you do." Camilla put the pillow under Jenny's head and slid into the narrow bed beside her so that her arm was beneath Jenny, who lay against her shoulder and shook, and soon the lapel of her dressing-gown was drenched with Jenny's tears, but they came quietly now, like rain. "Tonight was bound to be too much for you," Camilla said sensibly, smoothing back Jenny's soft hair, drying her face with the edge of the sheet, cradling her like a child against her own warm body.

"You aren't—angry with me—about Calvert?" Jenny asked pathetically.

"How could I be? People can't help what happens. I must say I never guessed, or I might have made it easier for you."

"He wanted it that way."

"Well, I think he was wrong, bless him, but never mind that now. You must get away for a few days—have a chance to pull yourself together."

"You mustn't tell anybody!" Jenny clutched at her with cold little paws. *"Promise* not to give me away!"

"I promise, silly. It's perfectly normal for you to have a bit of a holiday, everybody's been advising you to."

"Will you come with me—now that you know? I wouldn't want anybody but you."

"I'll manage it somehow, if you like. Where shall we go?"

"I don't care." There was a moment's silence. Jenny was calmer now, and warmer, and had almost stopped trembling. "It's not fair on you, Camilla, you've got troubles of your own."

"They'll keep," said Camilla philosophically. "It would do me good too, to get away. Shall we go to the sea?"

"I don't care." Jenny drew a long, quavering breath, and

Camilla felt the slight body relax a little in her arms. "I'm glad you found out, I think. I was going kind of crazy alone."

"I don't wonder." Camilla tightened her arm briefly, drew Jenny closer. "Don't you worry, now, we'll sit it out together. We'll go off by ourselves and get the kinks out of us, we've earned it." She heard the clink of the tray being deposited outside the door, and Melchett's discreet retreat into her own room. "Melchett has made us some tea," she said casually. "Shall I turn on the light and bring it in?"

"I must look a sight," said Jenny ruefully.

"There's only me," said Camilla, and got out of bed and fetched in the tray.

Melchett had made little Bovril sandwiches as well, and they had a cosy munch, Jenny sitting up in bed with a knitted jumper tied round her shoulders by the sleeves, Camilla on the foot of the bed with her feet under the eiderdown, discussing with determined composure now the best place for a short holiday.

And at the back of Camilla's mind a small new knot of worry was forming—this was the end of it, for Calvert. He would have to know some time, that it was Raymond who stood in his way. And she would be the one to break it to him.

━━━━━━━━━

Calvert took it very well, as might be expected. Camilla sat with him during a silence in which he put all further hope of Jenny away, for to hope now meant to wish Raymond dead when he might still, by a miracle which happened almost daily, be heard from.

At last he turned his face towards her, unsmiling but composed, and said, "Let's go home. To Williamsburg, I mean."

"All right," said Camilla readily. "Let's."

"Dinah and Bracken are sailing the end of January. Couldn't we travel with them?"

"I'll get Bracken to fix it."

"That suits me. But what about you? Do you mind too much—leaving here for a while?"

"I don't think it matters very much where I am, so long as you're there too."

Their eyes met bleakly, and then their hands, right to left, in a quick, life-saving grip.

"We're an unlucky pair, aren't we," Calvert said at last.

"Well, at least we're both in it together."

"Yes. There's an odd sort of comfort about that."

That evening in the drawing-room the twins announced their decision to return to America when Bracken sailed next month, and Sally spoke slowly out of one of her serene silences.

"I think that is a very good idea. I am homesick too." They sat staring at her while she turned to Sosthène, who was as usual within reach of her hand and seemed entirely unsurprised at her remark. "Would you like to see the place where I was born, my dear?"

"Very much," he answered gently. "If you think it would not make you sad."

"I have a brother," said Sally musingly. "It seems strange to think of Sedgwick still there, and Melicent, with grandchildren growing up now. There is no longer any need for me to concern myself about Fabrice—once I have seen her married to that lion-tamer of hers. I should like to go home, I think."

Camilla swallowed with an almost visible effort and managed to say, "Aunt Sue will be delighted, darling, I'm taking Calvert to her. There's no one at all in her big house, though Cousin Sedgwick's is pretty full." And then, at last, against their will, her eyes met Sosthène's in a long, troubled, searching look, and wrenched away again—anywhere—but away. What would it mean to them, not to be separated after all, she was wondering blankly. What would it be like to see him day after day in Sue's house, more intimately, more continuously than ever before, and under the eyes of the whole family? Surprisingly she found no pleasure in the prospect —only a sort of apprehension and uneasiness. Sue would know before long, it was impossible to conceal anything from her. Who else? Phoebe had been able to keep her secret because Oliver was not there. And how would Sosthène be explained in Williamsburg? How would they feel about him? It was a very different background from war-time England and Virginia's casual ways. People at home would want to know who Sosthène *was*. Who was he?

"Dear little Sue," Sally was saying dreamily. "I cannot imagine Sue old, like the rest of us. Is she still in love with poor Sedgwick?"

The low-voiced question, so lightly put, seemed to go off like a cannon in the listening room. It was not a thing the family ever spoke of. Bracken, who knew the story from his mother, had somehow not realized before that Sally must have known it too.

"Dear heart, we don't—you must promise not to ask Sue things like that," he said gently, rebukingly, and Sally looked at him with swift amusement and incredulity.

"Is it *still* a secret?" she asked, smiling. "Such naïveté from everybody! I had half forgotten how charming they all are, in Williamsburg. Sosthène, my angel, you have no idea—we shall put our foot in it a dozen times a day! Such discretion, it will demand of us! Bracken, you will see about the tickets for me? I must have an outside room, be sure, and not too many stairs to the promenade deck."

"There are lifts, darling. I'll attend to it," said Bracken, looking nevertheless a trifle floored, and the twins exchanged glances over this new glimpse into unsuspected mysteries from before their time.

Knowing that Sosthène was always down early to take Mimi for her walk before breakfast, and being an early riser herself, Camilla was already in the dining-room when he came in the following morning, before anyone else had appeared.

He joined her at the sideboard with his courteous first greeting of the day and his grave, lingering look, and their elbows brushed as they served themselves from the hot dishes. Camilla suddenly set her plate down with a little bump and faced him.

"Sosthène. I don't—know what to think about this, I don't know that I like it. I never dreamed that she would ever go back to Williamsburg too."

Sosthène put down his own plate deliberately, and laid one elbow on the sideboard, his kind, amused eyes at her disposal.

"Don't you want me to come?" he said, very low.

"I don't know, I—" She paused, gazing up at him helplessly.

"Were you running away?" he asked then.

"No, not exactly. It was Calvert's idea to go back, and I don't seem to care much where I am so long as I'm of some use to him. I must stick with him now, no matter what he wants."

"Mm-*hm*," said Sosthène, with the faintest hint of satisfaction. "So now you see how it is—how no one is free."

"*They're* free," she reminded him rebelliously. "*They* decide, and we're trapped."

He shook his head, still smiling.

"They need us. That is their prison, the same as ours."

"Don't you ever—" She broke off, and felt her eyes fill foolishly, and looked down, tracing the oaken carving of the sideboard with her fingertip, tongue-tied and insurgent as always in the face of his imperturbability.

"You will feel better if you say it," said Sosthène, and her head came up defiantly, to find his brooding face very near.

For a moment she stared back at him, very much on the defensive, and without knowing it utterly defenceless and pathetic. If he had moved, if even his eyes had showed what he was thinking, she would have been in his arms. There was a moment when they both knew that, and his continued immobility stung her pride like a slap.

"I was going to say, don't you ever feel an impulse?" she demanded, hurt and ashamed. "Don't you ever feel *anything?*" And then, because he would not be goaded or drawn, but an almost invisible tightening of his lips betrayed him, quick tears spilled over and ran down her cheeks. "Oh, Sosthène, I'm sorry—I didn't mean to be rude—" She could not meet his eyes now. "I wish I could take it the way you do, but I'm not like you, I never will be, I'm not patient and philosophical and detached and decorous like you, I wish—"

"My Camille—" His hand came down, firm and warm, on her faltering fingers on the oaken grooves, his words were barely audible. "Do not make any mistake about this, I feel the same as you do. But don't wish—don't revolutionize—and don't cry. At least not now, it is nearly nine. Just wait—as I do." And when she lifted a rather blurry but dazzled face to him, he drew his forefinger lightly across her lips, like a kiss. "Wait," he said, and turned away, carrying his plate to the table.

INTERMISSION

1. SPRING IN WILLIAMSBURG. 1922.

CAMILLA SAT IN THE DEEPENING TWILIGHT BY Calvert's bed, her head against the back of the chair, her hands lying listless on its arms, her eyes half closed. She was so placed that she could watch his sleeping face, and he could see her without moving his head when he woke.

For days now, since she had brought him back from the hospital in Richmond to Sue's house, she had sat like that, watching, and at last, only this afternoon, her reluctant intelligence had forced her to accept the fact that he was not going to get well. It was a family legend how Cousin Fitz had got well after Cuba, and everyone had given him up too. But Fitz had had Gwen to get well for, and a wife, it seemed, was worth more to a man than a sister, and had a stronger hold. Calvert's leg had got worse instead of better since they left England more than three years ago, and the Richmond doctor had finally insisted on amputation. But that needn't kill a man, Grandfather Dabney had lost a leg in '64, and ap-

251

parently been none the worse for it. Grandfather Dabney got well to marry Grandmother Charlotte. Perhaps if Calvert could have married Jenny Keane. . . .

Camilla turned her head restlessly against the back of the chair. You couldn't blame Jenny. Nobody blamed Jenny. But Raymond had not come back, nor been heard from. And it was hard not to wonder, had Raymond been positively reported killed, if Jenny might perhaps have seen things a little differently—so that Calvert might have had something besides his twin to live for—and never lost his leg at all. . . .

The house was very still, she realized gradually—almost as though Calvert were already dead. Until recently Fitz's children used to come to tea and make a cheerful babble, but now even Calvert admitted that family parties exhausted him. Rhoda, fourteen, Stephen, twelve, and Sylvia, ten—nice children Fitz had, well-behaved but spirited, a little inclined to dramatize. Gwen, who came of theatrical people, said ruefully that it was the ham in them, and worried about it. Fitz, who wrote musical comedies at a safe distance from Broadway and never went there except when he had a new show coming on, said he prayed every night that he had not begot a couple of soubrettes and a tenor, but Fitz never worried about anything. Camilla, who had helped the children get up their Christmas amateur show for two years now, suspected that Fitz and Gwen had something on their hands ahead, but was secretly on the other side. Her own music was still neglected, except as family entertainment and to amuse Calvert. Her voice, she supposed, was rusty and getting old by now. You had to start young or you never got any place. So the music was gone, along with Calvert. Sosthène was gone too, back to Cannes with Sally.

Even now, Camilla could smile at the memory of Sally's impact on Williamsburg. Sally had arrived there rather in the Bernhardt tradition, in a cyclone of trunks, furs, Parisian scent, jewel-cases, Pekinese, French maids, carriage rugs, and the mysterious, tranquil Sosthène, attentive, smiling, interested, untalkative, immediately adored by the young, who had never seen a live Frenchman before, or a Pekinese.

Sue, who had been a little prepared by letters, treated him as though she was an indulgent older sister and was not at all shy of him, and he regarded her with respectful delight. Not perhaps as well preserved as Sally, certainly not dressed nor made up with any such art, Sue was still quite irresistible, with her gay smile, her pretty voice, and her neat, slender figure. Sue and Sally kissed and cried a little, on that first meeting, and for days afterwards found endless absorbing things to talk about. Their conversation, which must have been mostly Greek to Sosthène, never appeared to bore him in the least.

Sally's brother Sedgwick, an irrepressible man, called his wife's attention to the fact that the wages of Sally's sins were obviously the shining exception which proved the dull old rule, and Melicent laughed and said who *was* Sosthène, but nobody knew. Somehow, without being put into words by anybody, certainly not aided in any way by the family, the impression had seeped through Williamsburg that Sosthène was Sally's son under the rose, which was the one thing the family was sure he was not, but as everybody else seemed to like it that way and went out of their way to be kind to him in that belief, there was no point in taking any notice of it. And Sosthène, taking Mimi for her daily walks in the quiet side streets of the little town, was greeted with a sort of tactful tenderness by the elders, gazed at with friendly curiosity by the young ladies, and followed by the children, who were permitted by Mimi in a disdainful sort of way to pat her.

But Sally had found Williamsburg more ravaged by time than were the faces she had known when they were young, and when she had once viewed the ugly paved main street

with its gaunt telephone poles, dirty garages and filling sta-
tions, the corrugated iron buildings and tawdry shops which
the war-time population of the works at Penniman near by
had brought into being, she took refuge in Sue's big house
and well-tended garden, which were still unchanged, and refused to go out again, and told Sosthène not to look, for it
wasn't the same.

She stayed on through the summer of 1919, and they tried
to coax her to stay for Christmas. But she had heard from
friends in Cannes that everything was much as she had left
it there, and from her lawyers that her fortune had not suffered as much as might have been feared—and a longing for
her own possessions of a lifetime and for intimates who spoke
French and thought in the French way and remembered the
things she remembered which had happened since she was a
girl, grew upon her. "It is no use," she said to Sue, rather
sadly but with a Gallic lift of her shoulders. "I do not belong
here, really. I am only playing at coming home. My home is
there in France, where I lived so long. Here I have been dead
for forty years. I feel like a ghost." She shivered. "I haunt
myself. We will go back to Cannes."

And a week later she was gone, and with her went all the
trunks, and Mimi, and Elvire, and Sosthène.

Camilla had been in Richmond with Calvert, seeing doctors, when the decision was taken, and they hurried back to
Williamsburg at the week-end to say good-bye. Sally gave her
a diamond ring, and said she must come to Cannes as soon as
Calvert was well enough to travel with her, and make a long
visit, for the climate might do wonders for him. Camilla,
who at that time thought such a thing might be possible,
promised to come. The invitation, so sincerely meant, was
about all that gave her courage to see Sosthène go from her
like that, for they had had very little time in each other's vi-
cinity after all, owing to Calvert's continuing bad health.

None of the situations which she had dreaded had arisen, therefore, which could only be regarded as a blessing, even though at the same time it meant that she hardly ever saw him. And they could not make an opportunity during those last few days for a dozen words alone together without becoming obvious. Their good-bye was said publicly in the flurry of departure, and she had to avoid Calvert for the rest of the day for fear his unspoken sympathy would break down her precarious self-control.

And now she knew that only too soon she would be quite free to go to Cannes—alone. For what? To hang about, waiting for a look, a few words from him, while Sally's friends looked on with perhaps too knowing eyes? That wouldn't do. What was there, then, when Calvert didn't need her any more? Nothing in Williamsburg, nothing in Richmond. Their mother had got used to doing without them, and had her own social set and gave dull little luncheons and card parties. All the girls Camilla's age had married the boys they grew up with and had babies, or, accepting spinsterhood prematurely, had dried up. She was twenty-eight. An awkward, in-between sort of age, especially if you weren't married. Thirty-ish women weren't very exciting to the average man who encountered them for the first time at dinner parties or dances, unless they were like Phoebe at that age and had accomplished something outstanding. The nursing Camilla had done and her war experience didn't count. Everybody had forgotten the war. Nobody wanted to think about it any more.

When faced by any sort of dilemma, the family always thought first of Aunt Sue and then of Bracken in New York. It seemed to Camilla that there was no sort of point in burdening Sue with belated revelations concerning Sosthène, since so far her state of mind had apparently gone unnoticed and could be covered over by the perpetual anxiety about

Calvert. But Bracken might hold the solution this time. He and Dinah always spent the summer in England and then went on to the Continent, while he had a sniff round his European bureaus. Camilla seemed to remember something about a new correspondent on the Vienna post, which meant that Bracken would be going there. Vienna had the best music in the world—or used to have. Perhaps some time— perhaps next year—she might ask Bracken to take her with him to Vienna. . . .

She may have dozed, in the big chair. She roused to something like a draught of cold air and sat up, glancing towards the window which stood open beyond the bed. The sun had gone down. Her eyes went back to Calvert's face—she leaned forward, listening—she reached to lay her hand on his—and knew with a despair too deep for tears that he had slipped away in his sleep.

For another ten minutes she sat there alone, dry-eyed, numb, and cold. It was too soon. She had not expected it quite so soon. She was not braced for it yet, she had not had time to find something to lay hold of beyond the day when she lost him. There would be nothing—nothing to *do*. . . .

Sue's light step had made no sound outside the door, but Camilla turned to see her standing there. When their eyes met, Sue knew, and came into the room, came straight to the chair, not to Calvert. Camilla laid her arms around Sue's waist and hid her face against the soft blue dress.

"There, there," Sue whispered in the foolish formula which had soothed so many griefs. "There, honey, there, I know, I know. But it's easier for him like this."

2. SUMMER IN CANNES. 1922.

BRACKEN HAD ALREADY GONE ABROAD TO OB-
serve the Economic Conference at Genoa, and was expecting
to join Dinah in London at its conclusion. The season there
promised to be the gayest since the war, as most of the big
houses which had been hospitals were by now restored to
normal, and the first regular Courts were being resumed after
a seven years' gap. Virginia's Irene, just eighteen, was being
presented, and Winifred, who had no girls of coming-out age,
was giving her a ball at the St. James's Square house.

Camilla sailed on the new *Berengaria* with Dinah, who
was delighted to have her as a guest, and Sue gave her a generous check for spending money and new clothes. It was
Camilla's first experience of the fashionable world without the
shadow of war across it, and was much the best tonic which
could have been prescribed, for Calvert had long ago made
her promise not to mope and mourn, if anything—the old
pitiful euphemism—happened to him. Virginia had taken a

house in London for the Season, and everything was in an uproar there with Irene's fittings and Court curtseys and parties and beaux, so that Phoebe, remembering with nostalgia her own first arrival in London from Williamsburg, said there might almost never have been a war.

Daphne had married Adrian Carteret in the summer of 1919, and the following year produced a son, and thought very highly of herself. Nigel was entering Eton next year, which made everyone feel very elderly, and Evadne at eight was still the beauty of the family, with Virginia's dark eyes and Archie's fair hair. Oliver and Phoebe were at their wits' end about Hermione, who had been put into a good school and hated it and was being very difficult about everything. It had been decided that Jeff should receive at least part of his education in England, and he was doing well at Oliver's old prep school and seemed to enjoy himself there, but he was such a silent, self-contained creature you couldn't be sure. As he was Bracken's adopted heir and destined for the newspaper business, it was secretly hoped that his admiration for Oliver would not breed in him Army ambitions, and his nine-year-old writings were surreptitiously searched by Phoebe and Bracken for signs of inherited literary talent. Letters, they would remind each other, were deceptive. Any fool could write a good letter, and remain incapable of any sustained effort.

Jenny was living with her father in what her letters to Camilla had described as a pokey flat in one of the dowdier squares south of the Park, and working at St. Dunstan's Hostel where people learned to be blind. Overcreech House was let to a man with a very recent knighthood whom Camilla gathered one didn't know, somebody who had made money out of the war, and Winifred, whose money came from coal and was therefore legitimate and safe, said that the Duke's death duties when that time came would probably necessitate an outright sale of the estate.

Jenny was a particular favorite with the sightless soldiers at St. Dunstan's, for her sweet voice and patient ways, and she had a faculty for giving them self-confidence. She taught them music, and how to walk beside her through the streets without her hand as a guide, with only the brush of her elbow and casual, interpolated directions about steps and turnings. Jenny did not approve of walking-sticks for the blind when they could be dispensed with. On their excursions with her, sticks were left behind, and when there was no mutilation her escorts were usually supposed by passers-by to be able to see as well as she could. Jenny knew how to chatter along about the things they encountered on the way and the small happenings in the streets around them so that memory and imagination came into play and it was almost like seeing again. Jenny urged them to use logic and hearing and smell rather than touch alone, and the men she had had charge of learned not to betray their blindness in any of the usual ways —they located the seat of a chair with the calves of their legs, instead of stooping pathetically to find it with their hands; they kept their food in the middle of their plates without trying to rely on the raised edge, and they never set their water glass on the blade of their knife and then upset it by picking up the knife. She insisted on their developing their sense of obstacle, located in the nerves of the face, instead of groping for walls and obstructions with outstretched hands. And her tactful advice to the families the men would return to was considered invaluable.

This was the Jenny Camilla found when she returned to London—busy, cheerful, useful—plainly dressed, her short, bright hair burnished with brushing, her face quite innocent of make-up, her eyes a little shadowed but very blue. They had tea that first afternoon together, filling in the gaps between their letters, linked by poignant memories, not shrinking from mention of Calvert and Raymond or Sosthène, not ashamed of the tears that stood in their eyes. And then Jenny said, with her usual directness, "What are you going to do now?"

Camilla confessed that she didn't know.

"After you've had a rest, I mean," Jenny pursued matter-of-factly. "Will you go back to your music?"

"It's been so long," Camilla sighed. "Compared to you, I feel very—incompetent. I'm not much good for anything."

"You had Calvert to think of. But you should fill his place now, as soon as possible, with something very exacting, for your own good. Go to the Conservatoire in Paris and study piano seriously, or something like that."

"Yes, I know I should. Bracken wants to stay here for the tennis at Wimbledon—that's for recreation, he says—and the Air Pageant at Hendon—that's business. After that they've offered to take me to Paris with them, and we might all go down to see Sally at Cannes. I'm afraid it sounds very idle and expensive and selfish, except for Bracken, of course, he always has his ear to the ground. Jenny—what's all this talk about another war?"

"It's the Russians," said Jenny simply. "They aren't on our side any more. They're hobnobbing with the Germans who naturally hate us because we won—or at least kept them from winning. It's a sinister combination."

"But I thought Germany had been disarmed by the Versailles Treaty."

"Theoretically. But it's difficult to enforce a thing like that, apparently. They've hidden stores of arms, and they're supposed to be inventing new weapons—gas bombs, and germ warfare, and other mysterious horrors."

"Oh, Jenny, not *again!*"

Jenny shook her head wearily.

"Doesn't it seem futile, after all we went through to stop them a little while ago? I was hoping for a chance to ask Bracken what he thought."

"Bracken will depress you like anything! Johnny Malone came to Genoa from Berlin for the Conference, and got him all worked up about German civil aviation. According to Johnny, they go right on building planes, and they've invented one without an engine, that *glides*, but they call it sport, because of Versailles."

Camilla had thought the war was over, till Bracken came back from the Continent, where he and Johnny Malone, his Berlin correspondent, had witnessed together the débâcle at Genoa. The Conference there was the first since the war at which German delegates had been invited to sit as equals at the Allied Council table. Russian delegates were also invited, and had accepted with alacrity, but as the Bolshevik government was not recognized they had no political significance and were not to take part in the discussions, though a restoration of trade with Russia was one of the objects of the Conference. So the international poker game had begun—Lloyd George for England, Barthou for France, Rathenau and von Maltzan for Germany, Tchitcherin and Litvinoff representing Russia—who were expected to be grateful to be present at all, and who began by demanding double representation on the steering committee "because Russia had so much at stake." Barthou then inquired if Russia wanted twice as many delegates as anybody else, and Tchitcherin replied acidly that he did not care how many anyone else had but he wanted two. At this point even Lloyd George had to take a stand.

From the first public session there was a poisonous atmosphere of national selfishness and fear, and things became steadily more acrimonious with each meeting, in an orgy of intrigue. No one was at the time quite clear, said Bracken, how one thing led to another, for the Press arrangements were atrocious, but Lloyd George apparently with some idea of playing *deus ex machina* attempted some sort of personal negotiations with the Bolshevik representatives at his own villa. The Germans got wind of it, imagined trickery, waited on the Russians' doorstep ready to concede to them everything the Allies so far refused, and announced on Easter Sunday the conclusion of a two-power treaty with Russia behind the back, as it were, of the Conference itself.

It was very hard to find any excuse for such behavior, but the Germans were highly elated and felt that they had got even with the French. The news was like a bombshell in the diplomatic world, and the way in which it was released was provocative to the point of nose-thumbing, said Bracken. Germany had thus alienated all the sympathy which was beginning to be extended to her, and Russia had thrown away her chance of being accepted into the civilized family of nations. After a few futile discussions, the Conference broke up in confusion and more hard feeling than when it began in gloom and a spirit of criticism. Everyone felt that Germany was up to her old tricks again, and Russia under the Bolsheviks had become an enigma and a menace. Whenever you picked up a newspaper now you found headlines like *Is Germany Planning a War of Revenge?* and *New School of German Aviators Develops Engineless Aeroplane.*

But London was full of dinner parties and dances, and everyone was going to the theater to see Fay Compton in *Secrets* and Henry Ainley in *The Dover Road,* and lots of other cheerful or touching plays with not a word about war in them—and there was an amusing innovation called Cabaret. Ascot was very gala, though the weather was unkind; the new tennis court at Wimbledon was opened with ceremony by the King, and Mlle. Lenglen beat Mrs. Mallory;

the Prince of Wales came home from India to a fervent welcome and was present at the third Court, when Irene made
her curtsey. Virginia said it quite took one back, except that
the dresses were nothing like so pretty now as they were when
she came out, as nobody was allowed to have a waist line
any more and it didn't really matter what sort of figure you
had.

Bracken attended the glider competition of ex-war pilots
on the South Downs with considerable interest—Fokker flew
his own machine and stayed up something like three hours,
engineless—and then Dinah said they had best think of something else for a bit, to which Bracken agreed and hired a big
Daimler with a G.B. plate on it and they set out with Camilla
under their wing for a motor tour of the Continent which
would bring them eventually to Cannes.

Sally complained that whereas Cannes had once been considered a winter resort, nowadays one had outsiders there
the year round, because of this new craze for getting sun-
burned.

She had changed so little, aged so little, that Camilla was
reminded again of the inevitable comparison to Queen
Alexandra, also perennially young. The house where Sally
lived stood above the water on the Juan les Pins side of
Cannes, snow white in a bower of bloom. Its gardens ran
straight down to the gulf, edged with great brown rocks which
had mercifully been left in their natural rugged state, alone
in the surrounding elegance. You left the house in your bathing things, crossed the lawn and the rocks and bathed, and
then sunned yourself on bright mats laid on the rocks. The
less you wore, the more fashionable you were.

It was said that no guest ever succeeded in mapping out in
his own mind the complicated geography of the house, which

burst out in balconies in all directions, and rambled off in wings, and had steps up or down between the rooms. It was the most any visitor ever accomplished to learn the way from his own room—complete with exotic colored-tile bathroom and flower-hung balcony—to the main living-rooms and entrance hall of the establishment. Where his fellow guests disappeared to or came from—except in certain tactfully adjusted cases—to bed and breakfast remained a mystery, some said on purpose. Nobody—unless it was Sally—knew how many rooms there were, but six or eight guests of assorted sexes and intimacy were usually in residence. Fabrice and her American lion-tamer, who had set up housekeeping in a little château just outside Paris, made frequent visits, bringing with them their entire nursery—two babies, a nurse, and a maid. The children were never seen outside their own quarters, but Fabrice said it kept her mind at rest to know that they were there. The family were all fascinated by Fabrice's evolution into an apparently perfect wife and mother without the loss of an ounce of her good looks and spirits and Phoebe had been heard to speculate more than once on whether Kendrick had actually carried out his threat to lay her across his knee. In any case not even Philadelphia could have found fault with her single-minded devotion to her husband and offspring—though her habit of flirting outrageously with the man she had married might have made talk anywhere. Kendrick showed no desire to return home, preferring the home he had made for himself in post-war France, entertaining with unending hospitality and delight all itinerant pre-war and war-time friends who turned up in Paris, and all the more amusing members of the American colony there. Sally in turn extended the hospitality of Cannes to anyone the Kendricks chose to bring or send there, which meant that the place boiled with the pleasure-bent young international crowd carelessly superimposed on Sally's own somewhat flamboyant coterie from before the war. As Bracken said, it all had to be seen to be believed, and even then Camilla often felt as though she had somehow got caught between the pages of a particularly lively French novel.

The expense of running such a household with an always amiable staff of well-paid servants, with unlimited food and drink at all hours, with a multitude of cars at everyone's disposal, fresh fruit and flowers daily in all the rooms, fresh linen before you could turn round from having washed your hands, streams of telephone calls, telegrams, and cables, which no guest ever paid for, was something not even Bracken liked to contemplate.

Most of the conversation—scandal, politics, sport, clothes —even when conducted in English, was completely above Camilla's head, but before she had time to find this an embarrassment she realized that Sosthène was as silent as she was— not because he did not know what they were talking about, or because he was bored, but simply because there was no necessity in the midst of all that babble for him to speak. After that, Camilla was content to watch and listen, unless directly spoken to. Dinah had seen to her wardrobe, Virginia had taught her to do her hair, and there was no need to keep her up to the mark on her make-up—lipstick, she discovered, made more difference than anything. She had an interesting mouth, with long, sensitive lips, and she learned to make the most of it with bright, neatly applied color, and a honey-toned powder which brought out her grey eyes. Properly made up, she ceased to feel thirty-ish, and consequently ceased to look her age.

To see Sosthène again, where he seemed now always to have been, from where he had been only briefly uprooted by the war and thrown across her path, was a lesson very hard to learn. Camilla bit on it gamely, convinced that to see him at all was worth the cost. Her faint hope that she would find the old obsession outgrown or at least dulled by time and separation soon gave up the struggle. From the day she arrived, with her heart pounding in her ears because when she stepped out of the car he would be there, she knew it was going to be just as bad as it ever was, and worse, for here was where he belonged and was obliged to remain—this was his life and Sally's as she had always shrunk from imagining it. Each day underlined anew that he was Sally's, and that he had made himself content to be. Now and then his eyes would meet Camilla's with a look so grave and kind and so impenetrable that she never knew if he meant to reassure or to warn her, and she would try to look away before her own eyes gave away too much. Her perpetual consciousness of onlookers, her pervading sense of inner guilt, an unfounded illusion of her own intrusion where she was as a matter of fact completely welcome, made her unduly reticent and cautious in her contacts with other guests in the house, and laid a restraint over her every waking hour which was attributed by strangers to shyness or possibly inadequate French.

Other people were in love, at Sally's house, often quite shamelessly so—it was in the hot, scented air and the whispering nights. Sometimes Camilla only wanted to escape from it, and told herself that she would ask to go back to England tomorrow. Other times she surrendered to it, dreaming dreams which made the barren reality all the harder to bear. But it was still Sosthène—always Sosthène—so that she was brusque or cool to advances from friendly, curious men who might have done her a world of good if she had let them, instead of hugging her emptiness to herself.

It was not long before she discovered that Sally's guests were nearly all very good at something, and were accustomed to being called on to entertain the rest. Professional musicians with widely known names poured out fortunes in box-office value, playing and singing in the vast, flowery drawing-room after dinner. Novelists brought her their latest autographed copies, and could be persuaded to read aloud from them. Theatrical people performed for her, impromptu, their most talked-about scenes. Impresarios introduced to her their latest sensations. And Camilla, who had fallen back into the Williamsburg way of thinking of Cousin Sally as perhaps a trifle demi-mondaine, was jerked into a realization of Sally's unique position here in her adopted country.

Never knowing who was who, because of Sally's careless ways about introductions, Camilla was only moderately nervous at being requested to play and sing for the guests one evening when the gathering was comparatively small and intimate. After one panicky glance at Sosthène, who nodded serene encouragement, she sat down obediently at the piano and sang to her own accompaniment some simple *lieder* and then a new song or two that she had picked up in London. It seemed to her that she was being kept at it a little longer than most people were required to perform, and that she was being listened to with closer attention than such amateur entertainment warranted, but confidence grew in her and she could not help but know that she was doing well—quite as well as could be expected from her.

She was astonished to hear, in the silence following her last song, an authoritative voice saying, in strongly accented English, "The touch is good—the tone, the feeling—excellent. The voice will not last."

"Then she is for Delorme," said Sally.

"Yes. I should get Delorme to hear her."

"He's coming next week. Thank you, my dear, you will want some refreshment now," said Sally to Camilla, who sat transfixed on the piano bench, and the listening room broke up into conversation, movement, and the handing round of iced drinks.

Camilla found Sosthène, smiling, at her side with a glass in his hand—for her. She accepted it rather ungraciously, with something like a scowl.

"That was hardly fair of her, to trick me into playing for somebody important, without my knowing I was on trial."

"You were less nervous, not knowing," said Sosthène calmly. "You didn't try too hard. It was the best way."

"Who is he, anyhow?"

When he told her, the name meant nothing. Nor did Delorme, who was coming next week. But if Delorme took her on as a pupil, said Sosthène, she might go far.

"Go where?" she asked, still rebellious. "As a concert pianist, do you mean?"

His shoulders rose a little. If she chose, perhaps. Anything, perhaps, if she chose.

A slim-waisted, sleek-haired young man sauntered up on the other side of the piano and leaned on it intimately, bending towards her.

"Do sing that thing from *Pot Luck* again," he said.

"I'm afraid not now, they've finished listening, they want to talk." She glanced nervously round the oblivious groups, already absorbed in their own conversation.

"Tomorrow, then—the first thing in the morning."

"And wake everybody up?" she parried perversely, aware that Sosthène had drifted away, leaving her to cope with it alone.

"You're marvellous," said the young man tenderly. "You're exactly what I've been wanting for ages. I must know all about you, and what it was that broke your heart."

"*Well!*" said Camilla, with a cool look studiously unimpressed by his almost excessive handsomeness, his romantic dark eyes, his full, smiling mouth, his tan, his tailoring. "And who might you be? Or should I know?"

"I'm Kim St. Clair. I write songs. You should know, as a matter of fact."

"What sort of songs?"

"The sort you can sing. Sad, sultry, sexy stuff. With that face and my music you'd knock them endwise."

"What's the matter with my face?"

"It's got a starved sort of haunted look," said the conscienceless young man. "I'll write a song for you, and show you what I mean. Will you sing it?"

"Here?" Her eyes went again around the room.

"In Paris, eventually. In a cabaret show."

"I can't sing in French."

"That's a lie," he said flatly, and the corners of her mouth deepened because he knew it. "Anyway, Americans are all the rage now. We won't pretend you're anything else."

"Are you English, or what?"

"My mother was. But I grew up here. I'm bilingual. It's very useful. Shall I tell you the story of my life? I'd much rather hear yours."

Now, Camilla had seldom been flirted with in her sober life, and this time she found it rather stimulating. Her commonsense told her that Kim St. Clair, if he had actually been born with that name, always flirted with women, automatically, and that his bright, consuming gaze and impetuous-seeming approach were nothing more than a bad habit with him. But there was an answering gleam in her own eyes as she sat looking up at him, waiting to see what he would say next.

"Mine's very dull," she said.

"*Why* do you look so sad?" he murmured, bending nearer.

"I'm *not*—I *don't!*" She tried to laugh, and found that she could not hold her eyes to his.

"You do, as soon as I saw you I thought you were the most *bereft*-looking creature I had ever seen! Did they kill your lover in the war?"

"No. They killed my twin brother."

There was a moment's silence, while she sat looking down into her glass, and the outrageous young man produced rather sudden good manners.

"I'm sorry," he said quite sincerely. "I shouldn't have said that."

"It's all right."

"Come out on the terrace. It's cooler there, and we'll talk about songs and—things that don't matter."

She rose, carrying her glass, and walked beside him through the long windows which opened onto a flagged terrace with cane chairs and soft cushions, and the garden and the sea beyond. When she sat down in a white armchair he took the glass from her hand and said, "Let me freshen this up for you and get one of my own. Shan't be a sec," and returned to the drawing-room.

Camilla leaned her head against the back of the chair and looked up at the Mediterranean stars. Soft light from the room inside lay in yellow slabs across the stone floor, but her chair was in shadow between two windows. It was disconcerting to be taken possession of like this, but rather comforting too. She supposed that he was a friend of the Kendricks, who knew all sorts. Did she want to sing in cabaret? Would the family object? Would it perhaps be a way of making her own living? Would it be quite—respectable? And did she care?

She was smiling at such spinsterish qualms when he returned with two tall glasses which clinked and sweated. His fingers brushed hers as he gave her the fresh drink, and seemed to linger. He turned another chair and sat down close beside her.

"This is marvellous," he said. "I'm only here because I'm recovering from an appendicitis operation and supposed to rest. Fabrice warned me it might be dull this week, with none of our own crowd here, but thank God I came anyway."

"Were you very ill?"

"Not very, it was one of those bothersome things one has to get over and done with. Now, why are you looking at me like that? Tell me what you are thinking."

"I was thinking," she said deliberately, returning his gaze, "that perhaps you are nicer than I thought."

"Oh, I *am!*" he assured her without blinking. "You didn't like the way I jumped down your throat, did you."

"Well, I'm not used to it."

"That's marvellous," he said. "You *are* marvellous, is it because you come from Virginia that you have a sort of other-world thing about you?"

"There you go again, why must you talk like a silly book just when I'm beginning to like you?"

"Do you really?" he cried unrepentantly, with exaggerated joy. "Thanks for saying it's a *silly* book, I can't help the way I talk, and it's you that are bookish and far-away, you know." He leaned forward, his glass held between his long, too-graceful hands. "I think you're the *realest* person I ever saw," he remarked earnestly, and added, "And the most defenceless."

"You say the most extraordinary things," she began, stiffening, and he laid one hand on her bare arm, his face so close to hers that in the dim light coming from behind her she could see the whites of his brilliant eyes and the shine of his teeth.

"Camilla—lovely name—*darling* Camilla, you make me feel very old and smirched and sinful. But you need somebody like me, if you're going to stay here. You need me—don't laugh—to protect you."

"Oh, nonsense, in my own cousin's house? If I need protection it's *from* you, not by you!"

"You won't be in Sally's house when you come to Paris to sing my songs."

"How do you know I can? I've never sung professionally."

"You've got that thing," he said, and his eyes went freely over her face and hair and throat. "You've got whatever it is—personality, we'll call it. There's a shorter and easier word. But it's all—waiting. No brother ever made you like this, Camilla. You're in love. And I wish to God it was me."

Camilla sat up and pushed him from her with a hand on his stiff shirt-front, but he caught the hand and held it there with unexpected strength, so that she could not rise.

"All right, you can kill me in a minute," he said. "But first—are you going to marry him?"

"It's none of your business!" she gasped furiously, but he held her where she was.

"You aren't," he said. "I thought not. You can't, is that why? It hurts, doesn't it. It hurts like hell. That's what it is about you, you're in some little hell of your own and you can't get out, can you, and you're ready to bite and claw everybody that tries to help you. How do I know, that's what you can't see, isn't it. I don't need second sight, Camilla, good God, it's written all over you! But mostly it's in your voice when you sing, and in your eyes now, this minute, you can't hide it, not from your Uncle Kim, I've been watching you for two days, trying to see what made you tick, and you never even knew I was there, did you. Shall I tell you who he is?"

Camilla wrenched herself free and stood up, and her glass shattered at their feet.

"Now look what you've done," she said inadequately, and because she could not face the drawing-room eyes she walked away from him towards the balustrade at the end of the terrace and leaned there, staring out towards the black water. It had to be only a question of time, of course, till some one saw, she had known that before she came to Cannes. But she had been so very careful, she and Sosthène had hardly spoken to each other, had never been alone for more than a few moments and by accident—

Kim arrived beside her, soundlessly, and lounged against the balustrade, his shoulder touching hers.

"I shouldn't have said that either," he remarked in his casual way. "I never did so much apologizing in my life as I'm doing tonight. You do strange things to me, Camilla. When I began this I thought I knew what I was up to, but—I got carried away. I'm not such a bad sort, really—and I'm learning fast, with you. Will you forgive me?"

"There's nothing to forgive," she said wearily, and dabbed at her eyes.

"Nobody else has noticed it," he murmured.

"That's very comforting!" she flashed.

"It should be. I wasn't sure myself till tonight." Still he lounged, his shoulder firm and persistent against hers. "I shall now cut my own throat by offering gratuitous advice. Get out of here, Camilla."

"How can you—" She turned on him, angry again, and he faced her, straightening slowly to his full height, which was not much above hers, so that she faltered and was silent.

"Get out of here, I said. Next time it won't be just old Uncle Kim who sees. Next time it might be the wrong person. You wouldn't like that, Camilla, not the way you are. In fact, things could happen that would make you pretty sick. Understand?" He left a silence, which she could not break, and then went on in his theatrically casual tone. "I don't know how things are with you—or what your plans are—were. If you do want to come to Paris and sing my songs—I'll write you some new ones. That's a promise. Shall we go in now, or don't you care about your reputation?"

━━━━━━

Camilla had been living in the house some days before she discovered the library, a small corner room rather dark and cool in the afternoons, with windows masked by the shrubbery on the east terrace. Nobody used books much at Sally's, but the library was well up to date with the latest fiction in French and English, and dozens of detective stories. As she was not very good at sleeping, Camilla was becoming addicted to who-dun-its, which could be read in bed with no mental effort.

Sally always disappeared for a siesta between luncheon and tea time, and her guests were left to themselves. Some went to the Casino, some played golf if it was not too hot, some just sat on the terrace of the Carlton with a drink, and some also took siestas. Anyway, the house seemed quite deserted that stifling afternoon as Camilla crossed the living-room towards the passage which led to the library, and she savored her solitude gratefully. Kim had coaxed her to sing again after lunch, and had played a bit of the new song he was devising just for her, he said, and then he strolled away down to the Casino with some of the others, a little vexed because she refused to go along.

"I suppose you either have a headache or want to write letters," he suggested, putting the stock excuses into savage quotation marks.

Camilla only laughed and would not argue, intending to get a new book and lie down on the chaise longue by her bedroom window, which caught a breeze from the water. She entered the apparently empty library and wandered along the shelves fingering the titles undecidedly, and jumped in a guilty sort of way when a voice said, "I thought you had gone to the Casino." It was Sosthène, who had risen from a high-backed chair in the corner with his finger holding the place in the book he had been reading.

"No, I—" She glanced at the door, which she had found closed and had closed again behind her.

"Come and sit down." He laid his book aside and moved

towards her and the sofa set facing the flower-filled fireplace which was between them.

Camilla stood still and watched him come, dumb and waiting. He paused, and then moved forward again and she was in his arms, their faces pressed together without a kiss, and she felt his hands claiming her, one at her waist, one gripping her shoulder. Neither of them could speak, but after a moment his lips slid down across her cheek and found hers. Camilla gave him the kiss gladly, generously, with a kind of triumph in the reckless response.

"My Camille," he murmured, still holding her. "What becomes of us like this?"

"I was going to tell you that I think I had better go away."

"Yes." He stood looking down at her in his arms, his gaze travelling slowly over her face like a caressing fingertip. "Yes, now it becomes impossible. You will have to go."

"Do you want me to go?" she challenged.

"Don't ask me a thing like that, when you know the answer so well." They spoke almost in whispers, their lips close gether.

"I was never sure about the answer—till now."

"You had no doubt, Camilla, from the beginning. What is it between us that will not starve to death?"

"I love you," she whispered, and with a little sound like pity he kissed her again, and then could not seem to stop, going from gentleness to violence, and quite suddenly let her go, and sat down on the arm of the sofa, not looking at her, staring at the rug under his feet. Camilla, who had not known quite what it would be like, took a few aimless steps around the room, feeling reckless and ablaze and ready for almost anything, until his silence brought her back to him and she laid her arms around his shoulders and her cheek against his and said simply, "Have I made it worse for you?"

"Not you, no," he answered, motionless. "I have destroyed

myself entirely. You had better — go up to your room."

"Yes. But give me a minute first."

"That door is not locked behind us."

"I know. Sosthène—couldn't we talk—couldn't we go for a drive together?"

"Alone? There is no excuse. We don't want her to know, do we."

"Are you sure she doesn't?"

"Quite sure—so far."

"But—you are so close to each other. I wonder she doesn't *feel* it somehow if—if you feel like this about me."

"It is not a thing which would ever occur to her—now."

She left him again, wandering about the room in a ferment. Finally, with her back to him, she spoke again into his silence.

"Sosthène—are you—married to Sally?"

"No." His answer came without hesitation. "But we have been together longer than most marriages last nowadays."

"If you were—both the same age—"

"Once it seemed as though we were. If we were, perhaps I could do differently than I must."

"She depends on you. So I must go away before—"

"Yes."

"Kim wants me to come to Paris and sing in his cabaret show. Do you think I could?"

"Probably."

"Could I make a living that way?"

"Oh, yes—if you're good at it. But you must make up your mind to one thing first—he will be in love with you, and not for marriage, you understand. You must be prepared for that."

She returned swiftly to the sofa and knelt up on the cushions, catching at his sleeve impulsively, her face against his shoulder.

"Oh, Sosthène, you don't think for a minute that anyone like that could make any difference between you and me!"

"That door," he reminded her without moving, "is not locked."

"Oh, damn the door!" cried Camilla, and flung away from him again, blindly, down the room. "I shan't be young myself forever," she said then, sullenly, and waited. He made no answer. She turned and looked at him, the room between them. He met her eyes again steadily, compassion and resignation in the droop of his thin, curving lids. "There isn't— anything you can say or do, is there," she realized at last.

"No. Nothing."

"Then I'll go to Paris with Kim."

She walked out of the room, and left him sitting on the arm of the sofa looking after her. Heading heedlessly for the stairs and her own room, she ran hard into Kim coming round the drawing-room doorway. He caught her by the shoulders and his knowing, sympathetic gaze raked her face.

"Not that way," he said. "You'll meet them all coming in just behind me."

"Kim, get me away from here, somehow, quick!" Tears welled up and ran down her cheeks.

"Stop it, I say, they've all come back early because of the heat. Do you want that Eugénie cat to see you like this and start guessing at reasons? Here." He swung her round and pushed her towards the piano bench. "Sit down beside me and play treble." His fingers were noisy on the keyboard as the other guests flowed into the room fanning themselves and looking for iced drinks. Her right hand followed his listlessly an octave higher, and she gave a piteous sniff under cover of the music. "When shall we start?" he murmured. "Tomorrow morning?"

"Yes, please."

"What will you tell Dinah?"

"Dinah doesn't interfere. I'm grown up."

"Are you?" said Kim, with an impudent *glissade* which swept her hand from the keys.

"What about my song?"

"You'll get it. More than one. What about your Delorme career?"

"I'll choose my own career. Can I make a living in Paris?"

"Why not?"

"Singing?"

He gave her a sardonic sidelong glance.

"Camilla, darling, don't you trust me?"

"Not altogether."

"You can," he said casually. "I'll never try to corner you. Take your time."

"Kim, I don't promise anything—ever. You do understand that."

"Perfectly."

"Then why do you bother?"

"Curiosity," he said, with another *glissade*.

"Suppose you're disappointed."

"I'll take what comes."

"What's that you're playing now?"

"Your new song. One of them. Try it."

She hummed along with the melody, experimentally.

"Pretty low, isn't it?"

"Your best notes are the low ones. Leave it to Uncle Kim."

"Has it got any words?"

"Not yet. I've got a glimmer, though."

"I think it's awfully clever of you to write both the words and the music."

"Darling, I *am* clever. You'll see."

"It's lucky you were here, isn't it," she said thoughtfully after a moment.

"I think so." He was humming the new melody himself,

"Especially just now. What happened, anyway? None of my business!" he answered for her before she could speak. "All right, all right, don't tell me, I can guess."

"I'd rather you didn't guess. You'll get it all wrong."

"Does it matter, to us?"

"Yes, it does," she said earnestly. "I don't want you to think—"

"After we leave here tomorrow," said Kim, "I swear never to think again."

"You know, half of what you say doesn't mean anything at all," she accused. "Like musical comedy dialogue."

"Thank you, Camilla," said Kim, inclining his head with dignity while he played. "This is my first act finale. Like it?"

3. AUTUMN IN SALZBURG. 1925.

CAMILLA FOUND THAT IT WAS POSSIBLE TO keep very busy in Paris, and being busy is the next best thing to being happy, and sometimes amounts to the same thing. She was always welcome in the lavish Kendrick household where Kim St. Clair was already entirely at home. The young international set who were the Kendricks' friends adopted her with enthusiasm and she sang nightly at their favorite dance club just off the Champs Elysées, and appeared in a rather mixed Paris revue which caught on for a time.

Not overnight, but almost imperceptibly, she and Kim became an established fashion, and parties were given especially so that newcomers from overseas might hear them, and their devotees might hear again their own choice among the songs. Admiration, pursuit, even, was a pleasant novelty to Camilla, and in a way she did thoroughly enjoy herself. It wasn't long before her professional engagements with

Kim provided enough legitimate excuses not to return to Cannes.

When she went to England for a few weeks in the summer of 1925, it was rather like Cinderella coming back to her chimney-corner, for Kim was left behind and she played her own accompaniments in the British drawing-rooms where Winifred's parties and Virginia's were somewhat different from the lively gatherings across the Channel. Camilla's hair, short now, with curls, and her make-up and her clothes all became a little extreme when seen against a London background, and a good many of the more popular numbers had to be omitted from her repertoire.

The family were proud of her glitter and success, but at the same time a trifle wary. They could not help but wonder just how far the sophisticating process had gone, and they felt a certain responsibility, though they were privately agreed that Camilla was by now certainly old enough to take care of herself. But with Sally's spectacular record before them, it did just occur to them to wonder. Bracken and Dinah, entertained at her comfortable flat on the Boulevard Suchet in Passy, had reported everything in outward good order, at least; unless, Bracken's conscientious postscript ran, one took exception to a slightly *bijou* drawing-room with *chartreuse* highlights. But even Kim seemed entirely under control. Of course she had met him at Sally's in the first place. . . .

Kim could have told them, if he had chosen, that they needn't have worried about that part of it. Camilla had not promised anything when they left Cannes, and he wasn't sure even now that he had actually expected anything. His main consolation was that nobody else appeared to succeed with her any further than he could, and he knew plenty of other people himself who were more obliging, and he was not one to pine. Their partnership at the piano was financially profitable to both, and was artistically satisfying to his creative side. He still made love to her when he got the chance, and took No with good grace. They had had a few dust-ups, but no reproaches, and on the whole their very informal, *laissez-faire* association was mutually beguiling.

When she got to London that summer Camilla lost no time about hunting up Jenny Keane, and found her a little thinner and more plainly dressed than before, a little quieter, a little pathetic, still absorbed in the work at St. Dunstan's. The old Duke had died the winter before, and her cousin Godfrey had inherited, and had at once put Overcreech up for sale. Jenny had found a small flat on the less fashionable edges of Regent's Park to be near St. Dunstan's, and she lived there alone with only a daily char to look after her, and not even a cat to keep her company. How different we are, in the way we take it, Camilla thought. Both of us left dangling, without the thing we want most—but Jenny is at least some good in the world. "Whenever I see you I feel ashamed of myself," she said suddenly, as they sat drinking tea in Jenny's rooms.

"That's a dreadful thing to hear from your best friend," Jenny objected lightly. "And it doesn't make any sense. Look at you!" Her eyes went wistfully over the groomed, exotic figure, dressed by Vionnet with an almost arrogant elegance and restraint, sitting on her sofa wth a buttered scone in its manicured fingers. "You make me feel and look like a sparrow, if it comes to that!"

"It's only skin deep," sighed Camilla, with a restless movement which set thin silver bracelets tinkling on both wrists. "I should have found something worth while to do, I suppose."

"Except for my blind," Jenny said slowly, "the world still needs pretty ladies and music and fun. You make people laugh and relax and forget their troubles. That's good enough, isn't it?"

"I don't know—is it?" Camilla brooded a moment. "What's become of Gerald?" she asked irrelevantly, and Jenny smiled.

"He's round and about."

"Not married yet?"

"No."

"You don't mean to say he learned a lesson!"

"Perhaps he did. It was about time, wasn't it!"

"Jenny, you wouldn't—wouldn't be going out of your way to teach him—and rather overdo it?"

"Et tu, Brute?" said Jenny, but she still smiled.

"Was there ever a word about Raymond?"

"Never. We moved heaven and earth, and ploughed up Geneva, but he was gone."

"I might be playing an engagement in New York this winter. And I was just thinking—would you like me to go up to that town he came from—what was its name?"

"Indian Landing."

"Lake Champlain, wasn't it? I could run up there—they might have heard something."

Jenny shook her head.

"Well, I only thought it might put your mind at rest a little," Camilla said apologetically. "I'd have gone there on my own before I left America if I'd had any idea that you were still—that you'd go on feeling this way."

"I don't think about it much," Jenny said after a moment. "Not any more. I keep pretty busy."

"But—perhaps there might be somebody else, if only you—"

Jenny shook her head.

"But, Jenny, it's not even as though you'd been married to him—"

"Darling, don't get any idea that I'm eating my heart out over a ghost, or anything like that." Jenny set down her cup and tried to speak levelly. "Raymond's gone. I'm used to that now. I don't—grieve for him. But if there was ever anyone else, he would have to be—*more* than Raymond. And I've just never seen anyone half as big as he was. That's all."

"So you'd rather do without."

"Well, what about yourself?" Jenny demanded. "What about this Kim St. Clair I hear so much about? How does he look beside Sosthène?"

"Rotten."

"So you're doing without, too," Jenny pointed out, with no triumph.

"Yes—but nobody's very sure of that except you and Kim! And as for me—just possibly—there's some hope some day. I try not to think about it, but it's there, all the same." She grinned ruefully into her empty cup. "So I keep pretty busy too," she said.

"Well, there we both are, then," said Jenny, and lit a cigarette.

"Just a couple of old maids," Camilla remarked reflectively, and Jenny laughed.

"You look it!"

"Anyway, we haven't got that war yet," said Camilla, reaching for a petit beurre and biting into it.

"Give us time."

"How much time?"

"Nobody knows that, but Bracken says we won't be ready. He and Dinah took me with them to the Air Pageant at Hendon last week. The King on the ground spoke to the pilots in the air and directed maneuvers by his voice. Wireless telephony. That was one of the things Raymond used to write about from France—direct communication with the ground, for a lost pilot, or an injured one—a way to guide a plane home through cloud or fog by question and answer, when there was no visibility. It was one of the things he wanted to work out." Jenny sat a moment, looking back. "I thought of that at Hendon. If Raymond had lived he would have spent all his time on things like that—not on bigger bombs or—or chemical warfare. He was thinking about ways to make flying safer for the pilots, not deadlier for the people below. Next time if they drop gas on us from planes—apparently it can be done now—nothing can function at all behind the lines. Trains, hospitals, anti-aircraft defence—it would all be completely paralyzed, and all they'd have to do is land."

"And bury us."

"It would be tidier, yes."

"Does Bracken think it will happen?"

"He thinks it *can*. He says the Germans are flying all over the place, under the heading of sport and commerce. All their big cities are linked by air lines, passenger and freight. Their schools teach aeronautics, like mathematics. They won't let other countries fly commercial routes over German territory —you have to get out at the border and change to a German plane. And we let them!"

"Jenny, are they going to try it *again?*"

"Bracken thinks they will, because we are not handling them right. He says we're letting them get away with murder, and it's becoming the fashion to coddle them. They don't understand our excessive sense of fair play, to them it's just a sign of weakness, an invitation to take advantage of us, because they haven't got any such thing themselves. He says they're a lot smarter than we are—and a thousand times more ruthless."

"Then Calvert and Raymond might just as well not have *tried!*" cried Camilla. "They might just as well still be *here*."

"They might be here," Jenny said realistically, "but it wouldn't be the same world it is now, you know—if Germany had won the war and walked in."

"But then by the time Jeff is grown up, and Nigel—and Evadne—"

"Let's not think," said Jenny. "Our statesmen are still trying. Sir Austen Chamberlain seems to have some sound ideas. There's another conference coming in the autumn. Bracken is staying for it. They're going to Salzburg in the meantime."

"I know," nodded Camilla. "Reinhardt and the *Miracle*. They want me to come and I think I will. Why don't you come too? You must need a holiday."

"We'll see," said Jenny, for she had long since learned the convenience of that ambiguous promise which from Raymond had always made her furious.

Camilla always forgot about war till she saw Bracken again. He was not a Cassandra, but neither did he have any belief in general European Couéism about conferences. Johnny Malone had returned to his Berlin post at the end of the war, and was under no delusions concerning the German state of mind, which he said was entirely unrepentant and quite indistinguishable from the state of mind which had resulted in the declaration of war in 1914. Except that it was worse, if anything, for now it was necessary for the Germans to prove to themselves the universal German myth that their army had not been beaten at all in 1918, but had merely been betrayed by a home front weakened in morale by the starvation imposed upon it by the inhuman Allied blockade. More even than in 1914, the Germans desired to assert their own superiority to all the rest of the human race, in order to make up to themselves for any vague shadows of doubt which they had experienced before the Armistice, and because they had now convinced themselves in their colossal *amour propre* that they had been *wronged*, but that they had never been *wrong*.

Johnny Malone came down to Salzburg to see his boss, and was waiting on the terrace of the Oesterreichische Hof when Bracken's party arrived there by motor. Jeff had had an illness—no one seemed quite sure what it was—but he was still something of an invalid, rather pale and listless, with spurts of energy which left him overtired. They were all sick of the London doctors, who only mentioned frightening things like rheumatic fever, and advised rest and good air—no exercise, no study, no excitement. Bracken had taken a house on the shore of one of the blue lakes near Salzburg, where the rest of them could swim and climb and Jeff could lie in the sun and breathe mountain air—and where, if they took the trouble to drive into the town, they could hear superb music. They hoped that this would put Jeff right again, and incidentally he would have a chance to pick up German. Dinah was determined not to fuss and make him think of himself as fragile, but the family was much concerned about him, and Camilla could see that the illness had been serious.

The journey to Salzburg was made in easy stages with delightful stops along the way, and nobody but Jeff was tired when they arrived in the middle of a sunny August afternoon. They were spending the night at the hotel, and Dinah took him away to rest upstairs on his bed, and the others sat down at Johnny's table on the terrace and ordered fresh coffee, and Camilla looked down at the river and began to feel relaxed and glad she had come—though they had not been able to get Jenny to budge from St. Dunstan's.

Camilla had heard about how people could sit for hours over coffee at a table in Salzburg, too contented to move, and she began at once to see how that would be. The mountains which ringed the dreamy little town were turning pink in the afternoon light, and the fortress on its crag rose sharply in the middle distance. There was a faint lingering fragrance in the warm, still air—woodsmoke, or was it incense, hot tar, coffee, and something else which might be cowsheds. And then the vesper bells began to ring from all the churches.

Gradually, almost unwillingly, she became aware of the conversation going on beside her.

"Don't for one minute think I'm being an optimist," Bracken was saying, his hands cupped round the lighted match above his pipe, "but if this meeting at Locarno can bring Germany into the League, it's just possible that Russia might get lonely enough to want to come in too—if invited. I don't say that it would get us anywhere if she did, but it might. Nor I don't say that we want the Russians in the League, but Europe now consists of ex-allies, ex-enemies, and Russians. Maybe—just maybe—if the ex-enemies and the Russians were allowed to join our club and play on our team in our game, they would find themselves without a grievance. They'd hate that, of course—but it might be an interesting experiment."

Johnny shook his head.

"Germans can't live without a grievance," he said, and Bracken laughed.

"And the Russians?" he queried.

"Russians even less. If the League had any teeth in it I'd be more of an optimist myself, but your premise is a little too Wilsonian for me. What is there to prevent a wilful nation from walking out on the League and going its own wilful way, even if it is a member? How does the League prevent a wilful nation from sending its army to wilful war? Where is the Big Stick? Wilson always seemed to think that accepting membership in the League was like entering the Kingdom of Heaven—where automatically the most hardened sinner simply put on the wings and halo issued to him at the gate and became a changed soul, pure white, with only the loftiest ideas from then on. Human nature doesn't work like that, at least not before it's dead. Germany in the League will go right on being Germany as it is today and was yesterday— only more so. More so because in the League she can stand on her aggressive right to equality in everything, and re-arm openly instead of in a corner with her back turned as she's doing now."

The bitterness of his quiet voice, the way the words came out as though bitten off in his teeth, caused Camilla to turn and look at him with more interest than he had at first aroused. He was about Bracken's age, but greyer, and his compact, powerfully built body was lounged easily in the iron chair, his feet stuck out, one hand in his pocket, his eyes—a cool blue—fixed moodily on the mountains, 'way, 'way off. That so much vehemence could come out of a creature out-wardly so relaxed was astonishing. She noticed too that Bracken, who in the family was always regarded as the ulti-mate authority about everything, was listening to Johnny Malone's views with the utmost respect and waiting for more. As more seemed not immediately forthcoming, Camilla could not resist putting a question of her own.

"Then the League isn't really going to be any good?" she asked uncertainly.

"No," was Johnny's blunt reply. "Not only because Amer-ica refused to join it. That was bad enough. But before that, they let the German army *march* home, as though it had won. There was no surrender, as such, no occupation of Berlin, nothing to drive it through their German skulls that they were licked. It's an idea no German can assimilate without a club. The Allies' pretty ideas about not hurting the German feelings, not rubbing it in—because Wilson was so sure the German people were an essentially peace-loving nation who had been misled by a few wicked leaders—and how did he know, why *should* he know?—Clemenceau was in a position to know otherwise, but Clemenceau was overruled—that idea of the Allies to play dear old Mrs. Doasyoudbedoneby to the Germans simply won't wash. There's a thing called *furor teutonicus* which the Germans are very fond of invoking. They can't get along without playing soldiers. They're playing soldiers now, with their sports clubs and their aviation clubs and their hiking clubs. The old Officers Corps is still there, running these things, still kowtowed to, still strutting. Hindenburg is President. Ludendorff is still around too, organizing trouble. He's picked up a little tramp somewhere, a neurotic-looking little rat called Adolf Hitler, who isn't as funny as some people would like to think he is. With Hitler's gift of gab and Ludendorff's prestige, they can go a long way in Germany. A civilian government has palled on the Germans in no time. Not enough show—not enough bands—not enough uniforms—not enough tin soldiers shouldering people into the gutters in the good old Prussian way. They're at it again, I tell you, and who's going to stop them the next time? Poor old France? Not without Poincaré! Poor old England? Not with Lloyd George! America? *Who* did you say? Oh, no, not *America!*"

"My God, Johnny, you have got a nasty way of putting things," Bracken murmured after a moment, while Camilla sat in stunned silence.

"Oh, hell," said Johnny, and sat up, pulling in his legs. "Isn't it about time for a drink?"

———

For a month they lived in a picture postcard, motoring slowly through the little mountain villages, making day excursions by car or steamer; to the Wolfgang See, where the White Horse Inn was, and where they went sailing and fishing; to Ischl for the cakes, along a narrow winding road which Bracken said could not be done after drinks, at least not by him; to Berchtesgaden, because it was the prettiest place of all—and even as far as Grundlsee. They heard Bruno Walter conduct *Don Pasquale* in the handsome little Stadt-theater, and attended the *Everyman* performance in the Cathedral square, and went to concerts in the Mozarteum hall.

Camilla, caught up and dizzied and drunken with music, going round in a haze of remembered or newly encountered enchantment, wrote long, lyrical letters to Sosthène about how Salzburg was fairyland and she hoped she never woke up, and how she wished that he could be there too. For even now she saw everything in terms of Sosthène, and always imagined him at her side when she was particularly happy, as well as when she was particularly not. And Sosthène, who never expected to see Salzburg because Sally did not care to go there and he never left her, wrote most satisfying letters in reply, missing out no detail of the stories and the pictures she sent him, having obviously pored over them for hours. *At least I see it all with the eyes of my heart,* he wrote, so that she could make almost anything she chose out of the phrases, *and I hear it with my soul.* And always he asked for more letters.

They lunched at their favorite Baustubernlm, sitting on hard benches and under glorious trees, eating Knödel and Sauerkraut and hunks of bread smeared with golden butter, and drinking beer. They walked the little slanting streets of the town, and kept finding one more fountain. They bought Weisswurstel sausages in the old market place and ate them as they stood on the bridge watching the river in relaxed and companionable silences, they visited the catacombs and the marionette show, and saw the Capuchin monastery, and bought old pewter in the Kaigasse. They didn't even mind the rain.

Then Bracken popped off to Berlin with Johnny for a quick look round, and Camilla found Dinah and Jeff ideal com-

panions for further holiday. Each day it seemed to her that
she came a little more unkinked, and life looked a little
easier even without Sosthène, and things mattered a little
less intensely. She slept better than she had for years, and
actually put on several pounds. Jeff was growing, and had got
quite brown in the sun, and his spirits were high—but he
was learning Austrian instead of German, and would open
a conversation with anyone he encountered, entirely unself-
conscious and with irresistible friendliness.

It was not raining the afternoon late in September when
they sank into chairs in the garden at Tomiselli's and ordered
coffee, with chocolate for Jeff. They had been up to the Fes-
tung again, because Jeff adored the funicular, and Camilla,
who didn't, confessed to a comfortable sort of exhaustion.
Most of the tables were occupied, though the season was at
an end, and while they were waiting to be served Dinah said,
"There are the Shenleys, only a month late, they were coming for the music—at the table in the corner."

Camilla glanced at the corner table, where a girl in a big
hat sat between two men with a third man facing her—she
glanced without much interest, looked again, gave a queer
little sound, and sat very still.

"Who did you say they were?" she asked, and her tongue
felt stiff and cold.

"Paliser Shenley, young Dan Shenley, and Kate, who is one
of my best friends. She—"

"The other man," said Camilla in the same stiff, controlled
tone. "Who is he?"

"Never saw him before," said Dinah. "Would he be a
German, with that scar? They say that student duels are still
the thing, and—"

Just then Kate Shenley turned her head, as people so often
do when they are being discussed, and saw Dinah, and waved,
and they both rose and went to meet each other. Camilla

waited, gripping the edge of the table, feeling sick and queer, while they linked arms and strolled towards her, and Dinah said, "This is our cousin Camilla, Kate, she's travelling with us."

Camilla returned Kate's greeting automatically, and because she could do nothing else for this paralysis of shock she sat still while Kate greeted Jeff with affection, took the extra chair, and said she had just lunched, and began answering Dinah's questions.

"My dear, don't scold *me* about being late for the music!" she cried, and Camilla thought how young and carefree and confident Kate looked, with her wide open blue eyes and rather toothy smile, beneath the expensive, sophisticated hat. "I've been punished enough already! My dear, those brutes of men of mine have dragged me all over Europe, *flying*, if you please, and *factories*, from Sweden *down!* All they know is *aeroplanes*, I hear nothing else from morning till night, and now this infernal *Conference*, and then on to Pisa where they make *more* aeroplanes! It was much nicer when Father just made automobiles, at least then we stayed on the ground!"

Camilla, staring stonily past Kate's chatter to the table in the corner, had caught the eyes of the man with the scar—and saw it flame up crimson to where it ran under the edge of his hat. For a moment more he sat as motionless as she was. Then he rose, moving in a wooden sort of way as though against his will, and came towards her. Camilla sat looking up at him helplessly until he stood before her, and Kate Shenley's voice faded away into surprise.

"Hullo, Raymond," said Camilla gently, and held out her hand.

He took off his hat.

The scar blazed upwards along his left cheek, past the outer corner of his eye forward of the temple, across his forehead and stopped at his hair. There was no distortion of his face in repose, no sign of the scar from his other profile, but even at a little distance the marks where the stitches had been still showed when he faced you. And when he smiled the scar drew upward, kinking his eyebrow into a peak almost the way a pantomime comedian would do it on purpose with make-up—instead of repelling the beholder, the unexpected twist gave to his dark, sombre face an involuntary Puckish fascination. He smiled now, and no one could guess what it had cost him to learn to do that, abandoning rigidity without thinking of the scar.

"Hullo, Camilla," he said, and his hand was warm and firm on hers. No self-consciousness, no evasion, no apology, no guilt—just Raymond. But still he had changed. His clothes were the best of the right kind, and he wore them as though he had forgotten about them. His manner was completely easy, the rather old-fashioned courteousness of his army days a little toned down. He's arrived, thought Camilla, for she had learned things too, in the interim. He's Somebody. Who?

"Well, Raymond," Kate was saying on the other side of him. "What *is* all this, we're dying to know!"

He let Camilla's hand go, and stood bareheaded facing the sun to be introduced to Dinah, smiled again, man to man, at Jeff, who was frankly staring, and then said to Kate, "Camilla and I met in England during the war. She's kind of surprised to see me alive."

"Thank God you are, or Father would still be firing his engineers faster than he hired them," said Kate, and added to Dinah, "Raymond has got Father tamed. He's the only man who ever made engines at the Shenley works that Father can't find everything wrong with. I only hope it lasts, because everything's so peaceful now around the house! But it's all because of *him* that I didn't get here for the music! This whole trip is just for Raymond to see aeroplanes, not for me to hear concerts!"

"Sit down," said Dinah to Raymond cordially, "and defend yourself."

He laid his hand on an unoccupied chair near by and swung it round to face the table and sat down beside Camilla.

"I'm sorry about all that," he said sincerely to Kate. "It was those gliders."

"We came to a place in Germany where they were *gliding*," Kate took it up. "And Raymond and Dan over there went completely *nuts*, and Father and I had to sit on the ground with a crick in our necks and watch and pray! I thought they'd never stop having just one more day at it! And now I suppose you'll start building them!"

"We might," said Raymond, as though it would be fun to try.

"There we go again!" said Kate cheerfully. "Dinah, darling, it's wonderful that you're still here, and where are you staying during the Conference?"

"Stresa. Bracken can motor from there to Locarno every day."

"So are we at Stresa!" Kate crowed. "What luck! Not that we *belong* there, but Father and Dan are just so curious about what's going to happen they can't stay away! Father says it can change the whole equilibrium of the world."

Dinah made a rueful face.

"Don't let him expect too much," she said. "Bracken and Johnny are in Berlin, both very grim."

"Not half so grim as *mine* can be!" Kate asserted with her gay grin. "We all sit around like a *wake,* and wait to bury civilization! In the meantime, I'm going back to the hotel and have a hot bath before somebody drops a bomb on the plumbing! Are you finished swilling coffee here, and can you dine with us at the hotel tonight, or what?"

Dinah explained about the house on the lake, and suggested that they all dine there, and Kate thought that would be lovely, and they all rose and drifted towards the other table. Raymond at Camilla's side said, "How is Calvert?"

"He died. At Williamsburg."

"I'm sorry."

And then there were more introductions, and a reminder of dinner at eight, and directions about how to find the house, and Raymond was gone with the Shenleys.

"Do you want to tell me about it or not?" said Dinah, as they walked back to their own car and Camilla kept a musing silence.

"It's not me," Camilla hesitated. "It's nothing to do with me, really, he was a friend of Calvert's—"

"*Raymond!*" said Dinah suddenly illuminated. "Of *course,* I wasn't thinking! I should have made more of him. I will, tonight. How did the Shenleys get him?"

"I haven't the faintest idea. He was missing. That's all we ever knew. Who are the Shenleys?"

"Oh, come, Camilla, you've heard of Shenley cars! He's built a big new factory somewhere upstate in New York, and they're making planes now—something very special. If Raymond has got a job there he's done very well for himself."

"It's what he always wanted to do," said Camilla. But inside, she could only think of Jenny and what this might mean to her. He had asked about Calvert, not about Jenny. Must Jenny know he was alive? *Couldn't* Jenny know? What did Raymond feel now, about Jenny. . . . "Dinah—I want to talk to him. Do you mind?"

"Of course not. Will after dinner tonight do? You can have the study all to yourselves if you like." Dinah flashed a glance at her as they got into the car. "There's more to it," she said. "Am I not supposed to know?"

"It's not me, you see, I can't—"

"Oh, all right," said Dinah good-humoredly. "Let me die of curiosity!"

"After tonight," Camilla promised uncomfortably. "I must talk to him first."

Raymond's evening clothes had been built by Dan's tailor, and he had forgotten about them too. The scar, now that he was at his ease again, had faded almost to invisibility in the soft drawing-room light, except for the twist to his eyebrow when he smiled, which Camilla continued to find attractive rather than otherwise. During dinner, when the plates were being changed, she caught his eyes across the table and his left lid drooped briefly in the most unnoticeable of winks, as he picked up his fish knife for the next course. He knew his way through a formal dinner now. He called Paliser Shenley sir, in an unobtrusive way, and was Raymond to all three of them.

The talk was easy and in some ways confidential, with things earmarked to be reported to Bracken when he returned with Johnny in a few days' time on his way to Locarno. The Germans were flying again, all right, they said. And their commercial planes could become war planes with no loss of time. While the Germans built planes like those it was suicide for France and England to consider armament limitation. Germany had factories in Sweden, Russia, and Italy for the manufacture of planes with more engine-power than she was permitted under the terms of the Versailles Treaty to construct in Germany—the factories were German-owned, and Heinkel, Junker, and Dornier interests and research were entirely unrestricted on the soil of friendly neighbor countries within six and eight hours flying time from Berlin. Germany had ambitious plans for the construction of giant Zeppelins for passenger routes to Asia and America, as soon as the Treaty could be revised sufficiently to give her leeway to begin—that was one of the main objects now, in Germany, the revision of the Treaty and the erasure of war guilt—the Polish Corridor must be eliminated—evacuation of the Rhineland by the Allies must be conceded—restoration of the German colonies—there would be nothing left at all of the Treaty and of reparations and of atonement, if Germany had her way, and the war would be all forgiven and forgotten, and everything would be just the same as it was (for Germany) before the war began, and everyone would tactfully pretend not to n-o-t-i-c-e the part Germany had played in 1914—and then Germany would be quite free and more than ready to prepare to try it all over again.

It was not altogether a cheerful dinner.

When they rose from the table Camilla slid her hand through Raymond's elbow and turned him aside into the little room Bracken used as a study, while the rest went on into the drawing-room. For a moment he stood with his back against the door he had closed behind them, waiting while she snapped on some lights. She sat down on a sofa facing the fire and motioned him to the place beside her. As he took it, with the good side of his face towards her, he said with a sigh, "Tell me about Calvert. Was it bad?"

Camilla told him, and it was pretty bad. When she had finished he made no comment, gazing into the fire above his pipe, and the silence lengthened between them. She had told it without any mention of Jenny, purposely. But Raymond was not going to mention her either.

"Well, now it's your turn," she said at last, and he roused, and glanced at her rather wearily, and drew a long breath.

"I still don't like to think about some of it," he said. "But I guess I was lucky, at that." In brief, blunt sentences he told of being taken prisoner in the German retreat, with that wound in his face and minor burns—of being dragged, only

half conscious and full of fever, in any kind of transporta-
tion, from place to place as the Germany army moved east-
ward—no one reset the stitches, he rarely had fresh dressings,
infection set in, and he dreaded the loss of his eye. Finally he
was left at a convent along the way with a dozen other half
dead or dying men, and an elderly nun did the best she could
for him. There were days, weeks, in fact, when he had no
idea where he was, or even who he was—he had lost his identity disc, he said, and so naturally was not reported to Geneva.
It was the spring of 1919 before he was able to crawl about
again and remember a life before the crash of his plane.
And then they let him have a mirror. "It was nothing like this
then," he said without self-consciousness. "I've had three
operations on it since then. I'm not going to have another. It's
no use any more, it was neglected too long. And a face like
mine isn't worth bothering about, so long as it doesn't scare
the dogs and children." His money had been taken from him,
but he had picked up enough German to make his way—when
he began to get well he worked for a while in the village
where he had found himself when he left the nuns' care—
odd jobs—gardening—tinkering—farm labor—as long as he
made himself useful, people asked few questions in the
chaos of post-war Germany—gradually he travelled westward
again, towards France—walked across the border without
papers—

"But your *people*," Camilla interrupted at last. "It was
wicked not to let anybody know—"

"There wasn't anybody but you and Calvert," he said
simply. "My Aunt Emma had died in the summer of 1918,
and I had nothing to go home for. Calvert had enough troubles of his own, I thought—and naturally I didn't want anybody to see me—I hoped you'd just forget about me, in time.
I planned it that way."

"Was that fair to Jenny?" she asked softly, and he stared at her.

"Did she tell you?"

"No. I found out by accident. She was dying of it, Raymond."

"She didn't—she's all right now?"

"She didn't die, no."

"Poor Jenny," he said, and sat looking into the fire.

"Well, so you got to France and then what?" she insisted.

"I spoke enough French. I got along. Everybody was too busy to care where I'd come from or where I belonged. There were hundreds of men like me all over Europe then—men that for one reason or another couldn't go back home. Then I got sick somehow, on the farm where I was working—bad food, I guess—they thought I was going to die and a doctor came out from the nearest village. He was wonderful. He said my face could be fixed up a little—not like it had been before I was hurt, but better than it was. I hadn't any money, of course, but he sent me to another doctor, a surgeon, and they arranged for me to work out the money, driving their cars and gardening and things like that—I think they wanted some one to experiment on. Well, it was better when they finished, and that was two operations. And when I'd paid off that debt I shipped home as a grease monkey on an American freighter. I knew I could always make a living as a mechanic in America, and before long I got a job in the Shenley Long Island works. One thing led to another there, and they let me have a corner of the shop to do some work of my own. One of my gadgets caught on, and the front office sent for me. And so on. Mr. Shenley paid for the third operation on my face, in New York. I tell him it's no good going on with any more. Does it look too bad?"

"It doesn't look bad at all." There was another long silence, which he would not break. "You haven't—married, then?"

He turned to look at her slowly, removing the pipe from his mouth.

"Are you crazy?" he said.

"But, Raymond—aren't you going to let Jenny know—ever?"

"Looking like this?" He shook his head. "I was no beauty before."

"Is that the only reason?"

"There were always plenty of other reasons, without this one," he said patiently.

"Don't you want to hear about Jenny—now?"

He stirred uneasily, and would not meet her eyes, busying himself with his pipe.

"If you can honestly tell me that you're in love with somebody else now," said Camilla, "I'll shut up." She waited. "*Is* there somebody else?"

"You know damn' well there isn't. But by now Jenny will have got over all that, she wouldn't—"

"How do you know?"

His eyes came round to her then, wide and steady and knife-grey.

"She hasn't got married?" he asked incredulously.

So Camilla told him about Jenny, and the work she did at St. Dunstan's, and the last time she and Jenny had met, over the tea-cups in the three drab rooms where Jenny lived alone. When she had finished he was sitting very still, the pipe clenched between his teeth.

"I didn't know it would be like that," he said finally, with a visible effort to speak calmly. "Honestly, I had no idea—" He rose, and bent over the hearth, tapping out his pipe. When he straightened, the scar was a crimson zigzag from cheek to hair. "What do you think I ought to do?" he demanded directly.

"Oh, Raymond—not what you *ought*. What do you *want* to do?"

"I want Jenny, of course," he said with his often childlike simplicity. "Just the same as I always did. But I gave up any idea of that in Germany years ago. It didn't stop me wanting her, but it made me decide to lie low, so far as she was concerned. What would she say now if I walked in—like this? If I was going to expect her to be—I mean, if I'd meant to go back there I would have let her know before now. I've got no right to think she still remembers—what we said when I was at Farthingale. I've got no right to—"

"Jenny's got a right to decide that, Raymond."

"Do you think she'd forgive me?" The idea seemed to strike him with the first faint ray of hope.

"Raymond—have you forgotten how Jenny is?"

"No." He began to walk up and down on the hearthrug, not looking at her, looking inside himself with excitement and a lingering doubt. "No, I haven't forgotten anything about her. Not one single thing. I've thought about her till —all that time I was sick, I thought about her, and how it was the other time, when she was looking after me—I've thought about Jenny till I almost went out of my mind. And so I had to stop. I had to put her away, and think about engines instead—build engines in my head—go back to the shop and work all night with grease up to my eyebrows—I studied —I learned all kinds of things—so as not to think about Jenny. I'd just got it sort of lined up so I could get along like that—and then Mr. Shenley decided on this trip, and the first place we went was England, to the Hendon show—and it started all over again. I actually thought once I saw her there—"

"You probably did."

"Well, Germany fixed that, anyway—what we saw there, and heard them say, and the way I felt, to see what they're up to, in Germany—sort of took my mind off everything else for a while again. And now *you* begin!" He faced her on the hearthrug, almost angrily. "What am I supposed to do now?" he demanded.

"Why don't you go and see her?"

"But I *can't* just walk in on her, I—" He came and sat down on the sofa again, chastened and polite like the boy they had known in England. "You've got to break it to her," he said. "Will you write her a letter?"

"I think you're the one to do that."

"I'm not much good at letters. Will you help me?" he asked humbly.

"Really, Raymond, you of all people must know what to say to Jenny!"

"I never did," he confessed. "You see, in France my letters were all read by the CO. And anyway—I don't know how to write things down."

"Poor Jenny," said Camilla, smiling.

"You see, I'm afraid if I just show up again like this, out of the blue, she might think I—*expect* something. I don't want her to feel—*obliged* to see me again, if she'd rather not. That's why I thought if you wrote to her and said you had seen me, we could tell by what she wrote back—"

"Coward."

He laughed a little, the eyebrow kinked upward, and his eyes were candid and sweet.

"It isn't that," he said. "Not entirely. It wouldn't be fair to her to—"

"I suppose you think you've been being fair to her all these years!"

"I meant to be," he said unargumentatively, stating a self-evident fact. "I thought I was doing the best thing for her, honestly. I thought she'd marry Calvert—or somebody else, if she had the chance to forget me—if she wasn't sorry for me—"

"It's not you *I'm* sorry for," said Camilla. "It's Jenny."

"Do you honestly think she could ever be happy married to me?" he asked, between exasperation and patience, appealing to her commonsense as though he already knew the answer would be in the negative.

"She thinks so. That's what matters. But only if you want it yourself, Raymond—not if you've changed or outgrown it yourself."

"Well, what do you think?" he asked with his engaging simplicity. "Every time I've gone up a notch—when they called me into the office and began to talk about patents—when Mr. Shenley gave me a real job like this I've got now—when they fixed my face the last time—when he asked me to come on this trip with them, like one of the family, and I bought these clothes—I always thought of Jenny. Because it was as though she'd known it was going to happen, long before I did. I don't mean I've got much money, even now—not yet. I'm still learning, and I can't save. It takes all I get to keep up, the way I have to live now, the way I'd want to live—with Jenny, if I had her. But I never thought I'd see her again. I thought by now she'd have a family of her own, somebody her own kind, and I wouldn't want to embarrass her, I—but as it is, from what you say she's got a right to be sore at me. It's like not keeping a date with a girl, the way it's turned out. Maybe she wouldn't want to see me now, maybe—"

"Coward."

He laughed again, without resentment, and his eyebrow peaked grotesquely.

"I guess I am, at that," he admitted. "It's kind of like going over the top again. You wouldn't come along and blow the whistle for me?"

Camilla shook her head.

"Jenny won't bite you."

"And you're *sure* it's all right for me to—"

"You won't ask me that when you see her. Can you start for England tomorrow?"

"That all depends on Mr. Shenley. I don't think he'll need me every day while the Conference at Locarno is on. We were going on to the Dornier works at Pisa after that."

"Let's go and ask him." Camilla rose.

"You know—if anything comes of this, I'll never be able to thank you enough," he said seriously.

"I'd like to see her happy."

"And you?"

"Oh, me, I'm in a rut," said Camilla, moving towards the door.

The kindest of men, Paliser Shenley was very pleased to give Raymond leave to go to London and fix things up with his girl there. He even rang up Paris and got Raymond a seat in the London plane, and advised him to go the Langham Hotel, as it was nearer to Regent's Park than the Ritz, where they had all stayed before, and was very comfortable.

So Raymond found himself unpacking his bag in Portland Place before he had managed to formulate his approach to Jenny. His natural inclination was towards the telephone, but he knew that wouldn't do. Jenny believed that he was dead. He couldn't just ring up and say he wasn't. Nor he couldn't just ring her doorbell in St. John's Wood and be standing there on the mat. She'd think she was seeing things.

A hot bath and a change of clothes didn't bring any revelations, either. He sat down at the writing-desk in his room and began a letter to her—tore it up and began another—and tore that up. *Dear Jenny: I wasn't killed in the crash, but I let you think so, because—* No. *Dear Jenny: I thought you would forget me and marry somebody more your kind*— No. What on earth did you say to a girl who thought you were dead? *Dear Jenny: I happened to run into Camilla and she said*— He threw down the pen and went out into the early October dusk of London. He turned southward, deliberately avoiding St. Dunstan's and the St. John's Wood address which Camilla had given him. He went down Regent Street and came all too soon to Piccadilly Circus where it seemed that some decision was required of him before he went further.

He was unaccustomed to dilemmas like this which could not be reasoned out in a decent length of time, and he was getting angry with himself. Moodily he turned into a cheerful-looking restaurant and followed a head waiter to a table against the wall. Wine card and menu were put into his hand. He ordered a whiskey cocktail and a cutlet, and made a solitary meal, aware that he might have had Jenny's happy face across the table—he was wasting time—but after so many years, did a few more hours matter? He left the table without a sweet and emerged again into the Circus, which swirled with theater time crowds. He thought of going to a play —leaving further action till tomorrow. Coward, said Camilla. He stepped into a taxi and returned to his hotel. There he wrote out a telegram and sent it off and sat down in the lounge with the evening papers. *Dear Jenny: I am at the Langham Hotel. I met Camilla by accident at Salzburg and she said you would see me. I shall wait here for you to telephone and let me explain. Raymond.*

She might not be at home this evening, of course. He would probably have to wait till about lunch time tomorrow before he heard from her. Even then she might not want to see him —she might write instead—Jenny knew how to write letters —or she might want time to think it over. . . .

He sat with the *Standard* open before him, forgetting to turn the page, and thought about Jenny. Now that he had sent the message and burnt his boats, a mounting excitement gripped him, a real stage-fright. What should he say on the telephone about the scar, she must be warned. Or would it be best to wait and watch her face, so as to be sure if it was too great a shock at her first sight of it, unprepared? Jenny had a face you could read like a book. . . .

The newspaper blurred before his unseeing gaze and there was only Jenny's face, its parted, eager lips, its honest, trustful eyes. She always looked at you as though you were the King. The old, abiding ache of his longing for Jenny had hold of him again, and he could only surrender to it as he had not done for a long time. If he lost her now, if he lost her again . . . But Camilla must know. Camilla was so sure. Jenny had always been so sure. And it wouldn't be Indian Landing now, nor night school, nor greasy overalls. That was all behind him. His father's house was still there, his own house now, and the town was still there, pretty much unchanged, and always would be—he meant to go back to it for summer holidays. But Jenny wouldn't have to get a job and try not to be an expense—he was remembering that day on the terrace at the Hall and Jenny sitting beside him on the little folding stool in her blue VAD dress, with tears dropping down on her hands—*When this war is over dukes aren't going to matter—nobody's going to care who I am, we needn't tell them in America.* . . . But Camilla had told them that night in Salzburg, and nobody had seemed to think twice about it, not even Dinah, who was a ladyship herself. Of course things were a little different now, with Paliser Shenley behind him—no one but Jenny had foreseen Paliser Shenley in 1918. . . .

"*Raymond.*"

It was a sound barely above a whisper, and Jenny stood beside his chair.

He rose in a single movement, dropping the paper,

and their hands came together, and there were her parted lips and her shining eyes, and—she had had no warning about the scar. He smiled down at her, and felt the familiar, inevitable upward twist of his face, and Jenny did not so much as blink.

"You shouldn't have come here," he said, more in surprise than in rebuke, with amusement too at the way Jenny never could do things by halves. "I would have come to you."

"I couldn't wait for that," said Jenny. "I just grabbed my hat and coat and ran till I saw a taxi. I forgot to bring any money. He's waiting outside to be paid. It will cost you one and ninepence."

He laughed. He pressed the small, warm fingers in his.

"I guess I can stand that," he said, but before he could move towards the door she held him, with both hands.

"Or we could take the taxi back to my flat where we can talk," she said, with a glance round the quiet lounge and the people drinking after-dinner coffee and settling in for the evening.

He paused, looking down at her searchingly—and knew that it was all right with Jenny, that she wasn't holding anything against him, that he didn't have to explain and apologize, that it was enough for Jenny that he was there, between her hands again. She looked tired, he thought, and too thin, and so small, and she stood so straight—but tired. And sort of forlorn. Living alone, like that, earning her own living, or part of it, holding out for him, when she must have had dozens of chances to do better. Stubborn. Her chin was sticking out right now. Something like pity flooded through him, a warm tide of tenderness, and he made what was perhaps the most impulsive speech of his life so far.

"If we take that taxi back to your place," he said quietly, "it means that you're going to marry me—*now*, as soon as we can."

Jenny looked back at him gravely, without reservations or caution.

"Is that what you came to London for?"

"I came to London to show you this face. Camilla said—" He hesitated.

"Said it wouldn't scare me?" Jenny suggested. "Did you really think that would make any difference to me?"

"Doesn't it?"

"The taxi meter will say two shillings by now," said Jenny. "And besides, you can't possibly kiss me here, it would cause raised eyebrows."

But he did, a quick hard one, and the Langham lounge tactfully pretended it hadn't seen, and then watched them wistfully as they departed, hand in hand, to the waiting cab.

When they had seen Raymond off to Paris and the London plane, Camilla reacted in a vast desolation which she attributed to the basest reasons and accused herself of selfishness and envy. Jenny and Raymond had earned it. She ought to be glad. She *was* glad. But she had never felt so lonely in her life, not even when Calvert died. She knew that she was entirely unequal to preserving her usual equanimity in an intimate family party at Stresa. She needed some time to herself to get hold of things. She decided to stay on alone at the Oesterreichische Hof, and join them later, possibly for Christmas in London.

Dinah was surprised, but she was always willing that people should have their own moods and foibles in peace, and she advised Bracken to let Camilla be, as it was plain she wasn't happy. Bracken thought the thing to do in that case was to have lots of company and plenty to think about besides oneself. But Dinah said he wasn't to try to live Camilla's life for her, and he subsided with the proviso that if she got tired of it Camilla should send them a telegram at once and come straight on to the hotel at Stresa. Camilla promised, and felt relief mixed with her misery as she watched them drive away, the Shenleys in one car, Bracken, Dinah, Jeff, and Johnny in the other. At least she wouldn't have to put a face on things for a few days. She could moon about, and feel sorry for herself because things weren't so simple for her and Sosthène, and she must try to answer the letters Kim was writing from Paris, and sort herself out again.

She was still at it more than a week later when the new Pact had been initialled at Locarno and the Conference was adjourned in a general glow of optimism very different from the break-up at Genoa three years before. The nations of the world had forsworn war. Germany's signature was there with the rest. Not Russia's. But Russia might begin to feel lonely now. . . .

The Shenleys had gone on to Pisa and Raymond was to join them there, with Jenny as his bride. They would all come back through Paris and sail from Boulogne in November, and Jenny would be setting out for America with a Paris trousseau as a gift from Kate Shenley. The happy ending, Camilla thought, with a sigh. And I helped. Well, God knows Jenny would have done as much for me.

Dinah's broadmindedness was not quite sufficient to take the observant Jeff into Sally's household at Cannes, so they were going straight through to London, and Bracken suggested that Camilla come with them to Farthingale and stay for Christmas. Camilla shook her head, but confessed under pressure that there was nothing else she had to do instead.

"Ever been to Switzerland?" Johnny asked her unexpectedly.

Camilla said she hadn't.

"You ought to come to Switzerland for winter sports," said Johnny. "Can you ski?"

Camilla said she couldn't.

"I'll teach you," said Johnny. "Of course you may break your neck, but in that case you wouldn't have anything more to worry about."

Camilla said she thought that might be a very convenient state of affairs.

"And if it's only your leg you break," said Johnny, "You get a nice rest and time to catch up on your reading."

Camilla said it all sounded most attractive.

They were having cocktails before dinner in the sitting-room of Bracken's suite at the Oesterreichische Hof, and just then a page knocked on the door and handed in a telegram for Bracken. Nobody took any notice, because Bracken was always getting telegrams. Johnny was in the midst of a lively description of Chamonix in its valley at the bottom of Mont Blanc, with enthusiastic footnotes by Dinah, who had been there at the same time last winter, when Bracken said, "Oh, dear," in an odd sort of way, and they all stopped talking to look at him.

He passed the telegram to Dinah, who said slowly when she had read it, "You and Camilla will have to go, I can't possibly take Jeff there."

"Where?" Camilla asked, and Bracken said, without thinking to break it to her, "Sosthène died suddenly last night— heart, of course, we all knew it could happen, but Sally is prostrated. We'll have to go and see to things for her, I suppose, she's counting on it." And he and Johnny began talking about trains and whether Dinah should stop in Paris or go straight on to London with Jeff.

Camilla sat very still, waiting for the room to stop going round, waiting for some sort of equilibrium to return. She felt as though something had fallen on her, and her stomach was cold and queasy, and her heart seemed to be trying to come through her side, and her face felt stiff and white, like a stone. . . .

"Camilla—" Dinah's voice came to her from a long way off. "Camilla, what *is* it?"

"I'm sorry, I think I'm going to faint," Camilla said quite distinctly, and the room reeled again, and she shut her eyes.

"Oh, nonsense, nobody faints nowadays," said Johnny's voice, and she felt a vigorous arm between her sagging shoulders and the back of the chair, and the rim of a glass pressed cold against her lips. "Drink this down, quick." The icy liquid struck her throat, and she strangled and leaned against him, coughing and shaking her head. "That's better," said Johnny. "Got to learn to take your liquor, though, and you from the South."

But still she clung to him, the rough tweed of his sleeve the only real and stable thing in a world which heaved and swung beneath her like a ship at sea. She kept her head down, in dread of the moment when she must show them her face, white and stiff like a stone, and even while she thought *I can't*, she was doing it, and saw in their eyes only concern for her sudden collapse, and not suspicion, nor comprehension —not yet.

"You mustn't be ill now, Camilla," Bracken was saying in a practical tone of voice. "You've got to come to Cannes with me in the morning."

"I can't—go to Cannes," she said, clinging to Johnny, and felt herself begin to tremble.

"Darling, what is it, you seemed perfectly well till just now." Dinah was holding her other hand, and patting it briskly. "Have you got a pain?"

Camilla looked round at them helplessly, Johnny's rough sleeve clutched tight in cold fingers, while the trembling ran all through her so that Johnny felt it too and tightened his arm reassuringly.

"Dinah, you've got to help me. You'll have to say I'm ill, or think of something better. I can't go to see Sally now."

"I'm afraid you must go, my dear," said Bracken, still not comprehending. "You were always her favorite, and you can't fail her at a time like this. Besides, after Sosthène, you are her sole heir."

"Oh, *no!*" cried Camilla, shrinking closer against Johnny's shoulder.

"I've known about it for some time because I am named executor," said Bracken. "The Will is very simple. Everything was to go to Sosthène, for his lifetime. And at his death you were to inherit everything. Elvire to be provided for as long as she lives, but beyond that there are no obligations, restrictions, or bequests. It's a very substantial fortune, even without the jewels, which also come to you. The least you can do in the circumstances is to go to her now when she needs you."

"But—don't you see—" Camilla began piteously, the tears raining down her face, and they all suddenly caught on, and Bracken said, "Oh, Lord, you and Sosthène? My dear girl, I'm terribly sorry about this, I had no idea."

Camilla sat there trembling, with Johnny's arm hard behind her, and her face streaming with tears, and her eyes went slowly from one to another of their three anxious faces.

"I don't want you to get the wrong impression," she said with difficulty. "There wasn't anything—except that he knew I loved him—ever since that first Christmas at Farthingale. We never—had much time together. There was nothing—to keep from her—except that we loved each other. We tried—not to let her know that. He thought she didn't. So now you see why I can't go to Cannes. I can't face her like this. I should give myself away."

Nobody said anything. Bracken turned and walked to the window and stood there with his hands in his pockets looking out towards the snow-capped mountains that ringed the horizon.

"It would be a pity," he said at last, "if anything—untoward should happen now to make her wonder, wouldn't it."

"You mean—if I don't go—she might think—"

"She'd be bound to think it very queer—wouldn't she," said Bracken reasonably. "Much queerer than if you broke down and cried at the funeral."

"I can't—*I can't!*" said Camilla, and hid her face against the nearest thing, which happened to be Johnny's tweed shoulder, and sobbed and trembled and shook—and knew, as they all did, that she would go to Cannes with Bracken in the morning, in order that Sosthène's flawless kindness and care of Sally should not be wasted now.

━━━━━

Johnny was to drive Dinah and Jeff to Paris by easy stages, while Bracken and Camilla took a train to Cannes. Dimly aware of his abiding surprise, his tactful lack of curiosity, and his sympathetic silence as he sat apparently engrossed in the welter of books and magazines which always accompanied him on even the briefest journey, Camilla stared out of the window of the railway carriage and saw nothing of the spectacular scenery through which they passed on the way to the French border. Her whole being was knotted up in the effort for composure. She had cried herself out during the night, the way Jenny had cried at Farthingale—hopelessly, bitterly, without dignity in her despair. This was what one got for trying to do the right thing. Wait, Sosthène had said once, as I do. And now it was too late. Too careful even to take what little joy of each other they might have had, now they had lost everything. Had he known, that day in the library at Cannes, that it would be like this? Had he perhaps kept the knowledge to himself, even then, and let her go, perhaps to make it easier for her, just as he had denied himself all indulgence in her love, to keep Sally's world safe for Sally?

I must know how it happened, Camilla thought, staring out blindly at the mountains around Innsbruck. I must know what he said last, where he was, how long it took—they can't just snatch him away from me like this—he wouldn't have left any word for me—but if I had been there—oh, no, I couldn't have been there, that belonged to Sally. . . .

The old savage rebellion against Sally's unchallenged possession of him rose and overwhelmed her again—it was never jealousy, you couldn't hate Sally, who was so innocent of being in the way—and you couldn't blame Sosthène for his tender care of Sally's peace of mind after all those years together. It was herself who was the interloper, and jealousy of Sally couldn't come into that, only an angry futile striving against the Way Things Were, no thought of changing them, no plan for circumventing circumstance, no chance for anything but patience and an obstinate, nameless, guilty hope that some day Things would be different, not through any careless or desperate act of one's own, of course, but just with the inevitable passing of time.

And now that hope was dead, along with Sosthène. Staring out of the window, Camilla realized that her cheeks were wet again with the slow, relentless tears which seemed to have no end, and she wiped them away impatiently, and hoped that Bracken had not noticed. She could not behave like this at Cannes. She must find composure somewhere, or everyone who saw her would know. But to enter that house again, where all the rooms would seem newly emptied of the quiet, smiling presence which was a part of them, was an ordeal she still could not face with anything like courage.

Bracken said Sally meant to leave the house to her, and all that went with it, which seemed the final irony. She would never be able to bear the sight of the house, she would have to shut it up, sell it, or give it away, when Sally had finished with it. Perhaps Bracken might like to have it himself, for Jeff. She only wanted to get away from it now, as soon as it was decently possible, back to Paris, back to Kim, and the noisiest, most superficial, fly-by-night crowd she could find.

In her desolation, still resembling anger more than grief, as though a trick had been played on her by something there was no other name for but Life, unless you blamed God Himself, Camilla found herself thinking of Kim, who always knew too much, and guessed the rest, but was on the whole tactful about it, and knew how to make one laugh and feel better. It was for Sally to mourn, even that was denied to herself. And nothing would last very long for Sally now. But if you were thirty-one, you still had a life to live, somehow, with whatever you could find to live it for. You couldn't just sit around and mope for another thirty years, nor you couldn't just comfortably die of it, like the Lily Maid of Astolat. Kim would understand about that. I am a fool, she would say to Kim with due humility when she got back to Paris, and I would rather be dead than go on being a fool. Show me, she would say to Kim meekly, how not to go on being a fool. And Kim would laugh, but affectionately, and write her a new song full of deep notes, and find her a new job—and when he made love to her, what would she say now?

Sleepless and white-faced and in a precarious state of composure, Camilla entered Sally's house at Bracken's side. Sally was in bed, tended by Elvire, whose eyes were red-rimmed but who showed no visible emotion. Sally, with her hair becomingly dressed and her *masquillage* in place, wearing a lace bedjacket, received them at once. She lifted her face to Bracken's kiss, and held to Camilla's hand so that it pulled her down on the edge of the bed. Sally in her tearless grief had a pitiful dignity. But she had become very fragile, almost transparent, and her voice, which had always been so rich and young, was as though some one was sleeping near by.

"It was good of you both to come so fast," she said, holding to Camilla's hand, with her eyes fixed on Bracken's face. "I haven't much time, and I wanted to see you." She said it so easily—I haven't much time—as though she was catching a train. "Bracken, there is a lawyer somewhere in the house, and a couple of doctors—please see them for me, and make them let me alone. You know all about the Will—you can explain that to Camilla later, nothing is changed. I would like to talk to her now."

Bracken kissed Sally's cheek again and left the room. Camilla sat still on the edge of the bed, thinking Here it comes, and dreading whatever it was that she must hear.

"If I were you," Sally was saying in that odd, muted way, as the door closed behind Bracken, "I would prefer just to think of Sosthène as gone away. I would not want to hear the last details, and I would not want to see him as he is now. Although I will tell you at once that it was very quick and easy, and he looks at peace. But it is not Sosthène as you knew him."

"Perhaps you would rather not talk about it," Camilla said uncertainly, and Sally replied at once, "It is not what I would rather, Camilla, it is what you wish to carry with you for the rest of your life. As it is now, you can always remember him alive, if you try—there will be no other picture of him in your mind."

"Yes," said Camilla after a moment, whispering too, and Sally's fingers tightened on hers, and somehow it was Sally who was comforting Camilla, and not the other way round. "Perhaps that would be easier."

"It is the way he meant it to be, for you," Sally said. "And I want you to remember me that way too, when the time comes. Let them do what is necessary. Elvire will look after

me as she always has. I don't want you to inherit a lot of
ghosts, my dear, along with this house, which has always
been a happy place, full of people and music and laughter
and love-making. I would like to think that you will keep
it like that, when it is yours. Don't let it pine for us, Camilla.
You may not want to live here all the time, as I have done
—at least not yet, while you are young. But come back to it
now and then and bring friends with you, and keep it company. Will you do that for me?"

"I'll try," Camilla promised, clinging to Sally's fingers, and
there went her selfish intention of never setting foot in the
place again.

"It is easy to be happy here, you will find—easier than you
think now, perhaps," Sally went on. "Always remember, my
darling, that happiness and love need not die till you do—
that life renews itself if you allow it to, as surely as the year
comes back round to spring after winter. Some years are not
so good as others—sometimes you love less, sometimes more—
and you can never be sure that the best is not still to come.
So many times I have thought This is all—now I have come
to the end—now there will be nothing to live for." Her fingers
moved on Camilla's, caressingly. "So many times I have been
wrong. And for me, the best came last. Always remember
that."

"I'll try," Camilla promised.

"To love only once in a lifetime because things go wrong
is stupid and selfish and short-sighted," said Sally against her
pillows. "It is wilfully to waste what happiness *le bon Dieu*
allows to us and to those we might make happy. It is wilfully
to wear a blindfold over eyes that can still see, because once
they beheld a perfect sunset or a sublime view. The sun will
go down on another day—the road will make another turn—
one should always be willing to look again. Do you understand?"

Their eyes met in a long, wordless intimacy, and Camilla thought, *She knew,* but there was no guilt, no apology, no embarrassment in that swift conviction, because Sally, knowing also that there was nothing to forgive, had only an immense compassion, without any hurt or resentment. And that was thanks to Sosthène.

"You will not always be happy, my dear, however wise you are—I wasn't—but always take what comes to you—don't fight life, Camilla, accept it with grace. Don't strike attitudes about how brave you are, or how tragic you are, or how hard done by—nobody is looking, unless you are in front of a mirror. Don't lunge at life and try to bully it into doing things your way—it's bigger than you are, it will do as it likes with you. Don't sulk, either, and turn your back on it—it will go on without you. Sit still, Camilla, not facing the light, and always looking your best, and let life come to you—think before you speak—smile when you want to cry—don't score at some one else's expense, even if you feel justified, you will lose more sympathy than you will gain satisfaction—never refuse love lightly, and never try to revive it when it fades—and never, never tell Everything to any living soul."

"I'll try," Camilla promised, with a wry little smile.

"Some people there are who would say that is bad advice I give you," said Sally. "But it is the way I have lived, and I have had in my time everything a woman could ask for. Perhaps it would not do for everybody. But for those of us, like you and me, who set out alone, it works very well, on the whole. Take what comes to you, Camilla—and when you give, use both hands. No man can love a stingy woman, not forever. It is no disgrace to be humble when you love a man—nor to be grateful to him that he loves you. It is no one's birthright to be loved—so never take it for granted. Sometimes it comes by surprise, but to be kept it must be earned again each day, by kindness and thought and always with tenderness, my dear, little words, little laughters, little glances—do not be afraid to show him, do not be afraid that some one else will see—let them see—they will only envy you.'

"Yes—I know," said Camilla.

"And now go and wash and rest and put on some more make-up. And send Bracken here to me."

"Thank you—for everything," Camilla whispered, and kissed Sally's cheek, and left the room with a backward glance and a smile at the door.

And she never saw Sally again.

THE LIGHTS ARE DIMMING

1. AUTUMN IN CANNES. 1930.

ALMOST AGAINST HER WILL, CAMILLA TOOK her legacy seriously. After what Sally had said that day, it was impossible to sell the house, or give it away. She felt responsible now for keeping it cheerful and amused. It weighed on her mind like a duty to a living thing. At first she made hard work of living in Sally's house—later the task took on the ease of habit. The Kendrick family helped her, by spending time there with their travelling nursery, and their legion of transatlantic friends. Kim helped her by enlisting his own rather various acquaintances for house parties. The family helped her by running over from London with its young and acquiring a tan on the rocks between the garden and the water. Sometimes this program required a nice adjustment of time-tables and schedules, so that Virginia's daughters did not encounter Kim's more exotic associates, and the smaller children came at a time when it was convenient for them to have the run of the house. There was however one fixture which the family was expected to take in its stride, and at which it never openly boggled—Kim was always there, or had just gone, or was about to arrive.

Camilla had at last learned the geography of the house, but she occupied the same comfortable room with its blue-tiled bath and the balcony facing the sea to which she had been assigned on her first visit years before. Sally's own rooms, with Sosthène's bedroom opening on to the same balcony, were not closed off, but nobody ever used them. Their doors stood open to the passage, their windows admitted the sun and sea air, their vases were kept full of fresh flowers, and fires were laid in the grates and sometimes lighted to keep out the damp. It was just that nobody ever sat down in them. There were plenty of other rooms, and Camilla had also re-sisted a cowardly impulse to lock up the library. Its door was always open, the contents of its shelves were regularly added to, and its books came and went at the whim of any guest who wished to read in bed.

There were no haunted chambers in the house, no ghosts, no echoes, for that was the way Sally had wanted it. And Ca-milla, as Sally had foretold, was happier there than she had expected to be. She was not angry any more, though she still felt bitter and a little raw, and preferred not to think much, and sometimes made rather a business of keeping her mind occupied with trivial daily things and a perpetual chatter about nothing.

Almost imperceptibly, almost to her own surprise, Sally's pattern of existence at Cannes enfolded her. She became more and more the hostess, the queen bee, and spent less time in Paris, for Paris began to come to her. She gave up regular singing engagements, and invested some of Sally's money in a new revue for which Kim had written the songs, though she did not appear in it herself. The show was a suc-cess, and they did very well out of it financially, and an Anglicised version went to London and did better still. Kim and Camilla went along, of course, to attend rehearsals, and she was not really surprised, and certainly she never shed a tear, when Kim fell in love with the leading lady there. By then a very presentable but stage-struck young man newly escaped from Cambridge who would one day write very good plays wanted to marry her, but Camilla said she was old enough to be his mother, which was far from true, and after a few months they parted friends.

Camilla's partnership with Kim in show business continued to be mutually profitable, and their respect for each other and an abiding affection and understanding survived the end of their love affair. They did another revue in London together the following year, and Kim changed leading ladies, to Camilla's tolerant amusement.

Johnny and Bracken both came to Paris for the signing of the Kellogg Pact in the summer of 1928—sixty-two nations agreed therewith to outlaw war. But Johnny said it was very difficult to find any difference between the new Pact and the original League Covenant which had been signed at Versailles, and again at Locarno—and as usual it contained no single word about what measures were to be taken, or ever could be taken, against its violators. Why, asked Johnny inconveniently in the midst of so much international satisfaction, should it have to be all carefully written out and piously signed again? Where, Johnny wanted to know not for the first time, was the Big Stick?

Germany was in the League now. Tremendous foreign investments had been poured into the country until Germany could no longer with a straight face claim that she could not afford to pay reparations, to the great chagrin of people like Dr. Schacht. The evacuation of the Rhineland had been begun ahead of time, in the Allies' eager efforts to please their defeated enemy, who showed no gratitude for concessions nor penitence for past misdeeds, and who were known to be con-structing submarines in a Spanish shipyard, as such activities were still technically forbidden in home waters. They were training army officers in military maneuvers in Russia, and in return for this hospitality trained Russian troops in the same Prussian methods. But of course nobody would ever go to war again. The Pact of Paris said so.

Johnny and Bracken visited Cannes that summer, when they left Paris. It was one of the wilder weeks there, with the Kendrick family in the house and some of Kim's set as well. Johnny quite entered into the spirit of things, Camilla thought, and got along very well indeed with a golden-haired countess who had a Hungarian name and had done film work at the Ufa studios in Berlin, and who was returning there shortly for another engagement—the beginning of a beautiful friendship, Camilla remarked without malice to Bracken, who looked at her sidewise and said she would soon out-Sally Sally if she didn't watch out. But when Johnny said Good-bye he took Camilla's hand in his warm, hard grip and said gravely, "This has been great fun. May I come again?"

Two years went by before he came again, and it was Sep-tember, and the recent German general elections had left everyone in Europe a little stunned by the seemingly sudden eruption to prominence of the man called Hitler, the man with the funny mustache who was always talking—and people had begun to ask, "Who *is* this fellow?" and "What does Nazi *mean?*" Johnny knew who Hitler was, and Johnny told them what Nazi meant—militarism—uniforms—the goose-step again—blood red banners with a black crooked cross—and the slogan, *Germany, awake!* It meant the end of dis-armament everywhere, it meant no more reparations, no war guilt, no Versailles, no security in Europe. It meant revenge. It could mean war.

"But, man alive, they're in the League, they've promised to be good!" objected the film actor from Hollywood who was lying on his spine wearing nothing but scarlet bathing-trunks in the garden chair next to Johnny. "And there's this Kellogg Pact, whatever it is, they signed that like everybody else!"

"Did you ever hear of the scrap of paper?" Johnny asked ironically. "Or are you too young?"

"I wouldn't take Hitler too seriously if I were you," said a dark young man also clad only in bathing-trunks who was sunning himself on a beach-mat laid on the grass at Camilla's feet. "We need him—for a while—to keep the Communists in order. Later, we shall get rid of him, but he doesn't know that."

There was a slightly uncomfortable pause. Owing to Camilla's easy way with introductions, Johnny had no idea what the young man's name was, and he spoke English with hardly any accent, but he spoke, apparently, as a German.

"Aren't you rather overdoing it recently?" Johnny suggested. "Isn't Hitler rather a risk from now on?"

"You mean because of his army? Nah!" It was an ugly sound of disgust. "The old army will take care of that, when the time comes. The men of my father's generation are not asleep, I can promise you!"

"Victor's father was on the Kaiser's staff," Camilla explained to Johnny. "You may have heard of him—Prince Conrad zu Polkwitz-Heidersdorf."

The name struck Johnny with an almost visible jolt. He sat looking down at the outstretched form of the young German lying in arrogant golden-tanned beauty at Camilla's feet—a truly superb specimen, not typically Teuton, for his hair and eyes were dark. But now Johnny thought he could see a resemblance in the jutting nose and heavy, well-chiselled lips. He wondered if his own name would mean anything to Victor, and how much Prince Conrad's son had ever learned about his English mother. It was fifteen years since Johnny had driven up to the Schloss at Heidersdorf with a crinkle of nerves at the pit of his stomach, commissioned to discover what had become of the woman who had been Rosalind Norton-Leigh, and who was then cut off by the war from any communication with her former home in London. But Johnny in the sunlit garden at Cannes could still feel the Zenda-like atmosphere of the Schloss in war time, and the preposterous interview with Prince Conrad, who explained so logically and amiably why it was impossible for his wife to make a visit in neutral Switzerland just then—Johnny had forgotten no single theatrical detail of Rosalind's subsequent flight from Germany, veiled and luggageless and fantastically composed, in his charge. It might be interesting to know how much Victor knew—Rosalind had never had a word from Germany since her departure, not even in the form of a divorce action.

"It was His Highness's mother that I knew best," Johnny said experimentally, and Victor sat up with a jerk, leaning on one hand to face him.

"And your name is—?"

"Malone," said Johnny, meeting the aggressive stare of the man on the grass, and saw that the name rang a bell.

"You know her still?"

"I haven't seen her since she went back to England. She is well and happy, I believe."

"Living with that British officer for whom you once acted?"

"Colonel Laverham had nothing whatever to do with my action. I came to Heidersdorf at the request of Phoebe Sprague, who was your mother's girlhood friend."

"I know all that. But she went to him."

"Eventually. Why not?"

"It is shameful."

"There is such a thing as divorce. But apparently your father has not seen fit—"

"Naturally not." Victor rose to his feet, scowling, but moving with grace and dignity, and turned to Camilla. "I apologize for discussing my personal affairs in this way. Mr. Malone took me quite by surprise." And he made a majestic little bow, clad only in bathing trunks, and stalked away towards the house.

"*Well!*" said the actor from Hollywood, a second too soon. "What was that all about?"

"I never even knew he had a mother," said Camilla, dazed.

"Most people do," said the Hollywood man wittily. No one laughed.

"To think I've picked up Rosalind's son," said Camilla. "What will Phoebe say?"

"Where did you get him?" Johnny asked.

"Kim brought him. I suppose they met in Paris originally. Everybody does. I rather liked him, for a German, he's not got a straight back to his head."

"Darling, he's much too young for you," objected the Hollywood man, who was more mature.

"Well, there's no need to turn him out of doors because of Rosalind," said Johnny. "She wouldn't mind your fraternizing, I suppose. His father is still alive, obviously."

"Oh, yes, Victor often speaks of him. You mean Rosalind and Charles Laverham can't get married until he dies."

"Or gives her a divorce."

"Which he won't do."

"Naturally not," said Johnny with a German *r*. "Though it would doubtless pain him to realize that everybody over there in England has forgotten that they weren't married years ago."

"It would never get by the Hayes office," said the Hollywood man, and yawned luxuriously in the sun. "You seem upset, Camilla, what is this young Hun to you?"

"Oh, dry up, Bimbo, there's a dear," said Camilla impatiently. "I'm trying to figure things out."

"It's too hot," said Bimbo comfortably. "Does this make Victor illegitimate, or what?"

"Of course not."

"Good. The censors wouldn't stand for that."

Johnny was watching Camilla's face. He had grown very fond of her face, with its high cheek-bones and long, sensitive mouth and arching brows, and the way all its moods came through her make-up and were visible to the naked eye. The women of this family have a fatal fascination for me, Johnny thought ruefully. More than anything in the world, I would like to see Camilla happy. But she isn't. I don't think she ever has been. I thought it was Raymond she wanted, that time at Salzburg, and it was Sosthène all the time. There's no blinking the fact that Kim consoled her a little, but that's over now. Who else? Who next? It's the old Sally pattern, so incomprehensible in Williamsburg, U.S.A. What about this Victor, he isn't good enough. If I were ten years younger. . . .

"He's a Monarchist, I think," Camilla was saying slowly, to herself. "There are all sorts of wheels within wheels in this Nazi business. Do you think the Monarchists have a chance, Johnny?"

"Not one in a million now. He'd better drop that very quickly if he wants to live to a ripe old age."

She looked at him protestingly.

"He's not an agitator, Johnny."

"Hitler's gang will shoot first and ask about that afterwards."

"But surely it's better than the Communists! Look what Mussolini has done in Italy!"

"I know, I know, he's made the trains run on time," said Johnny wearily.

"Victor says a man like Hitler can't last in Germany. He's an outsider, to begin with."

"Anybody who gits thar fustest with the mostest men can last—especially in Germany!"

"What does Hitler want, do you think?"

"The earth," said Johnny.

"You are the *gloomiest* person!" Camilla objected with affection. "Are you and Bracken still prophesying another war?"

"Yep."

"When?"

"When Germany is ready to start it. We aren't doing anything to prevent her. And don't tell me about the Kellogg Pact!" he added raising his voice.

"Johnny, don't signed agreements mean *anything?*"

"Not to Germans. You'd think we'd have learned that, in 1914. Besides, Hitler didn't sign at Paris. That was Stresemann. He's dead now. Not but what Hitler would sign something too, if he could gain time by it. Germany has discovered the world's fatal weakness—which is that nowadays we will do anything, believe anything, promise anything, sign anything, to avoid unpleasantness. Nothing could suit Hitler better, because he can be very unpleasant indeed if he tries."

A deliberate, insulting, well-executed snore came from the recumbent figure in red bathing-trunks on their left.

"We're boring Bimbo," Camilla said. "He can't bear politics. Is it time for drinks? I suppose I shall have to smooth Victor down when he re-appears."

"It must be very inconvenient to him to have an English mother," Johnny remarked. "I wasn't sure he would admit to it."

"He never has before," said Camilla. "Though he has

asked a lot of questions about England, come to think of it
—where to stay, whom to get introductions to, and so on."

"At it again," murmured Johnny.

"I never know what to tell him," Camilla confessed.

"Say you don't know any of the right people," Johnny advised her. "Don't inflict him on your friends there, for God's
sake!"

"Oh, come, Johnny, he's not as bad as all that!"

"Maybe not, as you see him here. But Phoebe, for instance,
wouldn't care for him."

"Oh, well, she's prejudiced, she'd be on Rosalind's side!"

"If you married a German, you'd see Rosalind's side fast
enough!"

"I have no intention of marrying a German," Camilla said
coolly, and rose, and walked away into the house, rather
haughtily, as Victor had done, to see about drinks.

2. *SUMMER AT SALZBURG. 1934.*

WHEN DINAH AND BRACKEN ARRIVED IN EU-
rope in June, 1934, Jeff was with them—tall, lanky, over-
grown, and twenty-one. His normal boy's activity was still
somewhat curtailed by the after-effects of that illness nearly
ten years before, which was now known to have been rheumatic fever. He was going to be all right, they said. But he
had barely escaped a lifelong invalid routine. It had left him
bookish and thoughtful and gentle-voiced and oddly mature
—and with enormous quiet charm. It had also checked any
inclination he might have had towards an army career in
Oliver's footsteps, and settled him without any visible regrets into journalism as Bracken's heir apparent.

By now it was impossible for anyone in Europe to forget
war. A lot of people were still trying, and in Paris and Brus-
sels and particularly in London you could still find a brief
oblivion to the dreadful realities which were shaping up
across the borders of Germany. But even the *Illustrated Lon-*

don News reprinted a full page drawing from a German paper showing the presumable result of a gas attack from the air on a city—well-dressed women lying dead in the street, their skirts artistically disarranged, with dead children beside them, hats and handbags strewn about, every visible human being prostrate, though the surrounding masonry was only slightly damaged. You glanced at it with horror and turned the page—then paused to contemplate it again in cold blood—and then couldn't forget it.

Every Continental city of any size was holding realistic gas drills, with designated victims feigning casualties, ambulance routine, and other gruesome details worked out to the last degree. But not England. England was gravely giving the world her "magnificent lead" in disarmament. In Germany great parade was being made of training Reichswehr troops with the dummy arms and wooden cannon which was all the terms of the Versailles Treaty permitted them, but a reign of terror by Hitler's private army had begun, including mysterious shootings and disappearances which rapidly increased after he became Chancellor early in 1933.

It seemed as though Nazi propaganda was really too transparent to work, but it did work, and the deadline for entering the Party in March, 1933, brought a general last-minute scramble with no conviction behind it but a dismal dodge for whatever safety there might still be in Germany. The Monarchists went on blindly believing that Hitler would restore the Hohenzollern rule, and even the Princes joined the Party as Hitler-worship spread. The aged President Hindenberg was seen in public with Hitler now, and it was cynically said that the Old Gentleman was being softened up.

When Winston Churchill opposed MacDonald's plan for the equalization of the French and German armies as foolishness, Mr. Eden called him an unconstructive critic, and Mr. Lloyd George pointed out that to remove the Nazi in-

feriority and persecution complexes one had only to remove
their cause. And then, just before this last precious grievance
could be alleviated at the expense of what was left of peace
of mind for France, Hitler withdrew from Geneva in one of
his dynamic huffs—Wilson had never entertained the idea
that any nation would ever dare to resign from the League,
because, he said, it would become an outlaw nation. But
there was nothing for the Disarmament Conference to do
now but collapse in more or less confessed defeat, and the
shadow of despair began to lengthen in Europe. A good deal
was being heard about Danzig and East Prussia and the
Polish Corridor—last remnants of Versailles. There was an
air-school near Berlin where the students crashed in dozens,
but there were always plenty more, and Goering, who had
taken over von Richthofen's famous flying squadron in 1918,
became head of the new Air Ministry. Scientific research in
Germany was being prostituted to such horrors as a poison
gas of which ten planes could carry enough to wipe out a
million people.

Johnny Malone was Director of the European Service on
Bracken's newspaper now, and had a beat up and down the
Continent which kept him nicely in touch with Camilla in
Paris and Cannes. They had run into each other again last
winter at St. Moritz, where Victor was teaching Camilla to
ski—or trying to, for she hated it from the beginning and
soon gave it up altogether, remarking philosophically that
she had never been the athletic type and advising Victor to
go and be hearty and Nordic all by himself from now on.
Johnny, having had a very nasty fall the season before, was
not skiing either.

Camilla was incredulous when Johnny told her that Victor
was a Nazi now, whether from expediency or not, and wore
the Elite black uniform in Berlin. Victor hadn't said so, she
maintained, and he was still Monarchist in his opinions.

Johnny said Sure, sure, even the Crown Prince was a Nazi these days and wore the Storm Trooper uniform, as did two of his sons. Camilla looked more incredulous still.

"Come to Germany," said Johnny abruptly. "Catch up on things. See for yourself what goes on there, you don't have to take my word for it. Call me a liar if you can, when you've been there a while!"

"All right, I will!" Camilla replied aggressively. "Victor has asked me more than once to come and be presented to his father." And she looked at Johnny obliquely, her red mouth squared and obstinate, to see how that went down.

For a minute Johnny said nothing at all. Then he shifted in his chair with a sort of sigh.

"Lord, I can remember the good old days when we all thought Prince Conrad and his crowd were the absolute limit," he said. "They used to talk about frightfulness, remember? No, you wouldn't. Well, they were pikers at that kind of thing compared to the present day experts. Conrad *is* a genuine Monarchist, if you like. But for them the time is running out."

"How do you mean? Victor says—"

"They've left it too late. There's nothing they can do now. Hitler's gang has got Germany by the throat and they'll never let go. Conrad and his kind have bred a Frankenstein monster, and it will destroy them. The Nazis begin where the Prussians left off. These black shirt boys are real roughnecks, they aren't squeamish, I can tell you—they haven't what you could call scruples."

"I don't see any change whatever in Victor since I first knew him," Camilla asserted.

"Not here, no," said Johnny. "He's on holiday here."

"You mean I'd find him different in Berlin?"

Johnny gave her a long, speculative look.

"Come and see Berlin," he said.

"You mean about the Jews and all that? Isn't it exaggerated?"

"There are no words adequate to exaggerate it with," said Johnny patiently. "And I don't mean just the Jews. If any German steps out of line now he doesn't have to be a Jew to land in a concentration camp. And a short time later his family gets him back again—in a box."

"But aren't the Nazis better than the Communists?" Camilla persisted.

"Why?" said Johnny.

So in June of 1934 Camilla set out for Germany with Bracken and Dinah and Jeff, leaving the Kendrick family—now five of them—in possession of the house at Cannes. Johnny was awaiting them in Berlin.

Camilla noticed that as they neared the German border Dinah became tense and quiet, and Bracken, glancing at her anxiously more than once, said at last, "You and Jeff could still go back to Cannes."

Dinah shook her head, her lips pressed together.

"I want him to see it," she said.

"But *you* don't have to," Bracken reminded her, and Dinah said she could take it, and Bracken explained to Camilla that Nazis always affected Dinah the way cats did the people who were born with a horror of them. Dinah could *smell* a Nazi in the same room or railway carriage, he said, and it was like poison gas to her. Her hatred of the Prussians went back to the time Rosalind Norton-Leigh had married one, he said—she couldn't abide Prince Conrad even in the old days before the war. It was psychic, or something, said Bracken, rather proud of her.

"Perhaps she would feel differently about Conrad's son," Camilla suggested. "If she knew him well, I mean. Victor's harmless enough, and very attractive."

"I must see him," Dinah agreed grimly. "It's partly why

I'm here. I've got to know what Victor is like, on account of Rosalind. I promised Phoebe."

"It's nothing to do with her any more, is it?" Jeff asked with interest. "Rosalind isn't likely to meet up with either of them again, I should think."

"I hope not," said Dinah. "But we want to *know*."

"I wonder if anyone ever sees Conrad these days," Bracken said. "Johnny will know. One doesn't hear much about those fellows any more. Except von Schleicher, he still has influence."

"*I* shall see Conrad," Camilla told him confidently, and found Dinah's eyes upon her. "Victor has said more than once that he wants me to know his father. He admires him very much."

"Camilla, you aren't—*involved* with Victor?" Dinah pleaded, as though driven to it.

"Oh, no," Camilla answered casually. "Except that I've known him quite a long time, on and off, and I like him. He's much too stiff and proper for anything else, if that's what you mean!"

And now it was Bracken's eyes that she felt, and she returned his look levelly, with a perverse little grin.

When they got to Berlin they found that Johnny had got into trouble with the authorities there—had in fact been asked to leave Germany because of his habit of expressing himself too freely about its Nazi masters. Johnny could never stomach the roughing up of American citizens who did not salute the Nazi flag, or did not see it, or who simply looked Jewish and caught the roving eye of a group of Hitler's hoodlums.

Bracken's hackles rose at once, and he went to see the American Ambassador about it. Johnny was not the first foreign correspondent to be suppressed or expelled, and Bracken wanted to make a test case of it. But the Ambassador said

No. Bracken was riled, and prepared to go as high as Hitler in defence of his man, and this kept the rest of them sitting about in Berlin as June ran out. It was plain even to the most casual observer, which Bracken and Johnny were not, that an increasing tension gripped the city. The eternal strife within the Party, dog eat dog, had flared again, Johnny said, and something like civil war might come of it.

There appeared moreover to be something of a mystery about Prince Conrad, and even the von Schleichers, who were friends of his and with whom Johnny was on excellent terms, seemed a trifle vague as to his whereabouts. Victor himself was moving in some sort of smoke screen. He could not be found on the telephone, and there was a delay of several days before he replied to Camilla's note sent to the usual address which she had known for some time.

He then arrived unannounced at the hotel where they were staying, wearing the spectacular black SS uniform which added to his height and impressive carriage. He sent up his card with an invitation to Camilla to dine with him that evening. Dinah at once bristled, and said wasn't that rather abrupt, and anyway they were all engaged at the Embassy that evening and Camilla couldn't accept. They were just then starting out for an afternoon drive to Potsdam, but Camilla excused herself from that and after introducing Victor to the others in the lobby invited him to stop for tea with her in their private sitting-room as she could go to Potsdam some other time. He accepted with formality and apologies and apparent surprise, and the rest of the party went on while he and Camilla returned to the suite.

He paused just inside the door of the sitting-room while closing it behind him, as though noting in detail the position of the windows, entrances, and telephone in the ornate, impersonal Adlon apartment. Camilla removed her hat, chose a chair, and said naturally, "Well, do come and sit down and tell me all your news. Is your father in Berlin now?"

Without replying, Victor walked to the sofa, picked up a large down cushion, and placed it firmly over the telephone, which stood on a console table against the wall beneath a heavy gilt mirror. Camilla watched him with a growing amazement as he drew up a chair close to hers and sat down in it, leaning towards her to say in a very low voice, "Please do not discuss my father here."

"What on earth do you mean?" she asked blankly.

"What I say. You have a singularly clear and carrying voice. It is very charming, I'm sure—but Germany at present is no place for it." The trace of a smile touched his shapely lips, but Camilla went on looking blank, although she had the grace to speak almost in a whisper.

"Victor, are you mixed up in all this? What *is* going on here, can you tell me that?"

"What makes you think I know?" he asked, and her eyes went significantly over the smart uniform he wore.

"I thought you were in the Foreign Office," she said.

"I am."

"And this as well?"

"But certainly. One does not preclude the other." He was facing the light and new lines of strain were clearly visible on his rugged, striking face. His eyes looked heavy and sleepless, his color was not as good as she remembered it, his body was tense and ready to spring from the delicate gilded chair he sat in. "I have a request to make which I hope you will not think unreasonable," he was saying, in that strange inaudible voice. "My car is outside. Will you come for a short drive with me now?"

Speechlessly Camilla rose and put on her hat again, glanced once at the muffled telephone, left it for Bracken to see, and walked briskly towards the door. Victor followed. In silence

they entered the lift and passed through the lower lobby to
where his car stood at the curb—long, low, black, with shining metal finishings. Victor put her in beside the driver's
seat and slid under the wheel, and drove smoothly away from
the Adlon, heading for the Tiergarten. Once in the park he
allowed the car's speed to slacken and glanced at her thoughtfully before he spoke.

"You are thinking it is like something out of an American
cinema," he said without smiling.

"Well, yes, rather."

"I hope I didn't frighten you. But the Adlon is really no
place to speak privately."

"And what have you to say that is so private?" she asked
with determined lightness.

"I want to ask you to arrange for me to attend the Independence Day reception at your Embassy—to go with you,
I mean, as one of your family party."

"Is that all!"

"Will it be so easy?"

"Bracken knows the Ambassador quite well. He can ask for
an invitation for a friend of ours, or whatever needs to be
done."

"And he will not object to my being one of your party?"

"Of course not, if I want you to come with us."

"I would be most grateful."

"Why?" she asked curiously, and again he gave her that
long, thoughtful glance, and returned his gaze at once to the
road ahead.

"It is advisable these days to take a little trouble about
where one is seen—or not seen," he said coolly.

"And you think it would do you good to be seen with us?"

"In certain circumstances—yes."

"And your father?" she inquired, and saw his face harden.
"Would he care to come too?"

"My father and I are not now on terms," he said briefly, and the car quickened its pace.

"You mean you've quarrelled with him?"

"Hardly that. But many of the old Imperial Army officers, like my father, have held too long to ideas which have become —obsolete."

"You mean you've gone Nazi and he wouldn't? You're not a Monarchist any more yourself?"

"We have a Leader," he said stiffly. "We do not need the Hohenzollerns too."

"You *believe* in Hitler now?" she cried in open disillusionment.

"When did I not believe in him?"

"That day at Cannes—talking to Johnny in the garden, after the September elections. And you always said that Hitler could not last—you always said he was an outsider and would be got rid of—you said—"

"You are mistaken," said Victor flatly. "You have confused me with some one else."

"I have *not!*" she cried indignantly. "Johnny was there and he heard you too!"

"You will do me the favor not to refer again to a matter in which your memory obviously plays you false," said Victor with a rasp in his usually pleasant voice and the somewhat stilted idiom which sometimes betrayed that he had read English more than he had heard it spoken. "Especially at the American Embassy on the Fourth of July," he added more politely, and she was silent a moment, thinking it over.

"Victor, are you in some kind of trouble here?" she asked then.

He drove for what seemed like a long time without replying, and she waited, watching his rigid profile.

"I am sorry you have come to Germany just at this time," he said at last, choosing his words. "We are not—ourselves."

"I don't quite see why you think being seen with me can help you."

"There is still tremendous caution regarding American opinion. Your friendship would be a protection to me, if you would allow it."

"Victor, why don't you leave Germany for good, if this is the way it's going to be?"

"Nonsense. My place is here, with the Leader."

"Don't call him by that silly name!" she cried irritably, and saw his neck redden with quickly controlled anger. "You know I'll do whatever I can for you—gladly. But I think you ought to see Bracken himself and make the arrangements to go with us on the Fourth."

"As you wish."

"We're dining out tonight, as I told you. But you might take me back to the hotel in time to have a drink with us before we have to dress."

"Thank you."

"Victor, don't be cross, darling—it all seems so fantastic!"

"Fantastic?" He repeated the word as though he had never heard it before. "I don't know what you mean."

"All this marching and stamping and saluting and flag-carrying and sabre-rattling! It's so—so *childish!*"

"You use some very odd words," he said, offended.

"Why can't you *relax*, Victor, why can't you Germans ever enjoy life a bit, and try to see a joke, and make love, and behave like mere human beings instead of supermen?"

"You think a German never makes love?" he said dangerously. "You are always a little put out, aren't you, that I do not. And do you suppose that if just once I kissed you I would ever let you go again?"

"*Well!*" said Camilla inadequately, taken completely by surprise, staring at his immovable profile.

"I do not want you in my life, Camilla," he went on, driv-

"What are you, then?" she asked with a touch of flip
which he ignored.

"We are a revolution," he said solemnly.

"But I thought you'd had that. A bloodless one, when
ler came to power by elections."

"It was necessary, of course, to—regulate the voting,"
Victor, and added coldly, "There is no such thing as a
olution without blood."

"Oh, come, what about the English one somewhere ro
about 1688?" she challenged, deliberately trying to pro
him out of what she considered a melodramatic m
for the sun was shining and people were strolling in the
dens, and the world looked a very normal, pleasant p
even in Berlin.

"The *English!*" Contempt hissed through the word. "
nearly three hundred years ago, besides! As a nation t
are bloodless anyway, cold as codfish, greedy, two-faced,
decadent. The English are finished! It only remains for th
to find it out."

"Stupid about that, aren't they!" she flashed back rese
fully. "Very obtuse, aren't they!"

There was an angry silence in the humming car, for th
had argued about the English before, to no effect. Camil
realizing that she had asked for it, was the first to spe
making an effort to restore normal conversation.

"Well, who is revolutionizing against whom?" she ask
ready to take a polite interest in German politics and re
later to Bracken.

"It is within the Party, entirely. Espionage—tale-bea
—accusations, probably well-founded, of intrigue agains
Leader—it is useless to mention names to anyone who
not know all the nuances. Those of us who do know too r
in any direction—we can trust no one."

ing smoothly, watching the road. "Women, yes—but not a woman like you, whom it would be impossible to forget. Besides, you are too unreliable. I could not trust your discretion in Germany, either as my mistress or my wife."

"Well, *really*—!" gasped Camilla, beginning to be angry.

"That is why I never asked you," said Victor, his eyes on the road.

"You were so sure that I would accept!" she said, outraged.

"Would you not?"

"*No,* I would not!"

"Forgive me," he said formally. "I misunderstood."

She sat beside him, seething, while he turned the car back towards the Adlon. All the same, something inside her was gratified in a way. He had not been so impervious after all.

The June weather in Berlin was hot and beautiful. People sunbathed and took long walks and drives out to the lakes, and gave garden parties.

Bracken and Johnny with their friends and belongings were always welcome guests at the big house in the Tiergarten Strasse which bore the American eagle plaque, and the Ambassador's daughter was a gay, intelligent creature who liked to have informal gatherings of a rather mixed and undiplomatic nature. Camilla asked and received permission to bring Victor to one of these afternoon affairs a few days before the Independence Day reception. He was not unknown at the Embassy, but had heretofore attended only large official functions. His good looks and impressive carriage recommended him to any young woman's eye, and the Ambassador's daughter received him with her characteristic friendliness—but he wore the black SS uniform, instead of the lounge suit customary on such occasions, and it was the only one there that day. The party was a little constrained, but

no one could have sworn that that was the fault of the striking black-clad figure in its midst.

Camilla, who had known Victor only at his leisure on holidays outside Germany, began unwillingly to recognize that he
was now a badly frightened man. Everyone knew that something was brewing in Berlin—no one seemed to know what.
On their drives together, for a car was almost the only place
where there could be no dictaphones and no eavesdropping,
she tried to draw him out and come at the cause of his increasing inward terror. Nothing so simple as the fear of death,
she was sure, could act on a man that way—a man trained to
courage and self-control as Victor's kind were trained. People
were shot at, were spirited away to concentration camps in
the middle of the night, which was often worse, she was well
aware—but surely not anyone with a *zu* in his name—surely
not anyone in that uniform?

Victor seemed to think that he answered all her questions,
he seemed impatient that she did not comprehend better, and
he was furious if she blamed the Nazi system for the state of
Berlin nerves at that time. There was dissension within the
Party, he admitted—the men close to the Leader were in
some cases unworthy—Hitler had nothing to do with the
atrocities, they were committed without his knowledge by
people who took advantage of him. . . .

But how was it possible to take advantage of a man whose
power was absolute, Camilla would insist, and why were
these men retained—and why was Streicher the Jew-baiter
known to be one of Hitler's closest friends? To this Victor
made no direct reply. He had himself protested more than
once against the atrocities, he said, on the ground that they
would have a bad effect on foreign opinion of the Nazi rule,
just as better relations with other countries were beginning.
He was so explicit on that point that Camilla looked at him
oddly—it was not pity for the victims, it was not humane jus-

tice nor any sense of delicacy that caused Victor's objections to Nazi cruelty—it was what people outside Germany might *say*, people who were squeamish, he implied. Moreover, he had been reprimanded by his superiors for his impertinence, and dared not bring it up again.

Yet he clung to Camilla's companionship in a way which seemed to include a sort of gratitude for being allowed to take up her time, and which was very different from his arrogant assurance in the past, and which sat strangely on his uniformed prestige even now. He took her to all the most prominent and expensive cafés and dancing places, flaunting their friendship with a satisfaction so naïve as to have something of pathos in it. Victor was frightened. It didn't make sense.

As that hot, bright June drew to its close, Camilla and Bracken were linked by a rising mutual excitement which was not shared by their travelling companions—a tingling awareness, natural enough in an old newspaper man like Bracken who had been through the wars, but in Camilla it sprang unexpectedly from an intense nervous perception, a sixth sense of hidden implications and of the mounting hysteria in the air she breathed. Dinah went round looking white and apprehensive, Jeff confessed that his tummy was inside out all the time, Johnny was moody and profane. But Bracken and Camilla watched everything with bright, recording eyes, listened with ears almost visibly erect to what went on around them.

Camilla had long ago learned German to sing in, and had used it easily at Salzburg and in Switzerland for years, just as she had learned French for her life at Cannes. Tri-lingual now, she repeated to Bracken in faithful detail whatever she heard that he hadn't, in the streets, in the shops and restaurants, from the chambermaids, or at the French Embassy where she had a devoted friend in one of the young attachés.

And she repeated to him also whatever she extracted from Victor and other Berlin acquaintances.

There were rumors of Hitler's growing difficulties, even of his possible collapse—now?—would it come *now?*—and who would be his successor?—*which* Hohenzollern, the Kaiser was too old and had failed once, the Crown Prince was always unpopular, his sons were lightweight and unreliable, one of them thoroughly inoculated with un-German ideas after a residence in the United States—rumors of rising discontent among the German people, who were growing tired of tight rationing and long working hours—would they turn against him in time?—would they free themselves, offering martyrs to the cause if necessary, could they unite before it was too late and choose a new government?—and what kind of government?—Germany was not naturally a democracy, it was a nation of bureaucrats, big toads in little puddles, big fleas with littler fleas to bite them, accustomed to a system of pompous authority and obsequious underlings. People were saying that von Papen was scared within an inch of his life now—von Papen who always worked both sides of the street, and whose switch to Nazism was one of the first sure signs that it was a force to be reckoned with. They said a faction was ganging up against Roehm and his SA troopers, and that Hitler liked it that way. They said von Schleicher's number was up, though his easy, confident bearing had not changed, and von Blomberg's, and von Fritsch's—all the old guard were doomed. Conrad zu Polkwitz-Heidersdorf? Eyebrows were raised non-committally. Keeping very quiet, doubtless behind von Schleicher, whose views he was known to share. His son was a rabid Nazi, of course, and lived in Goering's pocket these days—good place to be if there was trouble. Maybe. Goering was too big for Hitler's pocket, though, and little Goebbels had got there first. Von Hindenberg? Senile. If Hindenberg died it would be between von

Papen and Hitler for the presidency. Odds on Hitler, yes, but von Papen had a curious knack of surviving. . . .

Camilla and Bracken would mull it over endlessly, speculating, rejecting, surmising—the keenness of their suspense left no room for personal nervousness or disgust. Like surgeons, they examined with academic interest the festering sore which was the German crisis and awaited what the knife would reveal. Johnny said with some respect that she had missed her calling, and should have been a gal reporter like Sigrid Schultz, and added that if she and Bracken had seen as much between them as he had in his time they would both be sick as dogs like him. But Camilla said, "I wouldn't miss this for worlds, it's the biggest question mark since the war." And Bracken said, with an awful satisfaction, "It won't be long now."

The Foreign Press Corps in Berlin mingled quite freely with Nazi officialdom and its most ardent sympathizers, and there was no Party ban on such association so far—in fact, each paper's office had its Nazi spy as well as its secret sources of information, most of the correspondents were shadowed constantly, and it was no novelty to any news man to be called on the carpet by the Secret Police or the Foreign Office and requested to explain a hostile dispatch, as a threat or a warning. To Dinah the fact that Johnny was regularly so summoned whenever he was in Berlin seemed each time like his death warrant, but Johnny was merely rather bored by the interviews, and his confréres reacted to them with anger or resignation or ennui rather than fear. There were seldom any social repercussions, and Goebbels himself attended the big Press parties and became quite jovial as the evening lengthened.

With Bracken and Dinah and Jeff Camilla was invited to the at-home *bier abends* given by the journalistic set for themselves. Norman Ebbutt was the dean of them all, and

Johnny by his long European experience was one of the out-standing figures, and gave marvellous parties of his own at his bachelor apartment on Dornburger Strasse. Liquor was plentiful and the talk was free, even when the company was very mixed. Everybody in the Foreign Office was suddenly too busy to bother about Johnny, and nothing further had been heard about his leaving Germany under compulsion, though it was pretty certain that one of these times was going to be the last.

June thirtieth was a Saturday, sunny and hot, and again a drive to Potsdam had been planned. Johnny arrived at the Adlon in mid-morning, late for their appointment to start, tight-lipped, and excited. They weren't going, he said. Some-thing was up. Even as he spoke there was a spatter of gunfire in the distance and Camilla flew to the window overlooking the Linden. The street below was full of uniformed men in groups. Two military trucks dashed by, with gun-muzzles pointing out, and the soldiers in them wore steel helmets.

"Women must keep away from the windows and stay in-doors," Johnny said crushingly, and pulled her back into the room. Bracken reached for his hat, Jeff did likewise, and the three of them left the suite.

Dinah and Camilla looked at each other blankly.

"This is it," said Dinah, and sat down as though her knees had given way.

"We only have to try for Potsdam and something always happens," Camilla said unreasonably. "Where are they go-ing? How long will they be away?"

"You never know," said Dinah, out of years of being a cor-respondent's wife.

"Well, what are *we* supposed to do in the meantime?"

"Wait." Dinah picked up a day-old copy of the London *Times*. "Occupy our minds. Twiddle our thumbs."

"I wonder what Sigrid Schultz is doing," said Camilla rebelliously. And then, as the thing began to dawn in its further implications, "I wonder where Victor is. I wonder what he knew about this."

"Everybody knew *something* was coming," Dinah reminded her. "He's surely had time to dodge, if he needs to."

"He was afraid," Camilla murmured, gravitating to the window again.

"Of what?"

"I couldn't find out."

"Must have had a guilty conscience," said Dinah heartlessly.

"I don't know. He'd broken with his father. Does that mean they are on opposite sides of whatever is happening now?"

"I'd rather be in Victor's shoes than Conrad's if they are," said Dinah.

"I don't think Victor was so sure—" Camilla leaned to the window. "That's funny, it's all Goering's men you see— the green police uniform. What's become of all the others? Hardly any traffic moving now, and there's a truck full of machine guns and their crews parked opposite. Johnny was right. There's not a woman in sight."

"Don't stick your silly head out if there's any more shooting. Come and sit down."

"Can't we have some coffee sent up, or something, just to pass the time?"

"A very good idea," said Dinah.

When the coffee arrived the china chattered on the tray in the waiter's hands, and his face was greenish.

"What's happening outside?" Camilla asked him at once. "Why all the police? What was that shooting?"

The waiter glanced at them nervously and away, his unsteady hands fumbling unnecessarily at things on the tray.

"There was a plot, they say—discovered in time."

"What sort of plot?" Camilla asked persuasively.

"A foreign plot, of course—in which German officers were involved—the Brown Shirts meant to betray our Leader, the story goes—that's Roehm and his gang—" The man's lips curled. "It was the French at the bottom of it, you be sure —the French again, always at work, like moles—" He glanced over his shoulder, tucked the napkin under his arm, and stood at attention, his gaze avoiding theirs. "Was there anything else you require?"

"What about the SS?" Camilla persisted. "I don't see them in the streets either."

"A few," said the waiter cautiously. "But it is Goering's affair here in Berlin, they say. If that is all, you will excuse? We are very busy just now." The waiter departed, walking jerkily, his head down.

Camilla poured out the coffee thoughtfully and realized that she was going to worry about Victor. But if Goering was in charge in Berlin surely Victor would be safe. Then what had he been afraid of?

She shook off the paralysis of dread which caused Dinah to sit vaguely stirring her coffee without drinking it. Camilla stood up, moved about the room with her cup, sipping the strong, sweet liquid. Would he let her know soon? Would he still think their friendship a protection?

"Should I try to get in touch with Victor?" she asked doubtfully, thinking aloud.

"Heavens, no!" said Dinah. "Keep out of it. You don't know what he may have been up to. If this is any sort of plot against Hitler, the gutters will run red!"

"But Victor is loyal to him!"

"How do you know? He only says so. It's death to say anything else. Victor was scared. Remember?"

"But if he thought I could help, even before it started, perhaps I ought to make some effort—" She noticed that Dinah was looking at her sadly and went to sit beside her on the sofa, putting down her cup. "Honey, don't think I'm in love with Victor. I'm not. I never have been, though I couldn't tell you why. There is something in him that holds you off, just as there is something that attracts."

Dinah nodded.

"Conrad was the same," she said. "Virginia always called it sheer brute magnetism in the old days when he was courting Rosalind. There was something about him that made us not quite sure that she would be miserable with him after all—but she was! Don't ever let it fool you, will you! There is no compassion in them. Rosalind found that out. You can't trust yourself to a man who has no pity."

"I know." Camilla was silent, thinking of Victor's attitude towards the atrocities. Dinah had put her finger on the thing he lacked. "But even so," she argued slowly, aloud, "one can't bear to think of him being hunted or—tortured. And it was something more than getting shot in a fight that was weighing on him lately. A fight would be all in the day's work. It was something *worse* than that."

A look crossed Dinah's tell-tale face, but she did not speak. Camilla caught it, and waited, and then said, "You thought of something. What was it?"

"Only guesswork," said Dinah uncomfortably, but Camilla went on waiting. "Well, I was only thinking—suppose his father was involved in this thing, on the other side—von Schleicher and his friends might be. Suppose Victor knew what was coming—"

"—and had a chance to warn his father—had a chance to *choose*," Camilla interrupted, and they sat looking at each other with parted lips. "It would be a terrible dilemma—it would explain the strain he's been under—"

"And how did he choose?" Dinah wondered.

"If he gave a warning—and then was afraid he would be

found out by his own side— Oh, poor Victor!" Camilla rose, and began to walk up and down. "I suppose they would execute him for a thing like that."

"Well, not—right away," said Dinah significantly, and Camilla put both hands to her face and shivered. "Perhaps we're just imagining things," Dinah suggested after a moment.

"We're not imagining impossibilities. It must have been something like that. Victor was—was quietly going crazy inside himself." Camilla deliberately poured some more coffee, sugared it, and raised the cup in a shaky hand. "What a country," she said. "Johnny tried to tell me, before I came. I made Johnny awfully cross sometimes, and now I see why. You can't realize, till you've been here and seen for yourself —and *felt* it, like damp from a graveyard! It's fear you feel— millions of people afraid. Nobody safe, nobody daring to speak freely, or trust anybody else—surveillance everywhere, spying, and tale-bearing—"

"They teach the children to repeat at school what they hear their parents say at home," said Dinah. "A child, not quite understanding what it is doing, or deliberately currying favor, or nursing some childish grudge, can condemn his own father or mother to a concentration camp. A lie will do it, even—a deliberate, malicious lie." There was a silence. "I doubt very much if Victor's father was warned," she added.

"Oh, Dinah, that's horrible! Victor isn't like that, whatever you may say! He had great pride in his father once, as one of the old school."

"But if Hitler says now that the old school must go—"

"No, I won't believe that! There is a limit to how low an ordinarily decent man could come, even if he is a German—"

They were still at it, futilely, when lunch time had gone by and their three men returned. Bracken glanced sharply round the room and saw that the telephone wore its usual muffling sofa cushion, and that all the doors were shut.

"Haven't you eaten?" he asked briefly, and they shook their heads. They had forgotten to. "Might as well have something up here. And a bottle of whiskey."

While the order was given, Jeff sat limply in the corner of the sofa looking at nothing, and Johnny smoked cigarettes. They said very little till after the meal was served and the waiter had gone.

"Oddly enough," said Johnny then, "I'm hungry. Excitement, no doubt," he added philosophically.

"What did you see?" Camilla demanded. "What did you learn?"

"Not much, first hand. Martial law in Berlin. Goering's men are cleaning up the city according to their lights, and a lot of old scores are being settled in an impromptu execution ground at Lichterfeld barracks, on the edge of town. One of von Papen's secretaries has been killed and his house is surrounded. He's had narrow squeaks before, but this looks bad for him. Not that I care much, about von Papen." After a pause, reluctantly, he said, "But von Schleicher caught it—and his wife as well."

"*Dead?*"

"His *wife!*"

"Shot. In their home this morning."

"But *why?*"

"Treason," said Bracken in quotation marks.

"Then there really was a plot? And he was in it?"

"That will be the official explanation. They were probably just afraid of him. He stood for something, with the better element in Germany. He was a healthy influence, as far as he went—and the Nazis can't afford to have one of those around."

"But why his wife too?"

"She probably saw who did the shooting."

Dinah was not eating.

"She was such a pretty woman," she said quietly. "And she loved him. You could see that she did."

"And nobody warned von Schleicher," said Camilla, and caught Dinah's eyes, and glancing at their rigid faces Bracken decided not to ask her what she meant.

When Johnny returned to the hotel after the official Press conference for the foreign correspondents at which Goering presided—for Goebbels was with Hitler in Munich, which some people said was the only reason he had not ended up at Lichterfeld too—there was something to add regarding the death of pretty Elisabeth von Schleicher. Goering had accounted for it in a few casual words of one syllable, as he rose to dismiss his already speechless and shaken audience. "Frau von Schleicher was killed in attempting to place herself between her husband and the police," he said.

For three more days the suburban neighborhood near Lichterfeld shuddered at continual volleys from the execution rifles in the barracks square. The bodies accumulated in a freshly dug hole outside until they were burned and the ashes mailed back in little boxes to the families—or something that was supposed to be the ashes.

A court-martial sat there, in which Goering was one of the judges. Only a matter of minutes passed between the reading of the charges before the prisoner, who had no opportunity to reply, and the volley which ended his life. The shooting was done by groups of SS men with one blank cartridge amongst them. Young troops and attachés were required to witness the executions as part of the Nazi hardening process —a few of them broke under the delirium of slaughter and were not seen again. Even members of the firing squads turned sick and were summarily replaced. The confusion was so complete that some of the condemned died believing they were in the hands of the opposite faction, and with a loyal Heil Hitler as their last words.

Lichterfeld was the most orderly part of the massacre. Everywhere in Berlin, in cellars, in alleys, in private homes, in all sorts of refuges and hiding places, wherever some one on the black list could be run down, there were shooting and terror and bloodshed. There were suicides too—and a few miraculous escapes. Social engagements were all cancelled, and even the Hohenzollerns took cover. People whose dearest friends had disappeared dared not make inquiries nor try to learn their fate for fear of jeopardizing some last slim chance of safety. And a cryptic greeting, which became a slogan, was recklessly used by friends who met by chance and had felt apprehension for each other—*"Lebst du noch!"* they would say, clasping hands, which meant, "What, you still alive?"

For three days no word came from Victor and with the von Schleichers gone Bracken had no private source of information as to Conrad. One assumed that he was in hiding. Then Johnny heard on his own grapevine that Conrad was dead—no confirmation, no details. Even Dinah was troubled. "Should we have tried to get him out of Germany?" she asked Bracken. "Some of them did get out in time." Bracken said something about her poor little conscience because she had never liked the man, and expressed the opinion that Conrad would not have thanked them for trying—nor would Rosalind, either. "She wouldn't have wanted it like this," said Dinah reproachfully.

The Fourth of July reception at the American Embassy was to be held as usual in Berlin, as at every other American Embassy in Europe. It was going to be a grim afternoon, especially for Johnny, counting up the missing, but the Embassy was gaily decorated, an orchestra played American music, and the Ambassador's family was smiling and composed.

With Victor's anxiety to accompany them weighing on her mind, Camilla had put on her prettiest frock and a big hat and slathers of make-up, and delayed her departure from the hotel as long as possible, hoping that he would still show up. When they finally had to start without him after all, she found herself sick with anxiety, her palms cold and moist, her heart beating thickly. I didn't think I would mind so much even if something happened to him, she thought in further consternation. It's only because I've known him so long—it's only that one can't bear to think of a good friend being murdered—it's only the effect of this damnable, deliberate terrorism on one's nervous system—but it isn't as though he was somebody like Kim that belonged, that one had ever been really close to—I'm sorry for him, that's all— I'd be sorry for anyone caught up in this nightmare—but suppose it was some one I really *loved*. . . .

When she caught sight of him at the entrance to the Embassy ballroom greeting his hostess, only a few minutes after she had passed through it herself, she felt the relief like a blow in the diaphragm and hurried towards him, almost falling into his arms.

"Victor, oh, thank God, *lebst du noch!*" she said softly, and then with her hands gripping his hard upper arms on either side, she saw his face looking down at her, drawn, red-eyed, the bloodless lips stretched in a small fixed smile.

"You must not say that. It is cheap and tactless," he said as his only greeting to her.

"I'm sorry. What have they done to you? Come and have a drink. Or is it food you need?" She glanced towards the buffet, pulled a little at his arm.

"I would like to sit down, if that is possible," he said.

"The garden—out here—quick, before Bracken spots us—"

He followed her out to a small table set on the grass and they sat down facing each other. He said nothing, only gazed at her haggardly, a muscle jerking in his jaw, so that she rushed into speech herself, trying nervously to put him more at ease before they were interrupted.

"I was so worried about you—why didn't you send me word? Where have you been?"

"At Lichterfeld."

The word lay there between them, cold like a snake. She stared back at him, stricken almost as he was into a sort of glassy horror.

"You—saw—"

"Everything. We have not had much sleep."

"And—your father?" She could hardly form the question.

"Dead."

"N-not—?"

"No. By suicide."

She made a sound, half pity, half shudder, and he continued woodenly, "I should not have come here and I cannot remain long. I came only because of you." His eyes burned into her, hot and sick. "I wanted to look again at the sharp, sweet thing you are, Camilla, so sure of yourself and the things you believe in, so damnably *right,* no matter what you do! No fumbling, no guesswork, no mistakes—eh, Camilla? No regrets, shall we say, to carry to your grave!"

"Is that the way I seem to you?" She had winced involuntarily at the savage undertone in his controlled voice. "It sounds more like a description of yourself. And why do you hate me for it?"

"I wanted to love you—that is why I am damned. It is too late now. Always I have hated the soft English side of me, which was always tempted by you. Always I have fought the

English blood in me, which I recognized as a weakness in my heritage. And I have won against it. I have proved now that I am German."

"But if you only *knew* the English, Victor—they are very different than you think. If you knew your mother you would love her."

"That is hardly possible now," he said stiffly. "However, at least I shall know the English, as you suggest. I am posted to the Embassy in London, when this is over."

"London!" She gazed at him a moment apprehensively. "But why?"

"No reason—except that I have my orders. There are to be some changes there."

She sat silent a moment, looking at his haggard, somehow dogged face and the splendid body sagging in the little iron chair. Something rushed up in her, warm and impulsive and protective. She couldn't bear to see him like this, as though he disintegrated before her eyes. She leaned towards him across the table and laid a quick, caressing hand on his sleeve.

"Victor—let me help you!"

"Help me?" he said hopelessly, looking down without interest at her hand.

"It needn't be too late, Victor—need it? This job you've got in London—maybe that's the answer—maybe it's come just in time—for you. Suppose I came with you?"

"How do you mean?" he asked dully, for the liquor he had drunk to steady him was gaining on him fast.

"However you like," she said recklessly, seized by a sudden private hysteria of her own, born of the mass hysteria all around her—a passionate wish to save a man from his own implacable destiny, as though she threw down a challenge to his Nazi masters: My woman's power, my beauty and wit and experience, all the things I stand for and believe in, against your tyranny of fear—all my cards on the table, against yours, for this man's soul. "Victor, you're going to get *away,* don't you see? Take advantage of it, for the love of God! Come and meet *my* people, come and see how *we* live, come and learn the difference, darling, between being free and being part of a machine! Victor, I'll do anything I can, do you hear—I'll give you anything you want, I'll prove to you that our way is best, and that people don't have to live like this, in mortal terror morning, noon, and night! Let them send you to London, by all means—and I'll go with you to London too—and I'll guarantee that you'll never want to come back to this!"

His bloodshot, heavy-lidded eyes tried to focus on the vivid face upturned to his. His dry lips opened slackly and his words came blurred and slow.

"Are you suggesh-ting that I should desert the Leader for you—a woman?"

"Not just for me, Victor—for a way of life that I could make for you, so much more worth living than this! I *dare* you, Victor—escape with your soul while you can!"

"My soul?" He gave an ugly snort of laughter. "There's no such thing. I saw them die at Lichterfeld." He wagged a clumsy negative finger confidentially. "There's no soul."

"What about the ones with the courage to commit suicide?"

"For them it was made easy. They had privacy."

"And perhaps time to pray."

"Pray for what?" It was a sneer. "Mercy? From whom? Pray or not, they're just as dead now." He wavered groggily in the chair, jerked upright, and tried again to focus on her face.

"Victor, go and get some rest now, and we'll talk tomorrow. Can you come to see me at the hotel? I want to hear more about this assignment in London."

"Lon'on." He said it with loathing, and then levelled an unsteady forefinger at her across the table. "Now, you keep

out of this, Camilla, un'erstand? I don't want any help from
you in Lon'on. I know what I'm doing there. The fact is—"
He rose, and caught at the chair-back to save himself from
falling, and stood leaning on it looking down at her. "The
fact is, I never want to see you again. And after today it's not
likely, is it!"

He let go the chair cautiously, and walked away from her
like a somnambulist, towards the house, without seeing
Johnny who was almost in his path. Johnny came on to where
Camilla sat numbly at the table and said, with all sincerity,
"The poor guy. The poor, goddamned son-of-a-gun."

"He's ill," she said, staring after him.

"He's drunk," Johnny said, sitting down in Victor's chair.
"What did he tell you?"

"That he was at Lichterfeld."

Johnny gave a low, comprehending whistle.

"He's done for, then," he said. "He'll know too much."

"On the contrary, he's posted to the London Embassy,
whatever that may mean."

Johnny leaned foward in the chair.

"Sure about that?"

"He said so."

"*Now* what?" Johnny muttered, and his eyes went thoughtfully towards the house, where the black uniform had already disappeared in the crowd. "Always up to something,
aren't they. This could be very interesting—and very nasty
too."

"His father," said Camilla, "committed suicide."

"I'm not surprised," said Johnny, who very seldom was.
"Von Papen is still alive, though. Another one of his little
miracles."

Camilla was looking down at the table in front of her with
widened, hypnotized eyes.

"Perhaps when he goes to England he *will* realize, even

without me there," she said slowly. "I thought perhaps if he met the right people, and was made decently welcome, and saw how free people live and talk and enjoy life, he would comprehend."

"It's too late now," said Johnny, and her eyes came up to his face.

"He said that too." There was a long silence, while she traced meaningless patterns on the table top with a fingertip, and Johnny smoked, waiting for her to regain composure. "Do you know what I think?" she said at last.

"I'm afraid I do."

"You think so too. You think he might have saved his father —and didn't. And that's what's been eating into him. He had a choice—and he let it happen."

"He ought to feel just fine about that, as time goes on," said Johnny with some satisfaction. "It's the kind of thing that's likely to grow on you."

"But now that he's going to get out of Germany—if only one could get at him—if only there was a way to rescue him —there's so much in him that was worth saving—"

"Have you got some idea of going in for a lifetime of Good Works?" Johnny asked ironically, and she gave him an odd, slow look.

"Not me, Johnny. It's not my job. He said he wanted never to see me again."

"And is that so hard for you to take?"

"I don't know yet." Her gaze fell to her beautiful, restless hands on the table. "Maybe I was fonder of him than I knew. Maybe I was just sorry for him. But whatever it was—I feel as though I'd just seen it die." She shivered a little in the warm summer air, and sighed. "Maybe I came close to making a fool of myself—again."

"Maybe you need a drink," said Johnny sympathetically.

Camilla sat on the terrace of the Oesterreichische Hof in Salzburg with the cable from Williamsburg in her hands. She had developed a nostalgic affection for the little Austrian town which not even the growing international popularity of the Festival could spoil with its influx of tourists unsuitably clad in native dirndls and short leather pants. A great deal had happened to her there, and yet the place remained a refuge, a sort of emotional fourth dimension, to which she retreated again and again when she needed sorting out.

This time she had gone straight to Salzburg from Berlin in July, shaken and unreasonably frightened, groping her way back to normal from what seemed like a prolonged panic, with its usual aftermath of shock. When the others went on to Vienna, Johnny and Bracken sniffing upwind while the Dolfuss Government struggled to maintain itself against the backstairs Nazi invasion, she had stayed behind at the Oesterreichische Hof, glad of a few days' solitude.

And then the cable came, forwarded from Cannes.

Still a little dazed and unbelieving, she had just read it again, wondering at the back of her mind if they had had the same cable in London, and if she must send it on to Bracken or if he would have heard by now through his own channels that Aunt Sue was dead. What would Williamsburg be like now, without that gay, wise presence? What would become of the lovely house which had sheltered them all at one time or another? She had never meant to be away so long. She had never meant not to see Aunt Sue again. . . .

She sat with her eyes on the encircling mountains, drifting, bewildered, lost. Ought she to go home to Williamsburg? For what? She wrote to her mother in Richmond once a month, but they didn't miss each other, it was no good pretending that they did. She had no knowledge any more of the Sprague children in England Street, and she had lost touch with the Princeton bunch. Like Cousin Sally a dozen years ago she would feel herself a ghost now in Williamsburg. There was only Cannes, and London, and Salzburg. Virginia's youngest had come out last year, and the other three were married. Oliver's Hermione was getting spinsterish and sharp and had developed political opinions. Somebody was being married in September—one of Edward's girls, wasn't it? Should she go to London for the wedding, or just send a lavish present? And did it matter very much?

Nothing seemed to matter very much, all of a sudden. Was that old age? Had Aunt Sue ever come to a dead end like this, or Sally? Yes—Sally had. More than once. *Some years are not so good as others—sometimes you love less, sometimes more —and you can never be sure that the best is not still to come.* From where, Camilla wondered idly, doubting and depressed, with an aged, listless sensation of having been everywhere and met everybody there was. *Take what comes to you, and when you give, use both hands.* Well, she had done that, for a long time now, and with some success, it was true. People had loved her, been kind and generous and grateful, and no one had ever parted from her in anger or with an ugly quarrel. Even Kim was still her friend. She had offered even Victor both her hands.

She found herself wondering again about Victor, and what would become of him, what harm he could do in London, what she could do about him even now. *The fact is, I never want to see you again.* That wasn't a nice thing to hear, from anybody, even a man beside himself with nerves and drink —particularly a man who had engaged more of your secret thoughts than you had realized, until on a sudden, reckless, imperial, crusading impulse you offered him yourself for his salvation—and got turned down. Was that what rankled and gnawed—that she had been turned down? Was that why she couldn't seem to forget Victor, and make a new beginning? Was it just her own wounded vanity that kept him there in her consciousness, a sort of hair-shirt memory, of a time when she had almost made a fool of herself—a supreme, idiotic, futile, world-without-end fool? Because she suspected now, unwillingly, that Victor could never have been changed, and that it would only have been at best a long, bitter, defeating struggle between them, ending heaven knew how, much better never begun, much better left like this, without a lot more things to forget. . . .

It was getting dark on the terrace, and a little too cool. She must go in, or else get a wrap. She should have gone to Vienna with the others after all, they would never be able to tear themselves away from this Dolfuss story till things had simmered down or blown up, whichever they were going to do, and she felt a childish need of company in the desolation the news of Sue's death had brought. So much of youth and security and old affections went with Sue, it was like the end of a century—one was left face to face with Time, and one felt frightened and alone. She wanted to shelter under the family wing, and there was so much confusion in beleaguered Austria one couldn't even get Vienna on the telephone. Should she leave a message for them here at the hotel and go back to Cannes and the Kendricks, they always livened things up. . . . But the Austrian frontiers were closed, and no one knew when travel would be resumed.

Added to her sharp sense of personal loneliness, was the uneasy feeling of isolation from the rest of the world in this dreaming, doll's house town—of being cut off from reality at a time when it was only sensible to be abreast of things and know what was going on. If there was another war, Salzburg and its music would be engulfed and out of bounds, it was no place to find oneself stranded, with only a passport between oneself and unthinkable disasters. She remembered how Cousin Sally had been caught in Belgium the last time, and barely escaped from Antwerp in a fishing-boat, with ashes from the burning city dropping in her hair. . . . And with Sally then, besides Fabrice and Elvire, there was Sosthène.

The sense of alone-ness grew on Camilla in a really devastating way, and an impulse to bolt for Cannes and lock the door behind her. Cannes had survived the war, intact, and Sally had come back to it and resumed her life there as though there had been no interruption. Sosthène had seen to that, she told herself with a twinge of the old insurgence against circumstance. Sosthène was gone now, and there was no one to make sure that Camilla's life at Cannes remained secure. . . .

She shivered in the evening chill, and sat on wilfully, tempting a cold, too listless and depressed to move. She had not thought of Kim for ages, but she thought of him now, with a sort of homesickness. Kim had gone to Hollywood, where he was dangling notoriously after one of the vivid ladies there. And Camilla had not lifted a finger to detain him. She now began to wonder why. She and Kim had suited each other, in a way. He was gay and good-tempered and wouldn't hurt a fly, and they had had some memorable times together. He would have come back to her, she was thinking, after that first London episode, like an affectionate but impenitent husband. And soon he would have been off again, no doubt, but always to return if she had wished it, if she had not been too fastidious and independent. . . . They had always got on together, and laughed at the same things—and they had not been so terribly in love that their tiffs and misunderstandings mattered enough for tears or remorse, and their reconciliations had always been easy and graceful and without rancor, which was really the right way to love, she had come to believe. There was never anything tense and tragic about life with Kim, you went with the wind, you rolled with the punches, you gave as good as you got, and you laughed— God, how you laughed, Camilla thought nostalgically, and you felt young and adventuresome and reckless. And you let it go lightly, without regrets, because the world was full of men who were more than ready to see that you had no time to miss just one of them. . . .

Nothing would ever be the same now as in those mad mid-'Twenties when everyone had money to spend and everyone thought the war was over. And I'm not so young any more, she thought, flinching. I'm not so adaptable. I wonder—Kim might not like me so much nowadays. Lord knows, I was pretty green in the beginning. Kim taught me a lot. And what is it worth now, I wonder! Victor—she was back to that again—Victor didn't want it.

I must get out of here and stop this maundering, she thought, with no move to do so. I must go back to Cannes as soon as possible—or to Paris—London, maybe—anywhere—look up people—hear some good music—fall in love again—but it's all so much *trouble*. And it doesn't last. The people one falls in love with nowadays take it so hard—not like Kim—or else they don't take it at all—like Victor. . . .

So finally you come to a time like this, when there's nobody. Nobody older, because they've died. Nobody younger, because you haven't had a child, And you wonder what's going to become of you as time goes on. Who's going to be there when you're ill and frightened—who's going to need *you* there if they're ill and frightened—who's going to answer if you call out in the night. . . . Sosthène doesn't happen to everyone—only to Sally. . . . And even Sally was alone at the end. . . .

There were footsteps on the terrace behind her, and warm arms were laid around her shoulders. Dinah!

"Sitting out here in the cold," said Dinah. "We came as fast as we could because Bracken said you would be feeling dismal. They kept stopping the car and asking to see our papers. I see you got the cable—we were hoping to get here first, the way things are."

"Bad news was bound to get through." Holding Dinah's hand, Camilla looked from one to the other of them mistily —they were all there, even Johnny—she brimmed over with relief and pleasure. "How nice of you to think of me—I was feeling *suicidal*, and a hundred years old! I never dreamed you could leave Vienna now, and I was wondering if the same message would get through to you."

"It's all over in Vienna anyway," said Bracken, sitting down rather heavily. "Dolfuss is dead, poor little blighter —they stood around and let him bleed to death on a sofa— Schuschnigg is in—frontiers re-opened—railroads running —and Hitler with a flea in his ear, thanks to Mussolini!"

"It won't last long, of course," said Johnny, sinking into another chair.

"Oh, no, just long enough for a few deep breaths," Bracken agreed at once.

"And then what?" Camilla asked.

"Then they will try again," said Johnny. "Meanwhile, how about a nice stiff drink?"

They went up stairs to a warm, lighted room, and there was the clink of ice in tall glasses and pipe-smoke and casual, comforting conversation till a late hour. They didn't say much about Sue—she had left her money to Fitz's children, and the house to Jeff, Bracken as usual having been named executor—Jeff was a little more silent even than was his habit, awed and solemn in his inheritance, which he took very seriously. Sue had suggested more than once that if he found he didn't want the house he might give it to the Williamsburg Restoration people, who would see that it was kept intact and in repair, as they had begun to do with other old houses in the town. But Jeff, who had gone down to see the reconstructed Raleigh Tavern and the Capitol and the Governor's Palace when they were put on exhibition and was most enthusiastic about the whole Restoration project, was still unwilling to let the old Day house go out of his hands. "I might have children," he said quite solemnly to Bracken. "I wouldn't like to have them have to buy a ticket to see where Grandmother Tibby lived." Bracken said he could understand that. "The Palace and the Raleigh had disappeared," Jeff went on anxiously, lest they might think he was just selfish about the house. "But our place is *alive*. It's always been lived in. We'll have to find somebody to go on living in it. God knows the family is big enough!" Bracken said it seemed as though there ought to be someone, certainly. "Stevie Sprague will look after it for me till I can do something myself," said Jeff, for Fitz's Stephen was his favorite Williamsburg cousin. Bracken reminded him that Stephen was in New York, dancing in a Broadway show. "Well, Sylvia, then," said Jeff obstinately, knowing that Stephen's sister Sylvia would do almost anything her Cousin Jeff asked her to. "I'll write straight off to Sylvia and tell her I want the place left exactly as it is till I can get back there." Bracken said By all means, and didn't they think it was time to go to bed now.

Camilla lay awake a while, turning over in her mind the talk of Williamsburg and the Sprague cousins, who had grown out of her knowledge and were all in their twenties now. She was contemplating with the first stirrings of new interest the idea of returning home to see for herself the rebirth of the little town which had been Virginia's first capital when she fell asleep. It would be something to do, she thought drowsily. It would be a *reason* for doing something, which she had seemed lately to lack. But it would doubtless make her feel very old. . . .

They had made no plans for the morning, promising each other to sleep late and recover from recent excitements, and Camilla breakfasted in her room. When she wandered into the sitting-room of Bracken's suite looking for company, she found only Johnny, behind the London *Telegraph*.

"Hullo," he said. "Waiting for you. Had breakfast?"

Camilla said she had, and asked where the others were.

"Gone out for an airing. Said we could find them at Tomiselli's eventually."

"That's good," said Camilla vaguely, standing at the window in full sunshine. "What a glorious day. Shall we go along after them now?"

"No hurry."

"I was sort of surprised to see you here last night. I thought at least you'd be watching the pot boil in Vienna."

"Complaining?" Johnny sat looking at her, his arms along the back of the chair, and his legs crossed, lounging, easy, friendly.

She smiled at him with sudden, grateful affection.

"No. Glad to see you."

"Good."

There was a pause. She stood by the window looking at him.

"What's the matter with you this morning?" she asked suspiciously.

"Me? Nothing. I mean no more than usual. Why?"

"You look sort of funny."

"Can't help that. It's my face."

She laughed, more than the joke was worth, just because it was there at all. She felt oddly relaxed and unaccountably at peace, considering the way the world was going. Unless—

"Johnny, you aren't holding out on me? There isn't something nasty afoot that you haven't told me?"

"Not so far as I know."

She picked up the *Telegraph* and scanned its headlines briefly.

"Are we really going to have another war?" she asked, her eyes on the page.

" 'Fraid so."

"When?"

"Soon. The soothsayers have picked 1938."

"Four years," she said thoughtfully.

"Mm-hm."

"Not long, is it."

"Not long, no."

"What will it be like?"

"Bad. You scared?"

"I suppose I shall be, when it comes."

"Oh, shucks, you've seen wars."

"Gas, and germs, and—things like that, dropping on us out of the air?"

"Probably."

"Johnny—where will *you* be, in another war?"

"Oh, here and there and roundabout. They always miss me. What do you plan to do in the meantime, that's the question."

"You mean, till it starts?"

"Mm-hm."

"I don't know. I've been wondering. To tell the truth, I don't seem to care much. That's bad, isn't it. After what they were saying last night about Williamsburg being rebuilt the way it used to be I sort of thought I'd like to see it. But without Aunt Sue—. I might go to London, of course, but the Season is over there, everybody's in the country."

"Going to be a royal wedding in the autumn—Prince George and pretty Marina. Very gala, no doubt."

She made an uninterested face, and threw down the paper, and went to stand again at the window in the bar of sunlight, looking out at the mountains.

"I must be getting old," she said. "I just don't give a damn."

"I think," said Johnny, without moving, "that this is the day I have been waiting for all my life."

Preoccupied, she hardly heard him, then turned slowly to look at him in a dazed sort of way.

"What did you say?"

"Think back," said Johnny, sitting still, and saw that she recalled his words with uncertainty. "You heard me," said Johnny, and rose at his leisure and went to her. "We've got four years," he said. "At the outside. And after that, God help us. Will you give them to me?"

"Why—Johnny—I—"

"I want you to marry me, Camilla."

"I didn't—I—never thought—"

"Neither did I. We're bright, aren't we." He laid his arms around her, and felt her slim body pliant and unresisting in his hold. "You were always the most exciting, mysterious, *perennial* thing," he murmured. "I kept coming back, like a fly, remember? Or didn't you notice?"

"I did, rather." She laid her cheek against his smooth shaven one with a sweet, melting movement, and he felt her hair soft against his face and the fragrance that always clung about her was warm and near. "But, Johnny—"

"Mmmm?"

"I—never meant to m-marry anybody."

"Neither did I, but the hell with that now, we're wasting time!"

And a long minute later, when he had kissed her and both of them recognized with surprise that it was real and right and should have happened long ago, she said with a sort of timidity that wrung his heart, "You're sure about the m-marrying part?"

His arms tightened round her so that she gasped and wilted against him to ease the pressure on her ribs.

"This is for keeps," he said. "Yes or No?"

"Yes, Johnny," she said faintly, and added, with her face hidden, "We'd feel awful fools, wouldn't we, if there wasn't a war after all! I mean—if we had more than four years to go!"

He shook with laughter, and rocked her in his arms with a cradling, reassuring movement, his cheek hard against hers, so that she laughed too, confidently, recklessly, feeling young and adventuresome and gay again, not empty, not frightened at what might be ahead, nor alone.

"We'll chance it," said Johnny. "We can't lose."

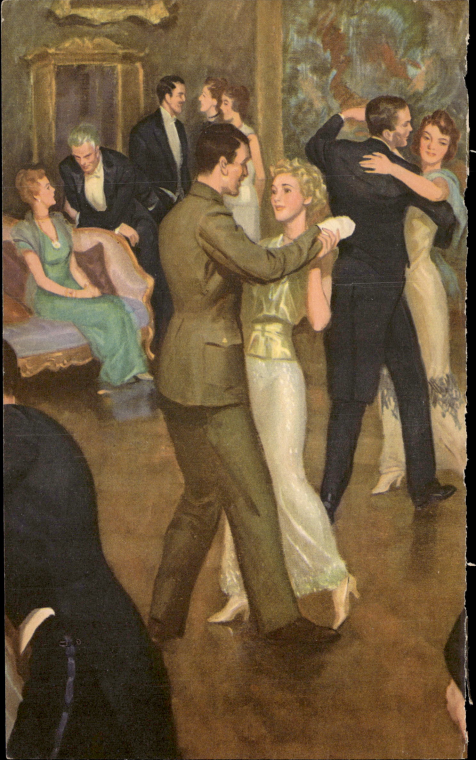